To Antonia —

I hope you find
this saga cinema-
tic and relatable.

My warmest best,

Sophia Hampton

The Crooked Little Pieces

Volume I

Sophia Lambton

The Crooked Little Pieces

Volume I

A Novel

THE CREPUSCULAR PRESS
London

First published in Great Britain by The Crepuscular Press 2022

The book is a work of fiction. Any resemblance to persons
living or dead is entirely coincidental.

Jacket design by Eloise G. Morgan

Set in 10/15pt Constantia

Typeset by RefineCatch, Bungay, Suffolk

Printed and bound by Clays Ltd., Elcograf S.p.A.

A CIP catalogue record for this book is available from the British Library.

ISBN 978-1-7397227-0-8
ISBN 978-1-7397227-1-5 (pbk)
ISBN 978-1-7397227-2-2 (ebook)

www.thecrepuscularpress.com

List of Contents

Prologue

2nd September 1968

The tapping of Isabel's spoon was beginning to irk her. It was a particularly idiosyncratic form of warfare, Anneliese inferred: her sister longing to drum into her a new responsibility. This so-called responsibility involved some happiness being thrust into her heart – a happiness she *should* have felt for Isabel.

The odds were hardly in her favour.

It so happened that the infantry that could have wielded joy in Anneliese restrained themselves from this invasion. They turned and became renegades, clinging seditiously to their objection. Gloom was the path that she was taking despite Isabel's unspoken pleas.

A memory bounced to the forefront of her mind. She and Isabel were four years old and at a park in Zurich. Crouched down in the little hut at the slide's peak, Isabel had wrapped her hands around the cold and shiny metal bar for fear of slipping. She was staring down at Anneliese in an imperious fervour: her way of commanding her to roll the ball along the slide. Anneliese propelled it to ascend the slope with all ten fingers. It tumbled with a bump before a nail of Isabel's could even poke it. But Isabel would not relent. With Anneliese's every try her glare grew meaner

– simultaneously more demeaning. Four minutes later she was staring at her sister to denounce her as a traitor. Her glance would have suggested she was looking at a person who had chosen to support the Axis powers there in Switzerland.

Now at forty-eight years old they played a new game. The rules, ethics and score were the same. Anneliese felt like the littler twin. Isabel was sure she was inferior. No victory was ever gained but both of them infallibly assumed the other won.

Isabel finished her ice cream. Crossing over to her purple music stand, she saw along its spine the strokes and dashes of a scribbled scarlet acronym: 'I.v.d.H; C.H.S.' She had no clue what could have urged her, aged eleven at the time of writing, to interpolate a semi-colon between two sets of initials. It was preposterous.

Quickly she returned to sit before her sister. Isabel's intentions were deliberately opaque; she simply didn't know that Anneliese's bore a hue of the same shade. Her eyes met fixedly with the clock's face.

'Is it safe to cross the date off now?'

Anneliese took her own turn to read the time.

'Ten thirty-seven.'

'That's an hour to go.'

'Well, it's over . . .'

The felt-tip pen was wandering already in her clammy clasp. Isabel drew a cross through the '2' and shrugged girlishly.

'The main part is over.'

There was something excessively timid about her; her voice was too soft. And after striking through the date she loosed a sigh so long and swirled it mirrored wispy smoke departing a volcano.

Isabel threw a half-smile at her sister. Yet her stock of weaponry appeared to be depleted. She couldn't make the effort and the smile was faint. Her mouth's shape quickly collapsed into an uncurved line.

Then she smirked on purpose – gently, not mockingly – with no ill will. She hadn't exercised ill will for a long time now. In Anneliese's eyes it had been far too long for Isabel.

'Liesa ...' She exhaled heavily through her nostrils. 'You're unimpressed with me.'

But it was one of the few times that Isabel was incorrect in that assumption. Anneliese's voice became breathy.

'No. No, Isabel . . .' She laid her hands down on her lap. Perhaps it would have stopped them from unwanted gesturing. 'You're acting ... your behaviour is guided by a smartness, resolution, cleverness ... so many features that I didn't know you – I mean, I . . .' She itched behind her ear. 'I wouldn't have expected so much.'

Isabel faintly half-smiled once more – feebly again.

'That's funny.' She leant her hands on the edge of the table. 'See, I worry for you, Liesa, 'cause I assumed you would have – I thought . . . I'm not speaking of accomplishment. I just meant . . . I had hoped that you'd be safe.'

There came the rebuttal:

'I'm not in physical danger, superficially it seems to be that way, but—'

'No, I meant . . . I just meant, professionally, erm . . .' She parted her lips noisily in nervousness. 'I imagined you in the kind of situation that would seem impressive on paper. I didn't expect you to be listed in the phone book with the same . . .' Isabel shut her eyes tightly. 'No, that was very horrible of me.'

Anneliese almost laughed.

'It's very understandable.' She crossed her legs the other way. 'Did he say something to you tonight – after the . . .'

'No.' Isabel shook her head. She picked up her felt-tip pen and started playing with it. 'I know it wasn't the best tactic but... he knows all of my routes. He's not going to...' Palpable fondness even percolated her description. She almost snickered from endearment. 'He isn't going to be surprised.'

'So you have . . . a sign of consent?'

'Well, yes.' The felt-tip pen tumbled onto the table.

The blue bowl in the corner of the room jogged her attention.

'Goodness.' Isabel effused as she stormed over to the bowl. 'Look how many sweets I put out, and the girls didn't want them.'

Back at the table she began picking them out and unwrapped one.

'Well . . .' Anneliese had been hesitant to admit it all evening. 'Isabel . . . the entire upstairs was locked.'

'That's impossible – I wanted all the rooms to be available.'

'You didn't unlock them, Isabel. At least – you didn't tell the caretaker to . . .' She folded her arms. 'They were locked, Isabel – that's why everyone congregated downstairs.'

Isabel's eyes appeared struck by hypnosis. Her voice emerged in a whisper.

'How did I? I could have sworn' – she used the expression of her fingers to help herself out – 'the—'

Something was off. Anneliese didn't want to remark it, she didn't want to vocalise her view. Her sister was too jittery for that. But it was tangible.

She didn't realise Isabel possessed a slender feeling of superiority. She didn't realise Isabel had the sensation *she* was stable; that her sister had cascaded into some obscured abyss, that Isabel desired most of all to yank her sister out of it and didn't know how to enforce such an extraction. Maybe the lighting in the room made Anneliese appear red-faced, but such was Isabel's impression.

'I check the papers every day.'

Anneliese was somewhat stunned.

'For what?'

'In case there's an announcement of the pregnancy. Penelope's pregnancy.'

Immediately Anneliese shifted in her chair. The tension simmered in her eyes. To Isabel they looked forlorn. They looked as they had once done in their infancy when Anneliese had burned her finger on the candle and extended sobs along Aunt Liesel's shoulder.

'Isabel, that is irrelevant to both of us.'

'It's *not*.'

'Isabel . . . that's . . .'

'Am I prodding too much?'

'Even *I* don't prod that far, and I'm the one who . . . yet it's not my situation, Isabel.'

'But he—'

'No.'

'I can't just forsake his existence, Licsa. The summer of '65 you told me—'

'I don't want to dwell on it. Verbally or otherwise.'

'No.' Isabel darted a sarcastic look at her. 'You reserve all that for conversations with Susanna.'

Anneliese slouched back in her chair.

'Yes. But you can't—'

'I figured . . .' Isabel picked up another sweet and unwrapped. 'What's wrong with your appetite?'

'*Mine?*' Anneliese gasped.

'You haven't taken any chocolate.'

Anneliese now had to take a chocolate to sustain an adamant impression of apparent normalcy.

'So I was . . . trying to realise . . . what . . .' Isabel was struggling to unwrap her golden ball. 'What they had in common.'

'Who?'

'Mine. Yours.'

Anneliese shook her head in embarrassment.

'I'd really rather not—'

If Anneliese insisted on abstaining from discussing men she would obliterate the possibility of any conversation with her sister. If she emphatically withheld her feelings when it came to *her* affairs their whole exchange would be unequal. She was trapped.

'You know . . .' Isabel pointed out. 'They're both killers, in some way.'

She was trying to be amusing. Anneliese only appeared shellshocked.

'OK, OK.' Isabel nodded. Her use of the two letters bothered Anneliese, together with other Americanisms her sister had picked up. 'Actually . . .' Isabel cleared her throat. 'I meant to ask, during the reception – what does Susanna think of my predicament?'

If only Anneliese had grasped Susanna's limitless capacity for lying. The latter's view of Isabel's 'predicament' was certainly among the numerous conceptions the psychiatrist had welded in her mind. But she cared not to divulge it – for that matter, even to *herself.*

'She has nothing against it.' was the phrase she flung off casually.

Isabel almost snorted.

'*Liesa.*'

'What?'

'The *credence* in your words . . .' She sighed. 'I was asking, because . . . I know what she has in her head.'

'You couldn't *possibly* divine what—'

'I meant to say – she *would* know.'

'About what?'

Isabel tossed a sweet to the side.

'Paralysis.'

Anneliese despised these foul intrusions – even more so when they obviously derived from such uneducated guesses.

'She doesn't make the correlation, Isabel.'

'He isn't anything like her.'

'I *know.*' Anneliese confirmed. 'But you can talk to me about it. I don't want you to imagine that I missed your life.'

Isabel paused. When she opened her mouth she spoke wispily.

'Liesa . . .' She grabbed hold of a sweet immediately to play with it as if it were a gadget. 'You were aware of the synopsis of my life; I wasn't even aware of the outline of yours. So . . . so, now that this is where I am, and you're not here . . . we'll just have to speak more regularly.'

Anneliese blinked. That was something that she *had* inherited from Susanna, albeit unintentionally. She looked at the clock.

'Oh . . .' Quickly she scratched her neck. 'My train leaves in forty minutes.'

'I know.'

Anneliese stood up. Gradually Isabel walked over to her.

'You should really come more often, Liesa. I mean . . . it's so sunny here.' She stroked her left arm with her right and sighed melodically. 'And I miss you.'

Anneliese understood this to be a bad sign. Had her sister genuinely been exulting, if the spring in her heart couldn't have resisted leaping, if she'd been engulfed by that extent of ecstasy it never would have been externalised in such a way. Isabel would have forgotten the words, 'I miss you'. She would have replaced them with a future tense; twisted the phrase into a hypothetical addendum: 'You know how much I'll *miss* you!'

They hugged.

'I'll wait until the taxi comes.' insisted Isabel.

They stood outside in pitch black darkness. The taller one barely discerned her sister's silhouette.

'We're going to keep each other more *abreast* of everything that happens, Liesa; be more obedient in this way. Set up a regime. And call me . . . er . . . I'll still be at home at seven. Call me then.'

'I will.'

A few minutes later they parted, squeezing each other warmly.

Both of them already knew the truth. If Isabel called every day her news would be the distribution of a reportage: a linear account of what her girls had done. His name would rarely pop up in the conversation. And Isabel had no doubt that her sister would be reticent to unstitch sentiments she kept sewn-up with fastened knots. At the same time they wouldn't settle for pretence and falsehood from each other. Instead they would glean substance from each other's intonations. These would be the only packages they sent that properly conveyed their inner states.

After a journey that encumbered Anneliese with five stops, seven periods of waiting and the missiles of a bristling cold, she was at home at half past six. Thirty minutes later she dialled Isabel's number.

Nobody picked up the telephone.

1.

Demons

Christmas was the second time each year when he felt morally permitted to indulge them. Clasping one hand of each, Josef led the pair around a gamut of boutiques on 23rd December 1925, ready to spend half his monthly savings on the six-year-olds' desires. Now a veteran professor of neurology at ETH Zurich, the fifty-year-old Dutch expatriate already lost his salary's gaunt other half on his twin daughters' nanny to obscure the indolence of their begrudging mother: the aspiring tenant of a mental institution.

Doused in the tips of dashing snowflakes, Anneliese's head of slick black curls was turning monochrome beneath her furry scarlet beret. Through the strength of some invisible adhesive once again her upturned raven lashes had grown stuck to both the lenses of her spectacles.

Propping them up her nose to ease her reading, Josef clutched the women's leather gloves with which he had regaled her hands. Since Anneliese's head kept facing what now looked like sugar-dusted pages of *The Snow Queen* as she roamed through hills and alleys, her father had to steer her miniature extension through the zigzag paths to stop the little girl colliding with the city's interrupting lampposts.

'You had a daughter. Now you have another daughter.' he recalled Dr Eichel alerting him after the birth of the second six days after the *first*: 8th November 1919. 'They will not be great mountaineers, sailors or soldiers – but they are *yours*, Herr van der Holt!'

He could identify the girls' respective trudging without pause.

There were times when, sitting in his study, Josef would disruptively hear Isabel parade around the whole apartment, stomping to a rhythm she was beating in her head. But if throughout his morning ritual of reading newspapers he heard a few creaks from the corridor crack timid pauses of slow, contemplative intervals, he recognised them as the movements of his Younger Twin – his *'Kleinste'*.

Now Isabel – who charged forth up the snowy ramp in leaps and bounds with the slick ease of bumping sledders sliding down – was forty yards ahead. Grabbing Anneliese's leather hand, Josef skidded up the slushy road and goaded the tenaciously absorbed, much littler twin to join her.

The significantly taller sister – a chestnut-haired and lanky girl who had long twigs of legs and hazel-coloured eyes of gaping almonds – halted at the stoop of an antique shop. Anneliese's blackberry bulbs were still steering their bolts to the page.

Isabel gazed at her father fixedly. Eventually she blinked three times behind her glasses, seemingly to gauge if he was able to divine her wish with the same power as a genie's lamp. A good girl she had been that day – not to have 'accidentally' misplaced her spectacles on a shop shelf, or in the middle of a mountain of amorphous rocks in her beloved park, or underneath the bench that held her dangling legs as they sat waiting for the train.

A bell rang as she pushed the door. Rushing to the back of the copper-coloured, dimly lit shop, Isabel neglected to greet the old lady who wished her a *'Frohe Weihnachten'*: 'Merry Christmas'.

Bedazzled, she stood with her ten fingers linked across her chest. After turning around coyly, Isabel trundled progressively to her father.

'Papi?' The pitch was unusually high compared to her habitual contralto.

'Yes, my love?'

They conversed in German.

'Can I show you something, please?'

This time she grabbed her father's cufflinks and took pigeon steps to lead him to the object.

It was a mahogany wooden construction; an oval shape curved inwards at the middle. She thought it was attractive and she wanted it for her and Anneliese's room.

Josef bent down to whisper in her ear:

'No, my love, that's an instrument. It's not furniture. You *play* it.'

Her eyes beamed. She shot her father a fearless expression.

'Good.' she said assertively.

'It's not your size, *meine Kleine*. We would have to get you one that fit you. But still, you don't want to spend your time on this. Practice is boring.'

Josef was not the kind of man to know this from a feat of personal experience. Music in his mind was either frivolous or a symbolic veneration of the Lord. It could be invited to the house after a solid period of labouring away at science, medicine, theology; subjects that incited goodness or well-being in their squalid town of Zurich or 'Downgraded Amsterdam' as he subtitled it: a hub of self-professed 'elites' who entertained themselves around the disc-shaped tables of their cabarets and downed liqueurs throughout discussions of that blasphemous intruder Sigmund Freud.

'Papi, I want *this* one.'

'Do you . . . do you want to *play* it?' Nervously he itched at his symmetrical, dyed auburn whiskers.

Fierce in her volition, Isabel nodded. Her voice became smaller and a net of red strokes now embroidered her eyes.

'Please . . .?'

That was the conclusion of the conversation.

Josef's rampant search to find the right size cello ended when his daughter burst into a spatter of impassioned tears.

Then it turned into a crazed and frenzied hunt. Finally at six o'clock, when the majority of shops were closed, they stumbled upon something close to two thirds of her height.

Erik von Gerber – a portly colleague of his from the Institute who taught biology and threw away his hours on carousing – was already stretched out on his sofa, spluttering and wheezing from his fat cigar when they returned.

Reeking of sickly perfume, his stiff collar was half-upright and half-tucked. Its sight became a toothpick prodding at the tender gum of Josef's conscience. Young lads who slouched and little children running hither-thither wedged sharp dents into his nervous system. He despised having to tuck in chairs of students when they sprang up carelessly at every signal of the school bell, scurrying outside instead of waiting for instruction.

'Good evening, Herr von Gerber.' He smiled as Isabel absconded to her room with her cello.

Josef's Prussian wife Elise – the daughter of societal belle Scharlotte von Preußen – had retired to her bedroom at three past midday.

Once again she had a headache. Perhaps her mother's chronic years of depilating the four corners of her scalp with every effort to coerce her daughter into playing the piano at the balls of Countess Prozorovskaya had borne into her skull an unabating migraine.

Of a merciful and empathetic disposition, Josef understood that he had salvaged from the zoo a panda invalid: its most unwanted creature with a porcelain complexion and a coat of raven hair who suffered from a lapsed and splintered psyche. Bent over despite being only twenty-seven years of age, among their company Elise would stick out like a thumb that was not only sore but crimson with a smear of violet bruises. Her literal one was reddish all the time; shrivelled from the crusty surface sculpted on it by her morbid biting.

Laws had long ago mandated that asylums teem with creatures such as these.

'That's Prussian aristocracy for you.' Erik von Gerber had explained.

In his dissension Josef was too ignorant to know that this may *not* have been the case. After extracting her from the incarceration of her life, he certainly had not expected this young woman to have zero interest in her polar opposite young daughters – over six years after their respective births.

Having finished *The Snow Queen*, Anneliese scampered to their guest; her flight inviting the skirt of her shimmery violet dress to make tents in the air.

'Do you know the stories of Hans Christian Andersen?'

It was Dutch. Josef had flung both his and his wife's native languages at the two girls but each was monolingual.

Isabel could socialise with Josef's colleagues in their mother tongue. She flattered them and snickered, flirted and showed off at the dinner table when she wasn't pointing out how much Professor Gerber 'needed to lose weight' or how Professor Abderhalden's 'tie has the wrong colours'.

Anneliese had taken to be tender when her father spoke to her in Dutch. Inexplicably it was this syntax she preferred, and Josef spoiled her with a vast array of Dutch books meant for older children.

The girl possessed a motley range of words in a vernacular that almost nobody in Zurich spoke.

'So . . . the little one's still resisting, heh?' The stench of cognac and cigar smoke fell along the tip of Anneliese's nose as she faced

Erik. 'She doesn't want to know the glories of Goethe, or Wagner, or Nietzsche's poisonous pen? Well – good on her. Who needs '*em*, anyway? Not when you can have a good ol' pair of *clogs*.'

Laughing smugly to himself, he took another puff before resuming the crass chortle. Its belting ripple smacked the little girl's naïve, underdeveloped soul: a ploppling puddle of black rainwater.

She could *understand* German because her older sister spoke it. She was deferential to the 'Older One': the 'Older One' had been expedient enough to beat her to the finish line of birth six days and nights *before* her.

Anneliese was sensitive to insults. Isabel was on the other hand a child incapable of recognising tact – which meant that Anneliese would lift her hand to mask her sister's mouth whenever she discharged distasteful comments.

Casting her glance at Josef, the Younger One anticipated a reaction.

Stroking her head, Josef insisted:

'*Kleinste*, you read books in Dutch intended for far more advanced—'

'Is that why Isabel doesn't play dress-up with me anymore?'

'Not at *all!*' He bent down so his height was parallel with hers.

Scrappy sounds of the smacked cello strings kept slicing through the air. At a loss without instructions from her older sister, the befuddled Anneliese looked down.

Lifting her up by the waist, Josef placed Anneliese beside him on the other sofa. 'Come and sit here with your Papa – that's a good girl. Isabel will play with Liesa after she has finished.'

'Liesa' was the first word Isabel had spoken. She had no idea her sister had another name.

After Erik reluctantly departed at half past eight, Josef disrupted Isabel's painstaking efforts. The tuneless strokes were starting to abrade his eardrums.

'*Meine Kleine.*' He bent down to face her. 'I'll find you a teacher in the morning. He'll tell you how it works.'

She looked at him as though he had suggested throwing it into the Limmat River and continued scraping one string with her bow. Again there emerged a quivering, diffident *mi*.

Anneliese barged in two hours later. Both of them had long been due for bed.

Isabel ignored her. Insisting she could help, the Younger One tried to take hold of the bow.

Isabel barked.

'You're not *holding* it correctly! You're not *touching* it properly! And it's *my* cello!'

Those were the last words Anneliese absorbed that night. Silently she cried off her upset in bed and fell asleep shortly afterwards.

At eleven o'clock Josef interrupted Isabel's putrid attempts once again.

'It's really time for bed now, *Liebling*.'

Her ferocious look suggested this time that he might be murdering her dolls.

'I'm not *going* to bed.'

'Isabel, your sister went to sleep two hours ago. It's really time that you—'

The steaming glare drummed fear into his soul. Too weak was he to call upon the power to resist.

That night he stayed up in his study though his morning lecture would begin at eight.

At half past five he heard her blubbering and let his index finger intercept the droplets gushing from her eyes.

'Papi, it won't *listen* to me!' she howled, irrespective of her sister sleeping in the same room and her mother tucked in bed in the adjacent one.

'Give it time, my love.'

Josef fell asleep with his head on his arms by the glow of the desk lamp. At thirteen to seven a collection of fingers drummed timidly on his arm. Faintly a voice stumbled forth:

'Papi?'

His head sprung up immediately.

'Oh, Isabel! You should have gone to *bed!*'

'Will you come to hear me play?'

Sniffling from cold, she appeared shy and exhausted. He insisted she put on a cardigan. She rebuffed him by insisting her performance was imminent.

Sat at her desk chair Isabel began to tuck the cello in between her knees. How she had deduced its intended position remained beyond Josef's banal understanding. Taking the bow in her right hand, she began stroking the strings. The sound was clean and enviable; its notes now fused together in a smooth *legato*. She was playing 'Twinkle, Twinkle, Little Star'.

'Where did you *hear* that, *meine Kleine*?'

They were too young for school and he had not exposed them to these melodies.

Isabel shrugged. She was shaken and anxious.

'Was it right, Papi?'

He looked at her, stymied.

'Of course, it was right.'

'No, Papi – tell me, seriously – was it *right?*'

'It was *right!*'

'Then why do you seem sad, Papi?'

He had augured it correctly. The new obsession kidnapped Isabel; dissolving the entire world into paraphernalia. It seemed as though his girl had morphed into another mammal. The six-year-old was suddenly withdrawn and secretive and introverted. Only during her fatigue did she now brim with electricity; storming the house when in the throes of games with Anneliese or coaxing from her dolls unusually aggressive conversations.

After three weeks of teaching her once every other day, Isabel's new teacher Senta Guidroz approached Josef and enquired tentatively if they could speak 'in private'.

In the kitchen the forty-something bespectacled woman confided in him of his daughter's condition:

'Herr Doktor van der Holt, I know this may come as a shock to you – but I can't teach your daughter.'

The man was flabbergasted.

'But . . . why not? Is she incompetent?'

'No. This . . .' The grey-haired lady took off her spectacles to polish them with a handkerchief. 'Herr Doktor van der Holt, these demons . . .'

'*Demons?*'

'If you want your daughter to have that kind of existence, if you want her to be a lady by nine, to know the roar of the audience before her first picnic – that's up to you. But I'm afraid I can't be party to such . . . that is not a level I can teach.'

Josef's shock commanded he be speechless.

'I-I . . . I'm sorry, I don't . . .'

'Your daughter has been practising for not more than two weeks. She just played me Paganini's Caprice No. 24. Without the notes.'

He spread his hands flat out.

'So? What is the problem?'

'Congratulations, Herr Doktor. Your daughter has embarked on her first love affair – aged six. She is a prodigy. This is a warning, not my flattery. If you want to subject her to a life of nothing but toil, a helping of early fame; to use her as a vehicle to make money . . . I cannot be privy to that. Frankly, I am not even qualified to train your daughter.'

Her words left him downhearted when he should have been rejoicing. Taking furtive steps towards his youngling, he beheld her labouring away at the caprice. The fingers of her left hand shuddered at the cello's neck; gyrating back and forth at a velocity beyond the scurrying of insects' legs. The bow, through her manipulation, seemed to penetrate the upper section of the strings; it worked so hard it was as though it sought to enter and eviscerate the surface.

In response to her the grave sounds throbbed like crystal vases, chandeliers and cut glass wine decanters jostling to the rhythms hammered by an earthquake. They were a set of thick metallic strokes fuelled by the fire flaring from a stack of burning coal. Every time that she released a string her father heard the tingle of vibration.

There was dissonance: it was deliberate. Between these notes there was no coalescence; they were biting, groping and colliding with each other. Something nether – a thing eerily infernal writhed within the piece; something inviting listeners to the macabre; maybe even the lascivious. He had to blink to shun a vision of the strings effusing slender strands of smoke.

He feared these outbursts would arouse God's wrath. A verve about her playing was insinuating that she wanted to transgress the boundaries of the earthly cosmos and the seat of all things natural; her incursion on the still, submissive instrument dislodged his comfort. He longed at certain instances to tap her on the shoulder gently, tuck her hair behind her ear and offer one demure request: he wanted her to make each phrase mellifluous and . . . *sparing.*

The kinsmen who believed and practised all he did would probably have burnt her in the sixteenth century; in Poland they would still have executed her in the eighteenth. Stymied by the inexplicable precision of her sorcery, they would have deemed it indispensable to toss her far across the sea.

It took him four weeks to acclimatise the serial explosions he felt going off within his bloodstream to this novel sound. At one point he felt valiant enough to trespass on her practice. Wandering over to the girl, he drew the hair back from her shoulders before whispering with caution:

'My love, perhaps you'd like me to read you some Aesop?'

There was no change. Pressingly she pounded the poor bow across the middle string whilst jabbing the adjacent one with her third finger. He repeated the proposal with extra aplomb:

'Maybe you'd like me to read you some Aesop – before you go to bed?'

Isabel politely declined with a shake of the head – her quest undisturbed.

He prayed to God to pillage his daughter of the sinister forces. The crux of this most painful quandary of his was that he did not know whether her competence was God's auspicious blessing or the handiwork of Satan's tapestry.

Anneliese trained herself to live independently. Aspiring to be near Isabel, she sat in the corner of the living room during her practice. Time was exhausted as she pored over the multi-coloured pages of one picture book or another; murmuring the words as she read: her velocious pitch rising and falling with each phrase's rhythm. Isabel's vicious grinding would never deter either *her* or her slumber. When Josef analysed her reaction, he found it was not one of hurt and abandonment – but none whatsoever.

'You don't like the music Isabel plays, *meine Kleinste*?'

'I am *indifferent*, Papa.' It was a new word she had picked up.

Routinely he began to spend two hours every evening sat between his twosome: one of them engrossed in a thick tome, her mind meandering in all its elasticity with the exception of the pauses saved to blow her nose; the other ablaze in an indousable cauldron of fire, menacing the instrument's bridge as she plundered her strings.

By the advent of February 1926 he relented and employed a new teacher: a former professor of the Paris Conservatoire.

2.

Ill Literacy

The mostly silent Anneliese had shopkeepers convinced that she was dumb.

At the age of six she had devoured *Faust* in Dutch.

Early on a Saturday morning Josef sat her at the dining room table and presented her with *Snow White* in the Brothers Grimm retelling. He spent hours listing German grammar points to her, telling her about the nominative, accusative, genitive and dative; striving in his patience to soften her accent.

None of this prevailed.

He and Isabel had rightfully assumed that Anneliese was slow. Yet when she did digest material she did so thoroughly. Adept at partly understanding German newspapers, often she would sit before the *Südostschweiz* and start examining the civil conflicts, epidemics and precarious global situations. Her familiarity with reasons for the Great War and its consequences triggered jolts in her whenever she read news about the international disputes.

These sensations weren't especially uncommon. She was reactive to the sound of tooting taxi horns as she lay wide awake at bedtime. Clicks and rustles of the paper boy distributing his smacking pages and his pedalling, the bell that jangled on his bicycle became *her* strokes of cello strings. She would cast hard glances at the sky and hear a whirring plane and listen to the fizz accumulate inside her, rushing to the surface just below her skin like rising bubbles in champagne.

Anneliese avoided telling Josef that her sleep was never one long fluent spell of senselessness. The next-door neighbours had an entrance of enormous oak Italian doors. Every night she heard the key thrust into them and click. Then she would hear the creak of one door flinging itself forward and an echo percolating through the hallway. She would listen to a pair of high heels clop first loudly then more softly as they stealthily retreated out of earshot. Following another creak the doors would fuse and clatter, rippling a vibration through the floor. No lethargy could overtake her when alertness rang to reinforce her concentration.

One day during the Easter holidays of 1926, Anneliese knocked on the door of Josef's study, her glasses sliding down her nose.

'What would you like, *meine Kleinste*?'

She kept staring at the open book in front of Josef: a thick tome about neurology.

'Papa, is that the brain?' She pointed to a diagram.

'Yes.'

'Is that where God lives?'

'God is everywhere.'

'But is that where He lives?'

He frowned. Of late Josef's career had taken a turn for the worse. Still refusing to believe the 'foul' idea that resolutions of the mind were predisposed because of huge webs of electrons, he prohibited allusions to neuropsychology during his seminars. For this reason he was now forced to acknowledge that his colleagues frequently belittled him.

Taking Anneliese by the hand, he offered:

'Do you want me to tell you how it works?'

'Doesn't God make it work?'

'Yes. Would you like me to tell you *how* He makes it work?'

She stared down at the picture of the mass cleft into different sections.

'Yes, please.'

The academic child was easier to please. Josef's reputation as an academic had contrarily become a tenuous affair.

Many factors now intruded on his honourable profession. Lavishing the larger portion of his time on his twin daughters and their torpid mother, he was trammelled by colluding causes that forestalled his punctuality. By the time Josef arrived to lectures, seminars and conferences it was ten or eleven or fourteen past the hour; his students were dispensing with their energy elsewhere. The gang was throwing paper planes, hanging out of windows or exchanging giggles and guffaws around the lecture hall – desperate to know if Hans was now the beau of Josefima and if Gert had really stood outside her window drinking beer in his avowal of undying love.

This wasn't unknown to Professor Klaus Gertzinger, the Faculty Head. He summoned the offender to his office for a tête-à-tête one evening. Josef was anxious that the girls would worry for his disappearance if he came home after half past five. He also feared that their experienced nanny would demand more pay.

Professor Gertzinger was in no mood to make exceptions. It was precisely five thirty when he surfaced to open the door of his office.

'Good evening, Dr van der Holt.'

Josef was staring at his watch.

'Good evening.'

'Please – have a seat.'

It was his first entrance in the man's dishevelled quarters: grey and murky was their shabby habitat. His floor was light grey and bestrewn with littered bits of dust, his papers were ascatter on the ring stains of his dented desk and his scratched, foggy window had eluded washing hands for years.

The only chair was likewise scratched and rusty looking; one leg bent a little backwards. Josef flicked dust away before he settled on its surface.

Klaus – a bald man with a beard and moustache – clasped his hands together with some thunder of importance.

'I understand that you've been having trouble with the nanny.'

'I'm sorry?'

'I have studied the information that is presently in my possession,' he announced, poring over his papers as though they were psychological profiles of Josef. 'I find myself unable to arrive at any other conclusion.'

Josef stroked the end of his moustache. His brows were bent downwards.

'I must say, it isn't true. Our nanny is quite competent. I simply am not fond of the idea of letting her monopolise their time. My daughters have two parents; they should not spend many hours in a nanny's hands.'

Klaus took a great breath normally reserved by Germans for a period of heavy contemplation. He let his chin rest between thumb and forefinger.

'With your timetable it would be almost impossible for you to spend a great deal of time with them. That said, it certainly explains your recent lack of punctuality, which has – suffice to say – *startled* some of our students.'

Josef puffed through his nostrils in a sign of heavy indignation.

'I have very rarely been late to lectures, Professor Gertzinger.'

The latter took out a chart from the drawer in his desk, popped on a pince-nez and examined the paper in front of him.

'According to our records, you have been unpunctual nine times in thirteen days. In most cases that counts as grounds for suspension. Given the length of your tenure however, I am prepared to make exceptions – *if*, let it be known – you take the necessary measures to ensure that your "family life" does not cost your work any further disruption. Schools open earlier these days.'

Josef turned his attention to another argument.

'Yes, I understand. But they have not yet started school. In any case they need their full eleven hours and I must be there to give them breakfast.'

'Eleven hours . . .?'

'They sleep the full eleven hours. I put them to bed at eight and awaken them at seven am. This routine has been in place for over three years now; a revised one would upturn their schedule.'

'A full-time governess could make all kinds of utile adjustments.'

'I will *not* hand my daughters to a governess. They have a mother.'

'Excuse me, but it doesn't seem to me their mother tends to them.'

'That is a *family* affair!'

Exasperated, Professor Gertzinger loosened his tie from fatigue.

'There is a teaching position in London. I understand you speak English.'

'Excuse me?'

'There is a great deficiency of professors in the neurology departments at London. They recently opened a new university for women.'

'I'm afraid I don't see how and why that should be relevant.'

'It would be relevant, for instance, hypothetically, if one no longer wanted you to work here.'

Josef sat back, by now helpless.

'I see.' He got up and extended his hand as a peace offering. 'I will do my best to ensure promptness every day, Professor Gertzinger.'

The latter nodded. Josef deemed his promise an inane one.

3.

Second love

Eight years had passed since Magdalena van der Holt had seen her son Josef.

They made the journey to Lisse by train and crossed most of western Germany in three days: hopping on at Zurich, travelling to Basel, disembarking at Cologne, catching the next train to Utrecht and finally getting to Leiden. There was one smouldering cabin for the three of them but only two beds. Elise had 'volunteered' to stay at home.

In Lisse it took the taxicab driver forty minutes to find Josef's old home. When they got out Anneliese staggered around in her drowsiness, barely able to walk.

Vrouw van der Holt waited at home, her eyes engrossed in knitting. At nine o'clock that summer's night she stepped outside. Her eyes meandered through the golden light until they stopped at a long creature with a bulky, instrumental case strapped down her back. Next to her was Josef with a bundle half her size atop his arms, her two peach-coloured legs propped on his hips and using them as pedals; raven curls adangle round his shoulders. Resting her head on him, she showed no signs of stirring.

Bobbing his head to the left, Josef introduced them:

'Isabel.'

Vrouw van der Holt nodded, frowning open-mouthed as she examined the contrasting figures.

Bowing his head, he asserted:

'Anneliese.' He turned around so that Vrouw van der Holt would see her face; at least, the half of it still visible.

Every morning the old, portly woman was abruptly startled in her sleep by the coarse sound of a molested cello. Every morning Vrouw van der Holt came to instruct Isabel on the etiquette of house manners.

She understood not one word of the language of her grandmother.

Nine days into their visit Josef was eating his lunch in the kitchen as Isabel dug her primed hands in the ruggedly deviant chords of the Cello Concerto's first movement: Elgar's. Vrouw van der Holt shuddered. Josef shot her an aggressively defensive look.

'She plays beautifully, Mama.'

'But . . . *that?*'

He heaved a great sigh.

'Modern music.'

She wanted those chords moody, dark: sounding both crooked and completely drained of hope. Each time her bow chafed at the strings it still lacked 'crookedness'. She recommened these two chords seven times, each time with more élan – much to the sorrow of her grandmother.

Thirteen minutes into her playing a sudden loud pop was succeeded by:

'*Ai!*'

He rushed into the living room expecting to see fingers bleeding from the scabrous pizzicato. Instead it was the string that had been plucked. The one on the extreme right was irreparably snapped and Isabel had bubbles foaming at her eyelids.

'Papi . . .' She offered her father the cello. 'Will you take it to the instrument repairman, please?'

'The nearest one would be in Leiden, my love.'

'Well – will you take it to Leiden?' She blinked several times.

He stroked her head. This irked her.

'Will you take it to Leiden, Papi?'

'*Meine Kleine*, I don't even *know* of one. And even if we did find one, it would take three or four weeks. By that time we'll be gone.'

She crossed her arms in a dramatic fashion. Suddenly she belted as though from her diaphragm:

'I want to go *home!*'

His voice became sterner.

'Isabel . . .'

'Papi – I want to go *home!* In Zurich the music man lives *in* our *building*. I want to go *home!*'

Her eyebrows dove inwards, almost touching the bridge of her nose.

He took hold of her hand.

'I know the Naaktgeborens. They're a lovely family who live less than one mile from here. I believe their son once played the violin—'

'The *violin?*' She looked at him as though he'd offered her putrescent grapes instead of strawberries and cream. 'I don't want a . . . a *violin?!* I want my *cello!*'

When he tried to embrace her she kicked at his chest with her foot before scurrying into the woods. Josef instructed Anneliese to go play with her.

But Isabel was slyer than her father could imagine: accustomed to obtaining any object of her zeal. Stampeding in the summery field, she was burning to win this dispute.

Unbeknownst to the clumsily wandering mind of her sister she clambered the tree; struggling to press her small feet on its bark and precarious branches.

Upon arrival on the first long branch she perched herself along the wood and quickly found herself engulfed by fear. Her pupils were dilated, drifting to and fro; hoping that a mode of transport somewhere in the sky could lift her.

Meanwhile Anneliese was strolling in the tulips. Scratching her knees amidst the nettles, she was striving hard to fight the potent urge to sneeze. Allergies vanquished these efforts. The little girl soon held a sticky handkerchief so moist it was beyond her use. All of a sudden came a high-pitched squeal:

'*Liesaaaa!!*' was the cry of panic. Twice she spun around to try to match a vision to the sound. No luck came. Another cry then hit her ears, more lengthily drawn out:

'I'm . . . *heeeere!*' Anneliese was quick to understand that 'here' could mean one of a number of locations. Haphazardly she looked up. Isabel was stuck on the branch of the tree, her legs swaying in spite of herself.

Anneliese was unsurprised. Young wisdom told her to expect and simultaneously ignore her sister's antics. At the same time Isabel gazed grumpily at her, expecting a great dose of sympathy. Anneliese exerted nothing but disdain and shook her head.

'Go and fetch Papi!!' the little girl insisted. Quickly her sister dashed into the house where Josef and Vrouw van der Holt were sitting comfortably, discussing all the neighbours' circumstances, sons and daughters.

Without regarding the small figure and her white drenched handkerchief he propped the girl up on his knee, continuing his chatter.

A shiny object on the table caught her eye. The rod was a metallic thermometer stick. When she put her hand on it, the red line grew; when she removed it, it mysteriously shrunk. This puzzled her and she elected to defy this law of physics.

To her misfortune and surprise it made her feel invariably powerless.

She eavesdropped on her father's conversation with her grand-mother – this being the first time that 'grown-up conversations' would ensue in Dutch. Josef assumed quite automatically that Anneliese possessed no interest in them. On the contrary, his tiny daughter's curiosity had spawned the offshoot of an eager cunning.

Her attention clipped on to Josef's words mid-sentence.

'. . .that we go to London.'

Vrouw van der Holt slammed down her cup of tea.

'To *London?*'

'I immediately dismissed the idea, of course.'

'*Why?*'

'Why? There's just been a war.'

'It was seven years ago!'

'Mother, I refuse to take my girls to that city. It's a dreadful, dreary place where even the most bourgeois of people feel entitled to defy morality. The women are becoming *doctors* there.'

'And how is *this* one going to learn to speak like all the other people in *your* city?'

He stroked Anneliese's head affectionately.

'When she starts school next month, I'm sure it'll come naturally.'

'But . . .' Vrouw van der Holt spread out her arms in confusion. 'Do they even understand they speak *two* languages?'

Anneliese knew very well she didn't speak 'the language'. She felt handicapped for it – as though she possessed *nine* fingers rather than ten.

'The division of languages somehow doesn't set them apart. In any case, Mother, that isn't the point. These girls are not just . . .' he whispered, '*young ladies*. They are very *feeling* girls. I worry about them not being cared for enough in Switzerland – the *neutral* terrain. It would be plainly immoral to take them to *England*. They're a cold, distanced and demoralising people. As said Napoleon, "nation of shopkeepers".'

Josef's dimmed volume provoked only a great one from Vrouw van der Holt.

'I fail to understand, Josef. What do you mean when you tell me they won't *suit* England?'

He covered up the ears of Anneliese and moved in closer to his mother as he spoke – but she heard anyway.

'It would be easier with another set of girls but these are not an average pair of sisters. They are so fragile, both of them ... wondrous. They're crooked little pieces of some kind of ... strange experiment. I have no idea how they could live without my guidance in this world – and you expect me to transfer them to *that* dangerous, gloomy place.'

Vrouw van der Holt rolled her eyes and tilted her head back.

'Josef, does it not occur to you that the reason they are fragile and strange is *because* they are young? You were not easy at their age.'

In a hushed voice bridled with anxiety, he confessed:

'But they are really . . . very, *very* sensitive!'

'*Schatje*, they're six year old girls. How thick do you expect their skin to *be?*'

Thanks to their lengthy interlocution, Isabel was now comfortably settled at her treeborne position. It suddenly occurred to Josef that his daughters had been separate now for an unusually long time. Looking inquisitively at Anneliese, he sought to know:

'Where is your sister?'

Anneliese's eyes grew and she quickly smacked her hand across her mouth.

'Ai.' she responded. Dropping from her father's knee, she led him to the miscreant. Upon seeing him the latter was hysterical:

'Papi – come *here!!!*'

Unsurprised, Josef surveyed Isabel in resignation rather than in horror. He insisted she descend the tree herself so he could take her from the bottom. But the young lady shook her head most vigorously, darting at him a severe expression that implied her disapproval. Growing more aggravated, he explained that there was no way he would trouble any of their neighbours for a ladder on the foolish grounds that his unruly child had climbed a tree.

This did not serve to affect her. He could tell his daughter knew that she was winning.

Finally he warned her if she didn't come down she would helplessly be left alone: as she grew taller and taller her weight would lower and lower the branch till it snapped and she tumbled down with it.

The young madam was stoic. She made a point of staring at her nails.

After two hours of alerting several villagers at home and asking if they had a ladder, Josef brought his daughter back to safety the exact way she had wanted. By that time she was bored.

Anneliese admonished Isabel and on this rare occasion voiced her cumbersome opinion: it was impertinent to ask so great a sacrifice from their exhausted father. She easily identified her sister's schemes and didn't like to see him cruelly mocked.

A quibble was unleashed. Isabel 'discovered' that 'Liesa loved Papi more than her sister', and how this was 'unfair'. Anneliese contended that she loved her father and her sister equally. But until she had discharged her share of wails and taken refuge in their room, Isabel would not be pacified. It took Anneliese three hugs and six biscuits to soothe Isabel. By the seventh she was quiet and the argument had been forgotten.

The Naaktgeboren family awaited their visit that Wednesday. After eating both her dinner and half of Anneliese's, Isabel helped herself to two servings of pudding. Then she sat back dissatisfied, attempting mentally to compose melodies for cello. Every so often while Anneliese sat with her legs straight and together, Isabel would shift her body to one side to turn her head and look behind her. Josef corrected her and told her off. At last in his frustration he enquired:

'Isabel, what are you looking at?' She hopped off her chair. 'Young lady, nobody *excused* you.'

She heeded him no notice. Within ten seconds she was stood at the piano in their living room. Josef didn't have to leave the room to check.

Swelling with humiliation, he faced the Naaktgeborens:

'Would you mind if my little one played a bit on your piano?'

Mr and Mrs Naaktgeboren looked at each other. Mrs Naaktgeboren asked:

'Does she play?'

'No, but she's . . . she's really very good on the cello.'

The Naaktgeborens consented. For the next hour no sound was emitted from the living room. Josef was puzzled.

Another hour passed. She dashed back into the room and tugged at his sleeve, whispering in his ear so that no one else heard:

'Papi, will you come to hear me play?'

'Erm . . .' He removed his napkin from his collar. 'Excuse me for a moment.'

Sheets of notes were splayed out over the piano stand. He heard the tinkling of the tender chords before he witnessed their quaint, docile execution: the dainty pitter-patter that her feet had not so long ago effused eclipsed by a solemnity. Having already mastered the *diminuendo*, she was using the soft pedal with her far-extended left foot to persuade select notes to demur.

Anneliese had risen from her chair after excusing herself. This time the child who had been apathetic to the grating cello's sound began to melt at slurs and intervals between the chiming notes.

Debussy's *Clair de Lune*. She grasped Josef's arm and smiled.

'Papa, our Isabel can *play* the piano!'

He knew well that he ought to have been overjoyed. The surface of his heart was met with the calm heat and crisp scintillas of a hearth.

Approaching it too closely, he was scalded by its fire.

It was happening again – and he had hoped that she would reach at least sixteen before selecting yet another lover.

4

A marble dropped

It took a baby grand piano and another music teacher to haul Isabel to school. Once Josef had adhered to all of her requests she clad herself in the school uniform without a squabble, followed him and proudly took her sister by her hand to march into the grounds.

With both of them behind the gates, Isabel took off her glasses.

Anneliese darted a disciplinary look.

'Papa said . . .'

'Papa won't *see* me!' she hissed.

Anneliese was eager to absorb new sights and people. Isabel was eager to return to her piano.

In their first lesson their teacher Frau Ziegelbauer sought to determine each pupil's level of literacy.

Twelve hours later Josef had been summoned to her office.

'Your daughter is unable to communicate.' was the announcement.

Her voice was unrealistically screechy – almost a male falsetto. Josef decided that the spectacles perched on the bridge of her nose were uncomely and owl-like.

'You see, Frau Ziegelbauer . . .' He cleared his throat. 'She understands most of what she hears. She understands what she reads. Speaking and pronunciation are her only struggle.'

'Speaking and *pronunciation* are what everybody else does very *well*.' She shrugged with the condescension of a prison security guard in the face of an inmate. 'Anneliese is both dumb and illiterate, Herr van der Holt. I'm not sure why you brought her here.'

This was the last drop. 'Illiterate' was a word that had lapsed from his vocabulary before kindergarten. He had heard it used regarding peasants, farmers; men who would never own property. He would not stand it being used about his little girl.

This spurred on impetuousness. If one of them could not articulate the native language she would not endure her sister as the competition.

Thus he fomented a new formula: Josef would take them to a land sure to subject them to an equal helplessness that would compel each one to start from scratch and for a long time make no progress. They would feel ill at ease, inferior and at a disadvantage.

Newly found egality would nonetheless sustain their *solidarity*. That was the main thing.

When Josef made the announcement Isabel spilled sobs that little by little became larger and louder. Like the successive whipping of a riding crop, Anneliese persisted:

'But we'll be speaking the same language!'

Isabel crossed to the other side of the room, withdrawing the chair from Josef's desk so its legs stomped on the floor. As she sat her arms conjoined to form a nook across the table and her head fell in its gap.

The sobs were raining down like water gushing from a punctured pipe.

'Isabel . . .' He tried hard to mould his voice into a soothing instrument. 'You are very, very young. At your age one learns a new language like *that*.' He snapped his fingers.

The prospect was too terrifying. She abstained from breakfast the following morning. Josef removed both girls from school, resolving to teach them the syntax and conjugations of English before their impending arrival. Their flight was scheduled for 22nd December.

Isabel rejected each attempt to be instructed. She stood up and bellowed, she stood up and sang, she danced around the kitchen on tiptoe, took her cello out on the balcony and practised in freezing cold temperatures. Nobody and nothing could impel her to desist. Anneliese had memorised nine sets of words already, among them her favourites being 'chemistry', 'sparkle' and 'vocabulary'. Before a mirror she practised her pronunciation four times daily.

Each deep breath of Anneliese's preceded another recitation of verbs that grated on Isabel's skin like an ill-tuned piano.

Two days before their departure Josef took one hand of each and led them to present their farewell to the city. Crowds were in a haste to do their Christmas shopping, crushing limbs along the way and grunting after each collision. Isabel peeked into gaps between the grey felt shoulder blades of people in the marching throng to swallow what she could of her beloved town. She beheld the triangular roofs topping red and violet rectangular prisms, fixated her eyes on the black sash windows; scrutinised small jewellers' shops and puny shrivelled men that gabbled in her mother tongue. She longed to brand into her memory the cornucopia of red, blue, gold and purple lanterns dangling in a row before the shop signs as her feet grew drenched in snow's entrenching slush: moisture was gathering at her toes and invading her soles.

The lanterns began surreptitiously to speckle by the dusky day; the sky was violet. Behind the blue apartment building Isabel could see a clocktower the colour of a pond; its arrowed handles fixed on the four and the one. As they trotted, careful not to smack the passers-by, she noticed that the compact, shady windows in each building were the same. The pattern continued as they came into narrower alleys, thinner streets and paved corners; as they descended a hill before mounting another.

Zurich was no flat city. Its texture was the principle of mountains alternating with the wells of valleys: the only kind of land that Isabel had known. If her feet did not encounter slopes her journey would become monotonous: amusical.

An hour later Josef took them on the Polybahn funicular. The little red crayon-like travelling hut carried them to the terrace of the ETH Zurich, Josef's former employer. They lingered there a while: the forecourt growing from a dark beige building boasting black sash windows glazed with cold, a few Greek columns finished with pale gold coronas and the shelter of a charcoal roof.

From this terrace a meandering maze of inclined, tightly-squeezed, semi-attached and individual towers was visible; each mottled with miniature windows and hatted with pitched maroon roofs. The Limmat River's wedge had cloven the vast city in two halves, each fortified by snow-topped Alps.

Isabel cast her eyes across night's landscape. When her feet collided with the bottom of the balustrade she noticed that small pebbles had amassed inside her shoes. Without the watch of Josef – busily engaged in yet another academic conversation with his favourite daughter – she crouched down and removed the shoe. Peering down, she suddenly beheld a speck of glint. Behind a few rocks, whirled in with the dust and sand there gleamed a purple sparkle. Isabel assumed it was a Christmas decoration. She reached out her hand and touched it with her index finger. It rolled into obscurity.

Through the sand her fingers rummaged and located it. It was a marble with a host of violet swirls. Immediately she put it in her pocket. Then she plunged her hand into the dirt and searched again. She found a red marble with the same pattern, then a dark blue one. Stealthily she tucked them both into her pocket, calling these her souvenirs of Zurich.

This displacement from her home would force her to remodel her existence. Her feet would slowly become numb without their wintry trampling over ice; the lack of hills would knock out all her sportsmanship. She had heard that certain people got sent to a nether world after they died: it was called 'hell'. And no distinction could be made between the unfamiliar city and this afterlife.

She was determined nonetheless. Isabel would not become a blackbird dethroned in its nest by a bloodthirsty cuckoo.

The morning they were due to leave she dressed in silence. After breakfast she approached her mother, who had nothing to advance except, 'What do you want?'

Isabel hoped she could look at her room. Elise had been deceived, unbeknownst to the girls, into believing they were going on holiday. Josef had surmised that soon enough she would forget about her hometown.

Twenty minutes later Josef entered the girls' bedroom. Anneliese was standing in her jacket, all her buttons fastened, her hands clasped behind her back.

Her voice was slim and tender as she spoke.

'Papa . . .'

'Yes?'

'I . . . I can't find Isabel.'

Josef began looking under beds and inside cupboards. He noticed that the door of their apartment was unlocked and headed out and scurried down the stairs. The echo resounded as his feet hit the steps; he was deaf to it. Anneliese ran out after him.

'Papa, can I help?'

There was no time to answer.

He plodded through the snow and alternated between left and right. No little girls were present without guardians; not three days before Christmas.

Down across the Limmat River he surveyed each building as he went. He peered through windows, intruded on his neighbours' private property, opened iron gates to houses where the sign 'No Trespassing' was hung. As he heard the splashes of the dark green water soak the bank the icy draught began to slice his spirit open.

No longer cold but petrified, he shoved his way through passers-by and headed back to the direction of the flat. Uneven streaks of tears criss-crossing down her face, his younger daughter was already on the lookout at the street's end.

'What are you *doing?*' he shouted at her. 'Get back inside!'

'Papa, I want to look for Isabel!'

Anneliese's breathing became heavier. Josef had to carry her up the exhausting flights of stairs that led to their apartment.

'Papa, let me look outside!' She kicked her legs against him till he had to put her on the floor. 'Papa!' she shouted over the apartment block so all the neighbours heard. 'But – let me look outside! I can go left and *you* go right . . .'

Her crying was enfeebling her. Leaving her in the apartment with the nonchalant Elise, he went back to resume unsparingly his vertigo-diseased pursuit.

Anneliese was sat in the corridor. After a few minutes of crying she continued her rummaging. She looked out of windows, fearing that Isabel might have decided she wanted to fly. All were closed.

She knew her father wouldn't like it but she left the building some time later.

It was already midday. She stuck her hands in her pockets and crossed roads by herself, travelling with haste to avoid strangers enquiring why she was alone. She didn't call her sister's name; she knew there could be no chance of response. Instead she wandered into alleys, entered every shop – even removed lids to scrutinise the rubbish bins.

Forced to wait for a neighbour to open the door of the building, three hours later she entered her home. When she got to their apartment it was open just as she had left it. No one was there except her mother. Her hands were red and grazed by cold.

She approached Elise: stoic as usual. Not knowing what to say, Anneliese scratched her head.

On a wall there hung a mirror. Her eyes were red, her cheeks were splotched and flustered. A thin red line across her knuckle was her proof of toil.

Two hours later she heard the door slam. It was dark. Her father had returned with empty hands.

'I went to the police station.' he told his daughter in a gasp. 'They said I could come look with them in twenty minutes.'

Anneliese began to tear up once again.

'But why . . . why would you tell the police?' Her weeping recommenced. 'I thought the police caught *bad* people . . .'

Despite her age the Younger Twin could understand how cumbersome her crying was. So she didn't seek a cuddle, didn't ask for reassurance. She simply went to Elise's room – a refuge in which no reaction was assured.

Stood with her back against the wall for over forty minutes, she was suddenly accosted by the trickle of a bouncing ball. Something bumped against her foot. She looked down at the sphere: a purple marble. Then another one gushed forth. They were emerging from the wardrobe in Elise's bedroom.

Anneliese thrust it open. There was her sister – trying not to breathe.

Anneliese broke her silence.

'*Isabel!*'

She squeezed her in a suffocating fashion. Isabel began to heave large sobs.

'Get *off* me! You weren't supposed to *find* me! Get *off* me, Liesa!'

It had not occurred to Josef to look for his daughter in his dormant wife's wardrobe. Elise had never even used her wardrobe; all her dresses were suspended from the hangers on her door.

Too furious to manifest relief, he dragged his daughter by the wrist and started yelling at her.

'But, Papi!' she moaned, still leaking tears, 'Why do we have to go? Because I didn't run away? I'll run away, you'll *see*! You'll never *find* me! You can't *force* me! Next time I'll *run away*! I'll run *away!!!*' she screamed.

Josef had no idea a child could be alarmingly hysterical and Isabel was almost wheezing.

Through the hissing simulated by his teeth he wanted to create a menacing and eerie tone.

'How could God have given me such an *unruly* child?'

'I'm not *going!* I'm not *going!!* I can't speak their language! I *won't* speak their language!!!' She kicked Josef's leg. Every time he tried to grab her she wrenched her arm out of his grip. 'It's *bad* in England!' she screeched. 'And I won't be *safe* there!! I could *not* be *safe there!!!*'

'Not safe? Why would you be "unsafe"? We're living in a house, a detached house, with no strange people in the area; a lovely suburb away from the centre . . . Why would you *not* be safe?'

She blubbered a little. Her lips quivered. Her energy faltered and she yielded to gloomy fatigue.

'I don't know, Papi . . . but I won't be *safe* there – I won't be *safe!*'

He sat down and propped her on his knee. They had already missed their flight.

'No harm will come to you. I'm here, Liesa is here. No harm will come to you.'

Anneliese began to stroke her sister's head.

The flight they eventually boarded took off the following day. A set of grisly, bumpy cobbles greeted Isabel when next she stepped on land. Stretches of thunder zipped their webs along the sky and a few hundred pints of rain cascaded. Arriving at their new abode on Glenluce Road in Blackheath she saw rising smoke escape the chimneys, houses that were dull brown cubes, windows half-barred by flimsy white gauze curtains. Turquoise apartment blocks did not grace grey British suburbia.

5.

Atomic disarray

Common knowledge had it that the fog was hazardous for lungs. Josef had read in the Swiss newspapers that children from the British poorhouses – forced into labour at the age of eight – ran through the streets with palms and cheeks both smeared in dirt; that beggars were not choosy when it came to preying on potential patrons.

Taking their cue from sooty scenes like these, the colours of the school were uninspiring. Murky brown meshed with downtrodden, dusty carpets branded by the stamps of little footprints stubbornly resistant to all kinds of vacuum cleaner. Anneliese preferred the teachers to the tone palette.

One and a half years had glided by. Josef's ears had noticed that his girls were picking up an English accent. Their consonants were crisp, their vowels were somewhat nasal and the Older Twin at last no longer had a German aspirate on every 'h' and 'v'. Isabel was fluent yet reliant on peculiar expressions or her independent coinage of an English word.

Anneliese became more open when it came to her affection – and a tad demanding.

Stealing away from the lower floor at lunchtime one day, she climbed the stairs to the next level where the older classes were located. It was a large staircase plunging down into the middle of the corridor, approximately four feet wide. To help the little ones ascend it had a silver rail on the left side.

Arriving at the summit, the exhausted eight-year-old fell short of breath. Looking up at the vast ceiling she could see the nectar of the sun suffuse the window as it shot its orange bolts across the walls. Fuzzy was her sight before its splendour. It was twenty-five degrees outside in mid-July. Nobody was loitering nearby. Isabel was probably outdoors, tossing her legs over a skipping rope.

Warm and buzzing rays were being pelted at the rail. It sparkled, almost blinding Anneliese, and she recalled how many times she had seen mavericks attempt to slide along the length of its illumined surface. Most of the time they vanquished the potential risks and stayed unhurt.

Though Anneliese was not aware of Newton's law of gravity she sensed it physically through her corporeal limitations. The air was her opponent: a phenomenon that dared her to embark on a defiant challenge. Whenever she flung an arm through the waft of the vacuum, the sound of the swipe made it tingle. Some force relayed to her the view that she could puncture this oppressive atmosphere.

Sliding across the rail could slice the air in half. In her mind she saw a vivid diagram of particles – for she had heard that air had particles. Sweeping across this bar would cut asunder this large stratosphere of soldered dots.

These exercises weren't accordant with the well-behaved, demure young ladies of her age. The only members of the school who practised them were older, gruff, dirty-haired schoolboys clad in grass-stained shirts.

But as she imagined the swishing stroke of the bar on her thighs and the breeze flapping at the hem of her dress, stealthily she pivoted and reassured herself no one was present. The amalgam she was shortly to foment – a fusion of the daring and the situationally deviant – set free the teeming mites of her exhilaration.

Rustles of a coarse and bumpy noise began to ring out through the hall. They weren't her preparations; rather – the school bell.

An elephant-like stampede of youngsters spluttered unabashedly into the grounds. Anneliese took gentle steps down the pedestrian side of her targeted staircase.

Struggling irremediably at science and at maths, Isabel for the most part neglected their homework and devoted herself to piano. A while ago the cello had become for her an old and cranky husband she was forced to tend to out of obligation; the other instrument her virile, thriving lover.

Nataliya Rakovskaya, her new piano teacher, had decreed on their first meeting that the sole important object *was* piano – that Isabel should exclude homework, outings to anywhere but concert houses and all social meetings with her peers – much to her father's chagrin.

The middle-aged woman believed that she ruled in their household; Isabel was one of her subjects. Often she brought her Russian sweets and pastries; sometimes a gold or silver necklace she believed might match a certain piece in a performance.

To the beaming, smiling Anneliese she did not tip her hat.

Josef regarded her with some disdain. But Isabel was so excited prior to her visits that he made a point of not dismissing her – though even *he* began to feel neglected.

What could he expect? His twins had never had a mother.

One evening at the end of September 1928 Madame Rakovskaya called Josef into his living room after a lesson. Isabel had scurried upstairs.

'Mr *Vandolt*,' cried Madame Rakovskaya, 'I talk to you about *Isabelle*.'

Josef detested it when someone pronounced his daughter's name as though it were French; it made her sound Catholic.

He forged a smile.

'Your daughter have much talent. She – very, very, very talented. When Artur Rubinstein have four years – he already *genius*. This girl – she maybe *genius*.'

Josef was more intimidated than flattered. Though he could not quite suffocate the swelling pride he felt in his evolving daughter's artistry, he likewise didn't want to pawn her off to a cantankerous, gaunt Russian lady.

'Mr *Vandolt*,' Madame Rakovskaya continued, slurring the 'sh's through her speech, 'she should go to competitions. She *vill vin* competitions. Two years – she *vill* play concert – *sohlo*.'

Such notions fired bullets of anxiety into Josef. He still picked out which stockings Isabel should wear each morning; there was no way she would perform these concerts by herself in front of upwards of a thousand people.

'She's very little, Madame Rakovskaya. I don't want to give her the pressure of a competition yet. For now I think a lot of teaching and practising will . . . *suffice*.'

'And other children?' Madame Rakovskaya's condescension demanded to know. 'Other children, these part in competition – six years. She – almost nine. She is *la-ate*, already – *la-ate*.'

'Well . . . er . . .' Motioning with his left hand, Josef appeared extremely apprehensive. 'Still, there is time left. For now I want her simply to enjoy playing, and to have the luxury to rehearse and improve.'

She shot him the look a Siberian peasant might dart at the neighbour who'd taken her bread.

At one point Erik von Gerber had mentioned to him the black sheep of Elise's family who had run off to London to marry a Jew. Josef had been vaguely informed that she and her husband 'lived in the Jewish area of London . . . or thereabouts.' He had interpreted this to mean Bethnal Green, and the name that had stuck in his head had been 'Hotzen'. Of course, 'Hotzen' could constitute no complete Jewish name, and it was 'Reuven Hotzenplotz' that he found listed.

The Hotzenplotzes' daughter was named after her never-seen aunt. Elise Hotzenplotz was a year older than the girls, spoke English and no German, and was being brought up to be Orthodox and learning Hebrew.

Josef's attitude to Jews was not exactly kosher. Once he had made it clear he wanted no influence wrought over his girls – that he did not want them to hear of the Torah, that he wanted Liesel to hide their menorah and mezuzah should they ever come over – only then was their first meeting arranged for the first week of August.

Isabel's eyes fell on the bale of carrot-coloured cotton standing just before their door, donning a pair of glasses to precociously resemble an old spinster. Elise's cheeks were spattered with the clusters of compressed and blending freckles; her orange locks were thick as bear fur.

Liesel – a woman with a vocal twang of high, atonal frequency – crouched down to address Isabel warmly in German. The latter found her patronising.

'My little *Wunderkind* . . . you're not so little, eh?'

Isabel hardly budged.

Anneliese liked Elise at first sight, gathering that she – unlike Isabel – was lacking in mischief; her attraction to a scheduled regularity persuaded her to hover near her cousin. They would discuss the Earth's rotation, interferometry, *Three Men in a Boat* and other names eluding Isabel's cognition.

Isabel pretended that the 'ginger person' was not there, retreating to her keys and pedals. Nevertheless Anneliese and Elise liked to linger in the corridor and exchange their ideas within earshot. Hearing the diction of her cousin's crystal English – and now even her sister's largely accentless speech – Isabel was tossed into the middle of a savage tribe's kerfuffle. All of it made up some form of rotten music to her: one in which the vulgar timpani bashed out of rhythm and the cymbal's rattle of vibration persevered in perpetuity.

She drowned out their voices with her playing; it unclogged her soul and rinsed the dregs out of her system. Yet every twenty minutes she would lean back on her stool and very surreptitiously begin to spy on them. Disgruntled, Isabel would huff and start to play more viciously.

Two weeks later Josef and the Hotzenplotzes took their girls to see *Eugene Onegin*, the opera. Isabel's eyes had moistened at the end; coaxing the girl to hide her shiny glance and wipe her tacit tears on an extended sleeve.

He found her still tossing and turning in her bed three hours later, pursuing her drizzling lament.

'But *meine Kleine*,' he assured her in German, 'that kind of thing doesn't happen in real life.'

She sniffed and looked at him in newfound hope.

'It doesn't?'

'No.' Josef whispered dismissively. 'They create that for stories. In real life, it's much easier. A man and woman love each other, they get married, they have children. It is God's will. It doesn't happen that a man and woman who adore each other are, for some reason, meant to be apart.'

Isabel glowed with refreshment. Josef stroked her knee and hugged her before leaving her in a good-spirited and sanguine state.

'Thank you, Papi.' she observed.

Poor Josef on the other hand was not so fortunate this time. Fate's trident had its newly sharpened prongs primed to relate to him a different story.

6.

Cascading trail

Pedagogues at Westfield College were the children of a different century. Most of the professors in the faculty had come into the world post-1900 and just recently obtained their doctorates.

By accepting his post at the new Westfield College for Women Josef had thwarted his principles. It meant that he would have to accept women as potential scientists. And that alone for Josef was too coarse and overcooked a piece of meat to swallow.

It was a case where ends would justify the means.

Independently from that the scenic change was indefatigably scarring: a vision that had surfaced so far only in the bleak back alleys of his nightmares. As he had heard so often, the crass city was a hub for careless, rowdy drinkers crowding public houses every night. It was a place where they played vulgar, locally known musical refrains so that the drunks could croon along instead of working. Tobacco-ridden music halls were crowded with dishevelled bands of miscreants arrived to see a lewd, offensive man tell sordid jokes before he juggled. Sometimes they threw knives; sometimes they swallowed them.

On a quiet evening in the paths of Covent Garden he could simultaneously encounter in the same square mile an educated, bowler-wearing, middle-aged professor and a pack of bottle-wielding hooligans who chirped tone-deaf: 'My old *ma-an* said follow the *va-an* . . .' a song whose lyrics Josef still stopped short of understanding.

As for intellectuals, it was they who festered in the tortured angle of his psyche. Those in Bloomsbury – Josef had been warned – were a vibrant, hapless herd of ill-conceived barbarians. They convinced themselves they knew more than a little about literature, wrote rhymeless verse and prose abundant with crude jargon and inhabited domestic situations seeking to subvert the course of nature.

Too raucous were his colleagues: loose and open. Every time he heard loud voices surging he would yearn for a retreat into his fogless, smogless, ill-advanced, regressive, backwards land: the small Dutch town of Lisse he had bitterly abandoned almost thirty years ago.

The rest of the staff picked on Josef, not viciously and not unkindly – they were English, after all – but it was clear that somewhere in the backgrounds of their minds they deemed him 'funny'. He never had in his possession the most recent 'in vogue' papers. Many works of his would only cite a host of nineteenth-century sources.

And yet the university did not exactly bear prestige. Its influx of professors was a challenging development in progress; hence their reasons for recruiting Josef van der Holt. The least popular of the college's science departments was this infant one four years of age.

As of September 1928, only two other professors beside Josef were neurologists: Professor Swenson – obese and puffy with a double chin, of old age and small stature, who interspersed each seminar with coughs from his cigar smoke – and a skinny lad just over thirty, Dr Anvill. The latter had been addled to hear Josef's swift refusal to accompany him 'for a pint': 'I thought you ol' cloggies liked a bit of Dutch courage,' he had nudged him with his tapered elbow.

By the beginning of that academic year the second had already vanished. There was a woman at the university. She was a professor *and* a doctor who had been the first choice for the post: a recruit from the more reputable St Mary's Hospital Medical School.

Josef's worst nightmare was being realised.

An awkward and misguided sense of her had stirred in him since his first learning of her presence.

For the past few weeks he had begun to sense a missile darting past him as he lingered in the corridors: it flew with all the valour of a fired rocket spearing into battle.

Someone was busy digging an extensive tunnel through the atmosphere; the figure seared through air as though there were a copious supply of it. He was quite certain she was capturing and hogging – even hankering to actually *monopolise* it. It was a presence he had never seen, although at one point he had felt the sharp bulk of a shoulder blade extemporaneously strike his own.

It suffocated Josef – striking his few moments of tranquillity. Another element began to aggravate this taut compression: the lanky missile gliding with propulsive fury used the rhythmic clop of high heels to announce itself.

He never turned his back. In part he associated this unbending reticence with his dismay at the idea of women teaching. In part he felt it was an outrage that a woman could comport her frame so violently and briskly. And finally it was because the perfumed waft that trailed behind this clop of heels was some tonality of rose and jasmine and the notes of oriental spices; its absorption was intoxicating and alarming to him.

Ajitter every time his nose came into contact with the scent, he feared she wouldn't be repellent to him. It was burdensome and inconvenient because he wanted her to be an ogre.

She was hardly *not* privy to it. Every time he had a chance to meet with her he exercised the caution of avoidance. Tangibly and olfactorily and auditorily he had a strong perception of her and he longed to ward off supplementing 'sight' to these four senses.

It was already late October and increasingly unlikely that he could prolong his distance from her for the next nine months. On a languorous, summery afternoon he felt the clopping had desisted, felt the perfume drifting near his nostrils, felt the air especially depleted.

Needless to say she was standing behind him. In wait.

He heard the clock strike two and came to realise it was time for him to be accosted by the spectacle of his tormentor. Evidently it was she who wanted to deflect adjournment of this meeting.

'I don't believe we've met.'

Second only to the aural palette of her shoes was this discovery of her by ear.

He had no choice but to confront her. The hope that he had nurtured in his arsenal was now upended by a ruthless onslaught of attrition.

Compact figurines Josef had come to know in Europe – both the hapless doll of Annemieke and the pocket-sized Elise – were little more than stunted seedlings in comparison to her. Edificial, pliant, she had flat, extended shoulders that ensured her posture the capacity to shun all evidence of discomposure.

Soon his greatest weakness got the better of him once again. Josef was immediately hurled into the messy puddle of a gross discomfort.

These were not eyes he looked at; they were objets d'art. Anneliese may have inspired his affection through endearment she inherently enkindled. This one – this one whose name he still awaited – had a pair of eyes no rare collector's doll could warrant.

The eyes in paintings of Dutch Masters he had known of Flemish or Germanic women had been circular or narrow or the shape of hazelnuts. Josef had always deemed that labelling eyes 'big' served only to imply a *form* of prettiness: these ones were almond-shaped and vast; encompassed width and stature. They alternated between grey and green and blue with each of her head's subtle tilts. Uplifted outer tips regaled them with hypnotic magnetism. Emblematic were they of a work of Modernism by an artist like Picasso; something in the realm of Cubism or decadence where human beings were deliberately illustrated with distorted features.

Josef had despised those artists for their daring, their *improbability*; their wanton craving to subvert God's natural work.

Now he learnt their models featured in real life.

In those corners there resided some exhibit of a sly foreknowledge: overflowing wells that sourced her cunning. As she amplified her smile the mischief only grew in palpability. Its gleam spread to her cheekbones, dusting them with the pomade of silver.

The impolite enormity of her collation of extruding features didn't finish there. Between those instruments there was a rounded triangular bulk of a nose with the rigid small ball of a tip; below it a pair of wide lips. Fluffed flaxen waves were hovering an inch above her shoulders: strands sealed glossily in place to look as smooth as golden satin.

But why he was conversing with himself about this was beyond all understanding. He was no artist, kept no paintbrush and he wasn't going to go and buy himself an easel.

Her hand was still outstretched as she put forth:

'Sara.'

Nervous as he hastily beheld the five extensive fingers, Josef watched the curling set of long and slender tendrils stretch to clasp the trellis of his own.

With a clearing of his throat he took her hand and finally produced an apt response.

'How do you do?'

The grip of her fingers was somewhat misplaced, strong and stalwart. Furling over Josef's digits with an infantile dependence, they were a koala bear's slippery claws. Slowly and tenuously she released him.

Despite what he perceived to be solemn timidity, she did not dote long on formalities.

'It seems Professor Swenson's mind escapes the tasks it doesn't document.'

To this Josef could only nod vigorously. Then something clicked in his mind.

'I'm sorry?'

'I've been here almost seven weeks and we were never introduced.'

Her tone was a little commanding and tinged with surprise. Nonetheless she walked away a few steps and as though by way of a reminder uttered:

'If you do need something, you will come to see me upstairs.'

He didn't understand it. *She* was the new one at the university.

Lingering a few steps back, she tacitly awaited some endeavour of a confirmation. Her eyes flitted hither-thither till she finally relented, turned her back and quickly launched into her skimming pace.

Successive weeks provided him no balm of relaxation. Isabel was spending supplementary hours at Madame Rakovskaya's merciless helm; Anneliese was exhausting the books in his library. In addition she was anxiously and obstinately warding off her sleep – so eager was she to discover from her father 'what exactly happens after death'.

He could struggle with the premise that his girls would have a future that would evidently change them. He could struggle with his fear of how he had to build some rampart to protect them from the outside world. And he could struggle with the fear of what might happen once they started questioning their mother's mental state.

Alternatively, he could struggle with the premise that he kept on musing about unrelated matters ... like those eyes. In all respects he didn't have a clue which ailment was the easier to cure.

A little while into the week her voice's memory began to dawn on him; the purity of an embroidered, slick contralto.

Gone was the conventional ribbed texture, the infirmness and the gravel sound associated with the timbre. This crusty layer had been scrubbed away in favour of unbridled fluency. A sleek, embracing instrument of slowly trickling honey, it reserved the smack of its authority for scarce and select intervals.

He rightfully assumed that one day he would witness other variations of the tone: a bolder execution, a mellower, more airy efflorescence, maybe a throatier and damaged sound. For now it remained lingering, expectant: aglow like a cascade of liquid oil trailed by the wispy sound that slithered from its base, its subtle whoosh surpassing the stale air.

In the middle of November Professor Swenson gestured to him in the corridor. Stroking the tip of his moustache, he advised Josef:

'I'm sorry to say that Sara might be leading some of our less independent-minded students ... er ...' Dithering, he almost wheezed. 'Cognitively *astray*, so to speak. They are *girls*, after all, and she is their superior in age and learnedness and ... well, they are quite ... *impressionable*, if you like.'

Josef was suddenly quite short of breath.

'Well, Professor, I really think ... I think ... I'm not sure that I ... it's not for me to say.'

'You see ... it appears she's quoting Ladd.'

'Ladd?'

'He wrote a book on physiological psychology.'

His heart plummeted some several miles: the customary reflex he experienced upon consumption of the word 'psychology'.

'We've had her giving lectures in neurophysiology. But some of the students have noticed that . . . well, they say she's putting quite a spin on them. They're hardly *orthodox*.'

'I see.'

'I want *you* to discuss this with her.'

Josef's eyes were still.

'I?'

'Yes.'

'I barely . . . we met only once.'

'Yes, but I have a feeling she's ever so slightly *pestered* by me.' He inhaled deeply and all of a sudden a lightbulb grew bright in his mind. 'I'll tell you what, old boy – why don't you attend one of her lectures . . .' Professor Swenson stroked his thumb with his rapacious forefinger. 'Make your own calculations and – if you assume that her material is *wanting* in . . . do go and have a little chat with her.'

He was stymied. But Professor Swenson was the head of the department. Spurning his requests would be interpreted as insubordination.

'Very well.'

That afternoon he walked into the Mendeleev Hall. Only a few girls were seated there: neurology was hardly popular. For that reason the lectures occasionally took the tone of a seminar rather than a formal, organised speech through which students refrained from projecting opinions.

She was standing on the podium to demonstrate her point on the enormous diagram pinned on the board: a brain.

'The orbitofrontal cortex is where . . . they say . . .' She was looking at her diagram inquisitively, almost with smugness, almost as though one could imply she was in doubt of it. 'They allege that's where our moral wherewithal resides.'

One bespectacled brunette lifted her hand.

'Yes?'

'Our conscience resides in the orbitofrontal cortex?'

'It inhibits action of the amygdala.'

'So . . .' the brunette held her pencil just below her face, 'do you mean to say that if a man wants to commit murder, *ergo* the oribitofrontal cortex must be impaired?'

The other girls attempted to suppress their laughter.

Sara kept on looking at the diagram with condescension. With a resigned air that lined her alto voice with dryness, she eventually spouted:

'I don't think that's what happened when Pozdnyshev killed his wife in *The Kreutzer Sonata*.'

The girls were confounded and still. Facing them anew, Sara reattempted the answer.

'"No" was the answer to that question.'

'Do you mean . . .' (it was the impatient brunette again), 'I'm sorry – are you using fictional examples to support your points?'

'Would you rather I mentioned Jack the Ripper?'

The eyes of the girls grew.

'I simply meant that . . . No, I don't believe an impaired orbitofrontal cortex and enlarged amygdala could explain an errant moral conscience. Certainly not . . .' She blinked for a little while. '*Murder*. It's too elementary.'

The brunette raised her hand another time.

'Yes, Miss Whittaker?'

'Would you say you reject Darwin outright?'

'No.'

'So you reject Christianity outright?'

'Yes.' The girls attempted to process this knowledge. Sara pondered for a short while, as though groping at the answer with her hand. After some timid sighs she confessed.

'No.'

'Well . . . but Professor, excuse me if I may – but you seem indecisive in this matter. That wasn't . . .' The brunette scratched at the back of her neck. 'Your answer isn't concrete.'

'No, it's not.'

'Why don't you give us one?'

'I don't see how it bears any relevance. You study Darwinism. I don't lecture on it.'

'You're suggesting human conscience is driven by natural selection, random mutations, physiological . . .' Miss Whittaker scoffed with indignation. 'Spontaneity.'

Sara swayed a little on the spot and accidentally stomped with one of her high heels.

'Girls . . . I can't tell you for sure if there's a *soul*, if that is in the scope of your requests.'

'And yet you're telling us that immorality is the cause of an impairment in the orbitofrontal cortex.'

'No, I was informing you that in the case of damage to the oribitotfrontal cortex, it wouldn't be surprising to see cases of a lapse in self-awareness; which in turn could . . . trigger some immoral acts.'

'But that isn't its cause?'

Sara looked up and her eyes appeared on fire.

'Its cause could be a woman stealing someone's husband.'

A spread of gasps began to flutter through the hall.

'Or perhaps a man has far too many complexes; he wants to practise his one-upmanship. The *cause* is not what's up for discussion at this point.'

'Then, what *is*?'

'The neurophysiological diagram that shows an impaired orbitofrontal cortex.' She heard the girls strike out a previous note and write anew. Coated more thickly with aplomb, her voice beseeched them to consider: 'But even if you *want* it to be psychological . . . How am I to know what *caused* it? I don't even know *who* caused it. The diagram is hypothetical. In any case – he probably just tumbled on his head. There is no *chance* you're going to find life's meaning there.'

An hour later Josef went upstairs to find the little enclave he believed to be her office. Left fractionally ajar, the door allowed him to espy her bent down at her bookcase lining spines of a long row of tomes with her right forefinger.

He knocked three times.

'Come in.'

She didn't turn around. He wondered if she even knew who stood there.

'Excuse me—'

'Yes?'

'I, erm . . .'

'Take your hands out of your pockets.'

Rigid in their stance, her eyes were still glued to the books.

'Professor Swenson asked me to inform you . . . he told me to pass on the message . . . not to promote this . . . this . . .' It was one of those instances when the English translation escaped his vocabulary; many motions of his hand now had to goad him to remember it. 'The . . . *omission* of the soul too . . . *vastly*.'

Only now did she spring up – and he remarked that she was wearing an enormous pair of glasses. She swung her head in his direction.

'Was I doing that?'

'It *seems* so, yes.'

'When?'

'At your lecture this afternoon.'

'No, I was . . . I don't believe I ever *omitted* the soul.'

'You told your students you did not believe in Christianity.'

'No, I actually confused them – quite deliberately.'

'So – you are a deist?'

'No.'

'You believe in metaphysical matter?'

Blankly she looked at him. Snatching the glasses from her eyes in one fast jibe to let them dangle from her fingers, Sara let her lips curve up into a smile.

'Where?'

'I'm – I'm sorry?'

'When you find it, let me know.'

The fixed stare melted and became a nurturing, compassionate and somewhat playful scrutiny. She had to look down for a second to restructure her facial expression. Then she turned away again to find the volume that eluded her.

Having grasped the book she targeted the page she needed, swallowed some lines briskly and abruptly slammed it shut.

'I don't believe in anything that disregards the recent findings in neurophysiology. It's those I teach.'

Her exit from the room was quieter and more elusive than the book had been. It would have left the objects in its space unruffled had it not been for an open window whose crazed wind propelled the door to clatter.

In the next two weeks they exchanged only visual communication. He never deigned to go knock at her office door, which was bizarrely always open. He never deigned to sit in on her lectures. He always ate lunch in his office and he almost never spoke to the professors.

But his uncompromising curiosity seduced him into snatching eyefuls. Traipsing through the corridor, Sara would halt at intervals to wipe her glasses with a cloth. Much of the time she seemed phlegmatic and unoccupied by any thought of people presently existing. She possessed an irksome habit of placing, adjusting and removing her glasses like the five-year-old Isabel.

And yet she dressed far too alluringly to be an academic. He saw so many long silk skirts of white and blue and – later in the season – cotton ones of brown and black; sometimes maroon and ruby red; he witnessed long-sleeved robes of different colours and it seemed that she selected them to compliment the weather. He only usually saw ladies dressed for lavish Sunday luncheons in the same attire.

Since Sara had some inexplicable propensity for keeping doors a little open, he was sharpening the habit of espying her at work. During those moments of experiment he wondered whether her demeanour became severed from reality. Her focus seemed to lack acknowledgement of beings; it was as though she wished not only to avoid all humans but all mammals *generally*. As she allowed her eyes to scrutinise a piece of *gyrus rectus* she appeared to have escaped the earth's dominion. Mesmerised by her contraption, the submerged young woman was displaced: not lost and not disturbed – rather, located *elsewhere*.

Expressions of joy she derived from a successful analysis or winsome experiment would embellish her eyes with the sparkle of self-loving glee. It sprayed over her irises some shiny glitter that he mused could either be her cunning or a trace of some naïvety; it fused the hints of both. The sight of it alarmed him so much he could not sustain the mental power *not* to think about it.

Josef had to get away. He struggled to identify his persecutor – yet 'away' he had to go.

7.

Metamorphoses

With Anneliese and Isabel in tow the three of them journeyed to Drury Lane to watch *Hamlet* one night. Bustling huddles clogged the entrances of the sold-out production.

Isabel slept through the first act. Positioned squarely on her shoulder, her head spouted inhalations too loud through 'the slings and arrows of outrageous fortune'. Periodically her father had to wake her up.

Anneliese sustained her focus on the stage. During the interval the girl insisted she had read 'the better part of it in Dutch aged six'.

The twins needed to go the ladies'; the queue was exhaustive. He awaited them at a short distance from it.

Meanwhile his eyes dashed through the room surveying those injurious types: men on their fourth glass of whiskey, untucked shirts, ladies whose perfumes left a lot to be desired. Only through the inescapable absorption of these nebulous aromas did he come across a musk he could identify: the one he had sought adamantly to avoid.

Supposing she had seen him, witnessed his blunt negligence and then begun to wallow in her upset? Women were so *prone* to wallow in their upset.

So he let his nose convey him to the source of that familiar trap. Yet he did not expect that source to have that semblance: sedentary at a table where the other chair was vacant, letting fingers curl around the rim of a half-empty glass.

She was wearing a black, floor-length gown whose train trailed slovenly along the ground. It clad her arms but laid bare both her shoulders.

The sleeves extended to her hands so that they too were half-draped in Alençon lace that finished with a hook suspended from her middle finger.

A long and daring slit conspicuously clambered up her knee. Crossing one leg on the other leant the pair an unavoidable exposure; both were crowned with black high heels that added some three inches to their length. Her flaxen waves had grown and now were coiffed and splayed across her shoulders.

Spotting him, she faced him with a wily look, eyes narrowed, twisting her mouth a little bit as though devising some connivance.

In this glare there was a touch of sinister; the tinge of some premeditated ruse.

She did not say 'hello' because she knew *he* wouldn't. Turning to the glass in front of her, she picked it up to take a sip.

He wondered whether rumours would be stirred if Josef neared a woman of her current *genre*.

Simultaneously he feared for Westfield's saintly reputation. In any case it would be giving off an air of dreadful impoliteness if he snubbed her.

Taking care to check the premises for possible familiar faces, he examined lengthily the queue outside the ladies' to make sure his twins were out of sight and then approached her speedily. By now she was staring at him, faintly curious, her chin perched on a laced hand. As he proceeded to sit down before her, her mouth almost curved in her bid to nix possible giggling.

Nonplussed, he spoke more plainly than he had expected.

'Women and science . . . is not the most appropriate collision.'

Nervousness tended to scramble the flow of his language.

'That's a rare piece of philosophy coming from someone who teaches at an all women's college.'

He cleared his throat.

'I understand there are exceptions.'

She did not disagree:

'Exceptions. Not many examples.'

His eyebrows were raised. She smiled and only now propelled her eyes to dance with playful glee. It was a close-mouthed smirk that indicated he was very funny to her.

Josef failed to comprehend it.

'I'm not sure that you . . . *befit* such an example.'

'I'm not sure either. I looked for an appropriate test,' she said, swaying her glass, 'but I passed all the academic ones and nothing told me I was wrong, given my two titles of "doctor" and my three and a half other qualifications.'

Her eyes were still beaming.

'You have other quali—' He gave up and sighed. 'A lady in such a position should not be . . .'

'Well, I know. But I am, and I'm waiting for someone. So if you could kindly just . . .' She motioned rhythmically in circles with her right hand.

A towering gentleman was heading to the table. It was far more knowledge of her private life than was his limit and immediately he rose.

'Dr van der Holt,' she addressed him hurriedly, 'it's amino acid that you're looking for.'

'I'm sorry?'

'I took a look at your paper this afternoon. You want to find amino acid.'

Slowly the equation clicked into the confines of his mind.

'You came into my office and you took my—'

'Well, I was going to tell you, but I was in a mood of feeling mean and so . . .' Her voice drifted in volume and she placed her chin atop her hand; perhaps a little ill at ease.

Soon enough the male figure sat itself opposite. Instinctively she embarked on some fiery exchange: bidding her eyes flit up and down and left and right; straddling her glass with both her hands, letting a chortle lapse from time to time and sparkle.

The next morning he passed her by in the corridor clad in a white jacket and skirt, her hair neatly pinned-up. In the interim she had secluded the sly creature she unfurled at night. Again there rose her lofty academic figure as she breezed her way through corridors with a high pedigree of ease.

When Professor Swenson stopped her with a tome of some three thousand pages at the threshold of her office, she immediately let her handbag slide onto her upper arm and took the book from him with all ten fingers. Her gratitude now left her flustered and she struggled to relay a typical reply:

'Yes, you see, well, I've been looking for it for five months now . . . it's a huge surprise that they don't stock it anywhere in London. I tried to go to Oxford for it – but the time is lacking in the day.'

'Isn't it *so*?' Professor Swenson sprung forth to respond – this being the sole grievance he could understand.

'I shall have it returned within six days.'

'No need – my father was the only one who used it and he passed away four months ago.'

The conversation splashed into the commonplace exchanges Josef heard at luncheons and he witnessed how exquisitely she dabbled in it like a married mother or a governess – far from the calculating vixen he had chanced upon the previous night.

Twenty minutes later he was toiling away at some long chemical equation on the chalkboard in the Mendeleev Hall. It wasn't long before it became clear to him that she had coiled her way into his whereabouts again.

Stood against the door, Sara attempted to feign patience with her wringedly clasped hands. Inexplicably she had let loose her hair but it was still a little ill-arranged compared to its condition at the theatre. After an irritated period of examining his poor attempts she told her colleague in a dry, lethargic tone:

'It should take another three minutes.'

He set the chalk and rubbed his chin.

'Well, that won't help.' she pointed out.

Eventually she walked up to the board, took Josef's chalk and scribbled an equation that extended to six lines. Her eyes were swiftly checking as she handed him the chalk.

It took Josef seven minutes to deduce her answer was correct. Once he admitted his agreement she seemed scarcely interested and exited the room.

That afternoon before he left to pick his girls up he resolved to lay the grounds for moral reconciliation. Stepping outside, he nervously awaited her emergence from the doors.

Instead he couldn't help but overhear a conversation from some yards away. There it was that he caught sight of her – her hair pinned-up again.

She was standing by a small young lady with black hair, lips coated in thick rouge, accoutred with the sartorial makings of exactly those women he desperately longed to avoid. Any reason to consort with such a woman would be scarcely justifiable.

'Mmm . . . *but* the soap – they use – *c'est un cauchemar.*' came the undesired's throaty instrument.

Awkward in her vigilance, Sara hastened to touch her on the forearm and insist:

'You'll have to tell me about it . . . on Saturday.'

'*Mais, oui!*'

She replied as though it were apparent:

'Indeed.'

'*A samedi, ma chérie!*'

Sara's accent remained cautiously and deliberately English as she replied:

'A samedi.'

Walking to her car, he trailed her steps as they grew louder. She was the only woman that he knew who had a car. There he distracted her – since she had not yet noticed him – and asked with spurious naïvety:

'Do you receive them in your house?'

Sara had already opened the door. She let her hand rest on it and gave him a straight, undiluted response.

'Occasionally, on weekends – yes. They feel safe there.'

'And, er . . .' He parted his lips noisily, resealed them, swallowed and then spoke. 'I heard that you . . . I heard you had a daughter.'

With the dawdling tone that he had used she shrunk her voice to half its volume, imitating lightly:

'A daughter . . .'

'You receive these women in your home with your daughter . . . in the same house?'

She was a little bit taken aback. It took a giant inhalation and a few blinks to finally issue the phrase:

'I'm not worried about her taking after their style, if that's what you mean.'

'But why do you . . .'

'The reasons are legitimate.'

They stood at odds about how to address each other. The way she gazed around suggested that she was indebted to him. Finally she offered:

'Do you need a lift somewhere?'

He responded with a lack of understanding.

The Christmas holidays arrived and Josef had no place where he could posit Anneliese and Isabel except for leaving them at home with 'mother'.

One late December morning he took both the girls to work,

brought them to the largest library and dashed off to a lecture – intermittently returning to ensure that the librarian was supervising them.

At five o'clock Josef performed his seventh routinely inspection. With no instrument at hand, Isabel was perfunctorily restless. Huffing and puffing was the captain of time's vessel. When he kissed both girls and left them to attend a meeting with Dr Pilkington she pressingly pursued him; footsteps started storming down the corridor.

'Isabel.' He bent down and commanded rather softly. 'Stay here with your sister.'

'I want to go with *you*.' she insisted.

Leaving Anneliese with the librarian, they traversed the corridor to the Department of Neurology. There he met Dr Pilkington in the John Hughlings Jackson Room. The latter was at his desk surveying some papers, a young boy in a rugby kit standing behind him.

'I'm afraid my little girl wanted to come with me.' he explained to Dr Pilkington apologetically.

'That's quite all right. My son just dropped by to tell me his exam results – all ninety per cent and above.'

'*Very* well done.' Josef offered a polite smile.

'Oh, I haven't introduced you.' Dr Pilkington noted. 'Josef, this is my boy, Vincent.'

'How do you do?' the boy asked most politely, extending his hand. He had a radiant smile and curly, ginger-brown hair that glowed under the light from the ceiling. Josef returned the greeting and presented his daughter.

'This is my 'Older Twin', Isabel. I left Anneliese in the library; she is most interested in visual agnosia, strangely enough. Say "hello", Isabel.'

The nine-year-old was struck by stupefaction. She gawped at the boy as though he were an alien from a country on the other side of the equator, dressed in other people's clothes and bearing mannerisms quite exotic in comparison to those she knew.

'Say "hello", Isabel.' Josef repeated.

Very faintly she let out a weak 'hello' then had to clear her throat. The boy was quite amused and grinned at her.

Josef began to feel a little nervous for his daughter.

'Isabel,' he calmly suggested, 'you really won't have anything to do here. Let me take you back to Liesa.'

She shook her head quite vigorously with her eyes still obstinately on the boy.

'Isabel.' He began to head back to the door. 'Come on, *meine Kleine.*'

She was rigid everywhere except her eyes, which fluttered quite conspicuously. He had never seen a girl know how to bat her lashes at the age of nine.

'Excuse me.' Josef apologised to Dr Pilkington, who found the sight enchanting. He picked Isabel up and swung her over his shoulder. By the following month her height and weight wouldn't allow him that.

'I think it's best we take you to the library again, yes?'

She didn't answer. As he turned around to carry her across the corridor her head poked out above his shoulder. Dr Pilkington and Vincent saw her smiling beamingly, still forcefully reluctant to unstick her eyes. Only after losing sight of Vincent did she gradually recover her tranquillity.

'Papi – when will we see those nice people again?' she squealed as he set her in front of the lift.

Obsessed with pressing spots, she pushed the button before Josef even asked her to.

As the doors opened turbulence rocked Josef's entrails. In the lift's corner she was wearing some black and white jacket and skirt combination he strove not to look at.

She gathered he was loath to make an introduction between such a virulent young woman and his unadulterated daughter. So Sara smiled at Isabel quite warmly and expected no response.

She turned around to press for the third level: the location of the library.

Impetuous and violently exhilarated from her episode, Isabel tugged at her jacket.

Josef immediately scolded the girl in a whisper:

'*Isabel!*'

She heeded no attention to him. The woman was looking down at her inquisitively, rummaging around in her mind for an answer. Isabel eyed her with a menacing glare.

It wasn't long before Sara retreated from the buttons and addressed Isabel:

'Oh . . . sorry. That was insensitive of me.'

The Older Twin then seized the opportunity to press the button. A fierce stare served to admonish the strange woman; reticently humbling Josef in her presence. He found himself addressing her with struggling effort:

'I'm sorry.'

Purposely ignoring his whisper, Sara replied with more volume than usual:

'Why on earth are you apologising?'

This caught Isabel's attention just a little bit. She looked at her father and Sara but – engaged in her private anxieties – quickly returned to the buttons.

Isabel enquired about 'those nice people' five times a day – even on Christmas. When Josef finally relented and confessed that probably she would not see the boy again, her bitter heartache sent her spinning into juvenile depression.

For three days before the New Year she excused herself early from lunch to go practise her crying. The whistle of her wailing, although stifled by her head and arms, prevailed and was distinctly audible through her closed door.

Refusing her porridge, she justified fasting with a glum 'I'm not hungry'. Every time her father looked at her she sat with a lugubrious and melancholy glare: the replica of a young bride whose beau had just gone to the front.

Anneliese began to think it was an act and tired of it. The attention Isabel was hogging from her father was depriving him of time to spend with her discussing cells and nuclei and corporal decay.

Moroseness was still plaguing her on New Year's Day of 1929. That afternoon she sat down to play Liszt's transcription of *Ernani*, Verdi's opera. Listening to her performance, Josef heard her bass notes emanate malicious omens that had hitherto gone undetected by his ear. Watching her fingers sprawl across the keys, he found himself at loss to understand the reasons for the differences in tone between the rival hands.

While the right could scale the keyboard with mellifluous arpeggios and scales, the left preferred to lower gloomy iron gates that throbbed in one compulsive leitmotif. She was embarking on constructing two opposing entities. The right hand pranced with a light-hearted flair while its antagonist contended with an augury of doom.

Split in this dichotomy, the piece's executor didn't give one hand a chance to dominate the other. Josef saw her eyes wince, narrow and then widen as she interchanged the jovial with her oppressive bleakness.

After enlacing straits of misery with lilts of lightness Isabel inanely looked at him. She was unchanged and still so far from burgeoning into a woman. Coolly she threw off the remark, 'It's from a Verdi opera, Papi.' before turning to the sheet music to mark something in with her pencil.

Something vociferous was rumbling in him. She was already too old for her age, and this – God's gift – gave her a supplementary maturity.

It was not long before he entered Westfield College for another term that bolstered his persistent sleeplessness.

This blunt trauma he was suffering could not be diagnosed. For it was not desire; it was not a desperate need to have possession of this woman. Copulation constituted a straightforward means of reproduction: it did not occur to him that love could be its catalyst. He clung tenaciously to the idea that forcing women to endure it for the sake of males' hedonistic pleasure was the highest pedigree of insult.

Desperately he needed to decipher her. There were few codes in life that Josef had not cracked. And now he spent the better hours of his day in the exhausting exultation of analysis.

He approached Sara one morning before an expectedly boring meeting with Swenson. Josef began to rabbit on about his gifted daughter.

'She's going to be a Fanny Mendelssohn, you know.'

Sara nodded. She was obviously untouched.

'I wouldn't be able to tell, I can't stand music.'

Appalled by her near-nonchalance, he retorted with something aspiring to slight:

'I should think, considering the number of men you must . . .' (his English hurt him yet again), '*parade* with, that you must do a lot of dancing.'

'That's where I play truant.'

'But . . .' They arrived at the John Hughlings Jackson room and waited for Professor Swenson to arrive.

'It's an intolerance, Josef.' she insisted in a most straightforward way – as though he was supposed to understand it was unhelpable.

He went silent. After a few moments she resumed:

'The arrangement of notes is an algorithm . . .' Suddenly she went shy again, folding her arms. 'I can read music. I can't listen to it. It looks a great deal better than it sounds.' She closed her mouth and looked ahead for a long pause. Then, like any thorough academic, she decided that her declaration was in need of explanation:

'It's a cloud of instruments that clash together to create effects that mathematically match up. It's science, only without any productive outcome. If composers have to entertain themselves some way . . . why don't they just perform division exercises?'

Such a stand on her part could have led him to condemn her. Instead through a perplexing paradox his appetite for music coaxed him to enjoy her intonations. He started to anticipate the next occasion when their flexing waves would percolate his ear canal. The curves her voice made on its journey downwards were unprecedented darkened twists. The rising half were more staccato, jumpier and unexpected though he strived to memorise them.

Expressions on her face weren't even emblematic of the total treasury. He could scarcely count how many were included in it because each scene he experienced with her, every strange circumstance unmasked a new reaction.

How was it that her countenance was so proficient at being malleable? And how did it meander so magnetically through many metamorphoses?

Three decades later a much defter man – struck by his love of her – would speak to her of a symphonic poem Richard Strauss had written: 'Metamorphosen'. With its corrupt mutations and the yearning of its iterations, he would be convinced that its foreboding shadow had been sewn atop her feet.

But Josef in the bloom of ignorance reflected on these changes as a novelty. His soul was free from having to accommodate such prescience. Each new turn of hers he could regard as a resplendent fresh ravine appearing in an unshorn forest.

To look at her the way he looked at hordes of female students, without recognition, without specifying her – would have been a negation of reality.

And he was not a man who relished fiddling with illusion.

8.

The resolution of the magnifying glass

He almost ignored Sara for two weeks, uttering only 'hellos' and 'goodbyes' as he trekked through the corridors.

Then on one occasion as he headed to the Ramsay Laboratory, he saw her looking incontestably perturbed. She was leant against the wall without her spectacles, wearing her white laboratory coat; her golden tresses in a ponytail that hung along her shoulder. Her gaze faced downwards and her mouth was twisted as though paralysed by some relentless spasm.

Josef approached her out of gentlemanly duty. He stumbled with his English once again.

'May I . . . be able to assist—'

'No, no.' she insisted, patting the air. But she was too nervous and tired to make use of more words to convince him.

'Is there anything wrong?'

'Not at all.' it was a rapid answer uttered with a breezy spell of confidence.

He hesitated. His earnest hope was that she might at last move from the door since he wished to conduct an experiment.

'Is it possible to use the Ramsay Laboratory?'

Her hand travelled to the back of her neck, where it rested with the aim of scratching it. For the first time in their mutual acquaintance, it was she who had to clear her throat.

'Well, it's not occupied. I mean . . . well, I mean – it isn't occupied by humans.'

'I'm sorry?'

'There are rats loose. I did it.'

'How did you manage that?'

She felt that he was giving her a cold, accusatory stare.

'There was an accident . . .' She swayed a little in her nerves. 'One of them – started to nip at my hair.'

'Well, that is one of the reasons ladies should *not* be involved in such work.'

Her voice hushed a little bit.

'I ordinarily don't – it's just that – well . . .' She removed quite a few sheets of scruffy paper from the pocket of her white coat. They looked most unprofessional. 'I had a few ideas . . . the outcome can only be verified through experimentation, and I had no choice . . . You see, I went – I went inside, I unlocked the cage . . .' Stuffing her papers back into her pocket she began explaining with her hands. 'I took one out – just one, not more – I couldn't even . . .'

She shuddered and folded her arms to sustain her composure.

'The pest began to crawl on me and while I tried to get it off it bit my hair. So I swept it off my shoulder in a single gesture, and with that great swipe of my arm, I knocked the cage. Apparently I hadn't locked it properly or else . . .' She mused a little to herself in silent meditation. 'It wouldn't have come *open*. It was the one with fifteen inside it.' She exhaled as though the exhalation might eschew her worries. 'Fifteen rats in it; the one that Dr Reyfield uses.'

Josef could not see the problem.

'May I?' He pointed to the door.

Her expression was still paralysed. She murmured:

'You won't find them.'

'I'm not scared of them, miss.' he told her patronisingly.

'The window was open.'

He looked most disapproving.

'The window was open because Dr Reyfield – that's – well you *know* Dr Reyfield, he . . . he hates the warmth. He says it gets too stuffy. And so the window was open and . . . well . . .' This time she let out a dramatic, demonstrative sigh of almost content resignation. 'Sometimes procedures don't *unravel* in a polished way and that sounds . . . totally inelegant.' She looked at him with a decisive glare. 'I'm not my usual self today.'

'I've noticed.'

'It's only in the presence of . . . rats. So,' she stepped away from the door, 'in conclusion, you're welcome to enter.'

Her earthy demeanour stirred sympathy. He imagined that one day this might be Anneliese.

'It is not a problem; I could take the responsibility for this mistake.'

Her tone changed. She was adamant and turned to principle.

'No, no. Absolutely not. I was just giving you a precaution in case you . . . stumbled upon a rat. But most likely they all fled, so . . . you won't.'

Josef rubbed his chin.

'Would you like a cup of tea, miss?'

She stared at him, completely puzzled for a moment.

'Well, yes.' Her voice became smaller. 'I suppose.'

The laboratory and its contents were left to fend for themselves. He led her to the kitchen where he had a tin of biscuits he had bought for Anneliese and Isabel. When he presented it to her, it took her a long while to understand its relevance.

'Oh, thank you.' she said, taking one. She took out the clips from her hair and removed her white coat. The shedding of this medical apparel finally relieved her inhibition.

Now showing off her dress, she walked in a manner that was fluently regal, betraying her childhood of practising ballet. Her head was positioned a little higher than usual.

He took this opportunity to ask:

'What's your little one's name?'

'Hmm?' She smiled and stopped herself from laughing. 'Oh – Clarette.'

'That's really her name?'

'At the moment it is, yes.'

'She doesn't have a real name?'

'Lily's currently obsessed with *The Nutcracker*.'

Henceforth began multiple comparisons between their girls. A conversation had despite them both been triggered. They exchanged anecdotes about which colour dresses matched which eyes – her little girl had golden hair much like her own – and where the most exquisite dolls were cheaper; how demanding teachers were in schools nowadays and why their attitude was strictly bureaucratic. He heard that chortle of hers let rip once again in its melodic rhythm: a set of measures so pristine and accurate that only Isabel could play them.

Josef essayed another concept:

'Aren't you frightened, living by yourself with a small child?'

She shook her head, a little amused and bewildered, and slapped her hands together knowingly.

'I have all the provisions.'

'I'm sorry – I don't follow.'

She almost smirked but ultimately thought it would not be appropriate.

'When I left home . . . I stole my brother's gun.'

'I beg your pardon?'

'The whole family . . .' She took a great breath. 'I shouldn't – I wouldn't . . .' But suddenly her burden of uneasiness gave way to a squiggle of laughter. Looking at the curly bracket of his symmetrical moustache and his polished demeanour, she asked herself rhetorically – but aloud:

'What *could* I be afraid of? Anyway . . . my family used to shoot. I was a great shooter once. But Ferdinand was so reckless, and . . .' She became much tenser in her recollection. 'My father . . .' Her voice almost cracked. 'Well, for one reason or another, my mother persuaded him to store the guns elsewhere; we had no clue of the location of their whereabouts. But Adam kept one only *I* knew about. And so I took it with me.'

The pity poured into him like a creek flowing into a stream.

'Why did you feel the need to . . .'

A defiant glare of soreness lingered on him and he understood her message. Taking the conversation in his stride, he concluded:

'I see.' He decided that the pause in speech was meant for him to change the subject. 'Are you really so frightened of rodents?'

'Yes.'

'Are you allergic to them?'

She realised that the moment offered her a brief chance to retrieve her status. Thickening her voice with an air of imperiousness, Sara declared:

'The university wouldn't have taken me if they thought I was allergic to rodents.'

She stood leaning against the kitchen top, resting her hands on its edge.

'If you want, you can tell them.'

'Tell . . . whom, what?'

'You can tell Professor Swenson I lost fifteen rats. In truth, I don't even deserve to be here – my post should actually be *higher*.'

'Higher?'

'I came from a medical school. I left.' She hastened to add as an afterthought: 'On my own grounds. It was a demotion of my making.'

'Ah.'

'It might not even be the worst thing if I *were* sacked. You don't like women teaching. You've been dying to find fault with me since you first saw me . . .'

Following some contemplation she proposed with an uncanny satisfaction:

'Take the opportunity.'

Josef was silent. Sara knew she had to fill the quiet. The kitchen top began to hold her weight as she sustained her elbows on it. Standing on the heels of her shoes with crossed feet, she tapped the left with the right. Only then he noticed she had swung her eyes around. They'd landed in a new position slanted to the left; darting to him a penetrative, daring stare he knew not how to answer.

Unsurprisingly he didn't act upon the challenge. Her bank of wiles was far too large for Josef's expectations.

Across a span of several weeks and university-related social functions they embarked on conversations about waning intellect among the titans of psychiatry, discrepancies between the Old and New Testaments, wars giving birth to looseness in society.

Stood in the middle of the Great Hall one afternoon at a neurologists' conference, she told him about the drosophilists. Sara related to him an extensive history of Mendelian and classical genetics, the offshoots from an ancient language now termed 'Indo-European' and her difference in opinion with some famed hydrogeologist.

His cheeks reddened from ignorance and he felt profound shame.

Following a timid conversation in which Sara had requested Josef spill the details of his life, she started to enquire about Anneliese and Isabel. He admitted with reluctance that his wife was apathetic. She grilled him with a sample of interrogation he deemed beneficial only in police investigations. As a result of these discoveries concerning Elise, she sank into a flat and shady melancholy.

In a voice that was more hushed than full blown she suggested tentatively – almost to avoid his earshot:

'There are . . . *sections* for such women.'

The flood of embarrassment broke through her reservoir's banks. She scratched her neck and looked at him with eyes that demonstrated a surprise at her suggestion.

It was a while before complacency could find a way to settle in her. When it did, she put a hand on Josef's shoulder and assumed the role of the allayer:

'It was a fleeting thought, Josef. A fleeting thought.'

Fear searing through him, Josef decreed internally that what had happened in his spirit when it came to Sara had been nothing but a miscommunication between soul and mind.

According to his theory, in inane attempts to mitigate the pain of wounds incurred by problems of his twins he had resorted to the remedy of a new ailment. It had served in the form of a minor diversion: a fascination whose outcome would bear no enduring effect on his life or the girls'. The transient abode was just a temporary shelter for him.

He had examined all this through a magnifying glass. If this fallacious object had possessed the power to present its targets in their accurate proportions Sara would have been a relative nonentity. A glass that didn't magnify would prove that her minute star in the galaxy flashed so infrequently, it shunned the sharpest scrutiny.

The only problem was that the deceptive magnifying glass was inconsistent. One moment the small speck was almost indiscernible. But as he caught more disc-shaped glimpses of her, the slight star began to grow in gleam. He wanted to eclipse its light by means of some new moon or comet; to obstruct its glimmer with a dusky rock.

A month later only a black form of sorcery could have explained Josef's alertness at two o'clock in the morning one brisk Thursday night. It was well into the Easter holidays and he was sat in Sara's garden on a rough, unsturdy chair made of white stone. The seat almost punctured the back of his knees.

The girls had been invited to spend a few days with Cousin Elise: for only the second time in their lives Josef had permitted Aunt Liesel this courtesy.

He had arrived at half past six; eight hours earlier. It had been Sara who had summoned him to come before her daughter's bedtime so that he could meet her; it had been she who had informed him she would spend a great deal of the night conducting research and was *not* in dire need of his invited company. But here was Josef sat at Sara's garden table with another glass of orange juice before him next to her lime cordial. She didn't drink and didn't practise keeping spirits in the house.

Several papers she had written were laid out across the table. Her veneer was of the fussy academic this time, shooting him a pair of taller eyes whenever he referred to a demoded theory or a concept out of vogue.

Every so often she would excuse herself to disappear into the kitchen and bring out some item of food or another: at first an apple pie that she herself 'had not and *would* not have made', then a huge jar of iced tea, then a series of fairy cakes whose texture she berated for some thirty minutes as she had not made them *either*. None of this consumption showed its presence on her figure.

Never before had he espied her at once meddlesome, at once under-satisfied – and simultaneously smug and gleaming with contentment.

As Josef saw the big hand on the kitchen clock hit three, he rose.

'The hour really is most inaccordant. I must go.'

'"Inaccordant"?' She took a bite from a green apple.

'Yes.'

'Which word are you looking for, exactly?'

'It is not right.'

'"Inappropriate"'

'Yes.'

'The hour?'

'It's really very late—'

'You know, there's a hole in your English that ought to be darned.' She issued a series of blinks. 'And you're analysing all this through the lens of Freud.'

At this he became aggravated and haughty. It inadvertently provoked him to sit down again.

'I can't stand that name anymore.'

'The women in Lisse didn't have men in their gardens in the middle of the night.'

'They did *not*.'

'So . . . that would make me the reverse of "primitive".'

'I'm sorry?'

She couldn't resist smiling at the absence of any endeavour to hide his naïvety.

'If I have male company at night it must mean I don't expect him to leave . . . until morning.'

Josef deliberately cleared his throat in a manner that suggested importance.

'Well, one would think—'

'It was clearly a plan of seduction.'

'I really don't think that's accordant.'

'Especially the apples, since you know how dangerous they are.'

She yielded to a great smirk and her nose even wrinkled but she kept her mouth shut. Ordinarily such crude citations of the bible would have thrown him into fits of rage.

This one seemed to have a surface that was quaint.

She twisted a little on her seat, knowing exactly how uncomfortable these garden chairs were.

'I know perfectly well what you are, so you can remain seated.'

In a way that stamped a contradiction on the scene and what it might entail there was a little glint of reassurance in her intonation. He wouldn't have expected a potential Eve to eat so much in front of him or an accomplished Jezebel to have her locks half pinned-up by an amber oval clip, half loose. She took another bite of her apple, chewed and continued, taking one of the files they had been reading and opening it.

'Don't you see I'm using you, Josef?' She looked at him whilst leafing through the file and saw that he still lacked an understanding of her humour. 'I was wondering whether you had noticed there was other material on the back of these pages.'

She handed him the document. Once he saw how much she wanted him to read, he winced.

'You can take it home if you want.'

He scratched a corner of his moustache.

'I don't understand why it is *my* opinion you request. I really do think that if you took this to Professor Swenson, he would be of greater help.'

'He *would*.'

'So, it really would be best—'

'But I don't like him.'

Josef flung the file across the table.

'I'm sorry, miss—'

'My Christian name is perfectly "accordant", Josef.'

And yet it was no luxury he could afford.

'Miss . . . I don't really understand why you keep me here.'

'I could respond that I didn't understand why you came; you could be left stymied and embarrassed, I could invent something else . . . I'm skirting that discussion. You . . .' She very briefly scratched behind her neck then covered herself up with her shawl for some sort of protection. 'You have in your possession quite an iron will, Josef.'

'Erm . . . well . . .'

'Is it so bizarre to think . . .' In order to delay the verbal onset of the concept in her mind, she took the open file from him, closed it and tossed it on her pile. 'To think that I could recognise some of myself there?'

The wind was stirring westerly. On its journey it carried off one of her files, dragging it to the back of the garden. Josef – a cavalier – immediately rose to fetch it.

'No, no, leave it alone – it's – NH2, no. 43. I think I have a copy of it somewhere.'

After staring at the flying file for a few moments she directed her gaze back at him. Her face moved only to take another bite of the apple. When her eyes were posited this way he remarked to himself that their lids were as telling as the overall shape of their instruments.

Noticing he wouldn't speak, she took the task upon herself again, laying her arms on the stone table and simultaneously keeping a grip on her apple.

'We live in a time of quick communication. You haven't noticed that distances no longer exist? It's all this transport. It means that peoples mesh and work together.'

She heaved a rather melancholy sigh and continued.

'The diversity is greater. People from different countries all rub off on one another, so there are fewer niches, cliques, *milieux*? That causes individuality. It's what they *think* they want – but they don't want it. They don't want the conflict that comes with it; they don't function well with millions of these "individuals". Time will prove that. You come from a tiny village, an infrangible nucleus. You grew up in a collective morality where all of you were *acclimatised*. You don't know how I envy that?'

She quietened for a little while. He was uncomfortable and huffed somewhat.

'I'm sorry . . .' Josef rubbed his brow. 'I still don't understand.'

'You see me as a "modern" woman? Two hundred years ago, you and I would have been man and wife and run a farm together. You were born iron-willed, took it one way. I took it another. But if you unwrap the effect of circumstance and context, our bases are quite similar.' A lingering sigh came from her. 'There is . . . *too much* that you don't know about me.'

Josef saw the opportunity to hunt his target down.

'Well . . . you can tell me.'

'I can't. You wouldn't like me if I did; it would not *be* my character to tell you.'

He was stirred and almost fell dumbstruck.

'The way *you* settled . . .'

'Is foreign to you.'

'But . . . you must actually believe that you will go unjudged.'

She smiled. When she began to fear the smile would emerge as a laugh, she deliberately broke it and looked at the skirt of her dress. Some moments later she raised her head. Her voice was not complete but rather airy: her sore spot had been caught in an eyelet.

'A strange word is "unjudged". No. No, I don't think that.'

'So, like everybody else, you are scared of your Judgment Day?'

Sara blinked tightly and confirmed.

'Like everybody else.'

'The day you'll have to face God . . .'

'Not God. Myself.'

'But how can you be . . . afraid of . . .'

'Because I wield the greater power over me.'

She sucked in night air as though it might render her voice even wispier. The gesture was a logical endeavour given the slight melancholy lining her next phrase.

'We're all just waiting for the "bitter core".'

'The "bitter core"?'

In a premeditated move she looked at her chewed apple cork.

'The part that we can't swallow.' Sara threw the apple cork into a bucket on the table.' Once I'm faced with that, I'll go about . . . meting out punishment.'

They sat in silence for some moments. Finally Sara slapped her hands on her knees and stood.

'I ought to go and check on her.'

'Yes.' Josef heartily agreed. 'I really must be going.'

She accompanied him to her door. All he could surmise he remarked to her, whether he ought to have said it or not.

'Madam . . . You are overcharged.'

'Well, it's frightening sometimes.' she conceded, darting playful eyes at him that falsely asked him to feel sympathy for her.

He was a few steps away from her door when she stopped him and called out:

'Josef.'

He assumed he had forgotten something.

'About your English . . . you really have to learn the accent. If you don't, they'll never take you seriously.'

A lull followed the turbulence. Once they came back after Easter they barely acknowledged each other. It was as though they had agreed that all that could be said had been expressed.

Any other register of revelation would have snapped the image of each other they had painted in their minds.

9.

The curfew of the hourglass

Josef's schedule was a myriad of disagreeable events refusing to be joined by any thread.

His work load meant that it had recently become the task of Liesel Hotzenplotz to pick the twins up after school. Determined to found a new journal, Professor Swenson was expecting new papers from everyone. The girls would often dine at Liesel's until eight or nine and sometimes ten. His pain at missing them had almost quelled all thoughts of Sara.

With the lights off it was dim and barely visible within the long and narrow confines of the dining room. Anneliese sat at the Hotzenplotzes' table patiently and waited for her dinner; Isabel was in the room adjacent practising on their piano; Cousin Elise was in their study doing homework.

Overly hungry was the Younger Twin and – unbeknownst to Liesel – swinging her legs hungrily beneath the table.

Liesel had lit a row of candles. Anneliese investigated them with the exhilaration of her famished eyes.

The outermost part of the flame was its least interesting feature; always on the verge of dissipating. But the red inside above the blue that nestled on the wick kept her attention lingering.

Lighting candles at their church one Sunday, Anneliese had whispered to her father surreptitiously:

'Where does the wax come from?'

'The wax?'

She had nodded.

'The middle is where the wax burns. On the outside, where the orange is, the wax isn't hot enough; it's cool.'

Papa had told Anneliese on her fifth birthday that lit candles were for blowing, not touching. But this fascination of hers – much like the banister that she had almost straddled – was a fixed one. Not even her compulsive need to heed to rules could bend it.

Now she sat staring at the candle glowing parallel to the crazed beacons of her eyes, examining the sparring blue, amber and flaxen darts. A curiosity was flickering inside her as the flames were flickering amongst themselves. She couldn't help but ask herself what realm or life existed in those beams; what substance she could stroke by being in their contact. Although the peril and the truth behind it grazed the foreground of her mind she took her forefinger and put it to the fire.

A scream erupted from the dining room and Isabel stopped playing. Liesel's spatula and ladle stirred a clatter as she dropped them to dash forth.

Anneliese sat with her red and puffy finger, her eyes spitting tears.

'Now, Anneliese!' Liesel yelped. 'Did no one ever tell you that you shouldn't play with *fire?*'

When Josef arrived he blamed Liesel for his daughter's altercation with the flame. Liesel uprooted her arms from her hips, swung them up in the air and cried out:

'Oi, oi, oi! What have we here! And you don't want your girls to come to any *Jewish* influence?!'

He didn't understand this argument. Knowing the tendency of Anneliese to remain *tender* he rejected the idea that she could disobey.

Upon his return to the university that Monday morning of 22nd April 1929 he was scheduled to attend a faculty meeting with Professor Swenson. Josef was startled to remark how much the latter failed to notice him as he entered his office. Sitting at his desk, Professor Swenson addressed Dr Reyfield, who stood facing the window, cupping his chin between his thumb and forefinger. A ray of early morning sun beat down over the pair; it was impalpable to them. The time was only half past seven.

Standing at the threshold, Josef intercepted their conversation.

Professor Swenson grunted and scoffed noisily.

'No one can *foretell* these things, yet one neglects to note that they can leave a stigma on the university.'

Dr Reyfield turned to look at him, astonished.

'A stigma on the university.' he echoed neutrally.

'Well . . . I understand it doesn't sound very compassionate of me. But it is in our obligation to *protect* the reputation of the university rather than – rather than throw it to the gallows of the yellow *press*.'

'Alistair . . .' Dr Reyfield almost gasped. 'This situation doesn't warrant social commentary.'

'Well – of *course*.' He raised his eyebrows nonetheless. 'But social commentary is inescapable.'

'You say she *took* the lecture?'

Professor Swenson let out a gigantic sigh.

'It was a *two-hour* lecture.'

'And she carried on for the entire two *hours*? After all that . . . commotion?'

'Police all over the building . . . One could hardly allude to it as a "commotion", Geoffrey.'

Josef was aghast. An adhesive of sweat pasted his sleeve to the skin of his arm. He was reminded of the moment he had spotted Sara conversing outside with the French prostitute.

'Excuse me ...' he interrupted the discussion. 'Is this ... regarding Sara?'

It was a strange opportunity to employ her Christian name for the first time; with his reason loosened he now grasped at it.

Professor Swenson rubbed the corner of his left eye.

'Yes.'

Josef began to feel short of breath. All of a sudden he came over as tremulous.

'Is she suspected in . . . an incident?'

Professor Swenson and Dr Reyfield traded suspicious looks.

'Did nobody inform you yesterday?'

Josef wrenched his hands out of his pockets and grew even more agitated.

'Inform me . . . about what?'

Dr Reyfield assumed the duty of reportage.

'There was an "accident".' He let out an elongated swirling sigh. 'Police suspect foul play.'

By this time Josef was anxiously rubbing his hands on his pockets.

'Where's Sara?'

Professor Swenson let out a light yawn.

'Have a look at her schedule.'

Josef was befuddled.

'I'm sorry?'

'She's pressing on. In the Mendeleev Hall, I would expect.'

Professor Swenson motioned with his hand.

'Sit down, Dr van der Holt.'

Josef ceded and Professor Swenson pursued his account.

'Sara—' He cleared his throat. 'Sara is safe and well.' An inhalation followed. 'Her little one is dead.'

He told him the whole story.

Once all the details of the incident had been related Josef

dashed awkwardly to Mendeleev Hall. Sara was indeed lecturing and it was a two-hour session.

'Aloof' would best have described those two hours. There was no bounciness, impetuous spontaneity or the impulse to spring an audacious response. No slur or hesitation affected her speech; nor did she need to look back at her notes. All she had planned to recite had been memorised. She was transfixed not by a shot of pain or fear or fury – but the state she had intended to assume in case such torsions of the spirit warped her.

It seemed she had rehearsed the bearing of this damaged soul.

When the students pelted questions at her, she took care to receive each one, hear it out in its entirety, stare fixedly for a brief period to ponder and unleash a timely and well-reasoned answer. She was more patient with the girls now than she had been in the comfort of her *status quo*.

Yet the texture of her voice, void of its usual swings and corners, was discoloured by an eerie alteration. There was a heavy, crinkled, corrugated quality about it; the imprint of a fork's dents lined its surface. In between each tone was a rift: vocal waves were heard bumping the rings of the trachea.

Simultaneously her concentration barely seemed impaired. She gave off the impression of a sunken mood and yet she was not rattled. She was too mechanical; all her components were too slickly bolted to suggest a woman rattled.

He waited for the students to depart before approaching her. Stood in silence, he attempted to devise the right expression on his face and thus pre-empt the naturally occurring one. He was expecting her to stagger to him with the dim acknowledgement of 'I gather you heard', or the need of an embrace, or a useless, pathetic insistence that 'he shouldn't worry about her'.

Instead she packed her books into her case without the recognition of his presence. During these few seconds her eyes met his at odd, sporadic intervals; perhaps three times. But every time it was a blank look empty of significance.

As she passed him the unsteady timbre of her voice gave way to a resigned, stern frailty.

'You're scheduled to be in the Great Hall now.'

She opened the door and flitted out, her heels heeding to her customary clopping rhythm.

He came to every lecture but he heard that clop less often. Every time he stopped outside her office there was no one there and every time he went into the library he didn't see her poking head and every time he went to luncheon she was absent. Apparently she had elected to recede into a burrow. He just didn't know its whereabouts.

For the next two weeks he stayed his entrances to lectures, arrived late for seminars and carried out less research than he ought to have. He searched the university – rummaging around through all the buildings of the Faculty of Sciences before investigating the Humanities Department. He checked seven lecture theatres, asked students he had never seen before, wandered through halls of residence. Only sixteen days after the accident did he locate her sanctuary.

In a tartan skirtsuit she was hidden on a bench outside the philosophy lecture theatre. It was a tiny garden with some scattered silver rocks and a small olive-coloured pond. She could have cared enough to hide herself more furtively. She didn't.

Sara recognised Josef's approach from a few yards away. Her head was buried in a large tome posited on her crossed leg; five other books sat at her side. Crunching as he trampled over gravel, his footsteps' volume became louder as he trekked along. When he stood in front of her she still refused to face him. The extended voice was gentle:

'Sara.'

'And now ...' Effusing a languorous sigh of acerbic and dry

satisfaction, she suddenly slammed her book shut. 'He calls me "Sara".'

Outside the confines of a lecture hall her voice resembled something close to 'Sara': the print of a relief portraying an old self.

'If I weren't exhausted, I would find this foul attempt to ricochet my common sense amusing.' She squeezed her eyes together to prevent another sigh from taking place. 'You caught me at a bad time.'

Shifting the books away, he sat down next to her. It took him a few inhalations and a long period of stroking his knees with his hands to begin.

'I didn't want you to *assume* that I was going to *pretend* . . . like all the others . . . that nothing happened. I did not want you to think that I expected . . . you would behave – *normally*.'

Sara at last looked at him directly. For a fraction of a second it occurred to him that she might scrunch her face into a laugh.

'Again . . . it's amusing that you'd think, considering what's passed, that I would take the trouble to examine your behavioural etiquette.'

'I only wanted to explain . . .'

'The *truly* funny thing is . . .' She let an arm linger on the side of the bench. Eventually her fingers gave way to the drumbeats of a rhythmic tap. Watching them play, she uttered to him dismally:

'You don't even understand you're being selfish.'

The finger-tapping stopped; she looked him in the eye.

'You can't even see . . .' She took a great breath. 'You can't even see that if you had been steered by moral righteousness before – you'd have never offered me a cup of tea after I lost the rats. At least – you would have never come to my house, staying until almost morning. I toyed with you because I found you interesting . . . you fell into that loop. I'm sorry for it. But now . . .' She attempted to mould a smile with her mouth. 'Now something's happened and you feel you *have* to be moral, for the sake of self-justification. And

I understand it. But I'm telling you, the moral deed . . . would be to leave me.'

She effused a few blinks and managed to unleash one smile of warmth before resuming her place in her book. It would have been tactical to obey her commands, and he did.

After that she paid no more attention to him. The intellectual attention *he* devoted to her only grew.

The woman endured sorrows bitterer than any he had known or read about. She was an edifice whose frame was kept intact by grit and mortar sealing off disintegrated inner contents. The exterior façade of stone had kept the tumbling rubble that he knew was blustering inside those walls entirely mute. And yet it ruthlessly persisted – splintering, cascading and being chronically fragmented by a clangourous attrition.

Peasant women he had seen in Lisse carrying nine kilograms of produce on their backs were feeble in comparison to her. So domineering was her strength that though her voice had lost its yarn of silk and was now worn and grisly like a trodden carpet, it could still command despite its fractured hue; it could still execute imperiousness.

For the successive weeks she exercised her self-taught schooling: being cold and cutting off. She practised it with no conundrum spinning in her head. The Sara he met now was not the same as she who had insisted that he 'learn the English accent'; as the one whose tiny sparks of girlishness had polka-dotted his horizon, even as the woman who'd waxed lyrical about a string of publications on the ribbon synapses.

Yet it seemed to him that all her features past and present, decorous and damaged, could be found on the same route. It was a linearity with curves – but one that he could pinpoint.

All his life he had scorned mortals for their weaknesses, for how they had a tendency to yield to pleasures they could live without. Josef had convinced himself naïvely that he had defeated the same obstacles as all his peers, that he had always had a lot of somethings to *resist*; that it was not a case of being good by nature – but of calling on a greater inner strength.

Her speech to him had cracked an aperture of truth wide open. Only now did he regard himself as truly being confronted by temptation.

It was not the notion of temptation that he found unprecedented but its incorruptible attire. He had foreseen 'temptation' to be Satan's fodder; to be breaking a Commandment or engaging in a sin; to be the act of looking at another woman lustfully. Whatever tempest festered in his soul, it did not touch on that.

It was not the feeling Titian had described when he had pitted the 'Profane' against the 'Sacred'. All he was experiencing he thought as being selfless. In such a case how could temptation morph into Love's costume?

Thus Josef's understanding was eclipsed by this peculiar foreign power. He could at last serve someone else, at last extend a wealth of aid to someone worthy of his help . . . yet he was hindered from this action by a vow to God. It was arguable that he had made that vow persuaded by delusion. But even that idea was totally impenetrable. Knowing full well that Sara could have made a better mother to his girls than he a father, Josef still begrudged the notion of divorce. First and foremost, he believed that if man erred in front of God he would incur a rapid punishment.

He couldn't have predicted that its object . . . would be he.

In the quiet nights spent reading to his Younger Twin, a balm expanded at the bottom of his soul. It dictated that all else was putrid and excessive and unnecessary. Love for his children would surpass all other elements; even all other facets metaphysical. Listening to that glowing balm's enlightenment, he painfully exerted efforts to impel this one great love to quell another.

Then the next morning a faculty meeting would be on the

agenda. She would be stood outside the door waiting and dallying, mindlessly glancing at staff notices to avoid conversation. That sight would snap the balm in two, dethrone it of its seat and topple its location.

According to her wish he did not speak to her in these brief moments when they had to wait together. With an edition of *The Times* one day, Josef pretended to be deeply engrossed in an article about the arduous lives of aggrieved chimney sweepers.

Then he elected to half-cede to the temptation – speaking in part to himself, but aloud. He decided that his speech could be interpreted as being rhetorical.

'Isabel is growing out of everything I put her in.'

She kept strolling to and fro at a pace that was lagging. Her head was unfocussed.

He must have played his cards adeptly as the ruse eventually began to work. It cut into her soul that there were two small girls in the same town as she serially unattended by their mother; deprived because their father barely knew what 'woman' meant. Maternal warmth that had resisted surfacing for several weeks – one she assumed had been exhausted like a dusty well – began to seep towards the fore. In a weakened tone she asked, a little unprepared to undertake new speech:

'How often do you buy them new clothes?'

It took him a long while to remember.

'I think approximately . . . twice a year.'

For a short time the fresh perception holed her tragedy. It threw her so violently, she had to sit down.

'Twice a year?'

'I think so.'

'Twice a year . . .' She made the calculation. 'There are four seasons.'

The discrepancy left her disturbed in the distractive way she needed.

Still 'absorbed' by *The Times*, he continued in a polite although meaningless vein.

'Are you going to . . . stay with relatives during the summer?'

The weakness of his choice of topic discommoded her.

'It's May.'

'Yes, but . . . I've already heard students discussing their plans.'

She exhaled a puff of air as though she had a cigarette.

'I'm leaving.'

'Where?'

'I'm leaving Westfield College.'

'Where are you going?'

'Nowhere, Josef.'

'You haven't found a post yet?'

'I'm going *nowhere*, Josef.'

Professor Swenson arrived beside them and launched into his chit-chat. Sara feigned a smile at him; nowadays her eyes never extended to their full potential.

Time chewed up the next three months.

When he arrived at her home on the night of her last day, it was to foster a diligent, noble parting. No source of light could be found in her house. From outside he saw the furniture and objects placed as always. He discerned that not a single item had been moved.

It was not the case that she'd escaped. That would have been melodramatic; her mental condition was too cool for such a commotion. She was merely avoiding the finality, eschewing the hassle; precluding the debilitating pain the gavel's thud would hammer into them upon the case being closed.

He remained in awe of such a cunning. But the man in him would not withstand being outwitted in this way. And so he stood outside her darkened home and waited.

In the meantime Anneliese and even Isabel were getting restless. That day Josef had instructed Liesel to pick them up, stay with them at home for a few hours then leave them to be with their somnolent mother. They were old enough now not to burn the house down.

It was too hot to stay inside that July evening. Anneliese, who was the guardian when Papa was away, had permitted her sister to open the door to the garden. Still naïve and inexperienced in her role as chaperone, she hadn't counted on her sister going to play outside.

Now it was ten o'clock and dark. Isabel was still on the swing.

Anneliese wandered into the garden. Stood in bewilderment for a few moments, she finally fulfilled the long-repressed wish of scolding her sister.

'I don't think we should be in the garden.'

'That's because you're not adventuresome.'

'You mean "adventurous".'

Isabel snorted, huffed and puffed.

Anneliese went back to reading. Two hours later at midnight there was no sign of Josef. Anneliese looked at the clock and went downstairs to interrupt Isabel – this time in the throes of Chopin's First Sonata. She was distressed about her fingering.

'No, that won't do.' She heard her utter to herself. 'Two, five, back two notes to three . . .'

'Isabel!' Anneliese yelled. Her sister was not happy with this intercession.

'What do you *want?*'

'Go to bed.'

Isabel sniggered.

'Papi isn't here yet. I'm not going to *bed!*'

'We always go to bed at nine o'clock; it's *well* past our bedtime. I'm taking over while Papa isn't here, and I say that we ought to go to *bed.*'

Isabel rolled her eyes.

'Five *minutes.*'

One and a half hours passed before she heeded to her sister.

Anneliese lay on her bed and found her consciousness distractively abuzz. By two o'clock Josef had not arrived.

Worms of anxiety curled round her. Half an hour later Anneliese retreated to the landing and positioned herself there, dangling her legs between the balustrade's bulky black bars. Hawk-like she watched in case Papa should enter. He was still not there at three. At half past three she started weeping. Now it felt as though more putrid parasites were generously awander all around her limbs.

She considered waking Isabel but, conscious of her own anxiety, resolved that she would not subject her sister to it; at least – not for now. At four o'clock, worn out by crying she began – her legs adangle from the landing and her head bowed at the balustrade – to fall in gentle increments asleep.

A shut of the door and a light woke her up at a quarter to five.

She gasped in utter shock:

'Papa!'

'You're not in bed yet?' Josef asked her gently in Dutch. There was something nervous in his trembling voice; Anneliese recognised he was unusually shaken. Intuition could permit her observations such as these. He was overdoing kindness given her apparent misbehaviour; it kindled her warming suspicion.

'You'll have to miss the first half of school tomorrow, *meine Kleinste*.' he conceded. 'If you sleep so little, you'll get ill.'

After hanging up his coat he went upstairs and with his hands removed her from the landing, drawing her up to her full height. She was too heavy now for him to pick her up.

'Where *were* you, Papa?' she asked sleepily.

He let out a great sigh of discomfort.

'I was helping a friend.'

'What happened to your friend?' Anneliese asked in an inquisitive, high-pitched tone.

'*Shh*. You'll wake up your sister.'

When he had tucked her into bed and turned the light off she demanded once again to know:

'Tell me what happened to your *friend*.'

She heard him exhale very loudly.

'It's all very upsetting.'

'Can I meet your friend?'

'No, *meine Kleinste*, I don't think so. Go to sleep.'

Josef never saw Sara again, and that was principally her decision. For every one of these luxurious fancies in her life she readily imposed a curfew.

The time had come when all the sand had dripped out from the top half of the hourglass.

10.

The Covered Way

In the midst of summer 1930 Josef's desk at home was cluttered with a heap of brochures and thick pamphlets each in hues of either olive green, maroon or black. They promoted 'academic excellence', 'moral astuteness' and the promise of the birth of 'women of the twentieth century'. Persistently he asked himself what could be wrong with women of the nineteenth century; a year after their unfulfilled farewell he was recovering from love of one.

Every time he opened a school syllabus he found the same proposal: all of them sought to dispatch their young ladies to Oxford and Cambridge; all attempted to convince this man his daughters would be academic pioneers. And whilst he wanted Isabel to be a celebrated pianist, and whilst he wanted Anneliese to be successful in her art of science, he was not inclined to harbour thoughts about an early training. Josef desired nothing but for them to be looked after when they went to school: someone to ensure they ate their lunch and had their hair clips fixed in place. None of these prestigious secondary institutions with their hefty fees could offer him this comfort.

In spite of Anneliese's large portfolio of work, Isabel had naught to offer save for her musicianship. Most schools didn't value that unless a pupil could accomplish 'A's in mathematics. 'C's were awarded Isabel on lucky days.

That October Josef and the girls trundled around interminably spacious grounds abound in busts and effigies and shiny golden plaques bequeathed by donors. On half the benches he found names engraved such as 'Lord Gerald John Ponsonby' or 'Archibald Pennefather, 1st Viscount of Chelsea.' A sixteen-year-old pupil led him and the twins to watch a school assembly. The headmistress – a small and stout fifty-year-old matron with tufts of blonde hair that resembled a giant toupee – was addressing the front rows of twelve- and thirteen-year-old girls.

'I'm sure your parents care a great deal for the school's future. In virtue of this I ask that please, when you come home tonight, before your tea, do remember to ask your Mamas and Papas, very kindly, whether they would be generous enough to make a small donation for the Lady Geraldine Winchester-Ivey School of Biological Sciences. That's all for today girls, thank you.'

This wouldn't be the last time that day Josef would hear of the 'Lady Geraldine Winchester-Ivey School of Biological Sciences.' He was reminded of it every time he turned a corner either by a notice on the wall or by his tour guide, who had been instructed to report the news every ten minutes.

'Gloria!' a grey-haired skinny woman with a near-moustache cooed in an almost falsetto voice. The girl stopped in her tracks a few feet behind Josef. Her shirt was loose from her skirt and she appeared rather dishevelled. 'Miss Adams told me that you missed your meeting yesterday.'

Frazzled with chagrin, Gloria shook her head and looked down at the ground.

'I'm sorry, Miss Hodges . . . I had to go home and look after my little brother because Father was ill—'

'Now, now, young lady. I don't want to hear anything about your domestic affairs. You are to attend weekly sessions with your moral tutor, circumstances notwithstanding. Have I made myself clear?'

Gloria issued a great sigh, still addressing the ground:

'Yes, Miss Hodges.'

'Don't be late for your next lesson. And ensure you don't *run*.'

Josef inclined his head to Miss Hodges.

'Excuse me, er . . .' He cleared his throat. 'This "moral tutor"—'

'I'm quite *sorry*, sir; please do excuse Miss Suggitt there for, I'm afraid she's an *unfortunate* exception. You see, Gloria's mother was killed in an automobile accident a fortnight ago. We want to make sure that her pace won't slacken as a consequence; to ensure that she remains abreast of all her studies and meets the requirements of homework. In such a circumstance it is our policy to send girls to our moral tutor, Miss Raleigh.' Clasping one hand in the other, she insisted firmly: 'Here at Aylesbury we do our *best* to see that no girl lags behind.'

On his way out a sixty-something hobbling lady giddily reminded him:

'We do hope that you'll consider applying for Aylesbury, and do inform your peers that construction shall shortly commence for the Lady Geraldine Winchester-Ivey School of Biological Sciences.'

Isabel was half-asleep and barely walking. Anneliese was too busy keeping her head upright to focus on anything else.

'Papi . . .' A sleepy Isabel approached Josef that evening. 'Could we please have dinner now?'

He was too busy glaring at another brochure; already considering sending his girls to a school outside London. That would burden them with a two-hour commute. Isabel snatched an unusual prospectus. It was thinner and blue.

'*Meine Kleine*, that one's hardly interesting.'

He was reluctant for the Older Twin to see it since it was the only one that had been recommended to him by a flagging student. Meagan Riddleston was hardly any model for his daughters. He was never going to hand his girls to the establishment that had created *that*.

Obstinately Isabel kept poring over the prospectus. Josef decided that she liked the colours.

'*Kleines Zwillingsmädchen . . .*'

'Papi – *wait*.' Her tongue was sticking out of her mouth as she read. Josef flicked open another brochure. 'Papi—'

'It's very far away, *meine Kleine*.'

'Papi, let me read it to you.' He took the prospectus away from her. 'No, Papi!' she yelped. A second later she seized it again. '"We are a school for individuals with a range of talents, not always conventional ones."'

He stroked his chin musingly, imagining it might be an ambush.

'I don't think the brochure says *that*, *meine Kleine*.'

Apparently it did. It also wanted its students to 'reach for the highest personal standards in all spheres of life' and made no mention of a fund for new buildings or Oxford and Cambridge acceptances. Isabel stood nervously fiddling with the hem of her skirt.

'Papi, look at the last page.'

He leafed through the brochure. There was a sketch of a girl playing the cello.

'This school is over twenty kilometres away.'

She merely stood still with her fingers interlocked and shot at him a devious stare.

'Very well . . . we'll go to their Open Day.'

It turned out they had missed the Open Day but there was also something called an 'Open Evening'. It took them a train and a bus and another bus to arrive at Croham Road in South Croydon.

They landed just outside what looked like a wide house made from three separate buildings: two tall, white nineteenth-century homes with gable roofs headlined by casement windows at the top that counterbalanced large bay windows popping out from the two lower floors.

In the middle of this pair was a much smaller edifice adjoining them; its zenith stopped at its superior neighbours' second floor. This little hut, again honed by a gable roof, resembled a small chapel. It was white like its brother and sister. A single triangular triple bay window emerged from its core.

To the left of this triple home was another more modern building of two floors regaled with a flat roof and modest sash windows as well as another white home. The image was suggestive of a well-off family who'd split their lavish residence to have their offices installed between the two halves of this Easter egg and save themselves a work commute.

All was green and quiet in the suburb. Opposite them on the other side of the road was a large empty field; expansive unused grass. The air was more wholesome and open; cooler than their garden's in Blackheath.

Josef's eyes scoured for the school. He expected to have to walk a hundred yards to stumble upon a five-storey building in the Gothic design that was cleft by a lake, littered with monuments, peacocks and fountains and bordered by flag-hoisting parapets.

Anneliese tugged at his sleeve.

'Papa.' She pointed out a notice hanging on a tree before the school. It read 'Croham Hurst School Open Evening' with the date in smaller letters: 'Monday 3rd November 1930'. There was an arrow pointing to the right.

Isabel didn't wait for her father, rushing ahead. There was no visible door, entrance or gate. She turned the corner and went up a road called Melville Avenue, eventually perceiving it to be a hill. To the side of her she saw the house on the extreme left climb and widen. Finally she halted at an iron gate.

'Papi!' she yelled.

'Isabel, we're on a residential road – don't make noise.' Josef and his younger daughter followed suit. He stood confused outside the gate. '*Meine Kleine*, this doesn't look like a school.'

But on the left of the gate he saw a car park and a row of vehicles stationed all along the road. There was a bustle coming from inside; the sound of adults' chatter and a cluster of girls' squeals at an unfathomably high pitch.

A padlock requiring a combination hung on the gate. Josef stood before it, helpless.

The cool breeze was flapping a girl's blazer open. She was around five foot three and blonde in spectacles, standing before an outdoor stone staircase. Her uniform consisted of a light blue shirt clad mostly in a royal blue v-neck sweater with a navy skirt and stockings, a blue blazer and a small straw hat atop her head.

Approaching the gate, she asked Josef tentatively:

'Excuse me, are you here for the Open Evening?'

'Yes, yes – we seem to have got . . .' Rotating the padlock, the girl dialled the combination. 'Lost.'

'The public entrance to the school is just a little further up the road – but no need to worry.'

A thirty-something woman with long brown hair and a floor-length skirt passed by.

'*Sarah.*' she reprimanded gently.

'I'll escort them to the Hall, Miss Clarendon.'

'You know it's not a good idea to take the parents through the Covered Way. Excuse me, sir, this isn't the real *entrance*.'

As he entered Josef rushed into apology:

'We didn't mean to cause an imposition.'

'That's quite all right. What are the names of your daughters?'

'This is Isabel,' Josef pointed to his left side, 'and this one is Anneliese.'

'Please make yourselves welcome. Sarah will lead you to the Assembly Hall for refreshments.'

'Thank you.'

The girl waved her hand.

'Come with me – I'll save you the trek the other parents had to do outside.' She went forward and left Josef lagging behind. 'Oh – sorry, sir.'

She waited for him to catch up before ascending stone steps leading up to a long slope of some two hundred metres.

'This is the Covered Way.' Sarah explained.

'Why is it called the "Covered Way"?' asked Anneliese.

'There's no particular reason . . . It's concrete covering a hill, and it's a way. It isn't all that pleasant; you can always smell the vegetables,' – she pointed to what looked like a shed on the right of the path – 'that's where all the ingredients are kept for lunch. The Assembly Hall's the dining hall as well – we don't have separate giant halls like other, you know, "posh" schools. And it's rather bleak along this path, but you get used to it. It's certainly nice exercise each day!'

Isabel looked to her right and saw the grassy hill. The 'Covered Way' was sheltered by a roof; its left laid bare the entrances to several rooms. Most of its right side nonetheless was open and gave out onto the slanted esplanade. Centred on the grassy hill was a narrower walking path with a loose and precarious rail. At its other end there was another row of small one-storey buildings propped up by a stable staircase.

Ahead of her there stood a giant three-floor building of red bricks.

'That's the Centenary Building, but really it's just for arts and crafts.' Sarah pointed out. 'They had it built four years ago to celebrate the school's one-hundredth anniversary; I wasn't here then but my sister was. She said the noise of the construction would spread *everywhere* and drills would put a stop to Mr Humble's anecdotes – he teaches Latin. It's where we do sewing and cookery and sometimes pottery. That's also where the Upper Thirds are; you see the bottom room? That was my classroom the year before last. Are you all right, Anneliese?'

She was a little mystified.

'I'm sorry?'

'You seem puzzled. Is there anything you want to ask?'

'Erm . . .' She rubbed her right palm against her left. 'Where do you have science lessons?'

'I'll take you there in a few minutes. You see the block of buildings straight ahead – just to the left? The Covered Way leads to them.' (Apparently it led to everything). 'That's where the chemistry laboratory is; we have two physics laboratories, three biology. They're not the nicest rooms but they're, you know, adequate. I'm not so very keen on sciences myself, so don't know much about them. But when we bump into Jessica, I'll ask her. Sir, do you have any questions?'

She stopped outside a large blue door, using her hip to push it open.

'Er . . . No, not yet.'

It led to the Assembly Hall: a wide dark oaken room of a colossal height. The only windows were small rectangles lining the top; artificial light illuminated most of it.

'I'm afraid you missed Miss Butterworth's talks, sir,' Sarah mentioned (it was almost half past eight). 'But I'd be happy to respond to your enquiries.'

Dozens of prospective parents and their girls were clustering throughout the hall.

Anneliese spotted a long row of tables laden with doughnuts and cakes. She tugged at Josef's sleeve.

'Papi?'

'Oh, sorry, I forgot!' gasped Sarah. 'Let me get you something to eat.'

They were all warm – the cakes. Anneliese spilled some orange juice over her front so Sarah immediately skidded to fetch her a napkin. She dampened it under the tap in the kitchen and came back. 'We're not allowed to go there,' she explained to Anneliese, 'but once you become familiar with the school, you understand that they don't pay attention to these things.'

Sarah dabbed at Anneliese's blouse.

'Which science are you interested in?'

She had never been asked such a question.

'Biology.' she replied.

'My sister has a friend who's reading biology at King's College. Do you want to be a doctor?'

Anneliese shrugged.

'Never mind – you have plenty of time left to think about that. I'm sorry, sir.' She looked at Josef. 'I didn't catch your name.'

'Josef van der Holt.'

'Mr van der Holt – you're welcome to speak to any of the staff if you like.' Sarah looked ahead. 'Although . . . they do seem rather busy. You see, a lot of parents came at half past six so you can imagine . . . Anyway, where do you want to go? Shall I take you to the science laboratories?'

Anneliese eagerly nodded.

On their way back out onto the Covered Way Isabel was immersed in the radiant glow of the lighting. Every other school they had attended for an open evening had been black or dim; the Gothic architecture had imposed on her the shadows of a bleakly lighted penitentiary. Here street lights encircled the Centenary Building and the sports court beside it.

Strolling up the Covered Way, teachers went by and smiled brightly, questioning her:

'Have you had something to eat, little one?'

She could do nothing but nod. Strangers didn't usually treat her in a motherly way. Neither did anyone else.

When they reached the Centenary Building and science laboratories Isabel looked straight ahead of her and saw the apex of the Covered Way. There was a massive playing field.

'On the other side is the Preparatory School.' Sarah informed her. 'We share the field for P.E. with them. I went there, and so did my sister. But it's perfectly all right if you *didn't* go there; my best friend came from Regina Coeli.'

Gazing at the concrete of the path and looking at the wonky rail along the grassy hill, she heard the faint simmer of notes. They were bouncing up and down in some long chain she could identify as music. Suddenly Sarah shouted at another girl:

'*Bam-bas, Bam-bas.*' as though it were a greeting in an oriental language.

The other girl was going down the Covered Way and called back:

'Oh, no – it's actually *tomorrow!*'

'Fourteen hours.' Sarah smiled.

'Fourteen hour – oh, *cheese* it! Never mind!'

Sarah sniggered, facing Anneliese and Isabel.

'We have a thorough grammar test tomorrow; Mr Humble made up a song for the endings. You'll learn it if you come here. You'll like Mr Humble, even if you do poorly in Latin. He dresses as a woman for pantomimes.'

Isabel's eyes were suddenly lacquered in gleam.

'*Pantomimes?*'

'The Christmas ones. Sometimes also at the end of the year. His wife Penny sews his costumes. She's a lovely woman.'

Josef broke into the dialogue.

'You . . . do the pupils know the family of . . .'

'Well, yes – occasionally. It depends on the teacher but, I mean, we've all been to Miss Cunningham's house two or three times. Sometimes after school, sometimes in the holidays for practice.'

'What does Miss Cunningham teach?' Anneliese asked.

'She's the Head of Music. I'll take you to her in a little while.'

They entered the chemistry laboratory. A middle-aged woman they learned was called Miss Frobishire was demonstrating the effect of a single displacement reaction. Around her were compressed five or six girls: some of them sitting on chairs, others sitting on tables. Chortling, they were shaking their hands rinse-like in a futile effort to control themselves.

' . . .because it's irrefutable. And I'm not going to deny it.' One girl laughed so loudly that she snorted. 'On the way out from the Vatican – they begin singing.'

Josef assumed the girl was speaking of a pupil on a recent holiday. Instead he heard Miss Frobishire respond:

'Don't listen to her, girls – it's all a bunch of *poppycock*.'

'It's not! Everyone was really very jolly on that trip . . . *Some* of us were quite too jolly.'

Miss Frobishire darted a very focussed playful look at the girl.

'Come help me with this, Julia. Take the beaker.' She was alerted to the presence of Josef, Sarah and the girls. 'Excuse me, we're just . . . some of us are *overexcited* today. I can't imagine the impression this is making!'

'We were talking about the Rome trip.' a skinny girl with a long nose explained.

'Is this . . . was this a holiday for Christmas?' Josef enquired.

'No.' the skinny girl replied. 'Mr Humble – our Latin teacher – he organises trips to Italy once every two years, and we went in July. Miss Frobishire and he sang as they went out the Vatican; rumour had it the *Pope* heard.'

'This was *not* so.' stated Miss Frobishire.

'No – it was so; it was *so*.' the skinny girl insisted melodically.

Anneliese's attention was elsewhere. Miss Frobishire had taken note of her attentive eyes.

'Care to give me a hand?'

There was silence.

'Erm . . . *me?*'

'That's right. Come put some gloves on; mind that your *hair* doesn't get in the way.'

So Anneliese approached the table where experiments were taking place. Julia removed her hairband to tie Anneliese's locks with it. The latter was invited to mix in some hydrobromic acid. It was the first time she had handled chemicals.

'Is she allowed to participate, sir?' Miss Frobishire checked with Josef.

'Yes, of course.'

'I'm quite surprised really; usually nobody comes here on the Open Evening. All the girls want to sing with the choir and go to the Centenary Building for sewing and go up the Art Building staircase. That's why these four aren't even wearing their lab coats – these *four*. You see what I have to put up with? *No* effort.'

'Mine's at home.' a redhead insisted.

'We know about *yours*, Marjorie – where are the *others*'? Home sick?'

Julia spluttered in a laugh.

'At *sea?*'

'*Goodness* – I meant home, sick!' Miss Frobishire insisted. 'Not "homesick"!'

Anneliese watched her solution turn to salt and water. She wouldn't cease to stare at it until Isabel tapped her back.

'Liesa, Liesa – Sarah's going to take us to the Music Room.'

It was located in a building that resided at the summit of the Covered Way; a special set of stone steps paved the route. The closer Isabel approached the Music Room the louder the notes fizzled. When a girl swung the door open wearing a black skirt and white blouse with a treble clef and the words 'Croham Hurst' embroidered on it she grasped the rhythm of the bumping melody. It was a song she had heard playing on the radio: 'I Happen to Like New York'.

And sure enough when she beheld the Covered Way and the peculiar outgrowths of its buildings and the slanted stair rail sloping down the hill; as she inhaled the stench of moistened earth and heard the trampling feet of an excited throng a word leapt to the foreground of her mind. She had read of it and maybe seen some photographs. There was a place called 'Broadway' somewhere in America. So far this was the nearest she had come to its proximity.

The moment she entered the building she was coated in warmth – in spite of its standoffish, uncanny structure. It consisted of red bricks and one could *see* them; they weren't covered by a sheet of mortar, wallpaper or plaster. On the wall to the left of the door was a music board. Another girl in the uniform of the white blouse and black skirt stood next to it. A flute jutted out from her hands.

Isabel prodded Sarah.

'Yes?'

'Why are there two uniforms?'

'Oh, that's the choir's uniform when they sing abroad.'

The girl's eyes froze.

'*Abroad?*'

Sarah nodded.

'Mmm-hmm. We went to Vienna and Paris, and this year we're going to New York. We're singing at Trinity Church in Manhattan.'

Isabel's heart skipped a beat upon hearing 'Manhattan'.

Josef was tentative as he enquired:

'This choir . . . is it reserved for very talented singers? What is the fee for the, er . . . the audition?'

'Oh, no, no, no – anyone can sing in the choir. There are others: the Senior Chamber Choir, Junior Chamber Choir, and there's also the Jazz Ensemble and the Orchestra and there's the Flute Choir . . . but no, when it comes to just the Junior Choir and the Senior Choir, anyone can sing. And when I say that, I don't just mean anyone's *allowed* to sing, because Miss Cunningham will *make* you sing – she'll make you sing *well*. And while some of the trips are expensive, the Old Crohamians Association funds a lot of costs when families don't have the means. Do you want to go in?'

Isabel was seized by trepidation.

'Mmm-*hmm*.' came the diffident rejoinder.

Sarah's hand pressed down the silver handle. It was a thin wooden door whose opening exuded a swift, slender click.

When they came in they saw a band of girls – some of them eighteen, some of them twelve – all sat around. It was an odd construction of a room: a building in itself. The top was a gable roof finished by a great pyramid at its apex. All the walls were naked bricks; a variation on some new Art Deco theme.

There were boards along the bricks of photographs: students on tour and in concert, even some pinned-up manuscripts of compositions. The ground they stood on as they entered was one level on which girls were sat – but there was a whole second platform on which others huddled at black desks. Miss Cunningham, the Head of Music, stood at a piano on the tawny parquet floor along the bottom ground: the space was triple-tiered.

Blue folders decorated with a treble clef stretched out along the students' hands. Well above them – around three feet or so – was this floor on which Josef, Anneliese, Isabel and Sarah watched. A layer of dark pink had carpeted it.

Some girls confusingly wore Santa hats. Two large teddy bears were resting with their backs against the wall. Music stands were scattered near them indiscriminately.

A healthy aroma stroked Isabel's nostrils: lavender's scent.

A tall girl of around sixteen tapped her shoulder.

'Would you like to join in?'

And Isabel was handed a blue folder with the music and the words to another song: 'I Got Rhythm'.

Anneliese grabbed hold of Isabel's sleeve.

'I can't sing.'

'Liesa!'

'I can't sing.'

The tall girl whispered in the ear of Anneliese:

'Just sing quietly. No one will notice.'

So Anneliese obeyed. No other school had ever asked Isabel if she could *sight*-sing; in this one she could lend her innate instrument to ditties unapproved by Josef.

He in the meantime asked Sarah:

'Are there . . . many instrumentalists here?'

'Oh, of course. And the Orchestra, the Flute Choir, the Jazz Ensemble . . . Miss Cunningham encourages us to form any kind of ensemble we'd like. And there are scholarships.'

'Scholarships?'

An hour later Anneliese and Isabel passed by the outdoor steel staircase: a fire escape. A few of the choir singers in their white blouses and black skirts were sitting there munching on cake.

'Little girls!' a tall blonde shouted at Anneliese and Isabel.

'Emma – that's so boisterous of you; like a girl from Croydon High.'

'They can tell I'm a nice person.' Emma insisted. 'Do you want to do some painting?'

Anneliese had no inclination for painting. Upon catching sight nevertheless of that bizarrely black steel staircase, still aglimmer from the drench of that day's downpour, she accosted the wet steps.

'Are you allowed to sit here?' Isabel asked the blonde.

'Well – sometimes. It depends.' The twins approached them and were taken to the highest level of that building. 'This is the Art and Design Room – where we have our art lessons.'

Emma switched the light on.

The twins sat down and drew but both of them were thoroughly preoccupied. Anneliese was dying to descend the staircase to see more laboratories. Isabel was dreaming of New York.

When an hour later they entered the bus Josef examined his girls. Both of them were still and quiet till they started speaking.

'What do you think the coat looks like?' Anneliese asked Isabel.

'What coat?'

'Miss Frobishire kept saying, "They're not wearing their coats." Do you think it's blue? I really can't wait till I get my coat. Did you know scientists have coats?'

'Did you notice roses in their hair? Sarah said that they wear roses in their hair for concerts.' Isabel rejoined.

It was a sad feat to witness the twins old enough to cover their own way.

11.

Ignition and dusk

'The *Daily Express* reported yesterday that Mary Pickford enjoys bricklaying. If you believe that, you'll believe anything.' Miss Carolyn S. Butterworth adjusted her spectacles on her nose. A slender, petite lady with short, sandy waves, the headmistress offered a complexion that was pasty; phantom-like. Every motion of hers was a measured gentle gesture. They were not those of a brittle, fragile woman but the movements of a person delicate in manner, schooled in tact. Her arms were thin like twigs, her wrists scarcely two inches in their girth. Curious and owl-like, her blue eyes intuited a broader scope of details than the girls imagined.

Raindrops were spattering against the tiny windows at the top of the Assembly Hall; impending winter had submerged and dunked it in a dusky brown obscurity. During that dark, autumnal morning assembly of November 1932 Miss Butterworth wore a blue jacket and skirt. A lilac brooch jutted out of her upper-right pocket.

Thirteen-year-old Isabel leant in to thoroughly inspect the sparkle of her new accessory: its shape was the school's emblem, a cornflower.

Attending on account of a three-quarter music scholarship next to Anneliese's seventy-five per cent academic, she sometimes slept but also simmered in her laughter during Mr Humble's Latin lessons that advised her 'never to get tense about her tenses'. Her closest friend Daphne Munroe had notified her recently about the devilishly energetic, lanky teacher's antics on their trip to Rome the previous year: befuddled in the midst of his intoxication, he had zestfully called both Miss Hampton and Miss Hampshire 'sexy'.

'That's *correct* . . .' His eyes transferred from Anneliese to Isabel during that Monday lesson. 'And the *future?*'

Isabel was busy gaping at the bleak, bespattered window, listening to rhythmic beats descending from the heavens.

'Isabel . . .?' Mr Humble asked.

Her mind continued to be elsewhere – whereupon he entered the habitual conversation he would lead with his pretend twin:

'"And how are you today, Christina?"' – "Not bad, Chris." – "You?" – "Not so bad, either . . ."'

Anneliese elbowed her sister.

'*Hmm?*' Isabel was roused.

'The future of "mitto".' Mr Humble clarified.

'"*am*".' Anneliese muttered.

A sly grin spread on Mr Humble's chin.

'What was *that?*'

Eyes sealed like a kitten's, hastily Anneliese shook her head.

She was Miss Frobishire's puppet; apparently had pledged to be since their first meeting at the Open Evening. Miss Rowley deemed her mathematical abilities to be 'exceptional'. To Isabel the latter was a short, bespectacled thirty-something-year-old with straight brown hair and an obscuring fringe who would lend pupils unsolicited counsel: 'Well . . . you know what they say: "Why buy the cow when you can get the milk for *free?*"' Straightening a pile of homework, she would look into the air and stumble in her self-defence. 'Nothing to worry about for now; of course, simply – for future reference. Some girls at Old Palace . . .' The papers would be tucked into her briefcase and a hand would stroke the air dismissively: 'Never mind.'

Nothing could throw off history teacher Miss Clarendon – who spouted '*bear* with me' repeatedly like a librarian hard-pressed to find a book. She had a habit of standing at the front of the class with disproving eyes, her arms akimbo as she waited for a period of silence to suppress the chatter. It was with her that Anneliese discussed museums and exhibitions. In Miss Clarendon's company she spent half of her lunchtimes posing copious numbers of questions on an epoch in history: especially those that the syllabus didn't encompass.

To Isabel belonged Miss Cunningham. The different choirs all sang songs both Classical and modern: jumping from Brahms' *Liebeslieder* Waltzes to the 'Morgenblätter' piece by Strauss to 'Mack the Knife' in well under an hour. Before the raven glossy grand piano, the adored Miss Cunningham was on the highest pedestal for choir members. They spent their free time helping her arrange the music stands, scribing arrangements of the songs if copies were amiss and making lists of future morning hymns.

Often she would play a chord at the beginning of a piece only to make a brief humorous comment – then repeat that chord, throw off another anecdote, attempt the chord once more – only to burst out laughing and dissolve into distraction. At times she had to wipe away the tears emerging from her laughter. During the hours spent at choir practice she played stationary always – never sitting down – and never ceased to keep her right foot hovering an inch above the pedal, even between songs.

It was typical of her to comment on most incidents. When a girlish scream from outside hacked the silence of the working girls she casually remarked, 'Just someone getting murdered.'

In the middle of the Christmas holidays – a form of bliss for Anneliese because they let her mind absorb a multitude of concepts never touched upon at school – Josef sat with her for hours every day while the allegedly autonomous Isabel musically busied herself. Following these lessons her head would be filled to the brim with more and more fresh ideas, to the extent that when the clock struck eight that evening she felt overstuffed. The next morning she would wake in great excitement and descend the stairs in leaps and bounds. Isabel could never catch a name or subject – but one day she was especially perturbed to hear her sister cry:

'Papa – Papa you told me that today you'd tell me of Santiago Ramón y Cajal!'

Isabel frowned. It was offensive enough that her sister and Papi spoke Dutch where she knew none. Now Anneliese was adding yet *another* language to the conversation.

A new ritual began every Wednesday: Josef would teach Anneliese to play chess. Three weeks into the lessons, the latter succeeded at beating her father.

Evidently one of his twins had inherited more than the other.

All of these attributes clashed to expedite the underscored degeneration of the sisters' mutual understanding: their arguments would kindle in a host of fired lashings. The oppressed Anneliese would end up condemning her sister for 'not even letting her exit the womb – she so urgently needed to get there *before* me.'

These infuriated Josef to no end – not purely by the imbecilic phrases the sororal spats would spew but also by the vulgar breach of his domestic peace. Entering the room, he would clap his hands loudly to distract their attention as though they were cats.

'We are young ladies.' he would emphasise – and neither daughter would correct him and inform him 'no, you're *not*.' 'We do not behave like hooligans. If you want *anyone* to take you seriously and treat you like a lady, you will not yap constantly like *poodles*. Am I correct?'

Cradled by her teachers, it was at Croham Hurst that Isabel felt lavishly surrounded by a cohort among which her gift was fervently promoted. Their wrangling muffled, both girls were securely nurtured in the balm of an oasis.

So when they had to rise, open their hymn books to page sixty-two and belt out in full voice, 'And did those feet in ancient time . . .', while certain students scratched their heads or turned to ask their neighbour for the page number again, it was a rare occasion in which Isabel believed herself a patriot.

That January her on-again, off-again false friend Olivia Paisley was appointed her partner in chemistry. Anneliese hogged the materials and thus assumed all the responsibilities herself. It was the day they would be testing lithium chloride.

Once she had poured in hydrochloric acid she could still sight specks of lithium ajitter at the bottom; white dots whose components were about to be dismantled.

Electrons hopped into the air like bees aflight, now dancing at the queenly apex of their flame. The buzz they had fomented gradually exhausted them and – just as agitated insects feel compelled at times to drop into reluctant slumber – presently they swung down in a loop and scattered to some nether level.

The escalation started to ignite a flurry of disparate colours; the first of which was a fluorescent pink. With the ceiling lights switched off they coruscated with an iridescent gleam much bolder than both natural and electric light.

Concurrently with the electrons' fall was the swift darting of the pieces Anneliese imagined were her own electrons: they were jetting back and forth to draw a long slick flame along her entrails. Gripping the table, she began to fear she might keel over. The thirteen-year-old – often contented with emotional monotony – was startled upon contacting this otherworldly layer.

Its alien dimension was a force she longed to penetrate.

Jerks of the flame were as spasmodic as convulsions of an epileptic. It danced sideways and upwards and was pulled abruptly to the right; it sought to reach a touch of the celestial – then plummeted in mourning for its failure. Tugging at the air to stay alight with the fierce grip of a paw's clenches, the quill fought a zealous struggle before finally relenting, shrinking and submitting to the classroom's black eclipse. When at last it clashed with oxygen within the atmosphere to mould into a glowing ball of pink, it looked like rubber.

Within seconds it had vanished.

Anneliese ringed her right goggle with her thumb and forefinger and leaned across the dish to gauge the relics of her glints. There was complete obscurity.

Miss Frobishire switched the lights on. The electrons Anneliese felt jiggling ceased to bounce and she expelled a wealthy sigh. She had floated down to her sobriety again, and somewhere in a corner Isabel was fast asleep.

Boredom was the latter's opportunity for rest. It was the only calibre of feeling capable of soothing her.

Snow rained down like pelting bombs from fighter planes that Christmas. Most of the window ledge was swollen by it.

With the piano in the living room stood opposite the wall, Isabel could never see the outside view throughout her practice. She abandoned her instrument for a few minutes to position herself at the window. Dreamy and half-conscious with her chin residing on her palm, she searched for something that might pique her interest.

A fluffy, dishevelled grey kitten was passing by the fence of the house opposite. It dragged its way laboriously; not unlike a postman burdened by a sack of parcels on his back. Limping feline legs were inconspicuous to the pedestrians who swept ahead.

Isabel watched the kitten with a mellow anticipation; equally busy with the mutilation of paper made thin in her hands. If the kitten could just safely cross the road and reach their side she could convince her father it was in their moral interest to adopt it. The game had been conducted thrice before without a stroke of luck.

She followed every millimetre of its trail with her fixated eyes until the view of it had lapsed beyond her scope of vision.

At the age of eight she would have soaked the pillow on her bed aplenty and suppressed her upset with a glass of water from the kitchen. But her tears would have dissolved along the glass's rim. The next morning the grey slush originating from her glacial panic would have thawed, and by midday it would have melted.

In adolescence it was far less simple. Somewhere in her abdomen was a solidifying mechanism whose cruel task it was to freeze the onset of her misery: she would call upon it in her moments of unease. But recently it had assumed a stalwart stance of being dormant. When at this moment Isabel began to let the tears rise in her eyes, she felt an eagle piercing through her entrails to sweep down and snatch away this power with its lengthy beak. The shrieking bird took off with it the way it would have scooped a caterpillar in its mouth.

These stitches of her ordinary disposition come apart, Isabel developed a habit of sitting at her piano stool with her elbows bent over the lid of the instrument, awaiting the lapse of her fraught altercations.

Papi was always at work during these hours. Mama was asleep – but Isabel already knew her Mama was defunct in any case. Liesa was indulged in some 'extremely useful' book.

So the phantom occupying her would slide its way along the keys, transferring both its shape and texture to make seams around the music's contours. Yet its remnant simmered in her like the gas of a neglected oven plate; giving way to eerie ponderings still unfamiliar to her.

That winter she became conspicuously quieter.

The dusk would always come too early so she readily obstructed it. Isabel began to ask permission to attend Olivia's parties, await the moment someone of the other sex would ask her for a dance and fling her time away at doing almost anything. It occurred to her that she devoted too much energy to thinking and the nature of this exercise impoverished her soul.

The only time that thinking did amuse her was her daily walk with Anneliese each morning to the station. During this ephemeral trajectory her sister cultivated a strange habit of nearing the side of the road, liberally swinging her arms as she strutted astray from the pavement.

'Are you trying to get yourself *killed?*' Isabel yelled the moment that a car roamed by one morning, seizing her wrist violently to drag her back to safety. 'You're a *madman!*' she yelled, not even realising she was referring to the wrong sex in her speech.

She couldn't help but recognise that there was some audacity in this behavioural example that her sister's words kept undisclosed.

Yet Isabel would tell herself to each there was an 'own' – and this was Anneliese's personal ignition.

12.

Fighting the sheath

'Naumburg' was Madame Rakovskaya's favourite word. It came second only to the name 'Alfred Cortot', which was immediately followed by 'École Normale de Musique de Paris'. Isabel could never understand this since her French was non-existent despite scolding at the hands of Mme. Ravencourt at school.

Such an admission on her part was usually the cue for Madame Rakovskaya's habitual tirade:

'Musicians *must* speak European language. English? What is *English?* Have you ever heard great "English" pianist? You – you are not going to stay in this co-*un*-try, *Isabelle?*'

Vigorously Isabel shook her head. She wasn't going to risk becoming a rank amateur who studied at the Royal College of Music. Any mention of the Royal Academy discharged her laughter like a fountain.

On this occasion she dared to enquire:

'Do you think there's a conservatoire worthy of me in Zurich?'

Madame Rakovskaya's eyes grew so wide that Isabel hastened to sew up her lips. According to her wishes Isabel would go to Paris, then New York. Before anything she'd venture to America. The

Naumburg competition took place every spring. Preliminary auditions were held in March.

'How are we going to convince them when I'll only be fourteen then?'

'You have seen yourself in the *mirror?*' It was a deal. Madame Rakovskaya clapped her hands together. 'I think you are prepared, eh?'

Isabel mustered a half-smile that soon collapsed into the shy act of biting her lip.

'Mmm ... well ...' She puffed. 'It's a long time before I'll be applying to conservatoires ...'

'Three years.'

'Well, Papi wanted me to finish schooling when I was eighteen.'

'You, young *woman* – always do what "Papa" say?'

'No. I just think I would be better *pre* ... pre – *pared*, if I were eighteen and not sixteen.'

'You *heve one* problem. You are *stubborn.* Now sit down and play to me Beet-*hoven.*'

'*The Tempest?*'

'Did I *ask* you to play other piece?'

'I taught myself all of the others.'

'*A piacere* – then *you* choose.'

Her hands swayed on the keyboard with untethered freedom. Unlike all of Madame's other pupils she could easily employ the left hand for her right-hand chords. Appendages to the piano were her limbs; no less than its reactive hammers. She lacked that exaggerative pose of raising the wrists and then swooping them down the way Russians did. Madame even acknowledged the allowances of subtle and uncanny expression that Isabel granted herself; risky fingering and slurs her other pupils would have never dared.

'This is too easy for you, ah?'

Isabel nodded enthusiastically.

'I was trying to teach myself the ballade, actually.'

'Very good, very good. You can do presentation – Friday.'

That Friday Madame Rakovskaya had her own verbal 'presentation' to make.

Entering the room with her hands clasped together, she announced in glee:

'I have already booked tickets.'

'You...' Isabel was dumbstruck. 'For next year's auditions in New York?'

'Abso*lutely.*'

'How many?'

'One to me, and one to you, and one to your father.'

'But that's ...' Isabel slouched back on her piano stool. 'Anneliese will be very upset.'

'She vill have to get *personal* ticket.'

Preparation would take longer than a week this time. It would have to be performed for the whole year at *mezzo forte*, then a lesser *mezzo forte* and a greater *mezzo forte*; with greater usage of the pedals and with moderate restraint. They needed, as Madame Rakovskaya insisted, to find 'for the piece – the correct *temperature.*'

It may have been *the* Chopin Ballade, but it was only a Chopin ballade. It wasn't even Liszt's *El Contrabandista*: a piece she expected would bring her some obstacles. Her piano playing, she lamented, had never quite acclimatised itself to greatness in the way her cello playing had.

Two days later she interrogated Papi. His moustache curled upwards.

'I heard it last night at three o'clock in the morning – you play it really very beautifully.'

'Thank you.'

If she played it very beautifully she couldn't process in either the left or the right of her brain why it was that her nerves had usurped half her abdomen. They were clattering against her stomach like unwieldy baby pigeons bumping midflight into lampposts. She hadn't slept for five nights; there were two to go until the debut of the piece before Madame Rakovskaya.

Anneliese came and stood in the living room the following lunchtime with her arms folded. Isabel sat on the stool with her interlocked hands in midair. Lined with frost, they disobeyed all orders from their master. Anneliese said nothing.

Finally the former let out an exasperated sigh:

'Why are you here – *Anneliese?*'

Slow to catch on, the Younger Twin offered a shrug.

'Could you please allow me some privacy? I have only forty-two hours to prepare.'

'Papa said you play it very beautifully.'

Of course she and 'Papa' shared everything including – from what Isabel had gathered – communication in Spanish.

'I don't want to play it in front of you.'

'Why not?'

She was nearing aggressiveness.

'I *don't.*'

There was a pause of tension.

'Did I upset you, Isabel?'

'Did – ah – no – Anneliese – go away!'

So rhythmically punctuated were the words that Anneliese – impinged by Isabel's coarse voice – sped out and went upstairs to throw herself onto her bed and read Joseph Babinski.

Those forty-two hours were for the most part excruciatingly unproductive.

Each time Isabel positioned herself on the stool she was all of a sudden dissatisfied with her location on it. Shuffling herself left and right, she struggled to decide how best to fit into the centre. This feat accomplished, she would rest her left foot on the left pedal and keep her right foot upturned on the right.

Isabel used a hairclip to hold the score's pages in place. Gazing at the notes, she would inspect them and decide to add more pencil markings. Staves were crawling already with *crescendo* and *diminuendo* and annotations galore; stained with infinite slurs and unending accents on notes she had *known* should be accented.

Both hands would stretch across the keys to form the contours of their chords. It was the action of pressing the notes that began to impose a tenacious dilemma.

She played the first G-minor chord. It said *pesante* in the bar. She wondered if that told her for how long the first chord had to linger. She would've used her metronome if she had known that this would deal her such a heavy load of problems.

Isabel hated the metronome. Madame Rakovskaya called it a 'waste of time'.

Quickly her fingers slid down from the keys. She had played the chord abominably. The thought drummed into her with an increasing echo: *the execution of notes is not music*. This notion did its own *pesante* jig around her mind; the more it pranced and bounced the more her head ached so that sweat began to trickle from her temples.

It was already eleven o'clock in the evening. There was a tentative knock on the door. Isabel – without enquiring who it was – yelled 'no' in a slack manner.

He entered anyway.

'*Meine Kleine*, it's getting very late. Don't you think the piece will be ... *more fresh*, if you continue your practice tomorrow morning?'

Her face was fixed on the page and her ears were oblivious.

'*No*.'

He approached her and reached for her forehead.

'You're very feverish—'

'I'm *not*.'

'I think we must measure your temperature—'

'I don't have a temperature.' She did however wish she had one.

'Let me just get the thermometer—'

'Papi – go away. You're disturbing my practice.'

He left after three minutes, determined to stay up until she went to bed in case a moment might allow him the faint chance of sticking a thermometer into her mouth.

She tried the chord again. It reverberated like the gargling of a person overly obsessed with dental hygiene.

The second time she ceded to ascending chords that followed it. Too loud were they for her to overlook their crassness. An object in her stomach seemingly swayed back and forth; hurling itself forward like a tide after the passage of a ship.

Where obliged to play gently she played chords that knocked like a cucumber's chopping. The fourth time she snatched her hands from the keyboard and covered her ears, panting from the ghastliness that *was* her performance. Her runs and scales became a splash of accidental disharmonic chords. This wasn't how she played. A spider could play better casting a long, incidental web along the keys.

Her hands were clammy. When she touched the lid they slipped and glided on it like an untrained skater on the ice. It was too bright. Lights were on everywhere. She could wager that Papi sat somewhere awaiting her exit. Anneliese would still be awake reading. Isabel could not play with this crowd. So she shut the piano, peeled her hands from the lid and tossed herself onto the sofa. Running water sounded from the kitchen; Anneliese's steps the ceiling. She would have to wait for utter silence: in the meantime she could turn her mind to something else.

She wiped her moist hands on her dress and stealthily began a mental composition of prosaic leitmotifs: contemplating how Daphne Munroe would probably marry a daft and unhandsome fellow called Timothy; how Olivia Paisley might be debauched in her later years; how it would take many years for Anneliese to find a young man to her taste. She wondered why it was that Miss

Hampshire was roiled when obliged to explain reproduction. Loose threads were hanging at her dress's hem so she got busy picking at them. A headache started rattling in her skull. It was five past midnight when she fell asleep.

Josef entered the room at half past to cover the girl with a blanket. It was twenty-four degrees outside, the middle of July, but he still feared she might catch cold. He switched off all the lights.

By one am there were no creaks unsmoothing the night's silence. It was then that Isabel resurfaced.

She was heady; restrained by the obstinate ghost of her headache. Half-asleep, she dumped herself acrook on the piano stool, opened the lid and embarked on the piece. Lusciously the lissome chords grew in *legato*; staccatos ranged from stark to subtle while dynamics dripped sublime proportion. But Isabel dismissed all this. There were notes and expression markings, and there were two hands but she was not there. She needed only to calm herself; spill her anxiety elsewhere. She wanted to abandon the waves in her stomach that made standing a challenge. She sought to dig into her memory with her sharp nails, rummage around and yank the vision of her father lovingly embracing her small sister out as she would jerk a splinter sitting in her skin.

Most of all, she wanted to excise *that* opera – the Russian one in which the lovers never got together – with a scalpel. That stigma had been suctioning the vigour from her for two years now; flattening her usual mental texture of champagne.

She may as well have taken some solution to efface her ailment – but she played and it gushed out. All she knew once she had finished was that she had executed, quite impressively, the whole of Chopin's Ballade No. 1. That meant she could play it in the morning to Papi and Liesa.

Breakfast was at seven the following day. Isabel had slept for only four hours, awoken in a sweat, flung on a dirty summer dress with no desire for a bath or shower and then burst ajar her father's door to get him up. It was a Sunday. He had no excuse not to listen to her.

She sat down and bobbed on his bed, awaiting a sign of alertness. Josef was forced to blink in order to distinguish the tall twin.

'Isa . . .bel?'

'Mmm-hmm. Get up. You have to hear me play. I practised all night.'

She hoped the white lie wouldn't dare curse her performance.

Next was Liesa. Isabel kicked her door open and sat on her knee as she slept. She took hold of her right shoulder and jolted it.

Anneliese stared up at her. Isabel beheld a sour kitten still untrained in opening her eyes.

Instinctively she probed:

'Is Mama all right?'

'Mama's fine, Mama's fine.' Isabel sang in anticipation. She sprinted across to Anneliese's closet and picked out a blue summer dress. With one eye open Anneliese responded:

'I wore that yesterday.'

'So?'

Anneliese was out of bed and headed to the door.

'Where are you *going?*'

'To have a shower – according to the daily routine.'

'No – you can do that in the *evening!* Liesa!! You have to put this on now – I'm going to show you my piece. You know it's my lesson tomorrow – why are you being so selfish?'

Anneliese forewent the energy to look her sister in the eye with a corrective glance. She took the creased and rumpled dress from her and flung it on.

'Good girl!' Isabel grabbed her hand and delivered her out of the room. 'Come on.'

She shot down the stairs like an elephant hounding its prey through the jungle. Anneliese dragged behind her, almost slipping on the back of her dress.

Josef hadn't yet come down so Isabel now volunteered to make the porridge. Never had she managed to succeed in this routine so Anneliese could easily predict the outcome of this daring. So fatigued was she nevertheless – excessive hours had been spent unscrewing her brain's nuts and bolts to find out how the plantar reflex worked – that she resided on her chair, elbow shamelessly on the table, fast asleep with her chin on her palm.

The porridge spilled out of the pan in eight minutes.

'Isabel – I think it's ready.'

'Hmm?' She was too busy humming. Anneliese could barely recognise the tune. 'Oh, yes!'

Speedily Isabel grabbed the pan from the stove – without even an oven mitt.

'Ow!' The pan stumbled into the sink; half its contents escaped down the drain. Then Isabel switched on the wrong tap and shrieked 'Ow!' again.

'Did you burn yourself?'

'No – no – no, it's not serious. It's barely even red.'

She held it under cold water. Some of the cold water seeped into the porridge in the pan.

Josef arrived at the table at twenty to eight. Not even he had prophesised this medley. He removed the dripping pan of porridge from the sink and insisted on making a fresh pot. Isabel sat down at the table, her arms folded, sulking.

'I did it very quickly, Papi!' she yelled.

'Isabel, I would not let you have this if you were *starving*.'

It took twenty-five minutes for Josef's porridge to be ready: far too long a stretch for Isabel to uphold glances of contempt in his direction but her eyebrows nonetheless persisted.

Out of sheer discontent Isabel roused her sleeping sister.

'Liesa!'

She sprang up as though someone had yelled 'fire'.

'Hmm?'

'It's morning.'

'Yes.'

It seemed to Isabel that the consumption of the porridge took too long. She had swallowed her whole bowl in just two minutes, taking large heaped spoonfuls of which Josef disapproved.

'Anneliese, is that the same dress you were wearing yesterday?'

'Yes, Papa I—'

'Go and change, please. We'll be at church in three hours and you're not going to wear that.'

Isabel flung her spoon into her empty bowl, if only for the purpose of making a statement. Luckily the thought of her own dirty dress had slipped her father's mind.

Breakfast was finished at nine. Ten minutes later Josef and Anneliese were both sat in the living room. Isabel was in the process of attempting to position herself on the stool.

It was too hot. Though her legs clung to the folds of her dress she was sure she was stuck to the stool. She did her best to pull it up around her and peel skin away from the stool's leather. After three minutes of engagement in this task Isabel raised the piano lid. Leaning back, it clanged against the surface of the wood.

The sound signalled the onset of an anxiousness far more intense than one stirred by the ticking clock of an examination. She took a last peek at her audience.

Isabel remarked that they were both so calm – even *too* tranquil. Here was Chopin's Ballade No. 1: a tempest of clamouring furore; a gallery of bitter recognition, feral strife and enforced torpor. The piece resounded in her head as she inspected the beige wall before her. On it hung some innocent replica of an oil-painted vase. Crickets were chirping outside. These small black dots in front of her she shared with Chopin: a transmission to her from the long-dead master. No instrumentalist could lavish craft onto a piece if lacking the capacity to conjure the creator's feelings at the time of composition.

Anneliese was fidgeting whilst Josef was demanding that she put her legs together like a lady: that was what *all* ladies did.

Together they reminded her of strangers that she often spotted on the bus: pairs gabbing about matters immaterial inanely, coaxing her to wonder if they *had* any capacity. She asked herself if, as they bitterly complained about their taxes being spent on ugly new apartment blocks, or seriously engaged in voicing disapproval of some music hall star's scandalous affair, they actually encompassed any volume.

If so – what could this 'volume' of theirs easily procure? Did it supply them with a love or care? Did it inspire them to gaze at art or marvel at the ceiling of the Sistine Chapel? Did it imply that when they heard a Chopin piece they felt the buttons in them being hammered like the keys that the performer pressed?

Such individuals went beyond the grounds of Isabel's imagination. In these instances she felt like a small child against a cold glass window, hard-pressed to decrypt the meanings of the happenings inside. The warmth that toddlers could inspire, even the droplets in her eyes whenever she would read a headline that reported a child's death – were all phenomena as foreign to these people as the rituals of a parliament of owls.

During their rest the keys of the piano would be covered with an often dusty yellow cloth whose role it was to stop dust's infiltration. For the past four years the dust from irresolvable, ineffaceable memories had grown throughout her insides as they might on archived papers. A sheath was now in her possession to protect herself from them. It would determine most of her inflections during speech.

Touching the keys with her fingers, she heard Josef shush Anneliese. The slight rebuke dropped on her with the force of a comet; she had no idea why. It shone with the slick surface of a typical suburban family whose children played on swings.

Isabel played on swings. She *had* played, at one time. What would change if she could play this piece? Would the household be subjected to a quake? Would she blend in with life's misfortunes like the painting nonchalantly hanging from the wall – its striking colours totally assimilated to the bland surrounding beige?

She lowered her hands from the piano. The iron curtain of the theatre was being hauled down prematurely.

'Are you feeling ill, Isabel?' Josef asked.

She scratched her neck.

'No.'

She exited the room and sprinted up the stairs. Anneliese arrived two minutes later to find her face-down on her bed.

'Isabel . . .' She sat beside her and began stroking her head. It only served to unnerve her. 'It's normal to be nervous.' she whispered. 'But it works better if you try a little first, become accustomed to playing. Perhaps if you play it only *technically* first you can grow into the idea of being free and unencumbered when you finally perform.'

How stupid would one have to be – thought Isabel – to think an artist produced work when 'unencumbered'? Did she think that every piece or painting or short story came from people who were regularly in the throes of joy?

'No, Liesa . . .' she pleaded in a soft tone. 'I'm sorry, I . . .' her voice broke off. 'I think I have to work on it more before I can *perform* it.'

'I'm sure you don't.'

She hated these polite contradictions.

Isabel spent most of the day weeping and pretending to do homework whilst in bed. In fact she did no more than blot the ink across her documents with tears.

At two o'clock at night after three hours of sleep she and the piano at last reconciled. This intermittent sojourn offered the sensations of a worn-out mother watching her sick child recover. She patted her instrument with affection.

But it was summer and the nights were short. That Tuesday was the day the ballade would encounter its primary listener.

As she laid her hands along the keys to offer her teacher that grouchy chord she was struck with new terror. It was as though a stranger had abruptly yoked her wrist, pushed her onstage and ordered her to improvise a monologue. She could not invent so much. She couldn't even play for her own sister. It was not becoming to her style.

She executed something. The ballade was destroyed. Her chords were disjointed. Left and right hand scarcely met co-ordination. Staccatos became accidental chords and sharps and flats. *piano* was *crescendo* as she stamped her foot on the right pedal when she should have pressed down on the left.

Anneliese knelt outside the room, spying on her through a keyhole: a captive forced to watch her loved one tortured to reveal a hidden truth. Miniature tears pricked the tender skin under her eyelids. Helplessly they rolled down her face, slipping into her cleavage. She wiped her eyes with a clenched fist.

When Isabel had finished after twelve and a half gruelling minutes, Madame Rakovskaya kept her head bowed. A moment later she discharged a bout of raucous laughter. Clapping her hands together, rubbing them as though it might ignite a fire, she proudly announced to her student with an oval-shaped Cheshire Cat grin:

'I have no time for girls who prefer go to party. Go to party – all girl – any girl go to party.'

She snatched the score off the piano and stuffed it into her bag. It belonged to Isabel.

Not stooping to look at the pupil as she addressed her, she let the lion's growl in her voice express most of her thoughts.

'I thought you want to be great pianist. Clearly *this* is *not truth*.'

Isabel nodded quite viciously.

'I want to be a great pianist.' she clarified in a sombre, lower-voiced tone.

'You think you are special, yes?' Isabel's unwillingness to answer this only incensed Madame Rakovskaya *further*. 'Yes?' she said again, now imperatively.

'I hope so.'

'You *hope* so?' The jeering in her attitude was growing.

'That's as much as I can say.' confessed Isabel.

'I see nothing special here. You play – way many other girls play.' She snorted with a condescending huff. 'Also – other girls – other girls have *advantages*. For *example*, other girls – prettier, smaller; other girls – *elegant*. Who are you, *mmm?* Who are *you?* You think you are *pianist?* You are not even ... how do you say, "*horoshenkaya*"? You are not even . . . *attractive*.'

The eyes of the young girl were welling up but she was rigidly determined not to let a tear escape her lashes. Keeping a cold gaze on Madame Rakovskaya, Isabel meekly suggested:

'I could try the Beethoven again—'

'No try. Pianists – they do not *try*. Great pianists – *do*. This – this is not "doing".'

Her cheeks now flushed with scarlet red, Isabel insisted:

'Then don't waste your time on me – you should leave.'

Madame Rakovskaya was indignant. She made a slight stamp as she stood and headed to the door.

'But the score is mine, Madame Rakovskaya.'

'Hmm?'

'You took my score and put it in your bag.'

'*Who?*'

'The *score*.'

Madame Rakovskaya's eyebrows were still furrowed; she was looking at Isabel as if she were requesting a gift.

'The notes.' Then to make it even clearer Isabel proclaimed: 'You have my *music*.'

Another snort came from Madame Rakovskaya. She took the ballade out of her bag, approached the table in the room and slammed it down with unrestrained aplomb.

On her way out she lacked the dignity to notice Anneliese beside the door.

Josef returned home from work three hours later, catching Anneliese sat at the dining room table, peeling the tips off her fingernails.

Her cheeks were smeared with red; the ends of her lashes were dewy.

'*Meine Kleinste* . . . did something happen?'

She sprung up off the chair and ran across.

'Isabel locked herself in her room. Madame Rakovskaya said she played badly and left.' She sniffed loudly and rubbed her nose on the back of her hand. 'Madame Rakovskaya isn't going to teach her . . . she was *horrible*. She said our girl was unattractive.'

This was a sickening injustice; as immoral a defilement as when Frans from Keukenhof had taken off with Magda Groen, the sexton's daughter. He wiped his hands off on each other.

'Then it is very good she left.'

'But Papa, Isabel is in a state . . .' She sniffed more loudly this time. 'I've been looking in the telephone directory to find her another teacher, and I've marked several names.'

'It's better to enquire at the Royal College.'

'Hmm?'

'Madame Rakovskaya was recommended to me by someone at the Royal Academy. This was of course an *error*.'

Isabel spent the whole night looking at the ceiling, wondering when blotches on her eyes would surrender the chore of obstructing her sight.

She didn't play in front of anyone throughout the summer. Sometimes, wielding an ice cream and awander in Hyde Park in August, she was tranquil. Sunrays would coat her face and batter at her eyelashes. She rationed her time between her sister and friends – taking care not to let one's affixed slot overlap with the other's.

Taking Anneliese to see *42nd Street*, Isabel became transfixed by the number of songs that immediately sealed themselves into her memory.

She was nonetheless taken aback when she noticed her sister's head bowed and eyes closed.

From the autumn she had little contact with her instruments. Imitating her sister at a supreme level, Isabel took hold of their biology textbook and began spending time over vain exercises.

Three weeks went by, and six weeks, then nine weeks, by which time Christmas decorations lined shops in their manifold arrangements.

At the beginning of December Josef's sleep was hindered by the sound of murmured wailing carefully being smothered with a pillow. He strolled into his daughter's room to see her dampening her hand, long swirls of liquid rolling from her eyes.

He sat on the edge of her bed.

'Isn't it about time we found you a new teacher?'

She shook her head adamantly.

'I get enough help from Miss Cunningham.'

'But . . . all pianists need private tuition.'

She let herself chortle.

'All *pianists*?' She folded her left and right sleeves away from her eyelids. 'No, Papi . . . I can manage. I don't want another teacher.'

Josef unleashed a loud puff. He was oblivious to the extent his moustache amplified his every sound.

'I've heard that there is a French woman who knew Nadia Boulanger teaching at the Royal College.'

'I don't want another teacher, Papi.'

It had never occurred to her to tell Josef she was unable to play in front of Miss Cunningham. She was ashamed.

'I really think, Isabel, that if there are problems . . .'

'No, I don't have any problems, Papi. I don't. It's my fault. It's not . . . it's not important. I don't have technical problems, Papi.'

'Yes, but—'

'I'm not going to have another teacher.'

'It really isn't difficult to—'

'I'm not *going* to.'

He hugged and stroked her head and she insisted that he leave her.

For a fortnight Josef heard no noise emerging from her room: her subterfuge surpassed his perspicacity.

Two days before Christmas she was suddenly entirely incapacitated. Sleep had escaped her for almost twelve days now. Prior to that it had encountered her for maybe half an hour every night. When she looked at the clock it was 4.47 am.

Watching herself very attentively in her mirror, Isabel began to tie her mane into a French plait using seven hairclips. Then she took hold of the scissors used for homework, brought them to her hair and sheared off half her ponytail. Fluffing out the rest of it, she made a fashionable bob akin to vaudeville dancers of the time.

The next day Anneliese and Josef were astounded when she came down for her breakfast ninety minutes late.

'Isabel!' Josef shouted almost in a general's fashion, momentarily forgetful of her age. In German he demanded to know: 'What have you *done?*'

'It's in vogue this way, Papa.' Isabel answered in English. 'It's what all the other girls have.'

She skipped down and gently asked if he could make her porridge. Josef was not going to be fooled.

'Well, I'll do it myself.' she decided.

Anneliese intervened:

'I can do it, Isabel.'

'No, no, it's all right. I'll cook myself breakfast.' her independence insisted.

13.

The string section

Six months passed. By summer 1934 her sister had become more of a phantom than a regular at 97 Glenluce Road.

Isabel disappeared at six o'clock most evenings, staying out until her aging father was compelled to go and pick her up – an hour she would frantically insist was 'bedtime for a newborn'.

She had taken to attempting courtship. Anneliese espied how Isabel behaved around young men: taking care to question them about themselves, offering the royal flush of vapid anecdotes her sister found unfunny, fashioning the image of a woman quite selective when it came to choosing whose advances she accepted.

Her rhythmic laughter and the throwback of her head were gimmicks indispensable to her.

She suffered from no emblem of excessive gaudiness. It was a discipline: a blink as a response, her hands hugging her glass to indicate that she was wallowing in tedium, the brash insistence that she fetch her coat if some insipid boy was offering.

Anneliese could have admired this if they had been a little older. As they were still under fifteen she took it as a symbol of Isabel leaving the pack. At five foot nine the Older Twin would emphasise her need to be addressed as a 'young lady'.

Close friends who had once shared combs now stayed apart because one followed boys, the other was still 'papa's little girl'. Former masters in music and sewing would flick back their locks when a young man strolled past. So drenched were their faces in cosmetic gunk that every time she saw them at a party she would barely recognised them, wondering what the black rings around their eyes were.

Lunchtime conversations bounded like a herd of kangaroos around the classroom: which Hollywood actors were having 'affairs', *where* they could be 'carrying on' – how tight were the locks on their dressing room doors? Some girls organised wide polls across the blackboard to determine which they thought would be 'deflowered' first. The leader would call on a vote. When Anneliese once saw that Isabel had won the second-largest number – and that her reaction was to smirk and snicker – she abruptly left the room and headed to the library.

Two months after their fifteenth birthdays, Josef remarked that Anneliese carried herself with more diligence, shook hands more vigorously and comported herself with more poise. She had contrived an automatic smile prepared for application in the contexts that required it. Knowing that her voice was unconventionally low and louder than most people's, she was careful not to raise it.

The girl recoiled from hordes of company. She was the one sat in the corner waiting for commotions to die down at parties, scarcely noticing the young man next to her hard-pressed to start a struggling conversation. Even Josef was a little disconcerted by this. When he questioned her she answered earnestly:

'I'm polite with everyone. I just don't want to talk to them.'

Josef patted her head.

'Are they really so dull?'

'Duller than what's going on in my head.'

One spring day when Josef was still lecturing, Isabel put her sister on trial:

'You don't have any friends, Liesa.'

Anneliese continued tinkling with her spoon until she placed it on the saucer at the side.

'Well . . .' she was trying to speak in a whisper but it was beyond her. 'Girls in our form are hardly *fascinating* individuals.'

'Well – *you're* not.'

'I know.'

'So can you expect it of our classmates?'

Anneliese grated her left cheek with her nails.

'Erm . . . I don't. But I did try to be friends, in the beginning, with Daphne, and it didn't work very well.' She scratched her cheek again. 'I bought so many biographies yesterday. I found out Mendeleev gained his doctorate because of a study called "On the Combinations of Water and Alcohol". She blinked a few times. 'It seems so primitive now. And he became so obsessed with a woman, whilst married to another, that he threatened suicide. And ended up committing bigamy.'

Isabel was squinting as though light were pestering her eye.

'His old woman got the short end of *that* stick.'

'It's just . . .' Anneliese linked the fingers of both hands together. 'One wonders what kinds of spheres or dimensions must exist in *one* man for him to love a woman so manically and at the same time be so obsessed with his *work* that he proposed a fictional element: "Coronium". It doesn't exist. I just can't understand how one can go through life holding so *much* inside. I barely hold *anything*.'

Her sister wasn't able to catch on.

Isabel would never pick a novel up if it did not meet one of her conditions: it either had to be the basis for an opera or include three 'inappropriate' depictions.

Cousin Elise's visits exposed polar opposite ideas.

Handing Anneliese her scarf and coat one afternoon, she explained how her train had been delayed because a man had jumped under it. The thirty-seven-year-old fellow was now dead. Anneliese was silent. Her eyes betrayed a gravity they rarely did, her gestures became slower and more programmed. She proceeded to the kitchen to brew tea.

Isabel followed her to the kitchen and came back to slam the biscuit tin down on their coffee table. Looking at Elise with viciousness, she sat and crossed her legs. After a while they began tapping the floor rhythmically to convey her impatience. A few minutes later Anneliese came equipped with the tea.

Elise's perceptions took time to take hold.

'It was absolutely *ghastly!*' she gasped. 'To think . . . he probably has children . . .' She paused and breathed in deeply before pursuing the discourse in a more theatrical fashion. 'And a wife . . .'

Anneliese didn't say anything. Her look betrayed it all.

Isabel was staring at her cup of tea.

'Is the Victoria line affected?'

Elise was taken aback. Subconsciously she was a little sad that her performance hadn't spawned a great effect.

'Pardon?' she asked in a hushed voice.

'The Victoria line, is it affected?'

There was a pause in which Anneliese held up her cheek with her hand.

'I don't know.' Elise helplessly replied, at loss for words.

The conversation turned to literature. They discussed Flaubert and Stendhal, whom Anneliese lambasted for their unambiguous aversion to humanity.

'And when she dies . . .' Elise remembered *Madame Bovary*, 'The black bile that comes gushing from her mouth . . . .. It's so horrid! Mama tried to stop me reading it, but Papa tells her that it's best I be familiar with these things.'

With her cello strings stilled, Isabel was loath to let those in her heart be plucked.

'Yes ...' Anneliese pondered, replacing her teacup. 'The problem is, I don't think he *does* have sympathy. I think he makes it grotesque. He overdoes it. Like Picasso. Never liked his paintings.'

Isabel offered no comment. The tension boiled between Elise and Isabel: each time they met they had to re-enact an introduction.

'Have you come across anything, Isabel?'

'In *Flaubert?*' A little offended, she folded her arms.

'Come to think of it, I doubt you would have read Flaubert.' Elise admitted frankly with some awkwardness.

'Mmm-hmm.' was the maximum that Isabel could muster.

'Anything else? I would have thought . . .'

At that point Elise stopped. With Isabel's long, regal stature and too often condescending glance, it was not right to pick a fight.

'Everyone's waiting for me to start reading novels.' She sulked. 'I'm not going to do that.'

'She's very busy.' Anneliese sarcastically excused her.

'I don't like the idea of novels.' Isabel defended her position. 'Some . . . yes. *Winnie the Pooh* is not a bad novel.'

'It's not a novel.' Anneliese scoffed.

'Well, it's *fiction*,' Isabel emphasised, 'so I don't see how it *isn't*. And there are some – there's something French by the Marquis de Sade that . . .' She realised the kind of conversation her words might now spark. 'Anyway, what I'm trying to clarify is—'

'Isabel does not read novels as her head is *jammed*.'

Elise's eyes coursed from one sister to another.

'"Jammed"?'

Anneliese proceeded with her argument – using her fingers as a counting aid.

'George, Michael . . . there's Peter Riddleston, Ewan Smith and many others . . .' varying her tone with every name, she listed them melodically.

'I wasn't going to *say* that. I don't think it's . . . *appropriate* to write about matters like *those*. As news pieces, maybe. Information can't be a bad thing. But *describing* death? Black *bile?* Why should I want to correspond with all that?'

Elise nodded, desiring complacency. She buried her nose in the steam of her tea, taking a sip.

'Isabel, your problem is the *word*, not sadness. You've never written anything in your life except half a history essay. A book for you is the equivalent of agricultural labour for the rest of us.'

'Who wants vivid descriptions of decaying *bodies?* Children dying? Men and women not consummating their love for *no* reason? It's pretentious – like a circus. Circus of gloom. People with real emotion do not spill their woes out on a page; it isn't natural.'

Abruptly giddy, Cousin Elise had found a point to raise:

'What about music?'

'That's a *disguise.'* insisted Isabel. 'It's not the real thing. Whereas prose . . . why on earth should anyone consult the idea of a miserable outcome?'

'Because it *reminds* you you're human.' Anneliese lectured.

'You seem to think that I'm *not.'*

Isabel was certain there was no use asking for some help: Anneliese was Papa's girl. Nothing she would ever say or do would be too intrusive in her loving father's eyes. Not one already bound to study any of phrenology, cosmology or pathophysiology and other words beyond her twin's pronunciation though the pair had long ago disposed of foreign accents.

Josef struggled to avoid the act of taking sides. The Older Twin in recent times no longer heeded to his manifold requests to 'take the needle off that racket' – one of Noël Coward, Cole Porter or Gershwin. She hated how he condemned her for saying 'goddamn' when she heard *everyone* saying 'goddamn'. To rile him she paraded round the house performing 'Night and Day' and 'All Through the

Night' in an affected American accent. At the slightest rebuke she would explode in a full-blown offensive:

'How can you be *against* these songs? The songs are not immoral!'

'Isabel, we have discussed this many times.'

'Their lyrics don't *mention* anything—'

'I don't want to hear this music in our home.'

'You don't want me wearing rouge or backless dresses; you don't want me staying up at night to play piano – you don't want *any* of me at home. But you don't want me going out a lot *as well*; where am I *supposed* to go?!'

'Isabel – you know very well this isn't true.'

It took a lot of convincing for Josef to reassure Isabel that he loved her. It was always inane. He would often end up embracing her only to tell her:

'I don't "disapprove" of anything in you. You are going to be the greatest pianist. The greatest and the most beautiful pianist in the world.' He held her arms in his protective clutches. 'You should be most confident.'

She would hug Papi back and hang her arms on him, not seeking to express that all of this just lumbered her with extra stress.

While she engineered elation Anneliese tinged her perceptions with new cynicism.

She would witness a young woman gaily greet the octogenarian who worked at the post office. The woman would request a few stamps. They would exchange trite comments on the weather in an almost mimicable fashion:

'It's rather nice today, isn't it?'

'Oh, yes.' the man would reply.

'The petunias grow so well this time of year. Of course you can't water them too much, or they die out too quickly.'

As though the man would not.

It was not a thought that Anneliese bore easily and yet she wondered just how tedious the woman's life was if she spoke about petunias. She disliked the conceit that everyone 'cared so much for their neighbour': they didn't. Too engrossed were they in cleaning their beloved Rolls until it sparkled. This globe that she inhabited at times seemed wooden. Many daily phrases and accompanying gestures were bereft of worth.

It was during these dry, dreary moments that she started to investigate her earthly purpose. Most of the time she was empty. Sentiments she kept for others were both wan and few. She disapproved of her external being: of the hypocritical façade politely gabbing with her church's congregation, obstinately feeling nothing.

The sharpest wedge in her conscience was guilt for her lack of ambition. Anneliese reviled herself for never wanting more; for not desiring marriage and for lacking in maternal instincts. In her prayers she implored God to lend her volition. One evening as her father was being stimulated by an article about neuropathology she knocked on his door and, upon seeing him raise a smile, tentatively entered and sat.

'What do you want me to do when I grow up?' she asked him quite sullenly.

She saw his moustache curl as he replaced his paper.

'That's up to you, Anneliese. Is there anything particular you want to do?'

'No. You always speak of wanting me to find a husband . . . but I don't *feel* as though I want to marry. I don't know why. Isabel enjoys flaunting herself . . . and it doesn't occur to me. It's all so strange. People are people; I can't imagine boys we see as being potential spouses. I don't want to have children. I don't picture myself at a stove.'

Josef gently patted her shoulder.

'You're very young, Anneliese.'

'Well, I know.' she conceded reluctantly. 'But I don't understand . . . I should be in love with someone by now, shouldn't I? And attending great balls and looking around for a husband.'

'But you're not.'

'I'm not.' she repeated dryly. 'But there's a summit – there's . . .' She brushed the fingernails of her left hand for no reason. 'I have this image of who people *should* be; of who a *woman* should be . . . And you know, I've been reading about Marie Curie; I wish I could have met her. Sometimes I think I *should* have met her. It's been less than a year since she died . . . If I could be half of that, then I could live. But I'm not interested in radiation and . . . Papa . . .'

'But you spend a lot of time feeding your mind. You're kind to those around you. I don't see anything wrong with you, *Liebling.*'

'What if I never get married?'

He sighed and, slightly agitated, took a handkerchief and wiped the sweat along his brow.

'Then you never shall, I suppose.' He cleared his throat. 'But you'll make something of yourself; this is a *truth*. I know you will.'

Anneliese was disheartened. Realising she was meant to rejoice at these words, she found his avowal to be somewhat expectant: a subtle request.

'What if I don't?' her muffled voice enquired.

'What do you mean?'

'What if all I do, in my short time on Earth . . .' She sighed, 'is sit at home and read all day? Would that be such a bad thing?'

Again he smiled, although she noticed he appeared perturbed.

'Not necessarily. It sounds all right to me.' he reassured her, stroking up and down her arm.

Anneliese thanked and hugged him. Immediately she scurried up the stairs to open her new book. It was Johannes Peter Müller's *Handbuch der Physiologie des Menschen*, which she was determined to read in the original German despite not being able to speak it.

When two months later Anneliese announced to her father she was considering pursuing neurology, he was unprecedentedly rapturous. For a short while afterwards she found this soothing.

With her daily worries now dispelled, Anneliese was less than pleased to find a band of fresh anxieties awaiting her.

Slightly unprepared for each of Isabel's new beaux, she struggled to remember all their names, confusing previous with current.

'This is Eric.' Isabel announced one day when Anneliese had wandered in to catch her sister singing to the boy.

'Good evening.' Anneliese greeted him.

The introduction was unnecessary. Anneliese never heard of or saw Eric again.

She was tidying Isabel's room the next day. The latter was expected to clean it herself. Otherwise engaged, she was too busy combing party crowds to find a husband.

Removing the mattress on her bed to clear the dust under its frame, Anneliese stumbled upon a white sack. Curiosity compelled her to untie the knot and open it.

Inside was a bountiful array of books. At first she found herself delighted and surprised: how novel it was that her sister liked a *novel*.

Immediately she understood her joy had been unfounded.

Isabel's collection consisted of books concerning only one subject. There was Ovid's *Art of Love*, Apuleius's *The Golden Ass* (each in its English translation), *The Life and Adventures of Miss Fanny Hill*, *Lady Chatterley's Lover*, and worst of all a copy of the *Kama Sutra* – a title Anneliese misunderstood until she started leafing through it. She was dismayed and most of all perplexed. Could a rapscallion's physiological sensations be the rudder of her sister's conduct?

Escorted back from yet another social function by her father, Isabel found her didactic twin already stationed at her threshold. Anneliese was primed to execute a lynching.

'Nobody *asked* you to rummage around here!'

'That I grant as true.' she conceded. 'But . . . just – try to explain it to me.'

'*What?*'

'Why on *earth* would you need all this . . . *filth?*'

Isabel was visibly embarrassed and, in a dramatic gesture, raised her hands high in the air.

'It's trivial, harmless nonsense.'

'Some of them are manuals.'

'So?'

'Do you think they'll come in *handy?*' Anneliese asked her sardonically.

'I wouldn't know. I'm still too young to put something to *use.*'

Anneliese averted her gaze in disgust.

'A girl of our age shouldn't be thinking—'

'How *can* you be so dictatorial? You can't tell me what to *think* about. You can tell me if you disapprove of this boy or of *that* – and that's the limitation of your judgment.'

'I don't *understand* it.'

'It's the culmination of all our existence.' Isabel insisted.

Anneliese's eyes grew cavernous.

'You think that fornication is the "culmination of all our existence"?'

'Don't all those physiology books teach you that?'

'They teach me it's responsible for reproduction.'

'Yes.' Isabel agreed on this single point. 'It's also an act of love.'

'It's a physiological process.'

Grabbing her arm, Isabel stridently told her:

'*Liesa* – you don't want to be one of those women whose husband comes home at an unthinkable hour.'

'"Unthinkable hour"?'

'Because he's being denied his basic right.'

Anneliese snubbed this comment. Scoffing, she returned to her room.

Flopping herself atop her bed, she felt a poke persuade her soul to quiver like a harp string.

She had been sat on the landing at three o'clock in the morning, aged nine, with her legs dangling out of the banister.

Then her mind switched to another subject: her forgetful mother. She had barely left her room in recent times and Anneliese and Isabel never awaited her at breakfast, lunch or dinner.

Slowly the thoughts converged. After their fusion they fell down into a lump and thankfully stagnated.

It was almost midnight. Anneliese brushed her teeth and put on her pyjamas.

In bed she raised her pillow and sat up.

Eventually her tension lapsed in a short, breathy laugh.

'No . . .' she whispered to herself. 'Not possible.'

Switching off the light, she fell asleep a minute later.

14.

Gossamer wings

The air was labouring away at a humidity so heavy that it unlocked panting. It was 5th July 1935: the final day of the school year.

Red and flustered, Isabel trudged down the stairs. A grating tree saw slicing back and forth outside was chafing at her head.

'Are all the windows open, Papi?'

'Yes, I've opened all the windows.'

She sat down with her legs deliberately an inch apart.

'Can you believe they make us wear our blazers even *now*?'

'I'll speak to Miss Butterworth about this; it is rather unhealthy.'

Anneliese saw Josef bow his head and squint for a long time and immediately put down her spoon.

'Did you see Dr Walter, Papa?'

'Why does Papi need to go and see Dr Walter?'

'His angina.'

Isabel was bitter and accusatory.

'Nobody told *me*.'

'It is not serious.' Josef countered. 'I'll see him at the end of the week.'

Isabel stood up and traipsed to the refrigerator. Anneliese pre-empted her:

'There's no more orange juice.'

'How could there be "no more"?! Papa – you said you'd buy two cartons!' Isabel effused a series of vexed puffs. 'We ran out of Robinsons yester—'

'Aren't you going to sit *down?*' Anneliese enquired.

'It's too hot to sit down.' She dabbed at the bridge of her sweaty nose with her forefinger. I'm waiting for *you.*'

Anneliese insisted on eating at a moderate pace. Isabel's lips were contorted in a venomous grimace.

Four minutes passed.

'Have a good day, Papa.' Anneliese hugged and kissed him. Isabel stood by.

He shouted, 'Bye, bye, *Kleine!*' but she was already lingering too far to hear him.

The gossip in the classroom was being turned out at a faster pace than usual. Anneliese revised for their impending test. Isabel discovered Katy White was moving to America.

Olivia explained the reason in a most exaggerated whisper:

'Her mother's taking her to live with their aunt; she found out her husband was carrying on with the next-door neighbour but one.'

'My God!' Isabel almost squealed.

'He kept on coming home at midnight and she couldn't tell. I mean her *mum*. How could – what did he have to do to raise suspicion – see a *priest* three times a day?!'

Anneliese was sure this monstrous talk would drive her mad.

At home Josef was arranging items on his bureau. Opalescent with snow-coloured splotches and pale shades of periwinkle blue, the coat on the horizon had the coruscating glimmer of a milky whirlpool.

With the girls so weighed down by the onus of their homework, Josef thought they merited a summer void of chores and duly went upstairs to tidy both their rooms.

Throughout the years it had remained beyond his means to fund a trip for them.

He slipped all of Isabel's cosmetics back into her case and ordered Anneliese's tomes along her shelves. Straightening the photographs across her desk, he fluffed her pillows before changing Isabel's loose, rumpled sheets. The spores of a nostalgic fog sketched hazy nets across his mind.

Soon both his nurtured foals would start their halter-breaking; other men would be responsible for keeping them in check. Premature jealousy was a poisonous trough. And yet too many years had passed since Josef had persuaded Isabel to wear a bonnet in the scalding summer. Too weary and decrepit was he nowadays to understand his younger daughter's science homework after seven thirty in the evening; Anneliese would end up helping *him*.

He wasn't used to this disservice they rendered him: the one that meant needing him *less*.

It was almost eleven o'clock when he finished. School would be finishing just ninety minutes later; Croham Hurst's final days of term were never full days. Flakes of sunlight were disseminated through the window pane as he stood watching in the living room. Their older than Victorian house did not provide protection from the penetrating heat.

Josef sat down and sighed profusely, removing the handkerchief tucked in his sleeve to dab at his brow. It was seven minutes past eleven.

Jammed between the hurling shouts of Anneliese and Isabel, Daphne longed to cover both her ears back at Croham Hurst. They were entering afternoon assembly as the former defended the cause of Miss Clarendon:

'She never asked for it and so I didn't give it to her.'

'You never *did* it!' Anneliese came close to screaming.

Olivia Paisley budged in.

'She *did* it. She did the exercises yesterday at lunchtime; I saw her.'

'I *didn't* do it. Clearly Miss Clarendon knows me so well – I wasn't *expected* to. She knows how much to—'

'Miss Clarendon's *afraid* of you. She didn't ask you for your homework 'cause she fears you might transform into a *viper.*'

'Girls – *no talking.*' Miss Rowley admonished.

Isabel turned her head in the other direction and walked quickly ahead of her sister. Her lips were pouting but she didn't know it. She would have to wait a whole half-hour before passing on her grievance to her father.

When the twins exited the gate it was thirty-five minutes past twelve. Josef wasn't there. On last days he would usually arrive well in advance equipped with chocolate. They were going to see *Aïda* in the evening. Anneliese was eager to unload her oratory; demand that Papa teach her sister that respect towards their staff was *mandatory.* It was going to be the longest reportage that she had ever given: articulate and eloquent but to the *point.* It was going to be a *Ciceronian* speech without all the unnecessary repetition.

Fifty minutes later the twins were still there, sweltering under the sun on the small fence in front of the flowerbed. Miss Butterworth passed out of the gate.

'Are you all right?'

Isabel shook her head.

'Yes.' Anneliese answered miserably.

'Do you want to come in, call home perhaps?'

'No, no.' Anneliese insisted. 'He won't be there, anyway. It's probably just the traffic.'

Miss Butterworth didn't know where to dart her eyes.

'Well – if he doesn't come within the next hour, do go *inside.* I don't want you sitting here all by yourselves.'

'We will, Miss Butterworth.'

'And have a good holiday.' She eyed Anneliese forcefully: 'Don't do *too* much work.'

'I won't.'

Isabel felt a sour taste at the back of her mouth.

Half an hour later rodents scurried in her stomach: it became a haunt for rats exchanging flicks of dust with their extending tails. Exporting Anneliese's knowledge of the present, they were slowly mixing with the murky memory of six years previously when she had sat before the balustrade awaiting the return of her elusive father.

From his mistress?

The words were scribed in her – and yet it was in such poor *taste*. It was tawdry to imagine *that* kind of affair. Her father never had a mistress; he would *never* have one. If he of all people fell short of Josef's scruples – who did *not?*

Another half-hour went by. Fearing Josef would worry upon his arrival, neither twin was anxious to go back to school. The taunting thought began to jab its quill at Anneliese again. He couldn't *surely* have forgotten that it was a half-day? That was not the point. The point was that her father didn't have a mistress. His current tardiness was doubtlessly irrelevant.

It was at half past two that shock effaced the girls' distress and elevated yet another.

A Santa-like, burly seventy-year-old man with a white beard was trotting with coarse huffs of breathlessness towards the entrance. Tensing till she tremulated, Anneliese immediately recognised him.

She jumped up.

'Dr *Newhart?!*' It was one of Josef's colleagues from the college.

Nodding almost manically, helter-skelter patterns of sweat at his temples, he hurriedly answered:

'Yes, yes – that's right. Have all your teachers gone?'

Without thinking, Isabel grabbed Anneliese's hand. The latter understood this was a cue for her to speak.

'I ...' Anneliese's gaze began to rock; threatening in a pendulum's fashion to melt in a blur. Speech came out breathily. 'I think so.'

'*Ah.*' More out of breath, the bulky man shifted his head left and right before duly commencing: 'I'm afraid—'

'What *happened?*' Anneliese's nails were digging into Isabel's cold palm.

'I – I went to your house today to deliver a revised copy of a paper your father had been – your father was *working* on.' Dramatically he cleared his throat. 'Unfortunately, I . . .' Dr Newhart rubbed his sweaty hands down his jacket. 'Upon peering into the window I caught sight of . . .' He shook his head. 'He was flat – flat down, lying in the – in the living room. I had to call the ambulance . . .' His voice was strained. 'Your father had a heart attack.' He squeezed his eyes shut. 'I'm so sorry – I am really very sorry – he has – he has passed.'

Isabel was staring down. Her breath was cleft in two. Her nails dug into Anneliese's palm.

Anneliese persevered.

'There are bad paramedics.' the phrase emerged atonally.

Shaking his head to the left and the right, Dr Newhart elaborated:

'I'm – I'm afraid *not*. No – no pulse. He's – I'm so very sorry.' The doctor rubbed his hands against his pocket. 'He's died. The coroners will come at around – around *six*. Is there anyone who can escort you home?'

Anneliese could barely understand if it was right to move. Numb to the clammy hand of Isabel's that clenched her own, she didn't hear the latter's teeth were chattering. At the left of her Anneliese saw a pupil some twelve years of age. Clad in an oversized blue blazer and a flattened straw hat, she dropped one of her files on the ground and bent down to retrieve it. After that she scurried past the girls without observing them.

'No, I . . .' Anneliese began.

'You see – you see, I'm afraid I've – our grandson is coming to stay with us; my daughter will be dropping him off any minute now and my wife's gone to Tesco's with our—'

'We'll get home.' Anneliese flatly confirmed.

'Are you *sure?* If there's someone at the school then I could call a taxi for you—'

'No.' Anneliese shook her head. 'Go.' was her cold imperative.

Meekly but hastily Dr Newhart obeyed, trundling back at a painstaking pace along Melville Avenue.

The sun was blazing in their faces; simultaneously the younger daughter's limbs and neck were stiff with cold. Inside she was a tall crane paralysed amidst an operation. Owing to the freeze that rendered the machine defunct it was now forced to hold the heavy weight it longed to drop.

Her free hand was impaled by the brick fence. She closed her eyes for a few seconds. When they were open nothing was dissimilar.

For a short interval she let her consciousness fluctuate. She imagined being nine and challenging this statement; she imagined the desirable prosperity of half-perception. Six years ago she could have lifted the latch from her shock. Could have uttered some naïve rejoinder: 'That isn't funny,' or 'I don't believe you'. For maybe some twelve minutes the conviction would have held its sway.

Now she targeted her feet because she had to shift her focus to that site. Pushing the pressure onto them, she stood. Isabel was still sat. The air conveyed Anneliese's branded free hand to her sister's sloped shoulder. Still Isabel refused to stir. Her eyes were irretractably fixed to the ground.

'Isabel.' she murmured.

After a few moments the quaking girl finally stood.

As they waddled Anneliese's feet began to sense the clash of fibre against fibre: the way her skin cells rubbed against the leather and the bottom of her shoes scraping the surface of the asphalt.

The bus – which was due in three minutes and usually late – arrived right on time. Noise of the engine clattered against

Anneliese's ears; its stench assailed her nostrils. As she boarded she watched Isabel totter with every new step.

The lobes in Anneliese's brain responsible for understanding the familiar driver's jargon were all out of service.

Buckets of sun were being poured every half-second through Isabel's window; slitting their loads between trees. She steadied one hand with the other but it obstinately shook.

The passengers fanned themselves with rolled-up newspapers. Two middle-aged women attired in floral pink and white dresses were blithely engaged in their babble:

'My son couldn't play his trombone today.'

'The heat, *was* it?'

'They said it was going to be just twenty-one degrees. Ha! What twenty-one degrees? It's *Africa* in 'ere!'

'The day that Mr Davies' forecast is correct will be the day my Lewis cooks 'is *grub*.'

Once such a dialogue had squirmed its way into her head the frozen Anneliese suspended her alertness.

Isabel was silent. Pale-faced she stared out of the window. She hoped that she might miss their stop so that the bus would take her further, drop her off somewhere and leave her stranded.

Anneliese awaited the deluge that shunned her. She had read of parasites nesting in bone marrow. Perhaps it was the extra weight they gave her that deceived her into thinking she was carrying a chest of iron. The oppression had closed off her tear ducts.

When they disembarked to catch the train a question sounded in her head. She wondered if the coroners had come to take away his body. Hopefully they hadn't. Still she didn't trust the paramedics' diagnosis. Prognosis. Hallucinosis.

Isabel bumped into an advertising stand at the station. Anneliese automatically circled her waist with her arm, shifting her closer to her.

The train was delayed. When Anneliese finally heard the

hooting wheels thirty-six minutes had passed. Isabel sat by the window again, this time resting her head on the glass. It ambled at a sluggish, carefree pace. The driver must have been the victim of a slackened *joie de vivre*.

Twenty minutes later Anneliese felt the frame of her neighbouring creature relax. Still leaning her head against the window, Isabel cautiously whispered:

'He's isn't dead.'

The latter raised her hand to stroke her shoulder. In a dimmed voice Isabel commanded:

'He's not dead.' She let out a very faint and wheezy swirl of giggling. 'Newhart's an idiot. The heat – probably fainted from the heat; he isn't *dead*.'

As Anneliese opened the gate of their house its creak smacked relief into her. The noise always relayed to her a sense of comfort: coming back home after trips to the library, from one of Isabel's parties, for the school holidays' well-earned period of rest. Her instinct used a fleeting interval to tell her consciousness that she would soon be playing chess with Papa. For a period of seven seconds it clung arduously to this port of safety, applying ointment to annihilate the gnawing parasites.

Then it rebounded to its place of origin and there retook its seat.

It was stuffy as they entered the house. The smell of dust on the old wooden staircase diffused a particular musk. After disposing of her bag on a chair, Anneliese looked at the clock on the wall in the corridor. It was already thirteen minutes to five.

In an hour's time the body would be scooped away.

Her sister stood leaning against the wall near the door, eyes fixed on the carpet inanely.

Anneliese tugged at Isabel's arm but felt only her sleeve. She was hoping that her desperate look sufficed.

Gently removing her arm from Anneliese's grip, Isabel unlatched herself.

She murmured in a solemn voice that tried hard to be reverent:

'I think I'll go upstairs . . . take a nap.'

Anneliese pulled at her arm again:

'They're coming in an hour.'

Isabel's glance was askew.

'I'm tired, Anneliese.'

Placing one foot on the first step of the stairs, she then had to bring her second to the first. To check that Isabel retained her self-control, Anneliese watched her ascend until she got halfway.

Seconds later she traversed the corridor. For two minutes she lingered outside the closed door of the living room, gripping the handle. She started to expel large breaths and gradually embellished them with an aborted weeping. Squinting eyes sought to push forth the tears. There *were* none.

Despite the confines of her knowledge she knew nothing disappeared. Human beings could convey themselves from one place or one person to another but the object on which one bestowed emotions or associations was a presence totally immobile. One could throw darts anywhere across the board: the board itself could not migrate. Josef could not be dead because he was her *target*; she had selected him, therefore he was her undertaking.

If there were mystical and unexplained events that could have culled someone like Daphne or Miss Butterworth from her she could digest this knowledge over time in tiny portions with her father as her balm. No form of scalpel on the other hand – not even the most finely honed – could surgically remove her father.

If she opened that door she would enter and find him asleep, or unconscious but still with a heartbeat. She and her father shared a heartbeat. Their pulsations were more often in accordant rhythm than the disharmonic syncopation between her and Isabel. If he had truly died some part of her would have expired: there would have been no function in her legs, her arms would have been numb; a form of paraplegia would have struck her.

Looking down to scrutinise herself she found no change except a pair of shaking hands. Considering the physiological effects on her were minimal, there was no possibility that Josef was extinct. Far too alive was she for such a concept to be concrete.

At three minutes to five she turned the doorknob.

He was keeled over on the ground, arms resting by his side. The fingertips of his left hand were covered by a chair his fall had shifted; it had skidded and replaced its angle. That had happened by the time that Josef had collapsed, powerless.

Half the buttons on his shirt were undone. Anneliese remembered reading in her textbooks that the chest becomes so tight in cardiac arrest, one's instinct is to liberate it. She recalled discovering the organ's pathway to malfunction: how a blocked coronary artery obstructed the trajectory the blood made to and from the heart. It was an equivalent to loss of oxygen. The heart therefore became defunct; a damaged tool. Responsible no longer for the operations in the body, all its ties were cut. The function of all organs stopped. Anneliese had learnt this equalled death. Mentally she felt she comprehended it.

His static eyes were facing upwards and his mouth half-open. His forehead was agleam. A shiny layer of moisture had erupted over it. His complexion was white; close to gossamer. At this point it was only really being used to cover up the veins and blood beneath it; no longer serving any function social or aesthetic. It was just a roof intended for preserving matter lying underneath. It may as well have been a white net used to cover food: a shield to ward off flies' ingestion.

Anneliese crouched down and touched his arm. It occurred to her that this wasn't her father. Her father was a tall, imposing man who spouted learned arguments with vigour. He could easily stretch down to take his smaller daughter in his arms.

The doorbell rang. She studied the clock in the living room. It was now six.

In a sudden rush she stretched forth and fastened the buttons. He would have hated to have strangers see him in this state.

The gentlemen's voices could be heard from the corridor. They were expressing condolences placably to Elise; condolences quickly disrupted by an alien imploration:

'*Schnell, schnell; ich will keinen Gestank.*'

Entering the room, the men chanced upon Anneliese standing in stupor. Cautiously they all removed their hats. It seemed they hadn't reasoned there was someone else for whom their reverence was expected; the task of taking off their boaters once again was bothersome to them. Each of them took one of Josef's arms and promised:

'We'll be out of your way in just a moment, miss.'

Anneliese watched them place Josef on the stretcher.

She called in a voice that died down with confoundment:

'Be . . . careful.'

Concealed by a slim sheet of navy blue, the body was extracted from the house. It might have been a toxic-mould-affected armoire undergoing an emergency removal.

She heard the clatter of some cutlery. Elise had sat down with raw meat since nobody would cook her dinner. She had turned on the radio – the sole apparatus she knew how to use. Anneliese heard remarks about twenty-six degrees centigrade and an imminent heatwave.

Hauling herself up the stairs to the room of her sister, she caught Isabel fast asleep. Anneliese murmured her name. No response. She lay on her left side facing her bedside table. On it a clock was ticking forcefully.

But nothing would rouse Isabel. Not at this moment.

15.

The grainy pit

It was five o'clock and Isabel had been deprived of sleep for over twenty hours. She went downstairs in order to retrieve a rolling pin. Retreating to her bedroom with the heavy cylinder, she strove in vain to make herself unconscious with a knock against her forehead. The attempt was unsuccessful.

Pulses in her skull bounced up and down for a few moments. In one fell swoop they mustered at the centre of her head to form a boisterous throb.

After this travail she found herself a little dizzy and a thin bolt of euphoria zapped through her. Isabel was sure it was the extrication of the self from its untiring contact with the soul.

Yet the collisions in her head subsided; her adrenalin slithered away with the stealth of a rattlesnake. All that remained was this unending rendezvous with a tenacious, vaporising cold. Jittery beneath two woollen blankets, she was sure her frame embodied the reverberating engine of an air conditioner.

Sticking her hand out of her window, she watched it shiver in the confines of the musty heat's enrobing glove.

There was a bottle of Sauvignon Josef kept in his cabinet. Much to her chagrin he had never allowed her to closely approach it – not even to stroke its slim neck with the back of her finger.

So she made another voyage to the kitchen. She remembered reading somewhere in her volumes of erotic poetry that wine was a hypnotic; that it cooled the nerves and stilled dynamic rushes on the inside.

Her steadiness began to slacken across each step on the kitchen tiles. It took her an eternity to reach the drawer where Josef kept his corkscrew.

As she pierced the wooden stub the cork cracked open. Several elongated breaths ensued. After yanking the wood right and left she saw a garnet imprint on her hand: the instrument's red Circle of Hell.

Shaking her hand, she started again. After six minutes it was out.

Emptied of the necessary energy to find a glass, Isabel brutishly swallowed the red bottle's generous gulps. Her tongue could only taste a sour kind of oil. She stumbled over to the tap, turned it to unleash a timid pressure and cupped her hands to take water. Swallowing the contents of her palms, she tossed the bottle back into her mouth.

The dilution barely made a difference to the taste.

Seventeen minutes later she had packed away the half-empty bottle, recorked its top and shoved it back into the cabinet.

There was no luck. Half an hour after that in bed she looked down to observe her fingers still atremble. Rigorously she attempted to transfer her focus. Why did fingers only shake when curved? Why did they not shiver when erect? If Pisa's Leaning Tower could be slanted without shaking, could her fingers also tilt?

After an hour of mental deliberation she fell asleep.

By the time Anneliese awoke the next morning it was two o'clock in the afternoon.

The sun was at its wholesome frolics once again. For a second it appeared nothing had changed.

Then the parasites resumed activity.

On her way to the bathroom she crossed Isabel – already fully dressed in a summery floral white dress.

'I'm meeting with Olivia in Hyde Park.' she announced.

'Erm . . .' Anneliese could scarcely amplify the volume of her voice. 'Did you tell—'

'I called her this morning. I should be back by six.'

'All . . . right.'

'And Aunt Liesel rang. She told me to remind you to call when you awoke. Well – don't get too gloomy.'

Isabel stroked her arm. Gracefully she headed down the stairs.

Anneliese found herself alone in the kitchen with no need to prepare breakfast.

She sat down and spent time being sedentary. When she next looked at the clock it was four. Then it struck five. She didn't even notice how her legs got tired from being stuck in the same place. At six Isabel was nowhere to be seen.

Anneliese took hold of the black and white salt and pepper mills. Holding the white one, she stared at it. Josef had brought them from Zurich. She awaited a telephone call in which he would apologise for not coming home that night; he had been unable to avoid a trip to Bristol University for some neurologists' conference; the journey had compelled him to stay overnight. She aspired to receive a call from a woman, to hear the news that yes – her father did apparently possess a mistress – a French, dark, petite woman – he had abandoned them for *her*. She would have enjoyed being on the tail end of this call; Woman was a force that she could reckon with. Mortality was not.

The contest and strife between these fictitious events was too much for her mind to support. She fell asleep with her head on the table. Startled by a clinking sound, she raised her head to find that it was very, very dark. The successive noise was wood being clattered.

Anneliese wrenched her torso. There was light in the corridor.
Isabel trotted into the kitchen.

'How did you spend the day, Liesa?'

The latter gazed at her, dumbfounded.

'I didn't . . . I didn't do anything.'

'I met Olivia's second cousin twice removed. A *very* charming
boy. His name is Ewan Thomson.'

Anneliese should have alluded to the stench of wine arising
from the spot where Isabel was standing. The parasites precluded
such an action.

'Well – I'm off to bed now.' Isabel daintily proclaimed.

Her tread was too light to be comprehensible. When Anneliese
made her way into the corridor, she saw it was 11.27 pm.

She had forever been reading of antibodies. They were proteins
spawned by plasma cells; the infantry of militants whose role it was
to fight malign bacteria and infection.

Now her organs had been flipped. Given their base position in
her body they had likely drowned. Unlike human beings who could
sense endangerment and flutter arms and legs in the inane hope
that quick movement earned survival, these components of her
entrails were resigned. Deprived of oxygen they choked on
parasites instead of water, similarly sinking to a grainy pit.

It was no longer in the bounds of her capacity to rescue them.
They sustained acute awareness only of their lifelessness. Yet it was
this awareness that refused to go to sleep.

16.

Crushed beetles

'You barely know any hymns.' Anneliese murmured.

Seven days had passed; the funeral had already been arranged. She had convened with the vicar of St Bartholomew's; she had offered 'Abide with Me' and 'The Day Thou Gavest'. Isabel was rabid about not being consulted.

'I know them *all*, Anneliese.' Her cheeks were red and puffy and she was exhaling very rapidly. 'I don't care – don't tell me what you chose; I'm late.'

It hadn't taken Isabel too long to snap up someone of the male persuasion. She was, after all, a people-trader.

It was a picnic prior to the Proms she was attending this time. Ewan had obtained the most expensive tickets for them to the opening night; his parents were friends with the son of some otolaryngologist, one of the festival's benefactors. By five o'clock that evening she was munching her third toffee apple.

'Tell your mother they're *delicious*.' she instructed Ewan giddily. He watched her with puzzlement: an unidentifiable species.

'Are you . . . how are you feeling today, Isabel?'

It took her a few moments to annihilate the segment in her mouth before she began speaking.

'I'm perfectly fine.'

'Is that so?' He scratched his chin.

'Absolutely.' She blinked very tightly and effused a bright smile.

'If you ever need me to come over, help with the arrangements—'

'We've finished the arrangements.'

He nodded.

'How many people are attending?'

Isabel shrugged.

'Anneliese was in charge of the invitations. Not more than forty, I'd imagine. A few colleagues and former colleagues and some students of his.'

'If there's anything I can do—'

'Actually, I was wondering whether you'd like to accompany me to the Coliseum.'

He rubbed the left side of his chin.

'Well – it's a noisy place.'

'I'll be fine as long as the music isn't atonal.'

'I suppose . . .'

'You did say that your father knew someone . . .' She grew a little bashful. 'I don't mean to be presumptuous, if it's difficult—'

'No, no, it's not difficult. I just assumed you would want to have some time to yourself before . . . you know.'

She shook her head adamantly.

'Not entirely, no.'

He purposely lowered his volume.

'You ought to know that I'm respectful of your time and privacy. If you want to be alone, I wouldn't take that as an insult. On the contrary, when I lost my grandfather—'

'How old were you?'

'Erm – well, I was nine.'

She lowered her eyes.

'That's sad. Did you mention there being a kiosk near the hall?'

'Yes – I think so. I think there's one on Exhibition Road.'

'I'd like to buy a packet of Smith's.' She got up off the grass, dusting the clinging blades from her knees and smoothing the folds of her skirt. She then extended a hand which he took. 'Lead the way.'

It was difficult to say no to her.

On the morning of the funeral Isabel was spending superfluous time getting dressed. When Anneliese entered her room she saw her attempting to sew up her black jacket's flapping torn pocket.

'Isabel . . .'

'Just – one *moment*.'

The only thread available was blue. Anneliese could see this from three feet away.

'It's going to look very unneat.'

'Don't be *naïve*, no one will notice it.'

'Why do you need to sew it?'

'"Cause it's unreliable.'

'What do you have in it?'

'Just some pennies.'

'I can tuck them in my pocket.'

'No – I'll keep them.'

It came as no surprise that Elise wasn't going to the funeral. She didn't even take a peek out of the window when the hearse arrived.

The ride to St Bartholomew's in Sydenham was silent. Isabel had taken the sewing kit with her. She continued threading in and out and in and out, chinking and rustling till they had to disembark.

The pallbearers were Professor Swenson, Dr Reyfield, Liesel's husband Reuven Hotzenplotz and Dr Newhart.

Aunt Liesel had brought a huge wreath. She patted Anneliese on the back. The latter immediately hugged her.

'I'm really so sorry that Elise did not come.' Liesel began.

'Well . . .' Anneliese tucked her hair behind her ear. 'It was expected.'

'No . . . no, no, no. Not at *all*. She was feeling fine until this morning – *then* thirty-nine point six; fever and nausea and *ai, ai, ai...*'

Anneliese's eyes were loosened from their fixedness.

'Oh . . . she isn't *ill*, Aunt Liesel.'

A fresh idea jerked Liesel's mind.

'Ah . . .' Liesel nodded many times. 'Isabel did not *inform* you.'

'About what?'

'I called this morning to apologise. Elise – *our* Elise – is suffering from a temperature and cough and sneezing. We left her with a friend from temple. She is awfully, awfully sorry she was unable to come.'

'Oh.' Anneliese was struck with greater puzzlement than usual. She had no phrase at her disposal except, 'Never mind.'

Isabel was sitting in the second pew already. The vicar was to stand and read a speech in seven minutes' time.

Anneliese took her seat beside her.

'You didn't tell me about Elise.'

She seemed heavily preoccupied.

'*Hmm?*'

'Elise.'

'Probably snoring away.' Isabel grunted in a voice in its lowest extremity.

'She isn't *here*, Isabel!' Anneliese sneered in a whisper.

'What? Oh – oh, you mean *that* Elise. I thought you were talking about . . .' A swift exhalation escaped her mouth. 'No, I forgot.' She crossed her legs. 'Sorry.'

Professor Swenson was the first one to recite a eulogy. Anneliese had structured the occasion as an intimate and simultaneously commemorative affair meant to discourage soppiness. She detested funerals and regarded them as artifice. In the middle of the planned proceedings she was struggling still to understand the premise of this bleak, unnecessary ritual.

The Professor – making sure his monocle was carefully adjusted in his eye – was holding a manilla piece of paper.

'Josef van der Holt . . .' he belted like a minister addressing Parliament, 'was one of the finest proponents of neurology in modern times.'

He turned the page over. It seemed almost impossible for him to have recited a whole page; apparently this was the case.

'Astute, succinct, unfailingly destructive—' His eyebrows furrowed and he looked down at his script contemptuously. 'My sincere apologies – that *should* have been *"instructive"*, not *"destructive".'* He cleared his throat. 'He was a pioneer of treatment for aphagia—'

Abruptly two sounds chinked at her left side. They were followed by successive episodes of robust bouncing taking little leaps before it timorously started to subside. Then a third noise – this time of tumbling glass – enlisted in the fight to thwart the silence. She looked at Isabel and saw her bending over.

Professor Swenson's speech had been disrupted well beyond repair.

'What are you *doing?*' Anneliese whispered in a hiss.

'My *marbles.*' Isabel whispered back. Crouching on the ground, she began to look under her seat.

'What?'

'My *marbles.* They fell out of my pocket.'

'Get them *later.*'

'That would be bad *luck!*'

Anneliese appreciated how they risked encountering 'bad luck'.

At the wake they deliberately distanced themselves from each other. It was being held at Mendeleev Hall in Westfield College, which had funded the reception.

Anneliese was standing in a huddle of professors and their former students. Two of them were Professor Swenson and Dr Reyfield; the other two young women Josef had once taught.

Tedium was in her favour, sparing her a confrontation with her adamant aggressor, grief.

A few feet away in a circle of students was some thirty-something small woman. The only female in the hall neither a relative nor a familiar member of the faculty, she looked like Goldilocks.

Anneliese excused herself, alleging there was someone that she had to thank.

Approaching her more closely, she observed that Goldilocks was round-eyed and beaming in spite of her overall sense of moroseness. In the throes of some conversation with Professor Fielding, she comported herself with a soft, humble radiance.

'I remember he was so sympathetic towards all of the female students. I know they used to say he was a misogynist, but didn't they just underestimate him! I could never look at rats, so he began to carry out all the experiments on my behalf!'

'Now, Sarah – you didn't tell us that six years ago!'

'I couldn't!'

Anneliese was on the verge of interrupting when a tapering and sedentary figure caught her eye. Perched on a tall stool, a glass of Chardonnay in hand, Isabel extended her crossed leg to curl it round. This kind of fête was her fine chance to shine. Opposite her on another stool was a curly-haired, skinny boy: taller even than she. As Anneliese approached the pair she could discern her sister's squeals:

'How interesting. I never knew Edward III was a great fan of archery.'

'Well, you see – it was only really a rumour, *and*—'

It was the young curly-haired man who first observed Anneliese, his expression growing sterner as he studied her perturbed and wearied face.

'Oh, Liesa,' Isabel began excitedly, 'This is Edgar. He's Dr Reyfield's son – remember Dr Reyfield? And he plays the organ. *Him* – not Dr Reyfield.'

Lacking enthusiasm, Anneliese mumbled, 'How do you do.' She then turned her attention to the list of charges incurred by her sister. 'Are you *drinking*, Isabel?'

'Yes.' she responded, as though her actions were both natural and completely irreproachable. Anneliese seized the glass.

'How *can* you be so immature?' Isabel retorted.

'Do you even know what happens to the liver when a lady starts *this* young?'

Edgar looked at them both in confusion. Staring at Isabel, he wondered something aloud.

'You told me you were nineteen.'

Another roll of the eyes came from Anneliese. 'Goldilocks' had slipped her mind.

A week later she skipped church on a Sunday. It was a choice made without precedent – yet necessary.

She told herself in 'Heaven' Josef would rejoice in love of God and thank Him.

Then she wondered, given his untimely passing, for which gifts he had to thank Him.

There could have been no 'Heaven' for her father if a greater force had prised him from his girls. Eternally he had despised the notion that a woman should look after herself: thought it inhuman; subversive. She wondered what kind of a luxurious stronghold Heaven could be, short of a copy of Stedman's Medical Dictionary or diagrams of the parietal lobe. There was no postal address to which she could send him the globe Josef used to examine the world.

Adhering to tradition, one Sunday afternoon in August she invited Dr Newhart to tea. Her plan was to investigate this uncelestial tie to her departed father: the 'Goldilocks' she had espied at the funeral. It was still rattling Anneliese's brain that Josef might have had some ... *companion*, although now the reverse state of mind ruled her thoughts. She was entirely convinced it was false and *desired* the opposite.

After the customary chit-chat she lunged forward with her inquisition.

'I've been meaning to ask . . . there was a young blonde-haired woman at the wake – I think her name was "Sarah" . . .'

'Ah – yes, yes. Sara Asztalos.'

'"Sara"?'

'Yes.'

'Is she a professor at Westfield?'

Dr Newhart wasted too much time inspecting the ceiling.

'I'm sorry?'

'Does she teach at Westfield?'

He uncrossed his arms.

'Er . . . No, no, no.'

'Well . . . is she a student there?'

'No. She *was* a student.'

'So my father taught her?'

'No. No, no, no . . . she *was* a teacher. Also.'

'She moved on?'

'Er – yes. Yes . . .' His voice lingered till its volume expired. 'I think that's it, yes.'

For a few moments he examined the young lady in silence and sympathy. With calm and gentleness he placed his cup and saucer on the table.

'If you don't mind, Anneliese, I would be grateful if you might permit me to . . . to offer a . . . suggestion . . . or the like.'

The girl shrugged lazily. She was already too fatigued to respond. He clasped his hands and rubbed them together.

'Well . . . sometimes in these situations, those who experience bereavement . . .' He paused and cleared his throat. 'One who . . . *loses* a close one – doesn't *necessarily* . . . have the fortune to treasure a *confidant*.'

She dreaded the proposal that would obviously ensue.

'Thank you, Dr Newhart. I'll bear that in mind.'

'No, I'm afraid you haven't quite let me finish.' he proceeded. 'You're a very mature, clever young girl, and you've endured a *most* unfortunate tragedy. If you were one of my patients, I would advise, for your *own* sake, that you see a psychiatrist.'

For the first time since her father's passing something jolted Anneliese. Facing a propagandist of some recent school of thought, she was prepared to battle with this man intending to exploit her mind and blindfold her as though she was a mouse in his experiment.

'I'm sorry, Dr Newhart,' she explained in a tone indicating offence, 'but I am – as you say, "a mature girl", and I don't believe there's any *reason* to believe that bereavement engenders . . .' She became haughty. 'Mental *impairment*. I also don't think it's ethical for a doctor to be diagnosing someone who *isn't* their patient. And I hasten to add that my father *certainly* wouldn't improve.'

'Well, that's where you're right.' Dr Newhart concurred – neglecting her other words. 'Your father held great contempt for the practices of psychiatry and psychoanalysis. I certainly don't think you suffer from, as you say, a "mental impairment"; though I prefer to use the term "neurotic disorder". In modern times . . .' (she could forecast where this monumental speech was steered), 'psychoanalytical psychotherapy is not always intended for those suffering from a psychiatric affliction. But it *helps*, nonetheless, to consult a psychoanalyst in times of distress.'

'I would call that self-indulgence.'

'Well . . .' He smiled, 'At times like these, a little "self-indulgence" wouldn't do much *harm*.'

'Really?' she spouted with deliberate apathy.

'Well, forgive me for being *forward*—'

'I think you transgressed "forwardness" a while ago.'

He was unaffected.

'You're a girl who's highly advanced in her thinking and I don't think you're letting yourself *grieve* enough. You've appointed yourself Master of the House. That isn't the responsibility of a young lady of your ... *disposition*. And while I'm no psychiatrist, I have studied both psychiatry and psychoanalysis a great deal, and I think if you continue in this fashion to repress the *id*, it couldn't possibly be healthy in the long run.'

'"*Healthy?!*"'

'Why make life so much harder for yourself when you could make it just a little ...' He used his thumb and index finger to propose a pea-sized quantity. '*Easier?*'

By no means was she impressed.

'Could you leave now, Dr Newhart?'

'Very well.' he agreed, not the slightest disputatious. Walking to the rack to fetch his coat, she escorted him out.

When she had already opened the door he reached into his pocket and pulled out a small piece of paper. It was obvious that he had written it long in advance; something that galled her much *more*.

'This is the telephone number and address of Dr Westwood.' he explained in a hurry. 'If you do ever feel under the weather, it would do you no harm to—'

'I *understand*, Dr Newhart.' She snatched the paper from his hand and glanced at him emotionless. 'Goodbye.'

The door was slammed. She crumpled up the paper in her hands and threw it on the chest of drawers along the corridor, making a mental note to dispose of it later on.

Anneliese fell asleep at one thirty and awoke only at six. Doubting that Isabel would be at home, she called her name in order to confirm the notion's surreality.

When there was no response she headed to the living room to take a heavy tome she had been struggling to read for the past three and a half weeks.

On the sofa Isabel was locked in the enlacing arms of some young man with wavy hair. Anneliese imagined it was Ewan – but who knew?

They were in the throes of kissing when she entered. Isabel peeled the boy off her and greeted Anneliese in a higher-pitched tone than was natural:

'Liesa – I haven't forgotten about the dishes—'

By that point Anneliese had walked out of the house. At least outside the air was cool and uninfested. A stroll would lead her even farther from her sister.

It grated loudly on her nerves that the sole member of her family she still presumed to love now treated her as though she were a distant cousin. The rare occasions in which Isabel would help with dinner preparations, or returned home before midnight, or refrained from mentioning her boyfriend were mere clemency on her part.

Anneliese retired herself to a state of non-feeling. Recently she had grown warm to it.

People were encroaching worms that crawled each day to novel destinations; writhing, wriggling, struggling to survive the trampling feet of passers-by. She ceased to look at them as presences or spirits, viewing them instead as just another aphid visibly asplatter at the bottom of a shoe – crushed beetles, flies or ants.

This leant her supplementary insight. Worms marauded to find moistened warmth and shelter; Anneliese desired a return to her cool hearth of yore.

She found herself attempting to revive the free years of her childhood. Instead of walking in the middle of the pavement Anneliese waddled into the road again, strolling two feet away from approaching fast cars.

A greater voice commanded her to seek a challenge to ensure survival; opposition to potential fear. Obstinately nothing was alit inside; no satisfaction, daring or alarm could quench her thirst for feeling. Her movements inexplicably laborious, she was at loss to combat the consuming numbness.

A few minutes passed by uneventfully. Screeching as it swerved left to avoid her, a white Ford Deluxe fled in a panic out of sight as a pedestrian leapt forth to drag her to the pavement.

'You oughta be more careful!' the working-class man yelled at her. 'Walkin' like tha', ye'll get yerself run *ovah!*'

So out of sorts and unalert was she that Anneliese could hardly muster any murmur of a 'thank you'. Nodding to the man, she took note of his oiled, greasy shirt and surmised he was just an uncultured mechanic.

Afterwards she kept her footsteps on the pavement, staring at them. Fatigue and lack of sensitivity to what was real caused her to sway a little. Continuing to walk down Glenluce Road, she looked up at the sky to remember the time and the season. When she got home a loud noise woke her from her haze.

'Ewan!' bellowed Isabel. 'That's the same recording! That's – no, you can't *trick* me! I'm not-—'

The noise of such a musical voice – varied in stress and motley in its intonations – jarred on her vacuity. She didn't want to hear its source again.

After half an hour of walking up and down the stairs with a ponderous tread Anneliese halted at the third-from-top step, leaning her head on the banister. Sitting with her head adangle through the gap of its two bars, she fell asleep for twenty minutes. When she awoke she found the house was grey. This time some jovial jazz was being played. Ewan's protruding boyish bass voice filtered through the walls.

A pang of shame coursed through her stomach; she was obviously its culprit. What an idiot she must have looked awander amidst *cars*. She despised herself for having appeared clueless before somebody of that man's etiquette and origins.

There was no one in the world with whom she *wanted* to maintain association. With a frivolous sister and perfunctory mother in need of her, this was a problem.

Her dormant cells were wanting of a stirring rod.

She fostered enough strength to step into the corridor. There she picked up the crumpled-up piece of paper.

Drowsy, she approached the hallway telephone and dialled its number.

After a long period of ringing a word hit her ear.

'*Hallo?*'

It was a croaky, aged female voice. Also a distinctly foreign accent – maybe German.

Anneliese studied the digits on the paper again. Her blotchy consciousness had interfered with her numerical perception.

'Erm . . . I think I telephoned by mistake.' she said sleepily.

'You searchest . . . Dr Westwood?'

'Yes.' Anneliese responded automatically.

'You want – to make a *Termin*?'

'*Termin*'. That was it.

'Yes. Is Dr Westwood . . .' Anneliese released a great and heavy sigh. 'A . . .' She opened her mouth several times to speak, breathed in, swallowed and finally uttered: '*Psychiatrist?*'

'*Ja, ja.* You want *Termin*?'

She tried to make excuses.

'If there's time . . .' Anneliese began to scratch her forehead viciously.

'Time, time.' the woman insisted. 'Wednesday, seven August?'

Anneliese shook her head, unaware that the woman on the phone would not hear her.

'Wednesday, seven August?' she repeated. 'Do you mean . . . the seventh of August?'

'*Ja, ja.*'

'All right.' Anneliese unleashed an ill-conceived yawn. 'What time shall I be there?'

'Evening good?'

'Good evening?'

'Nein. Um Sieben Uhr.'

Anneliese nodded. 'I suppose ... But ...' She had awoken a little. 'If you can tell Dr Westwood that ... that if I stay, when I start school again – you see, I'm young – I don't know if that's all right with you people – but I'm only fifteen, and when I start school it'll have to be earlier because I'll have to get home in time to go to bed and ...'

'I want say Dr Westwood.' the foreign woman confirmed.

'Did you understand?' asked Anneliese, surprised.

'Oh, *ja*, yes.'

'Could you give me the address, please?'

Anneliese began to rummage for a notepad and a pencil.

She would have to memorise it.

'9 Eversley Avenue, near school.'

'Thank you.'

'Thank you.' repeated the foreign woman. 'Bye-bye.'

'Goodbye.' Anneliese heard the foreign woman replace the receiver.

17.

Red peonies

It was an arduous mount. Five minutes into her trek from Wembley Hill underground station Anneliese had begun counting steps. She found herself desiring the comforting hold of a lamppost.

Grasping the pole, she heard her breath gush forth in hurrying cascades. As she resumed the steep ascent Anneliese lifted her eyes and remarked the surroundings. It was a residential area with zero residents in view. No shops or offices dared interject. Every clop she made with her flat shoes rang like the first soft stirrings of a stage play.

Along the journey Anneliese was forced to climb a long and winding alley, holding on to metal bars to help her reach the other side. Half in respite, half in sorrow she enquired from herself: *Why such a sacrifice for some* psychiatrist?

It was another seven minutes before she arrived.

9 Eversley Avenue was a large detached house in the Tudor style. There was a ground floor and a top floor and a little window in the attic. Both flanks of its wide front garden were bestrewn with towering arrays of scarlet peonies divided by shorn grass. In between them was a lane of granite mottled with a row of separate silver tiles. This path led to the royal blue painted wooden door, which hid a porch.

With the feeling that an octopus in her stomach was bespeckling its lining with splotches of ink she took short, wary steps to the door and eventually sounded the bell.

Through the window of the porch was another door of mahogany brown. The short old lady – probably the one with whom she had arranged the session – finally emerged.

Almost overly enthusiastic, she was hard-pressed to employ whatever English may have been at her disposal. When Anneliese declared, 'Good evening, I'm Anneliese van der Holt,' the old lady scarcely heard her.

'Come, come.' she hastened, swiftly turning away.

The old lady immediately took her coat.

Before her eyes had caught the frame of any image an intense musk smacked her nose. The dose of this aroma was so strong it swelled around her throat like a desired aftertaste. Too long had passed since Anneliese had been susceptible to fragrances.

Her nostrils led her to the source: red peonies. The flowers from outside were here, aloft in lavish and ceramic vases; looming high enough to almost reach her length. There was one on the mahogany table spouting from the left-hand side staircase; another taller gold one on a twin table stood next to the entrance. The floor was of an amber wood obscured by a plush velvet ruby rug. It was elaborated with a host of gold and silver patterns.

A pungent warmth – the kind arising only from the flames of burning coals – began to radiate and tickle both her cheeks. So far was its extension that it filtered through the coating of her sleeves and stockings to envelop all her limbs.

Despite the presence of scant decorative lamps there was no artificial light because it was still summer. Anneliese began to notice that the peonies' far-stretching vases stood beside small gas lamps. Together with the central heating it was they that caused the simmering effect.

Before her a mostly red velvet carpet flowed over the staircase.

The old lady sniffed and pointed clumsily:

'There – first door.'

The walls were lacquered in dark gold and paintings hung across them. Mostly they were oil of murky brown and black, some were dirty-looking yellow; images apparently depicting individuals living in both caves and alcoves.

On the right side there were several wooden bookcases – mahogany again – equipped with tiny rows of paperbacks. There was Cervantes in Spanish, six volumes of a pocket medical dictionary, a lexicon of 'Idiomatic Ancient Greek' following a collection of essays called *On the External Characteristics of Fossils, or of Minerals*, something by the name of *Grundriß der Kolloidchemie* and a book two inches thick called *De Constitutione Artis Medicae*.

Closing her eyes, all she saw was plush red. With them shut she bumped her head on some huge metal structure and an 'ow' shot from her mouth.

Anneliese looked up to see a rack two-metres high of wooden shelves accommodating different shoes. She counted eight pairs lodged on each: all of them high heels. Categorised by a colour palette, at the top were classic black stilettos with extensive spears. Traipsing her eyes across the row, Anneliese located the brown shoes. There were shoes with fat heels, shoes with thin heels; shoes with thick ankle straps and shoes with two sets of thin ankle straps; court shoes. And when Anneliese had studied brown, maroon, violet and dark purple shoes; dark red, blood red, pink and peach-coloured hues, bright orange ones, light orange ones, yellow shoes with chunky heels, light blue ones, dark blue ones and green – it was then she came across the wooden ones along the bottom shelves.

She recollected that her sister called these new shoes 'Mary Janes'.

Yet she asked herself who could have found – and bought –

three rows of these shoes made almost entirely out of wood: like Dutch clogs – but sophisticated. The strap alone was leather.

This kind of footwear ought to have belonged to a museum.

The door was half-ajar. Anneliese stood peering through the threshold.

The room was a library. It was also a practice with a Freudian couch and two armchairs. But in the furniture's periphery there was a university athenaeum. Walls were invisible because the bookcases disguised them top to bottom, left to right. Seven feet high, each one was over-stuffed with tomes whose coarse arrangements were chaotic.

While the leather-bound volumes were colour-co-ordinated, recent editions stuck out in the confines of a literary entropy. Squeezed into tiny gaps, many of their spines were on the verge of breakage as they clung on for dear life. Anneliese could vaguely make out something called *Gamiani, or Two Nights of Excess* next to Herder's *Ursprung der Sprache*. Mentally cataloguing the books, she came to the conclusion that no principle had underscored their order. In the centre of the sofa and two armchairs was a tiny table made of patterned tiles of multi-coloured glass and glistening ceramic: it had no doubt hailed from Europe.

Positioned on smaller mahogany bookcases, the lamps flaunted tall and gold shades. The room's complexion was a dimmer one than that to which her eyes had been accustomed.

A monument was parked in front of one of the small bookcases. If she derived from a collection it was evident her contour hadn't gelled with that of other members of her company. She was an item too extraneous to be appraised at auction.

Perspicacious as was Anneliese, it was her shoes that first engaged her glare: akin to the style she had stumbled upon in the corridor, but of a mahogany colour. The heels appeared to be tall blocks of crimson wood. The strap was dark red leather with black buttons.

She pitied the cobbler beset with this ponderous order.

That was until she saw the dress. A long-sleeved gown of blood red silk topped with a low-cut v-neck, its bottom was a flowing skirt that stopped above her ankles. It was drawn in at the middle by a tall black sash around the waist. Just above the dress's apex was her hair: fluffed out in waves of honeyed amber. The thick gold locks dangled an inch above her shoulder.

Her head was fixedly engaged in menial manual work: the scribbling of some notes across her pad. Anneliese could see her eyes shift left and right across the page and blink at intervals enough to gauge their size was unconventionally large. Rimmed by generous sets of black lashes, they were a pair natural selection rarely touted on the market; mystically cavernous and finished off with heightened tips extending to the temples. A long bridge as straight as a gradient ran up her bulk of a nose.

Dr Westwood did not sit. Apparently the act of enforced standing was her idiosyncratic brand of discipline.

Each line she finished briskly. Anneliese could see the letters alternated between straight and curvy; stealthily contained in a calligraphy few humans could decipher.

Aloofness on her part profusely persevered. She crossed out all the words she had just written, tore away the sheet, scrunched it up and tossed it in a nearby bin.

With a great sigh of frustration obviously directed at herself, Dr Westwood now began anew. Her movements were too rigid; somehow too exact. Yet there was a melodic chime at odds with her adroitness. It consisted of the bangles on her wrist: one large chunk of genuine amber tinted by a red hue; one thinner cheaper-looking one of black, another of a bold beige colour next to one in silver and another of rich burgundy. With every move they tinkled.

Anneliese took one step forward and the door responded with a creak. Dr Westwood dropped her pen and fixed her gaze on the small specimen in front of her.

Drowsiness lingered in her numinous eyes. In the course of a brief episode of silence they went left and right, immersed in rapid calculation.

She paced out of the room at some unseizable speed, spewing some speech that Anneliese perceived to be affirmative:

'Just – wait here for a moment.'

She understood this may have been her cue to cross the threshold.

Yet Anneliese was grappling with a cold fear that had paralysed her instincts.

Muffled dialogue swam slowly through the corridor. The old lady was speaking German; Dr Westwood replied to her only in English. The latter's voice was louder and more palpable:

'"Vandolt"? What "Vandolt"? What kind of name is . . .'

Anneliese heard more rushed muttering exude from the old lady.

Dr Westwood now clarified it in a louder voice: she seemed resigned to present circumstance.

'"van der Holt".'

She returned so quickly that the young girl could have sworn her voice still echoed from the kitchen.

'Your name is three words, isn't it?'

'It's . . . four.'

'"van der Holt"?'

'That's three words, yes.'

'Mmm-hmm.'

It was not inert – her focus. The psychiatrist was too alert to be inert. But she was also too direct to bear a vague resemblance to a doctor whose profession was dependent on the grounds of tentative investigation.

It was she who sat down before Anneliese and crossed her legs immediately, and let her hands rest on the armchair's sides.

'You don't have to use the . . . the sofa. That's a template.'

Anneliese was thrown.

'Hmm?'

'Well – you're bespectacled, so I presumed you'd know. The sofa – the "Freudian couch". You don't have to lie down; its purposes are largely decorative.'

'Oh.' Anneliese nodded. She let her eyes dance till they landed on the other armchair. 'May I . . .'

'Of course.'

Anneliese couldn't help but look down at her own dress. It was an old corduroy thing out of season.

'Who told you where to find me?'

Anneliese was stunned.

'Your . . . your secretary.'

'I have a secretary?'

'That – that lady who just answered the door.'

She had to curve her mouth to keep herself from bursting into flames of laughter.

'That's – that's not a secretary. No, I meant which *doctor*.'

'Oh.' Anneliese's voice grew even quieter. 'My father was a neurologist; a professor at Westfield College . . . He knew someone who's apparently familiar with your work.'

'Who would that be?'

'Dr Newhart.'

'Newhart?'

'Gregory Newhart.'

Dr Westwood didn't pay a great deal of attention to the name.

'Is your father dead now?'

Anneliese compelled herself to overlook the lack of sensitivity.

'Yes. I don't suppose Dr Newhart mentioned the chance of my . . .'

'No. No – that was all Helga.'

'Who?'

'The lady who answered the door.'

There was a pause in which the doctor drew her bangles further up her arm in an inane attempt to stop them clinking.

'When was the last time you ate? It doesn't look as though it was this morning.'

Anneliese stayed her response. Her eyes were out of focus.

Dr Westwood wasted no time. In a manner split between imperiousness and urgency, she yelled:

'*Helga!*'

The old lady arrived forthwith.

Dr Westwood looked at her with eyes emphatic and a glimpse of mischief.

'Could you bring the rock cakes here?'

Helga responded with a phrase in German Anneliese could just about interpret as: 'Those you left on the stove for flies to eat?'

'The edible ones, Helga.' Dr Westwood emphasised with a condemnatory blink. The blinking was the true intensifier. 'The ones that are *edible*.'

Helga muttered something that sounded belligerent.

'Not those – no, Helga. No . . .' She let a huge sigh perforate the air and rose. 'Excuse me.'

So Anneliese waited, hoping to occupy the room alone for maybe a minute.

She was back within fifteen seconds.

They were huge cakes. They were warm.

Anneliese took one in the hope that her eating would save her from having to speak. Dr Westwood just continued gazing at her, internally examining; concocting some impression in her head to which the patient was not privy.

After a few moments of chewing Anneliese realised she hadn't said thank you.

'Erm . . . it's very kind of you.'

'You were beginning to look shrivelled.'

Chewing on the cake some more for her protection, Anneliese swallowed and, with her eyes cast down, summoned the bravery to dart a statement.

'I don't know how communication works in this.'

'Well, usually it's verbal.'

Dr Westwood almost curved her lips into a smile. Anneliese was slow to understand.

'When did he pass away?'

'My . . .'

'Your father.'

'Just over a month ago.'

'What caused his death?'

'An unexpected heart attack. Dr Newhart told us he was dead outside our school.'

The doctor was responding with two or three casual blinks and some scrutiny. Anneliese awaited the condolences. She anticipated the habitual 'I'm sorry'. Nothing came.

'Your mother is too busy with her own grief?'

'There was none to begin with.'

'Siblings?'

'I'm a twin.'

'She's not a "soulmate" then?'

'How did you know it was a girl?'

'"Divination"?' Dr Westwood looked up for a moment. When her head came down she gazed at Anneliese guessingly. 'I wouldn't imagine how a girl like you could possibly respect psychiatry.'

'Well . . .'

'Your father was a purist.'

'I'm . . .' It took some time for words to pop up into Anneliese's consciousness. 'Excuse me?'

'Most neurologists dismiss psychoanalysis as speculation.'

Anneliese took a great breath. She could learn something from Dr Westwood about confidence. Her eyes alone – both instruments of predetermined mischief – could erode a person's outer layers, gnawing at protective skin until no more than flakes were left.

'I'm sorry, but – aren't you the one who's supposed to listen to *me*?'

'Yes – but it's an area I know too well.' Her excuse was barely half-apologetic.

'So . . . all psychiatrists bicker with neurologists?'

'Is that a question about me or "all psychiatrists"?'

There again came the series of supercilious blinks. Anneliese attempted to direct her gaze elsewhere.

'That was a question about . . .' Anneliese slouched back into her chair. 'That was about you.'

'It wouldn't be natural if you didn't want to know about me.' Dr Westwood shrugged. 'I might just . . . rob you of your soul.'

She wasn't quick enough to understand. Dr Westwood recrossed her legs, attempted to purse her lips to quench laughter and lined her next words with gentility.

'Sorry – you're so young; it's wrong of me. I meant to say . . . It's healthy to possess a great desire to promote your father's doctrine following his death.'

'That's all you have to say to me?'

'Poor choice of words. Tell me what you *think*, Anneliese.'

'Of . . .'

'Psychoanalytical psychiatry. I'm not going to believe that you're an advocate.'

'Why is that relevant?'

'Because you're sitting here in front of me and while you think you can conceal your thoughts each time you think of something new to hide, your body submits to a tremor.'

She wanted to exploit her own artillery to fire back at Dr Westwood.

But she felt disarmed.

And there was something in the fluctuation of her speech and gestures of a soothing quality. Her contralto was not husky. It was a soft timbre of velvet lined with a smooth yarn of silk. A coat of wispiness regaled her vocal instrument with misappropriated warmth.

'Well – well . . .' Anneliese's nerves were hauling a great panic at her. Her hands were laced in frost. 'In my mind, there are two kinds of doctors. There are those who want to cure and do good. And then there are those who went to medical school on the advice of their parents, who want to make a living. So I suppose the advent of psychiatry was when the ones who didn't want to cure but rather earn some cash produced this pal- this *substitute* for medicinal treatment. You care no more for human life than life-insurers, mystics and astrologers, philosophers and other "healers" all designed to "cleanse" the soul. All . . .' Her hands were clammy. She gave up. 'You're either a shrewd businesswoman or you live on a great ancestor's estate.'

Dr Westwood shrugged.

'Whichever works for you.'

Because of her long-winded avowal, Anneliese was now puffing out breath in much shorter stretches.

'You'll get hiccoughs. Take a glass of water.'

Only then did she behold a full jar on the table opposite a glass.

'Oh . . .'

She wiped her head before pouring herself water she gulped down immediately.

'You left out the soul-keepers and matchmakers.' Dr Westwood resumed.

'The what?'

'The theorists who assume they've got your soul. You tell them just a single symptom or event from childhood and they . . .' She snapped her fingers. 'Something neatly fits inside their filing cabinet; they find a match. Conveniently it's also quite a match for the idea they're selling in their doctoral thesis.'

'Dr Westwood—'

'Susanna.'

'You want me to call you . . . "Susanna"?'

'It's the name they gave me.'

'"They"?'

'My parents.'

'Are you so informal with . . . all of your patients?'

She let a half-smirk make its way across her mouth then promptly straightened it.

'No – I detest my surname.'

'So much?'

'So much.'

A pause transpired. Susanna looked at her with eyebrows slanted slightly.

'What's your twin's name?'

'Isabel.'

'You came to me because she doesn't comprehend the loss.'

It was a comment proffered almost nonchalantly.

'There was one *recorded* loss.'

'What was the other one?'

'How did you know there was another?'

'Because you specified a *numeral*.'

'We lost Isabel as well.' Anneliese kept her head down before hastily adding: 'Not we, not we. *I* did. I would say that I'm the only member of the family who's left.'

'Your sister's interpreting death differently.'

'Mmm . . .' Anneliese sat up on the armchair. 'I don't know that she *has* an "interpretation" . . .' She cleared her throat. 'Isabel's on foreign soil.'

'You don't know who she is?'

'I don't.'

'Have you tried asking her?'

'You mean . . . have I tried to pin her down, demand to know why she's behaving like an idiot, why she's in a stupor, why she lacks awareness?'

'Yes.'

'No, I haven't.'

Susanna extended her arm over the right side of her chair.

'I don't suppose it would be of much use.'

'It wouldn't.'

'She is inflexible. So it's your judgment that you want to shift.'

'I . . . I understand that. But Isabel – doesn't – she doesn't seem – what kind of a loving daughter finds herself a boyfriend straight after her father keels *over* and dies?'

The blinks were quicker this time.

'You would prefer her reaction to be yours.'

'I would prefer it to be *human*.'

'It's not *going* to be in your eyes. Not until you switch your judgment.' Her bangles clinked again. 'Do you suppose your sister ever loved your father?'

'Well, of course I – no. I don't. I used to. I don't – *now*.'

'That's because you're only using "a" and "b".'

'Hmm?'

'Isabel is a monster. You're not a monster. And . . .' Susanna waved her hand at her side. 'There's nothing else between these two types. There are more letters in the alphabet, Anneliese. It's the most common argument I spout inside this room. Come to think of it . . . it was the most common argument I spouted when at university. And elsewhere.' She shifted her position in the armchair. 'If you're going to compartmentalise people, why don't you build extra *shelves*?'

'And yet I don't think I could build a shelf for *you*.'

'Hmm?' Susanna feigned incomprehension. By now even Anneliese could tell it was *simulated*. 'For *me*?'

'You know . . . You . . . didn't express any condolences.'

Susanna tapped the pen now in her hands. Matter-of-factly she replied:

'I know.'

'Well, isn't it unethical of a psychiatrist to—'

'See how people can have different *motives?*'

Her eyes took on fresh animation and her voice was higher-pitched; she was close to seeming giddy. Her glare was knowing, maybe even smug; the charm resulting from the pleasant outcome of her cunningly hatched plan.

This was all too rapid for the young girl to absorb.

'I'm . . . sorry?'

'I was catching you out; conscious of my actions.'

'So . . . are there patients who go through bereavement who . . . aren't?'

'Yes. And you should . . . Take a closer look.'

Anneliese almost snorted from laughter.

'Why would I want to do *that?*'

'You could rummage around to find the reason for her behaviour – rather than assume your father's death means that you don't have anyone and never *will.*'

She scratched her neck.

'Why would you assume I . . .'

'Anneliese . . .' She shook her head. 'You're hardly an *original.*'

As the patient digested these thoughts Susanna took this time to stare up into space, sideways; engaged elsewhere.

When she had floated back down to their circumstance she spoke again.

'Not everything computes together like an algorithm and I don't think that you're Ada Lovelace.' She let out a few more blinks before concluding, 'Maybe I'm just *assuming.*'

Anneliese was looking at her blankly. She gulped. Susanna explained:

'Byron's daughter. Mathematician.'

A black cloud of shame began to loiter over Anneliese's heart. She changed the subject to avoid embarrassment.

'I'm still barely sleeping, though.'

'Well . . .' Susanna looked down in a hint of sympathy. 'It can be a very taxing thing.'

'Are you authorised to prescribe barbiturates?'

'Yes.'

'Could you?'

'No.'

'Why not?'

'They interfere with the activity of gamma-Amino-butyric acid, so they dilate the blood vessels and decrease the heart's contractibility.'

'What's . . . "gamma-Amino" . . .?'

'A chemical neural transmitter; a chemical transmitted across neural synapses.'

Anneliese's eyes lingered on the wall opposite.

'I've never heard of that.'

'You wouldn't have.'

'I've actually read—'

Susanna bowed her head and steadied her gaze purposely.

'You *wouldn't* have – because that name doesn't exist yet.'

'You mean . . . the findings haven't been published?'

'No.' Susanna uncrossed and recrossed her legs. 'I mean the findings haven't even been *identified*.'

'So . . . *you're* going to publish . . .'

Susanna closed her eyes, shook her head gently and emitted a tenuous laugh. A little more air than usual was conveyed through her speech.

'No, no. If you knew the name it takes . . .' Anneliese frowned. Susanna pressed her thumb on her pen almost unwittingly. 'If one goes only by documentation, Acetylcholine is still making its way up the ranks.'

Anneliese's countenance betrayed a puzzlement much greater than the one she felt.

Susanna continued:

'That means that by the time they discover it, I won't be here.'

She stroked her left cheek with her forefinger.

'Where will you *be*?' Susanna narrowed her eyes in a semi-contempt. Anneliese caught on. 'Oh.' She swallowed then resumed. 'Is your husband involved in the—'

'Poor slyness, Anneliese.'

'Well – *is* he?'

'What you want to know is, I'm not married. As for the *topic*, I have weaker antidotes for insomnia.'

'Such as what?'

'Go out of the room and look on the right and you'll see.'

Anneliese rose and obeyed the instructions.

'It's a bookcase.'

'A basket of hypnotics. Last one on the middle shelf. It's not the one with Proust on it, as most of my patients presume.'

Anneliese heard footsteps rapidly catch up with her. By the time she looked on her left side Susanna was already handing her some heavy tome: *Geology of Petroleum.*

'I do *not* need it back.' she emphasised.

Taking her seat again, she was forced to wait for Anneliese to assume her position. Anneliese did this ten times more slowly.

'Well . . . I think that we can close this now.' Susanna concluded.

'Close what?'

'The session.'

Something itched at Anneliese.

'But . . . Well, I assumed . . .'

'We've found everything out.'

'Yes . . .'

'And now it's up to you to ponder it.'

'But . . . how can you know that I'm . . . well?'

'You mean . . .' She looked at her with her chin lowered and eyes raised. 'How can I know you're capable of managing yourself?'

'Yes.'

Susanna recapitulated:

'You furrowed your eyebrows when I didn't express my condolences, interrogated me about a chemical neurotransmitter that I may have . . .' she waved her hand, 'just spontaneously invented, managed to concoct a ploy to find out whether I was married. You're not even . . .' She sat up. '"Commercially viable".'

'What does that mean?'

'It means that if I tried to make a business out of you I'd end up shaking hands with something called "foreclosure". You don't just have your wits "about you", Anneliese; they're locked into position like a cycle's brakes. You don't need a psychiatrist.'

Anneliese got up and smoothed out the skirt of her dress. Nearing the table, she reached into her pocket to retrieve the sum that she had taken with her, accompanying her reverential gesture with the words:

'Forgive me – I had no clue what was acceptable. I hoped that this would be enough.'

'Why are you stretching out these arbitrary banknotes?'

'Would you prefer a cheque?'

Susanna's eyes hung long and low. She appeared almost solemn for the first time in their session.

'I don't take money from minors.'

'But—'

'I don't take money from minors.'

'You're only saying that because I accused psychiatrists of—'

'No, Anneliese – I'm saying it because I do not *do* it.'

Perhaps there was a kind of human species she was soft on. Anneliese was fortunate enough to still meet its requirements.

'Oh.' She tucked the notes into her pocket.

For a few moments she stood motionless – until she started itching at her sleeve quite inexplicably.

Susanna rose and offered her the parting gesture of her hand. Its shake was strong and quick – as though it had an autonomous desire of leaving her mark.

In a dry tone reluctant to express something, she weakly affirmed:

'It was a pleasure to meet you.'

Anneliese was struck dumb. She could still feel the peonies' scent in her nose. Letting her eyes drift in different directions, she couldn't help but observe:

'Erm . . . I still think my reasoning is . . . blotchy. Extra counsel might be beneficial for me.'

Susanna let her look linger sparingly on the patient. This time she exerted blinks more from uneasiness than any motive.

'Well, if you . . . If you should feel you want to come – you *can*. Wednesday is hardly a full day.' Anneliese nodded enthusiastically. 'You know . . . You should bear in mind that many people become overly dependent.'

Anneliese shrugged.

'It's not a narcotic.'

'No.' She looked down for a moment, gave out a short breath and then looked up again. 'It's also indulgence for those not in need of it.'

'But . . . You'll let me come back?'

For the first time Anneliese remarked Susanna's mind was pacing – awkwardly. In that infrangible gaze was the hint of a sombre fatigue; something Anneliese could not attribute to a source.

'Yes.' Susanna recovered herself. 'You can *come* . . . but I will tell you now that my professional perspective sees this only as a transient arrangement.'

'All right.' Anneliese smiled.

Susanna returned the smile, albeit half-heartedly. Quickly she froze her face, restraining it from further animation.

Anneliese's concentration was caught off guard. She was examining Susanna's bookcases in wonder at the juxtaposition of *Mrs Beeton's Book of Household Management* and J.W. Buel's *Sea and Land*.

By the time she looked straight ahead Susanna was out of the room.

Having stepped into the corridor she saw her waiting at the brown door leading to the porch. Her hand was on the latch. Anneliese eyed the psychiatrist wondrously and commented:

'You move so fast . . . I don't mean that – I don't mean that in a nasty way. It's just . . . you're always seven paces ahead.' Courage was now in her grip. On her way out she dared to ask: 'Did you never publish an article in the British Psychoanalytic Journal?'

Susanna looked at her, bewildered. It was an opportune time for her lashes to batter. 'Did *I* ever publish an article?'

'Yes.'

'No, Anneliese.' She laughed a little to herself. 'Not in the *psychoanalytic* journal.'

'But . . . you seem to be a fairly verbal person . . .'

'I wouldn't think my material would concur with their kind.'

Anneliese smiled again. Upon receiving it Susanna struggled to repress endearment. With a smile half-polished and half-tamed she asked:

'How old are you – fifteen?'

Anneliese nodded.

Susanna closed her eyes. Opening her mouth to speak, her voice was warm in spite of her.

'Well . . . there's not much else you're going to lose. Not soon.'

The patient barely knew how to respond to this. Finally she mustered:

'So . . . I'll see you next week at . . . seven?'

This threw Susanna's concentration.

'Come at five. It's Helga's scheduling that's . . . Never mind.'

'All right.'

'Goodbye.'

'Goodbye.'

Anneliese stepped out but then looked back.

'Susanna?'

Her eyes looked at her lazily.

'Hmm?'

'Did you make up that *gamma* Amino . . . that acid?'

'No.'

With that she shut the door.

18.

Poison ivy

The sun had reached its peak on Monday 26th August, 1935. Isabel and Ewan were strolling around Hyde Park: the former walking in diagonal lines, the latter shooing her away from herds of cyclists.

Giddier than usual was the girl as she related a history lesson with Miss Clarendon that had taken place weeks before Josef's death. In tune with her the birds were chirping much to her delight.

'And so, she looks at me and asks—'

'Careful.' Ewan brusquely interrupted, shifting her away from a bicycle's bell. 'Isabel . . .' he sounded quite frustrated, 'I *really* think we should reorganise our route.'

'They're just cyclists. Not motor vehicles. So, Miss Clarendon asks me,' (she turned around and placed her hands atop her hips) '"And where have you misplaced your glasses, missy?" That's really how she *stands*, you know, and I hate it when she calls us "missies"; it makes us sounds like we're – anyway, so I tell her in quite a bit of detail, and I know it made the girls laugh 'cause I heard them giggling to the left and right of me: "Miss Clarendon, I had an eye test two months ago, I went to the optician's and he told me that God had recovered my sight." Katy was having a fit. I don't even *know* if Miss Clarendon believed me, but at least I got away with not wearing the damn pair.'

They walked a little further before she remarked:

'And they're so *ugly* – the ones I got last year.'

Ewan huffed and puffed rather sarcastically.

'Honestly, Isabel, I really don't understand what your problem with wearing them—'

'I've *told* you – they make me look *unattractive*. They make me look like a *headmistress.*' She turned on her coquettish voice and sought to know: 'Do *you* think I look like a headmistress?'

A faint smile came into view. His lack of interest became palpable so she moved on, striding in a swagger.

'Anyway, so we come home; Liesa's blowing steam like a kettle. I've never seen her so furious. "How could you *lie*, Isabel? How could you be so *blasphemous?*"'

Ewan stopped in his tracks. Isabel stopped with him for the sake of being polite and proceeded with her argument, this time more briskly. She was in a race to conclude before he commenced with his own speech:

'And *she* – she has no right to berate me as though I'm her *inferior*. She spends all her time in *church*. Every Wednesday she tells me she's going there – and, Ewan . . . She's gone for three and a half hours at least – every week. Who would spend that much time at *church?*'

'Listen, Isabel . . .' He sounded ill at ease and held down by the pendant of a heavy albatross. 'I'm afraid that . . .' He reached to stroke behind his neck. 'I'm afraid I don't think it would be a good idea for us to continue our meetings.'

Isabel was rational but did not understand.

'*Why?*'

'Well . . . I'm sorry, it's my fault. When we met, Olivia told me that your father had just died. I took pity on you. And you seemed so . . . *strong* and sophisticated. I admired you very much. Most girls would be a blubbering mess in the same situation. But you carried on with life out of duty. I told myself this was a girl who couldn't afford to waste any time; prioritised looking after her family. I told myself this was a girl wanting to make the most of life who reserved grief for her own, *private* moments. I wanted to help you. But, but instead ... Look, I don't know that much about young women. But all the time we've been together, all that you've been going on about has been Liesa *this*, Liesa *that* ... What happened last year at school, and asking whether we can go to the pictures, mentioning odd subjects such as Ginger Rogers' legs ... I just ... I don't see that you're in agony and ... well ... I'm so sorry but, I think I just assumed that you were someone else.' He hastened to add in some flat bid for reassurance: 'It's *my* fault, really.'

Isabel stared at him, her eyes both long and still. In a voice that was deliberately calm she answered:

'All right.'

She took her hat out of his hands. In a most polite and even kind tone she observed:

'I suppose we'll see each other at Olivia's someday.'

Slightly alarmed at her resolution, Ewan mustered the courage to churn a reply:

'Certainly.'

She half-whispered:

'Good. Keep well.'

Distancing herself, she put the hat on and began to take large goose steps as though on a hike. Once she had turned the left corner he didn't see her again.

There was a cypress tree where she found comfort. In that area of shade the sun could not encrust its bark. Sinking to the bottom, she sat down and placed her hat on folded knees. The fading sky of piquant blue was visible.

There would be a man who'd understand she had no

ammunition: comprehend her constitution was no danger to the human aspect titled 'sensitivity'. In her soul's reservoir where all the weeds and poison ivy and the barren drooping foliage resided she was quite an advocate of it. *Someone ought to find that out*, she mused, before deciding hastily against it.

19.

Turning over the compass

It was a great surprise to Isabel that Anneliese had never been run over by a car. This she considered as they headed to the station soaked in the September sun, the Younger Twin as usual circumambulating on the road *beside* the pavement.

Too tired to run up to her, sluggishly Isabel bellowed:

'Anneliese.'

Her sister didn't hear. It had begun to seem to Isabel that Anneliese was going deaf.

'*Liesa.*'

There was silence.

'*Anneliese!*'

Isabel ran up to her and grabbed her arm.

'What?'

'You were skirting the pavement, Liesa.'

'No, I wasn't.'

'Somebody's Rolls was going to roll on *you.*'

Anneliese looked down. In recent times communication had been difficult with her.

At school she tended to spend all her time together with a German dictionary. Isabel was forced to clear her throat to get attention. Even then she wouldn't rouse.

'Is she all right?' Daphne approached Isabel that day.

'I have no *clue*.'

'She seems a little . . .'

'She's not here, Daphne – hasn't been for *weeks*.'

'You mean, she's . . .'

'Away with the dragonflies.'

Miss Butterworth summoned Anneliese at lunchtime after she had told Miss Rowley of their father's passing. At the end of school Isabel felt a familiar two fingers jump on her shoulder.

'Miss Butterworth wants to see you.'

'Now?'

'Mmm-hmm.'

She noticed Anneliese was yet again holding the German dictionary. Her sister may as well have been struck *comatose*.

When it was Isabel's turn to accept the same condolences, she relied on protracting her half-smile:

'Thank you.'

'I . . .' Miss Butterworth heaved a very pained sigh. 'I really wish that someone had informed me over the summer. Do sit down.'

'Well . . .' Isabel scratched her head. 'I hope I'm not being rude, but I was hoping to be excused rather quickly . . . choir starts in three minutes.'

Miss Butterworth looked up at the clock.

'It's *ten* to four, Isabel.'

'Mmm-hmm.'

'Choir starts at four on the dot, doesn't it?' Miss Butterworth smiled. 'Or have I been completely out of touch?'

'No, you're right; only, I wanted to go over some Bach with Miss Cunningham. I haven't seen her since July.'

'I would have thought that Bach for *you* was far too easy.'

It hadn't been a smoothly calculated lie on her part. She had always depended on 'Bach' as her escape route: a monosyllable.

'I *think* it was Bach . . .' Isabel shook her head in false confusion. 'In any case, unfortunately I don't have any time to spare.'

Miss Butterworth eventually succumbed.

'Well . . . all right. But please do come to see me if . . . there's anything you'd care to discuss. Related to school, or to anything else. Even midway through a lesson, should you want to.'

'Thank you.' Isabel reiterated. 'Good evening.'

'Good evening, Isabel.'

She quickened her pace with her exit. When it occurred to her to count she realised that she hadn't played an instrument in over sixty days.

Lately Anneliese and her amusing antics almost served as a distraction. After their last lesson of chemistry the following day she had requested that Isabel wait another ten minutes: dying was she to ask Miss Frobishire about some upcoming experiment.

Half an hour passed and Isabel was sure she had to yank her sister from the room.

'No – I'm certain.' Anneliese was emphasising.

Poor Miss Frobishire appeared exhausted.

'My dear, *all* neural transmissions are bioelectric. There is nothing "chemical" about it.'

'So you haven't heard of acetylcholine?'

The teacher let her eyebrows be symbolic of her sentiment.

'No. No, I haven't.'

'Well, maybe I . . . I don't know.'

Miss Frobishire contemplatively raised her hands.

'Tell me *again* what it was called.'

'*Gamma*-Amino-butyric acid. And it's a neural transmitter.'

The teacher heaved a heavy sigh:

'Somebody's pulling your *leg*, poppet.'

Isabel had rarely seen her sister so disheartened. She patted her shoulder.

'*Liesa!*'

It took Anneliese a long delay to suddenly recall who else was left at school.

Four sessions had passed. The air was always crisp when she departed from Susanna's; a light and dainty breeze resided there that didn't filter through her home at Glenluce Road. The sky would be reddish and purple and paving its indigo way to the sunset.

Every Wednesday she arrived armed with more German; every Wednesday there would be an interlingual sparring match between Susanna and her maid. Anneliese had detected that Helga was rustic; protected from life's urban charms. She breathed and sighed exactly like a peasant woman whose mundane existence could incorporate the skinning of a rabbit.

Anneliese expected the sophisticate Susanna to regard her maid with superciliousness and mockery. Quite often it was obvious that she did.

By now she had beheld three different gowns of black, navy and crimson, iridescent bangles, shoes and floral skirts. Every week Susanna's hair would be a little different; every week her patient looked down at her own inferior clothes.

It was the norm.

She was learning to engage in German dialogue with Helga: a feat most usefully accomplished once she realised how the latter gossiped. She kept remembering Susanna as a girl and yielding to great sighs. At one point Anneliese latched on to something in her speech that was anomalous:

'*Byla další dívka.*'

A mental note was made of Helga's phrase but when she then transcribed the words they came out as 'Bilada sidivka'. It was a phrase no dictionary could define for her when she spent hours poring over several in the local library. It sounded Russian. She would have to study the Cyrillic alphabet.

Lessons with Mary Ann Hampshire – the jittery, never quite focussed biology teacher – now cast a lull on Anneliese's spirit. It seemed her voice's jumpiness was little more successful at alerting Anneliese than might have been a pair of gently tinkling tree chimes.

In the middle of a lesson halfway through the term Anneliese opened her book to stare at some diagrams matching small samples of words. They swam from left to right and back again without her scarcely extricating what they meant. No impulses had been created; no thoughts could pop up uninvited in her mind. Where the investigation of a plant cell's nucleus had been the highlight of her day three months before, she now regarded this as little but the bland quotidian.

At moments when she found herself most penetrative in her insight she unwittingly began to ring a circle on a blank page with her compass. Pivoting her pencil several times around the border, she would make the thin line swell until it bled into ten blunt ones. Eventually Miss Hampshire felt she had no choice but to approach her:

'Anneliese.' she commanded. The other girls – now far less somnolent and more aroused than usual in biology – all turned to witness the unique exchange. 'Please surrender your compass.'

Without pausing to reflect on her misconduct Anneliese conveyed the instrument. It was then that Isabel – who had been sitting at the back with Daphne – began earnestly to fret about her sister.

20.

High voltage

'Liesa, not too long.' Isabel instructed her sister as she presided over a stove in the Cookery Room at Croham Hurst. Anneliese was holding a wooden spoon in her right hand and stirring her mixture of brown sugar and water. Suddenly she slid the pan off the heat.

'Liesa!' Isabel jerked the pan away from her.

'What?'

'It's going to solidify.'

'It's still liquid.' Anneliese surveyed the pan once more. The mixture morphed into rigidity. 'Oh.'

'We'll have to do it again.'

Isabel hurriedly dumped the pan's contents into the bin. Miss Wiltshire approached them, disgruntled.

'Still hopeless, I see?'

'Indeed.' Isabel confirmed.

'Well, if you do get there, come show me.'

'We won't "get there".' She began measuring the sugar out again. 'Liesa – let me do it this time. For the past four years we've failed this.'

'What do you mean?'

'Our cake, Liesa. Our birthday cake.'

'This isn't our birthday cake.'

Isabel put the bowl on the surface. It thumped.

'What the Hell else could it be?'

'I'm making this for church.'

She addressed her in disgust:

'For *church?*'

'Yes.'

'Liesa . . . I've already got you a present. You forgot my present even though my birthday was four days ago.'

'I didn't forget. I just haven't found it yet.'

'Jonathan Wilkes.'

'Is he your latest treasure?'

'No . . . The music shop on South End. That's where you went to buy my scores. It's where you always go to get my gifts. I don't suppose you've used much more of your imagination this time.' She pushed the bowl in Anneliese's direction. 'You simply *forgot*. You didn't forget about *your* birthday – but there's a hole in your memory where 2nd November previously bore significance. I was born six days *before*, not after.'

'I know *that*.'

'*Really?!*'

They were making an upside-down caramelised apple cake; a lavish notion Isabel assumed her sister had devised in a deliberate attempt to please her.

She was wrong.

'I'm going to see *Anna Karenina* tonight with David.'

'David?'

'Yes.' Isabel emphasised. 'Don't you remember? We went to see another Garbo picture last week?'

'Yes, yes. I remember.'

After Miss Wiltshire had agreed to make the caramel it took two hours for the cake's completion and was forty minutes after home time. By the time they exited Croham Hurst the corridors were empty. Anneliese was tightly holding the cake secured on a platter under a lid. With each step on the Covered Way it trembled.

'Let me hold it, Liesa.'

'No – I've got it. I'm catching a different bus anyway.'

'You're going straight to church.'

'Mmm-hmm.'

'Is it not in the same direction?'

'Not exactly, no.'

'Well – why don't you just find a church closer to home?'

Anneliese was smug.

'It's the community and atmosphere one chooses, Isabel. Once one is a part of that, one doesn't just *swap* churches.' They carried on a few paces before she decided to add: 'They're not *men*, you know.'

It was raining on that day, 6th November. Anneliese stood at the bus stop with her hands lying over the cake cover, an umbrella tucked under her arm.

Ordinarily she spent forty-five minutes at Susanna's since the journey back and forth was of a mammoth length. A few weeks previously when it had started getting dark Susanna had tasked Helga with a new assignment: it was now her duty to escort her patient till her final bus stop.

Anneliese devoured all the chances for exchanges it provided her. She had already learnt Susanna lived on two hours of sleep every night. She had heard about how stubbornly Susanna had behaved with her colossal clan of siblings (Helga had yet to specify the number). Anneliese had gathered Helga had been working for the family for years before Susanna's birth.

She had also found out that they shared a birthday. This was why the cake was now no longer Isabel's. Isabel's own present was a crummy one: some encyclopaedia that Anneliese had deemed designed for infants.

She stopped off at a florist's and persuaded him to close ten minutes later; scouring the scattered peonies and scrupulously choosing both the reddest and the largest for her generous bouquet.

It was quarter past seven when she arrived at her house. On school nights there was no 'late' for Anneliese; their sessions tended to begin when she arrived, which varied from six thirty to nine minutes past eight. All of Susanna's other appointments that day were finished by six.

As she stood outside her porch the sky continued drizzling. Diaphanous droplets were sprinkling the peonies' petals. Peering through the glass of the blue door, she witnessed the banter in the full throes of its swing: Helga unwinding loud spirals of German while arms-folded Susanna stood leaning against the brown door of her practice. Through the bespattered two doors Anneliese could arduously discern the lazy drifting of Susanna's eyes eschewing sights of the old lady cleaving peace with her cacophony.

In a few moments' time Susanna had remarked that Anneliese was stood outside her porch and briefly gazed at her. The latter heard her announce without movement:

'Helga – the door.'

Helga was tempestuous. Without so much as turning around, she headed upstairs in a fury.

Susanna peeled herself away and paced towards the porch. As she opened the main door Anneliese saw her white, long-sleeved dress.

She presented the bouquet.

'I noticed your peonies were wilting.'

Susanna looked at the flowers half-heartedly – as though to suggest that they might be a burden. Taking them, she drowsily informed the girl:

'I don't generally expect these.'

'Is there a rule about . . .'

'Patients aren't supposed to administer gifts to psychiatrists. Anyway . . .' She strolled down the corridor, entered her practice, dumped the flowers on the multi-coloured table and forgot that they existed.

Till she noticed Anneliese was carrying a cake.

A flush spattered her cheeks when she observed her psychiatrist next. The latter sat down on her armchair, arms flopped on her legs and hands loose at her knees. Anneliese was sure the only reason for their movement was their length. The arms of her chair were too short for Susanna's.

She was scrutinising Anneliese with a more supercilious air than was her wont, and when she spoke her voice was even more replete with the low cello timbre Anneliese had heard her sister spouting years ago.

'Helga told you about my birthday.'

'Yes. And . . . well . . .' Anneliese shifted the flowers to place the cake on the table. 'We have a cookery lesson every Wednesday.' She started taking off her coat. 'So I thought, since I was on my way here . . .'

'Did you get Isabel anything?'

'Yes. I got her some notes.'

Susanna sat back. A smirk effused across her face.

'"Some notes"?'

'Yes.' Diffidently Anneliese hung her wet coat on the back of the chair.

'Which?'

'I got her . . .' She finally plonked herself down. 'I found this piano arrangement of Beethoven's Tenth Symphony.'

Susanna gazed at her with her chin lowered and eyes raised. She was pitiful and tethered by endearment.

'There is no "Tenth Symphony".'

'Hmm?'

'He didn't write one.'

'Oh.'

Anneliese thought this an opportune moment to scratch at her wrist. After a few ticks of the clock an idea stumbled into her head.

'So . . . You must have been a good musician.'

Almost muttering, Susanna responded haphazardly:

'I never played.'

'Not anything?'

'The viola. Until I was six.'

Anneliese could do nothing but nod.

Susanna let her eyes dip for a moment, unleashed a trio of blinks and then recommenced after a sigh:

'But, Anneliese—'

'It's funny that you should have played the viola. Nobody plays the viola.'

'You shouldn't have—'

'Isabel makes jokes about it. And Miss Cunningham has them reserved for keeping parents entertained in breaks between the pieces at our concerts.'

Susanna offered her a look of incomplete amusement.

'If you're trying to make this a contest, you've come to the wrong person.'

'No, I was . . .'

'There is . . . *no* chance I won't defeat you.'

'Well, you're older.' Anneliese tucked a strand of hair behind her ear. 'Considerably.' She tapped her fingers for a little while. 'I didn't say that last part.'

'The cake.'

'Yes.'

'You're taking it back.'

'In the rain?'

'That's right.'

'Why? Because of formal rules?'

'Because I'm not your mother.'

'Well, certainly . . .' Anneliese tried and failed to laugh. 'Thank God you're not my *mother*, I don't think anyone would want to *be* my mother...'

'Anneliese, you're an observant girl.'

'Yes.'

'And yet – you haven't picked up on the fact that you've been coming here for over three months now – without a problem?'

'Well . . .' she dawdled, 'I came here because I needed to know myself better.'

'And that's your only problem.'

'So?'

'So . . .' Susanna took her pen off the tiled table and started to fiddle with it. 'I have patients who suffer from real neuroses.'

'You . . .' Anneliese chuckled. 'You're no Freudian.'

'How on earth would *you* know?' She threw the pen back on the table. 'Has it not occurred to you that this is your survival mechanism? That obviously you would have felt this towards anyone who offered you some comfort after Josef died?'

'Felt what?'

'Anything that stirred on cake and peonies?'

Anneliese was stymied. A millstone weighed down on her heart and sought to apply pressure so the organ under it would burst.

'But – you . . .' She breathed out heavily. 'This is no ordinary comfort. I haven't taken an interest in Daphne or Olivia Paisley just because they've given me all sorts of hugs and flowers.'

'Have *they* listened to you?'

'No, but – they couldn't.'

'And I *can*?'

'Yes – *you* can, since you're—'

'I'm a psychiatrist. Usually they pay me to do this.'

'Well, I've said that I can do that if—'

'No, no, Anneliese – I don't want you to do that. I want you to realise why this is happening to you because I think that you're intelligent enough to understand.' Another trio of blinks followed. 'I'm not "harassed" by the idea of your bringing me cake. I happen to like cake.' She swirled a hand in the air as though to prompt further speech. 'But you have to realise what's going on inside you before it spins out of control. Baking a cake for me for my birthday, when we've discovered in these sessions that you dislike cooking – that's . . .' Susanna shook her head, nonplussed in how she wanted to express herself. 'That's some profound affection, Anneliese.'

Anneliese was snivelling. She took her handkerchief out of her sleeve. Susanna began:

'If you need some more, Helga has—' suddenly she stopped herself and took a deep breath. 'This is partly my fault.'

'*Your* fault?'

'A fifteen-year-old girl whose father has just died comes to my practice seeking help. I'm of a certain age. If I appear maternal – I apologise.'

'Why would you . . . "apologise"?'

'Because it really – firmly – very severely – gives you a misleading impression. You cannot depend on me. It's like your school-teachers. You can like them, you can respect them and admire them – but you can't treat them like a mother or a sister or a chum. You're supposed to *use* me, Anneliese, the way I use my postman to deliver parcels.'

Anneliese blew her nose.

'I'm quite sure . . . you don't send parcels.'

'Either way you're not supposed to know. And any interest in my private life both simulates this "love" for a simulacrum that doesn't exist and interferes with the work that we do here.'

Anneliese tucked her handkerchief back into her sleeve.

'And . . . what are we supposed to find out?'

'How to place you.' Susanna folded her arms and focussed her stare. 'That's what you want – isn't it? To place yourself in the real world? I thought you came here not to end up vegetating in your grief. And so we're going to do it. But *my* becoming a part of your life . . .' She tittered very slightly, almost annoyingly and girlishly. Anneliese perceived it as derision. 'Psychiatrists are the surplus. We exist *outside* a life; not inside it. If that happens, I'll have to transfer you.'

'To where?'

'To a colleague.'

Anneliese was horrified.

'No one is forcing you to "make friends" but . . . have you done tests?' Susanna asked.

'Done tests on what?'

'Have you done tests to prove "all girls your age are clueless", that "their sole interest is boys", and that "they have no interest in or penchant for abstract ideas"?'

Anneliese missed the point. Too amazed was she at her psychiatrist's citational memory.

'Well, no . . . You can't conduct *tests* . . .'

'So . . . why don't we investigate to see where this outlook *does* come from, aside from your sister's behaviour?'

Anneliese was very tempted to say, 'You can go first.'

Though still scarcely familiar with Susanna's tactics, she knew well that what the woman practised was strategic.

'Why is it everything you say is non-negotiable?'

'If that is the impression that you get, then combat me.'

Anneliese scratched her nose before beginning:

'You accuse me of growing fond of you because you listen. That's not *all*. You think I locked myself inside a cage, although you're doing the same *thing*.'

Susanna appeared apathetic.

'You sit here alone practising the whole day when most psychiatrists rent offices. Helga says you spend the evening reading

all the time, never receive guests, never speak on the telephone;
from what I see you have no family, no friend to speak of – certainly
no *man* in your life . . . How can I believe that is neither a choice,
nor a mistake? I'm not going to sit here and think nobody wants
you, that they threw you out, abandoned you, neglected you. You
don't look as though . . .'

She realised she had said enough. Relaxed a little in her chair,
she laid one hand over the other.

After a pause in which Susanna allowed Anneliese to catch her
breath and push out a long sigh, she resumed in a cold, detached
manner:

'Anneliese, you are in need of a compatriot. Because of this
you're keen to pin a certain image onto someone who may suit that
idol even only by a *fraction*.'

'What's the "cure" for this?'

'The lowering of your standards.'

Her eyes dropped and she looked at her despairingly.

'Hmm?'

'Have you ever considered that your attitude may be a little . . .
haughty?'

'*My* attitude?'

'You never confronted your sister.'

'No, but . . . Why *would* I?'

'I assumed you love her.'

'Yes. But I – I can't . . .'

'Do it.'

There was a short pause.

'All right.'

Susanna looked down at her hands. The clock ticked for some
fifteen seconds before she directed her gaze at her patient again.
This time she was a little mellower.

'Is there anything you need to tell me? Anything that
happened?'

'No.'

Susanna sprang up.

'Good.'

'That's it?'

'The work is yours now, Anneliese.' The latter stood. 'And take the cake.'

A disjointed series of clangs ensued as the patient collected the dish.

With her coat on she opened the door. Then it suddenly occurred to her there was another weapon at her helm.

'Remember the first time I came here, you told me about "gamma-Amino-butyric acid"?'

'Mmm-hmm.'

'How did you . . . *ascertain* its existence?'

'In a laboratory. I taught at St Mary's.'

'So you wrote papers?'

'All of us wrote papers.'

'Could I see them?'

'You're not here to appraise my scientific contribution, Anneliese.'

'No, but . . .' She scratched the back of her head. 'You *have* no scientific contribution, Susanna. That's why I'm stymied.'

Susanna let out a whispering sigh.

'I had no idea that word was in vogue nowadays.'

'So you won't answer my question?'

'No.'

'Then – how would you expect me to believe you?'

She let a knowing gaze linger on Anneliese for a while. Finally she lapsed into laughter.

'Because you've become my adulating pygmy, Anneliese. There's something sweet about that – but the point is, there should be a *limit* to it.' She corrected her face and tried to look serious. 'Probably.'

Of so high a voltage was the slyness, Anneliese imagined there had been a time when she had been a wily seductress. She was paradoxical: hotly dispassionate. Coldness was not among her cards.

'I'll see you next week.'

Susanna retreated to one of the bookcases. She crouched down and started pulling out some tomes to order them again.

Anneliese was obstinate. She dallied at the door, stepping back and forth and left and right. Susanna continued repositioning the books. Without so much as looking at her patient she shot:

'Am I keeping you?'

Anneliese stopped moving and stood still. 'I was just wondering ... I'm not familiar with most foreign languages except, of course, my own, and almost, slightly ... Isabel's. But I saw Helga writing once when I came early ... was that ... Russian?'

Susanna sprang around, projecting a long face and a sorrowful look at the girl.

'You can't differentiate between the Roman and Cyrillic alphabets?'

It dawned on Anneliese only at that point.

'Oh ...'

She turned away and kept on rearranging books. After some brutal reluctance she noted:

'It's Czech.'

'Czech?'

Susanna stood up and smoothed out her skirt. Her face was bluntly nonchalant.

'Czech.'

When Anneliese returned home Isabel was sitting at a table chomping on a piece of cake the size of a small island.

'Didn't the church want it?' Her eyes met Anneliese's cake immediately.

'No.' Anneliese muttered under her breath, positing the dish beside Isabel who eyed it voraciously.

'The vicar doesn't like this kind of cake?' Isabel noticed her sister was glummer than usual.

'Why not?'

'Well . . . many children go to church; their parents wouldn't want their teeth to get . . .'

Anneliese was too exhausted to finish. She eyed her sister for a response, wondering if it was possible to gauge a little empathy.

'That's absurd.' proclaimed Isabel.

'Well, perhaps one should consider that—'

'No.' insisted Isabel to her sister's delight. 'That's so off-putting; cold. It was only a cake, and you did it out of goodwill.'

For the first time in many months Anneliese found it possible to comply with her sister's mentality.

'Do you want to share it with me?'

The latter nodded violently.

21.

Smoulder

The music was too soft. Loud music in these crowds – the pumping of French horns or blaring boom of saxophones – would allow Isabel to sensually submerge herself in mind-despoiled delirium. That euphoric clasp could have persuaded her to heave herself into the seat of a hot air balloon. Cider or wine when greedily consumed with jazz became her magnet: she depended on its inhalation for her upkeep. With it she could dye her soul a glimmering array of sparkling foreign colours. Whatever antidote was offered she would drink up like a drain.

At eleven o'clock on New Year's Eve the crowd was in the garden at the house of Olivia's older sister. Approximately two hundred in their number, Isabel had counted only eighty-nine, most of whom were male and years beyond eighteen.

It was the nineteenth party she attended that December 1935 – having come this time at Olivia's urgency.

The latter had begun to label her the 'tooter' since she sang with every drink. She was the only one of their companions who could sing in tune; unleash a Gershwin ditty with the liberty of some audacious starlet, fling her dress's skirt up with enthused abandon, tap her heels with Ginger Rogers' rhythms.

The most amusing part – Olivia would tell others back at school – was when, exhausted from fatigue, she would eventually keel over.

This time the air was clearer. Isabel despised rarefied air. Contrarily her claustrophobia served to refresh her like a sauna's buckets of cold water oozing over scintillating flesh. She only attended the bashes to have her face drenched in sweat; feel the film of a sweltering heat coat her legs.

Nowhere else could she so easily surrender to engrossment in the senses. Even the trickle of her perspiration climbing her curvaceous thighs ignited her exhilaration and she lay in bed recalling it. The vocal resonance of a broad-shouldered boy standing behind her, a vibrating growl tickling the hairs along her neck became the zenith of self-liberation.

The moment Isabel began to clop her shoes and fling her feet into the air would be a signal for the lock to teasingly unfasten. Bound to consciousness throughout the day – the thought of her glum sister or her sterile playing throughout music lessons – she discovered there was nothing she awaited more than the occasion when her body would prevail over cognition; undergo an evanescent carnal smoulder. At least she knew there was a part of her that manifestly couldn't be defective.

That evening Olivia kept jerking her arm.

'You *have* to play it, Isabel.'

The latter leant her red cheek on her glass.

'But . . . *why?*'

'Because you never know who might be at the *door?*' Olivia spluttered laughter. She had become inebriated long before the influx of her guests.

'Don't some of those young men have girlfriends?'

Very, very slowly Olivia shook her head – then burst into laughter at her own silliness.

'Well . . . I'd rather just watch.' Isabel admitted.

'But that – but that's not *fair! I'm* doing it. And *Clare* is doing it. For Christ's sake, *Valerie* is lining up.'

'What about your sister?'

'*Obviously.*' Olivia started hiccoughing. 'Oops – sorry.'

Imposing though her arduous persuasion was, Isabel abstained from the game. It was a two-hour session of Postman's Knock. Olivia had insisted that it was in vogue after seeing some Hollywood film. Addicted as she was to Bacchanalian rites, Isabel was not yet ready to allow a dozen strangers to share kisses with her.

There was a fruitfulness that came from being kissed by a young man. She had experienced it with Ewan and with David; wallowing in the sensation of a pair of rugged lips against her own and little bristles branding her soft skin. Flashes of coruscating images in her mind would ignite and immediately vanquish her *status quo* emptiness. She would have preferred the boys to be much older with shoulders much broader, of a statelier height and a less sensitive grip.

In order to obtain this gift for which she often yearned in the dark hours there had to be – as she was bitterly aware – a moral seal in place inside her skull: the word 'relationship'.

That night she came back earlier than usual. Anneliese was sitting in the middle of the stairs with a huge hardback on her lap and a notebook beside her. With her head still focussed on a page she murmured:

'I didn't expect to see you before morning.'

Isabel sought to outstrip her sarcasm.

'I wouldn't have expected you to *wait.*'

Stepping over Anneliese on the staircase, she observed she was reading a Czech dictionary. It only sought to hammer into her more violently the width of the great chasm between her and the slow-growing twin.

Isabel's early entrance reassured her sister that she hadn't lost her purity that night. Sadly it didn't ratify the theory that she wouldn't.

22.

Pop of the champagne cork

Rosy twilight swept the vernal gales to rise and crest like billows over and around her legs that mid-May evening. Perched on the garden swing, she swayed with a small copy of *Hard Times* across her lap.

Miss Butterworth, Miss Cunningham, Miss Clarendon and Miss Rowley had many times explained to Isabel that it was necessary to attain the Higher School Certificate if she still wanted to apply to the Royal College – and there couldn't be a 'Higher School Certificate' without a 'School Certificate'.

Trotting out with small and dainty footsteps was without a doubt her sister's vain attempt at espionage.

'You're not making notes?' Anneliese confronted her – but in a bid to be inquisitive rather than anyhow *accusatory*.

'No, Anneliese ...' Isabel answered melodically. 'I am not making notes.'

'Have you read it?'

'I'm reading it, Anneliese. I'm reading it.'

Every two minutes Isabel allowed herself a 'break'. Absconding to the kitchen, she fetched a biscuit and proceeded to top up her glass of milk poured for *dipping* the biscuit. Later on she made herself some tea and then some cocoa and returned to take her seat again. These zigzag treks would almost throw off balance Anneliese's own regime of study.

En route in the bus the following morning Anneliese counted she had studied *Hard Times* for a total of two hundred and forty-six hours; scraping off the need for self-reproach in the event that she attained a poor result.

Isabel initially sat next to Olivia whom she now regularly met on their way. Two minutes into the journey she plopped herself down at the flank of her sister.

'Liesa . . .'

Staring out of the window, Anneliese was focussing on benches, reeds, tall strands of grass, granite and other inanimate objects.

'Mmm?'

'Could you just, momentarily, recount the story of *Hard Times*?'

'You didn't read it?'

'I read most of it.'

Anneliese knew that if she started now she would undoubtedly find that she lacked the sufficient number of quotes, had forgotten a tertiary character's name or was missing a part of the socio-political context. Begrudgingly she offered the rejoinder:

'We studied it at school for two months then had three to prepare for the *exam*. Why haven't you read it?'

'It's not a music exam.'

'But—' her voice was on the verge of breaking. 'I'm not – *you* wanted admission to a conservatoire! You're already *doomed* to fail!'

Isabel remained unstirred.

'Well, good.'

'How can you *say* that?'

'I'm not going to be a great performer anyway. So I stay at school, don't stay at school. A conservatoire would give me its *name*, not my *talent*. I'll fail this exam and go find myself someone to marry. At least that's a valuable exercise.'

For the sake of her exams she had skipped sessions for a period of seven weeks. As Anneliese espied Susanna at the threshold of the practice that first Wednesday back in therapy she watched her take hold of her pencil and start jabbing its tip chronically into the armrest, loath to stop until it snapped. The psychiatrist then hauled herself upright, skidded to her great commode and wrenched the last drawer open.

Stealthily Anneliese took a peek. Susanna reached out Freud's *Psychology of Love*. From it there stuck out a small yellow piece of paper bearing the word 'Anneliese'. Catching sight of all its neighbours in the drawer, she saw that all of them contained a label lodged at some page of the book. Each had a patient's name.

She hastened to point something out.

'I finished it.'

Susanna turned around.

'I thought so.'

Anneliese settled down on her chair.

'I didn't know you kept a drawer with . . . are those all the books your patients read?'

'Mmm-hmm.' She was unwilling to converse about it. 'I gather your results surpassed everyone else's.'

'I think so. Olivia didn't do all that badly.'

'You got seven distinctions?'

'Six.'

'And your only "pass" was Latin.'

'How . . .'

'I *listen*. I take it Isabel passed everything.'

'Yes, everything—'

'But physics.'

'Yes.'

Susanna cleared her throat.

'Well – that won't do her any harm.'

'No.'

Susanna was now drumming the fingers of one hand on the flat of the other.

'What will Miss Hampshire teach you in biology with the exhaustion of the annual syllabus?'

She waited for the answer as Anneliese tucked her handkerchief back in her sleeve.

'Miss Hampshire . . .' The girl sighed. 'She's really very sweet.' She linked her fingers and stared at the ceiling before daring to tackle her next thought aloud. 'She barely knows what reproduction is.' Anneliese was wondering if this would gauge a comment from Susanna. It didn't. 'It's not her *fault* per se . . . she's a botanist. Last week she made us go into the field and do compost tests with broad beans.'

Susanna's eyes opened wide as she forcefully gripped the arms of her chair.

'Really?'

'Well – it's not *that* outrageous—'

'No, it's just – I didn't – I . . .' Her voice trailed off. She was meditating something altogether different. 'You're not taught that they offer anything . . . *medicinal*?'

'No. Why – why, did you . . .'

'*No.*'

'You don't know what I was about to ask.'

'Did I experiment with "broad beans"? Why would I have *done* that?'

'I don't know.' Anneliese sniffed. 'You seem . . . *round* in the areas of your knowledge.'

Susanna had already spread her arms over the armchair's own but this time Anneliese caught sight of her left wrist. A thick scar lay over it: pale and skin-coloured. Conspicuously bumpy, it must have been around five centimetres wide. Anneliese had never noticed it before.

'What did you . . .'

And she waited for Susanna's interruption. Instead it was some time before she spoke.

'What?'

Anneliese knew her well enough to understand that she wasn't pretending but clueless. She let her eyes linger a little on the scar. It looked almost completely faded.

Susanna was beginning to absorb this strange behaviour. A flat, open-ended look became that day's first missile:

'Anneliese, why are you looking at me as though I'm the Marquise de Merteuil at the end of *Liaisons dangereuses*?'

'Erm . . .' She rested her chin on her palm and attempted to find a digression. 'I know nothing about *Liaisons dangereuses*, except that it was written prior to the Revolution.'

Encountering distaste, Susanna effused in a breathier voice than her wont:

'Foul novel. Is there a reason?'

'For what?'

'Did something happen?'

Anneliese felt absent-minded. Susanna morphed the question.

'Is there something you're not telling me prompting this glare? Something you remembered?'

'Erm . . . Isabel is almost certain that Cousin Elise has a boyfriend.'

'Is this causing jealousy?'

'No, no . . .' She wondered for how long she could prolong the tale. 'No, it's just speculative . . . Rather – I . . .'

But there was no chance the heavens could provide her with the hubris and the clout to catch Susanna out. Sadly for her, compassion was the greater force. So it was *her* turn to be cagey.

'You know . . . it's always astonished me that when my father died, I thought he had a mistress.'

Susanna's point-blank gaze was unassailable.

'A mistress?'

'Yes.'

'You never told me this.'

'No.'

'Why are you recollecting it now?'

Her mind was fast awander to seek detours for this ill-conceived concoction.

'I found a letter.'

Susanna furrowed her eyebrows.

'A letter from . . . *whom?*'

'It was a letter that my father had—'

It was the first time Anneliese had seen her baffled as Susanna's eyes abruptly met her wrist. She looked at it for a few seconds with disparagement; purportedly in wonder as to how it got there. Immediately she turned it over.

Having surmised the reason for her patient's trick, her voice was more demanding this time.

'A *letter*, Anneliese? Because you think that your *father* was an *adulterer?*'

'No, I . . .' Her voice faded into a whisper. 'I . . .'

She awaited Susanna's reaction. There was none. She was too busy keeping her left arm pressed firmly on the chair. After a moment she resumed.

'Would you care to tell me of the gradient on which your current feelings for your sister lie?'

So they replastered and repainted the same walls. Anneliese promised again that she would try to prod her sister, knowing that she wouldn't.

It was still light by nine o'clock. This didn't stop Susanna entering the corridor with a commanding voice riddled with taut exhaustion:

'Helga – see Anneliese home please.'

Returning to her practice she immediately shut the door.

Anneliese yelled from the corridor:

'Erm – it's not really necessarily . . . I'm sixteen now, and by the time Helga gets back it'll be very late.'

Close to indignation, the psychiatrist boomed from the living room:

'She's almost seventy; what letch is going to *touch* her?'

Understanding her English, Helga shrugged from indifference.

It would have been unprecedented if she hadn't used this opportunity for an interrogation. Her notebook of German vocabulary bounced in her pocket with each of the bus's swift jumps.

'Doesn't Susanna speak German?'

Helga scoffed.

'Of course.'

'So she addresses you in English only with her patients there?'

She belted out a measured, rhythmic laugh.

'No, no, no! She hasn't talked to me in German since we got off the ferry.'

'The "ferry"?'

'Since we came from Vysoké Mýto.'

'When was *that*?'

'After the war. Missy comes to England, starts behaving like a hoity-toity London woman and we're all to think she never knew a *word* of Czech. All things considered . . . she had an accent back then.'

'*Really?*'

'No one can swap his origins. Although – you'd have to pick that bone with *her*. She hired tutors.'

'You mean . . . for elocution?'

'That's right – *nine* of 'em she hired.' Helga grunted rudely and stared out in front of her. 'She then sacked nine of 'em. Between you-me, I think she got the accent through a man.'

'"*Through* . . . a man"?' Anneliese wondered if this might be some euphemism for a venereal disease.

'A married man. Married professor. Used to come to our place nineteen times a week. *God*, he would itch my nerves.'

'Oh.'

It took Anneliese twenty minutes of silence to swallow this new information.

Then she plucked her courage once again.

'I noticed . . . she has a . . . a scar on her wrist.'

Helga's eyes stretched oval.

'You mean she didn't get that *past* you? I haven't seen it in six years!'

'What do you . . .'

'She uses make-up! Hides the thing. You wouldn't blame her, knowing where it came from.'

Anneliese let the tension linger for a while. A whole minute had passed by when she enquired:

'Was there an accident?'

'No, no, no, no . . .' Helga hastily replied – and then began explaining with her hands again. 'Her mother did it. That not-so-little girl . . . it was easier to move a hippopotamus than change her mind. She spoke German at dinner.' Helga complained, great scoffs interjecting her sentences. 'We all told her many times – and all her brothers, all her sisters – all ten of 'em – "No German at the table." At school maybe; not at the table. So when she turned fifteen her mother warned her. But every single time she spoke, it was – nothing but *German*. Not a *word* of Czech. All her school work, all her lessons – were in Czech. But no; no *dialogue* in it. Her mother let the other times go – when they were in corridors, in private. But in the company of guests, at dinner . . .' She tut-tutted to herself. 'So finally she started placing it on a hot stove. Four years of that – it left a mark.'

'On the . . . she placed her wrist – on the stove for four years?'

'Just the edge of it. And that was Frau Czernuska at her worst; she wasn't usually hot-tempered.'

Anneliese's eyes had lost all focus.

"'Czernuska ...'" A blast of fatigue shot the girl. This didn't puncture her desire for discovery. 'Did her father ... mistreat her also?'

Helga shook her head vigorously, insistently.

'No, no. He overlooked *all* of her faults. She was *spoiled* by him. The other girls, the boys ... it was not *fair*. It was *not* ...' She swiped her arm along the air diagonally. *'Fair.'*

'She was his favourite?'

'She did work for him.' Helga's left hand was astutter as she recollected: 'He forgave her *everything*. And I mean – *everything*.'

'What kind of work?'

'All kinds of work.' she continued to express elaborately with the use of all ten fingers. 'For that, she got away with – *everything*.' Helga let a great sigh lapse. Then she reminisced most wondrously: 'But then again, you *know*, she was so quiet when the time came.'

'I'm sorry ... what time?'

'For the stove. She always saw it coming. First she would made crude jokes about Czech people in German – you know, callin' her brothers "*prase*"'s and – heaven forbid—' Helga crossed herself. 'The *other* "p" word – you know, pretending to be all grown-up, drinking her troughs of wine, looking no more than eleven with her glasses on. She couldn't see a *thing* without 'em. Still can't.'

'But ... She never ...'

'Well ...' Helga shrugged. 'You *learn* these things.'

'Learn ... *sight?*'

'Yes. And here was this madam, who always thought she was the oldest of the children – well, suffice to say, she *wasn't*. She prattled and prattled like a parrot that wouldn't shut up – and every time she spoke her energy fizzed like champagne in a dropped bottle. But then – one yell from the mistress, darting all the way over the room: *"Enough!"* And that was it. The pop of the champagne cork. She always knew that it was coming. When she did go to receive her punishment . . . Well, she received it *graciously*.' Helga looked outside to check their stop had not been missed. 'Nothing has changed.'

'I'm sorry – how?'

'Nothing has changed.'

It was time for Anneliese to disembark. She longed to prey on Helga with more conversation but she knew their session had concluded. Holding a smile firmly on her lips, she wished her a good evening and hopped off.

At home inside her skull tectonic plates were busily colliding, simulating quakes and quick explosions; leaving remnants of debris.

Exuding yawns that made her mouth the size of a bear's cave, she opened the door to find a pink envelope in her name. Isabel shouted, 'In here, Liesa!' from upstairs.

Anneliese ascended the steps and opened the pink envelope. The squiggly handwriting was too familiar and the news quickly reoriented her.

Bemused, Isabel examined her sister. Elation spread across her face: the kind that Anneliese met during moments of enlightenment. Isabel watched as she retraced the course of the letter and started once more from the top.

She lay across her bed with a pocket-sized Verdi biography and was chewing on segments of orange. 'What's happened?'

Anneliese responded with embarrassed anxiousness.

'Cousin Elise is engaged.'

'To do what?' Isabel popped another segment of orange into her mouth.

'She's engaged to be married.'

Her listener's eyes were inflated with fury.

'She's . . . that – that little ice cube, redhead prude is getting *married?!* Elise? Of all the girls we – what, how – *Elise? Our Elise?* Our cousin who doesn't *smile?*' she scoffed very loudly, coughing a little and almost choking on her half-bitten orange. 'I didn't know the stocking had it *in* her.'

'Obviously someone has fallen in love.' mused Anneliese in contemplation.

Isabel sat up on her knees. A fresh concept now enrobed her mind.

'Well – how much does Uncle Reuven earn?'

'It's not about that.'

'How do *you* know?'

'She says he's a teacher.'

'He's . . .' Isabel had to cough a little again. 'You mean it's a *man?* It's actually a grown-up . . . on a salary . . . a *man?*'

She was speaking of this 'man' as though Elise had found the fossil of a dodo bird.

'Yes.' Anneliese nodded. 'His name is Richard. She didn't mention his surname.'

'Well . . .' Instantly her hand made a dismissive motion. 'That's a stupid name. Too common.'

23.

Tempted fate

They left Croham Hurst clad in blue blazers veiling backless gowns that late November evening. Aunt Liesel was hosting the 'vort': a traditional Jewish engagement party.

'Isabel, I'm really not sure you chose very correctly.'

'I thought you liked the dress.'

'I like the dress . . . but *we're* not the ones who're engaged.'

'By this time we *could* be. Seventeen and on the brink of spinsterhood. In six years' time they'll think that we're old maids.' The noise of their footsteps intruded on silence. Isabel hastened to correct herself. 'They'll think *you're* an old maid.'

Five minutes from the Hotzenplotzes' house in Bethnal Green, she began an inquisition.

'Liesa?'

'Hmm?'

'Is there going to be any . . . ceremonious action tonight?'

'What do you mean?'

'Don't they break glass on their wedding day?'

'Yes. On their wedding day. Not prior to the wedding day.'

'Is anyone going to cut hair, or . . .'

'Just remain seated, don't ask where the butter is—'

'Why not?'

'They separate their poultry from their dairy. And please—'

'You mean there won't be butter?'

'It'll be somewhere in the refrigerator, I suppose. But you can't touch it.'

'I'm not Jewish.'

'Isabel . . . Please don't make comments.'

There was a grave silence.

'Not . . . *any* comments?'

'No.'

Isabel unsealed her lips and inadvertently produced her proof of indignation.

'Then can I ask you something first? Liesa, is it true that all Jewish men—'

'Isabel!'

'So it *is* true?'

Anneliese's sigh was lengthier than usual.

'It's important for you to know this *now?*'

'Why not?'

'You're not marrying the Jew. *Elise* is marrying the Jew.'

'Well, maybe I should tell her.'

'Isabel – she – she's known this since . . . since before she knew everything else regarding . . . the said subject. And why *you* need to know it is beyond my understanding.'

'I don't. I'm never going to marry a Jew.'

'No.' Anneliese fiddled with her thumb. 'Papa would have killed you.'

'Exactly.'

Anneliese mused for a while.

'You're not their type in any case.'

'Hmm?' Isabel appeared deeply offended. 'How do you know?'

'Well, you're too tall, not blonde...'

'But . . . Jewish girls aren't blondes.'

'No. That's why, if they wanted a *shiksa*, they would never pick
you.'

'What's a *shiksa*?'

Anneliese opened the gate of the Hotzenplotzes' home.

'Tell me what a *shiksa* is.'

'Hush.'

'Liesa!'

'*Hush!*'

Elise opened the door. Since her arrival at Cambridge she had
become aloof and even supercilious; these attributes both clashed
with and augmented her timidity.

This time she was radiant and bashful. Isabel watched her hands
trembling when she reached out to hug her. It was as always not
the most affectionate reception.

'Thank you so *much* for coming.'

The words were uttered in a whisper. Already the twins could
hear loud groans and melancholy howls and jibes along melodious
dialogue. They entered the dining room.

Elise was wearing an apron. She sounded out of breath as she
spoke.

'You can sit anywhere. I'm just helping Mother with the
cholent.'

Isabel disliked the guttural pronunciation. She remembered
that Elise spoke Hebrew. Few skills were beyond Elise; she was her
family's dear, little, pious, airy, academic, erudite and lustrous
creature. On top of that she now had a fiancé.

Isabel's feelings towards her weren't tepid.

Sat at their table, she found herself barely impressed by the
males. With a throaty accent bordering on German they were
exhibiting excitement and endlessly muttering a gamut of theories;
colliding in long-winded, litigious exchanges. There would either
be no response and the continuous spillage of some verbal tirade or
the answer would be tangentially overwrought. Listening was out

of the question. One old man in half-moon glasses – his voice growling and hoarse as though lined with cigar smoke – spent over four minutes recounting a joke:

'Moshe Leibowitz is walking round Vienna.'

His bearded neighbour enquired:

'Who is Moshe Leibowitz?'

'He isn't *real*, this is an anecdote.'

With raised hands the bearded man lamented:

'*How* was *I* supposed to know he wasn't real? You tell me "Moshe Leibowitz". That's Revekah's son, he's going to be a dental surgeon, he just finished school—'

'But would you let me tell the anecdote already?' the narrator proceeded. 'Moshe Leibowitz is walking round Vienna. He stops a rabbi passing by – the rabbi of his shul. The rabbi's carrying a watermelon.' The old man paused to scratch his moustache. 'So he asks him, "Rabbi, could you tell me how to get to Walcherstraße?" The rabbi tells him, "Hold my watermelon." And so he takes the watermelon. The rabbi responds,' – the old man raised his outstretched hands to demonstrate – '"And how would *I* know?" Then he takes the watermelon back from Moshe.'

Isabel failed to understand what was funny.

Anneliese observed an absence at the table. She turned to Elise when she came in with the *challah*:

'Where's Uncle Reuven?'

Elise feigned a smile.

'He isn't here.'

'I hope he's not ill.'

Her voice grew hoarse.

'No.'

'Then . . .'

Elise shrugged. Hands trembling, she whispered in Anneliese's ear:

'Papa doesn't like Richard.'

'Why does—'

'He says he's too secular. He's probably right, but . . . But he'll be there on my wedding day. He said he would. He's *going* to.' She giggled somewhat anxiously. 'I know he's *going* to.'

Elise returned to the kitchen and Isabel turned her head to her sister.

'What's *that?*'

'Uncle Reuven doesn't like Elise's fiancé; I don't think he's Orthodox.'

'The *scandal.*'

'Isabel . . .'

'At least *that's* interesting.' Circumspecting the room, she whispered almost contemptuously: 'Why do they wear plaits?'

'What plaits?'

'The men. They have plaits on the sides of their heads.'

Anneliese inhaled deeply.

'You've never read *anything* about Judaism?'

'I know they're stingy businessmen.' she whispered. 'Is there much need for any more? Why would I want to know? It's the religion of the ginger ice cube.'

'She isn't the world's only Jew!' Anneliese hissed through her teeth.

'Our father would have hated being here as much as I do.'

Liesel had barely greeted them, so pressed was she for time. Bearing a fresh dish with every new entrance she appeared flustered, nervous, discombobulated: in a huff as though a fly were obstructing her personal space. Elise was still jittery.

'May I help with anything?' Anneliese offered.

'No, no.'

'What time will your fiancé be arriving?'

'Very soon.'

Elise forced a smile and afterwards maintained a long glare in the corridor's direction, awaiting the sound of the doorbell.

Every few minutes Liesel patted Elise's shoulder, reassuring her all would proceed as planned.

Every time Isabel caught sight of this she couldn't help but smirk.

When Elise finally took her seat it was quarter to eight. The girls had arrived at seven. There was no sign of 'Richard'.

'Elise, tell me – what does your *bashert* do?' asked another bearded man.

'He's a schoolteacher.'

The bristly, bearded man seemed hard of hearing.

'A doctor?'

Elise was taken by surprise.

'No, a schoolteacher.'

'But some teachers, you know … they are doctors; they have …' His hand motioned as if he were swirling a wineglass. '*Doctorates*.'

Liesel had just walked in from the kitchen, an apron still around her waist. Elise looked at her mother in panic to tell her to take over the reins.

'Let her *be*, Baruch. He is a schoolteacher. He is no penniless *academic*; he earns a decent *crust*.'

'Ah … well,' he raised his glass, 'mazel tov.'

Liesel eyed the man contentiously.

'*Mazel tov*? Enough already with your "mazel tov"; from now – that's no more till the *t'naim*.'

'You're waiting till the wedding?'

'Yes.'

'But *Liesel* …' He rubbed his beard. 'It is the *tradition*—'

Liesel waved her hand and spoke with bellowed, aspirated words.

'You with your *tradition*! The Greenbergs, Aldmans, Lewises …' she counted on her fingers, '*All* of them waited for the wedding for the *t'naim*.'

Baruch shook his head in despair.

'That poor young *man*.'

'Ah – it's the *man* that's poor? So it's the *man* that's poor?'

He opened his palms.

'It's *your* decision when to honour the *t'naim*.'

'It was *their* decision. Both of them agreed to it; they're old enough.'

'But, Liesel! How was I supposed to *know*? You have a vort – that means your daughter's getting married. Why don't you be *happy*? Very rarely in our lives can we declare we have good reason to be happy.'

Another ten minutes passed uneventfully. Liesel beckoned Elise to come help her 'tidy up' in the kitchen until the arrival of Richard.

Isabel excused herself, pretending she was going to the bathroom. Instead she waited in the corridor and eavesdropped.

Liesel was frantic and sighing.

'*What* kind of man? What *kind* of man?' she cried in a whisper, taking care not to let her exasperated words bounce off the house's walls.

Elise was timid and red-cheeked.

'Mama, I told you; he said he'd call before he got into his car.'

Liesel couldn't take it anymore. She slammed one of her dishes down atop the kitchen surface.

'*Exactly!* And it's eight o'clock! What are you telling me, Elise, hmm? Are you telling me this man of yours will arrive less than an hour late? There is left . . .' She darted a fierce look at the clock. 'Three minutes!'

'Well, Mama . . .' Elise appeared afflicted by a painful stomach ache. She was running out of breath. 'He probably forgot.'

'Forgot? *Forgot?!* You think *I'm* going to let *my* daughter marry a man who *forgets* how to use the telephone? You think *I'm* that kind of mother? I should have listened to your father.'

Elise's eyes were oozing tears. Her words were choked. Approaching Liesel, she placed a hand on her arm.

'No, Mama ... he's *so* reliable. He's so good. I just don't understand ...'

'What?' Liesel raised her hands in the air. 'What is it that you fail to understand, hmm? Because I'll tell you *one* thing: no man I have ever seen – not at the Greenbergs' house, not in the Mendel family with their nine married cousins – not one of those inflated Spiellman sisters – has a man who can't guess how to use the telephone. That is what *I* have seen. Perhaps among your Anglican friends, there is another custom, hmm?'

'Oh, Mama ... he is *not* secular! He knows the Torah off by heart!'

'"Off by heart", she says. We haven't seen him *once* at *shul*.'

'Yes, but I told you; he goes every Saturday – but somewhere else.'

Liesel grunted.

'This "somewhere else" does not exist.'

After two minutes of implorations and laments the telephone rang. Liesel sprang out of the kitchen and on her way pleaded with guests to 'excuse her'.

She returned in just a few seconds and quietly beckoned Elise.

Isabel, in the eyes of Anneliese, was still 'in the bathroom'. Already nonetheless she had transferred herself to the spot of the living room door, where Elise was now taking her call.

The ginger ice cube was gulping and speedily running out of breath. Isabel's hearing palpated her sobbing.

'But Richard, I think it's a little hasty ...' Her voice cut off. It was no longer full of air but thin and flimsy. 'You should at least come to the dinner ...' Her sleeve began to wipe away her tears. 'Everyone's waiting for you. Come tonight – tomorrow I will tell them.'

Apparently it was to no avail. After a bout of weeping almost silently, Elise replaced the receiver. Liesel dashed into the corridor to put her arms around her daughter. Isabel succeeded in her inconspicuousness.

'He said he was sorry . . . he was being dishonest. He blamed himself.'

'Dishonest? In what way dishonest?' the scorned Liesel demanded to know.

'I don't know . . . he said that marrying me would be dishonest in God's eyes.'

Liesel's eyes now seemed more oval than before. She held her crying daughter in her arms.

'Still . . .' Liesel gasped. 'I don't understand his problem.'

'Mama!' cried Elise. 'He loves another woman! That's his problem! This is what he's *hiding* from me!'

In such a situation Elise was due credit. She was at the very least astute enough to realise her fiancé was in love with someone else. The knowledge that she had that brand of wisdom somewhat rattled Isabel.

But Isabel had rarely welcomed such a smugness. Returning to the table, it was challenging for her to check the rising corners of her mouth.

Anneliese had gleaned her motives.

'Well?'

Isabel looked at her, swallowed in a weak attempt to close her smile and shook her head most slowly.

'You mean . . . it's off?'

'Oh . . .' Isabel let a cool breath escape her mouth. 'It is so *very* off.'

On their way home Isabel skipped down the pavement, whistling in a whisper slow to wane the opening lyrics of 'Let's Face the Music and Dance.'

Anneliese's voice was blunt in comparison.

'You're not supposed to find *your* merriment in others' misery.'

'La-di-da! No part of the Bible demands that, Liesa – no part!'

24.

Ruffled feathers

Toiling away at arduous thought, Anneliese began to click her mind into a range of different modes to ask herself if it was possible to unlock doors without their keys. It had been one of those white dismal English days on which midday was twilight. Looking out into Susanna's garden she watched balls of escalating snow surrender to the ground like the Niagara Falls.

Susanna had been standing at the window with her arms crossed for three quarters of an hour. Personifying this new storm as though it were an undermanned and wearied army, she was waiting anxiously for its retreat. London transport had come to a halt. Taxi companies were out of order. It was already nine o'clock at night. Anneliese stared at her, resisting the urge to chew on her nails but inspecting them seriously.

Finally she heard a great sigh leave Susanna's mouth. Without turning to face Anneliese she gave in, the usual languor vaporous across her vocal cords:

'Helga will find you something in place of pyjamas. Probably one of her own . . . dresses.' There was a pause until she added with a masked acidity: 'If she can call them *dresses*.'

Anneliese wanted to jump for all her radiating happiness. Instead she gulped this urge down and retorted shyly:

'It doesn't look as though there's another choice, does it?'

Susanna was disgruntled.

'No.'

'Can I call Isabel to tell her that I won't be coming home?'

'The phone is by the sofa.'

She exited the dining room to give Anneliese privacy.

It only took two rings for Isabel to pick it up.

'Liesa! I've been worried sick; you're going to be stuck there *forever!*'

Anneliese struggled not to sound gleeful.

'Mmm-hmm.'

'What – where are you staying?'

It was a rushed and ill-thought answer:

'In the church.'

Isabel was confounded.

'You mean . . . the vicar lives *inside?*'

'Of course not. It's the House of *God.*'

'Doesn't he live near?'

'He can't get home either, Isabel.'

'*God?*'

'No, *nobody* can. We're going to camp out here.'

'Well – tell me the address, Liesa. Maybe I can come and we can camp out together.'

'But – no, I don't think you *understand.* Nothing is going anywhere, so neither of us can move.'

'I'll walk there; it can't be that far. We'll trot our way back together.'

'It's *very* far, Isabel.'

'How far could it *possibly* be?'

'Harrow.'

The pitch of her voice grew to three times its size.

'*Harrow?*' Anneliese heard her gasp and pant on the phone's other end. 'What's so special about the church in . . . *Harrow?*'

'It's one of the most renowned Presbyterian churches in the country, Isabel.'

'What's it called?'

'It's called St – Listen, Isabel, I'm using up the church's donations with this telephone call. I'll call you tomorrow morning when I leave.'

'But—'

'Have a nice evening, Isabel.'

She slammed down the receiver. When she looked up Susanna was already there and scrutinising her with staid haughtiness.

'Sorry.' Anneliese gushed.

'Isabel thinks you go to church every Wednesday?'

'Yes.'

Susanna analysed this frostily.

'A slick machination.'

She crossed the room to look for a tome on the bookshelf. Anneliese followed her.

'What do you mean, "machination"?'

'We'll discuss it next week, Anneliese.'

As violent as a pigeon's tapping beak, heavier flakes of snow struck the glass.

Susanna had obtained a heavy hardback and was scouring through it.

'Do you have something to do? Homework?'

'It's two days before Christmas.'

'So?'

'And I've already done my homework.'

Susanna eyed her bookcase. A few moments passed before she reached out an enormous volume and extended it: Robert Tigerstedt's *Textbook of Human Physiology*.

'Make notes.'

'Why?'

'You said you wanted to apply for medicine at Lady Margaret Hall.'

'Yes.'

'So . . . you'll need that. Very much.'

'Where did *you* go?'

Susanna leant against a chair.

'St Mary's.'

'So then . . . Oxford didn't take you.'

'I refused them.'

'*Really?*' Anneliese saw this as a chance to shoot point blank. 'I would have thought they might have had a problem with your English.'

She was unruffled as usual.

'*My* English?'

'Yes.'

'Why?'

'You're Czech. Back then your English was quite minimal.'

Susanna looked fed up and so the customary row of blinks ensued.

'Both of them took me; I didn't like their style. I'm not pathetic enough to retrieve my acceptance letters to appease you. I've no idea where Helga even stored them.'

'What do you mean "both"?'

'Cambridge also. Read the textbook. You can keep it.'

'Don't you use—'

'No – I know it off by heart.'

Susanna left her to read over seven hundred pages.

Helga brought Anneliese beef and potatoes. After dinner she began to read. There was something to do with segmentation and peristalsis. After flicking through ninety pages she read through a long paragraph on the pyloric opening.

Two years before she would have relished any opportunity to

swell her bank of knowledge. Now she found herself incapable of being its receptor.

Living in another, foreign state, familiar with a jungle of all kinds of novel flora, fauna and exotic lakes, she could no longer undertake a pathway leading to her previous regime. Somewhere it existed – one day like a stowaway she would be carried back to her safe harbour; to the joy that had once gushed along her system from a reservoir of intellectual delights. For now there was no lighthouse in this sea that could illuminate it. Maybe she was blind to it.

These ponderings infused her skull with a thick mist. When she next looked up at the clock it was nineteen past midnight. She had spent over two hours . . . doing nothing.

Susanna entered and demanded to know:

'Are you going to bed? I'm not *commanding* you. I need the room.'

She rose and took the heavy medical compendium.

'Good night.'

'Good night.'

Helga handed Anneliese one of her nightgowns: it was twice her breadth. She sat in the bed of the guest room wondering how to unlock half the others.

Under no circumstances could she leave that house without Susanna's papers. She would go to any lengths to fetch them.

Helga was asleep; Susanna was downstairs engrossed in yet another tome.

Anneliese posited herself on the landing and looked down through its bars. She watched Susanna to ensure that she was not performing anything extraordinary.

As though in Anneliese's presence she would do something extraordinary.

It came to three o'clock and Anneliese was still divining a clandestine means to break and enter. There was a door on the other end of the landing Anneliese was sure led to the attic.

Susanna was flouncing in her bedroom, door half-ajar.

Anneliese espied her stealthily approaching what appeared to be her dressing table. The psychiatrist took out a small glass bottle containing a transparent solution. Then she removed a syringe from some small wooden chest. Dipping the syringe to fill it, she immediately stuck it in her wrist for an injection.

After storing away her equipment she went out of her room and raced once again down the stairs.

Never had Anneliese felt more devoid of hope. Here she was in the abode of all the information she could want – and it was resolutely unaccommodating. It seemed that there was nowhere she could move without inciting at least *some* rage on Susanna's part; no door she could crack open without fearing that Susanna might diminish her already insufficient frame with rabid eyes. Yet every answer she had sought was registered no farther than two metres from her whereabouts.

After vigilantly staking out the area on quiet tiptoe she approached the attic door. Its handle was of gold; the kind susceptible to noise with every touch. Anneliese enrobed it with her fingers and provoked a chunky squeak. Immediately she backed away.

A pen lay in her bag. Targetting the guest room, she procured her instrument before returning to the attic door. The shiny end was dipped into the lock.

It made a violent metal clang that startled her. She was sure Susanna would ascend the steps in a few moments and deliver some sardonic comment.

It didn't happen. Neither would the door come open.

Anneliese crouched down on her knees and peered into the gap between the threshold and the door. A small staircase was behind it with a slithering, pervasive draught that sinuously slipped along the steps. She had to pinch her nose to in order to curtail the possibility of sneezing.

Rising back up, she heard a jarring click. Dashing to her room immediately, she didn't close the door so she could eavesdrop.

It was Helga. She was on her way to the bathroom and tried turning the knob. The door wouldn't burst open. She tried again. It was still stuck.

Anneliese heard her mutter in German:

'That damn weasel.'

Helga returned to her room. When she came out again her hand was in possession of a key. She used it to unlock Susanna's room and went inside, leaving it in the keyhole. Upon returning to the corridor her hand was in possession of another key. The door was still ajar.

Anneliese's legs were cold. Too quivery was she to move. Helga came out of the bathroom and returned to her room. It took Anneliese's courage twenty minutes to determine whether she should go inside Susanna's unlocked bedroom. When she finally entered and switched on the light her eyes clapped on a desk in the corner. On it were around a dozen keys arranged in some peculiar order.

In her panic she was seized by an impulse. She had to obtain the solution Susanna had used intravenously. Miss Frobishire could identify it . . . possibly.

She headed to Susanna's dressing room table and began prodding around in the drawers. There were some glass bottles containing different solutions, some beakers, some cylinders: a hoard of equipment Anneliese would have never expected to see in a bedroom – especially inside a dressing table topped with an immense cosmetics case and an array of tall perfume flasks.

The recognisable bottle stood in the sixth drawer. There must have been three hundred millilitres there.

Quickly she rummaged around for an empty perfume bottle. All of them were noticeably large and crystal-like; their absence would be easily perceptible.

Anneliese crossed to different sides of the room; scouring hither and thither. In a chest of drawers she came across a wooden box. Inside it lay a small pink blanket that had black embroidery. Its letters spelt out 'Lily'.

She tried another drawer; it was to no avail. Finally she returned to the dressing room table and reached out a miniscule cylinder, wondering how to abscond with a glass beaker filled with ten ounces unnoticeably.

That problem she would deal with later. After performing the required decantation she traversed the room to study all the keys across the desk.

It took Anneliese a while to decrypt the construction. When she did a warm smile piqued her countenance. The keys were all arranged in order of their rooms: the top one was the attic's.

She clasped it in her hand and exited, turning the lights off.

Dropping the liquid-filled cylinder off in her room, she cautiously slid it under her bed. It struggled to fit.

The click of the attic door opening was softer this time. Shutting it behind her, Anneliese clambered up the cold stone steps in the dark on all fours. Upon feeling the absence of a consecutive step she began to crawl forward. The new ground was dank, wooden, creaky and dusty. Her knees kept bumping into cracks across the floor. Moisture was sticking to her fingers.

She stood up. Reaching her hand up in the air, she realised that the ceiling was much higher than expected.

In search of light she walked in careful little circles. There was none; only a window. Moonlit snow illuminated her vicinity. As she neared the glass pane she discerned the outline of a table with a handful of thin candles. A drawer inside stored matches.

Armed with a kindled candle, she now gleaned the contours of a host of Bunsen burners, beakers, flasks and Petri dishes, stacks of needles and syringes, two microscopes and strips used for thin layer chromatography. Next to those was a kymograph.

Anneliese rummaged through those graduated cylinders and beakers, taking them one by one, looking for signs of a drawer or a cabinet or a box. The wax was starting to pour down and scorch her thumb.

Gradually she crawled over the floor to inspect what lay under the desks. Still nothing. It seemed the attic was littered exclusively with equipment and candles.

Then the heel of her left foot was scraped by a sharp corner. Yelping in pain, she felt her skin assume a grated texture. It was a wooden chest of drawers. Her cut ignored, she opened the top drawer. Towels were in there. Feeling through its contents with her hand she had no luck. In the second drawer she found a set of undressed blankets. In the third she came across some supplementary bedsheets next to pillow cases. In the bottom one there were more bedsheets and a row of pillows. Yanking one out, she began smoothing its surface with her fingers as her wax dripped on its cover. Nothing but the sound of crinkled feathers. She turned it over. Passing her hand along the cotton she abruptly heard another kind of crinkle: the sound of a leaf.

She removed the case. The pillow was sewn together; seemingly stuffed with down. She began tugging at the thread. It took a minute for three stitches to come tryingly undone: a fissure into which she could stick just two fingers. She persevered. It took two minutes for her to be able to thrust her hand into the case. A flurry of feathers spewed out – along with a papery foreign object.

It was a file made of card. Susanna's incoherent scribble on the front read:

Quisqualamine: 41.

Anneliese stuck her hand in and thrust out more files, each of them heavy. They contained labels such as *Dopamine: 212*, *Vicia Faba: 74*, *GABA*, which Anneliese deciphered: '*gamma-Amino-butyric Acid.*' The heaviest one was called simply 'Niemann'.

Anneliese had heard of 'Niemann' in the medical field only once – as a fatal children's disease.

Taking all of them into one hand, she stuffed the damaged pillow underneath the others in the drawer. Clasping the heavy files Anneliese closed it, collected some loose feathers in her hand, blew out the candle and proceeded down the steps.

Never had she been so fruitfully self-pleased. The remainder of the night was spent stood on the landing spying on Susanna.

Two hours into the inspection she watched the psychiatrist loosen the pen from her hand and then rise from the table, taking care to tuck in the chair. She left her book and notepad there. It was five thirty in the morning and she looked neither famished nor tired. Swooping into the kitchen, the train of her dress brushed the floor with no lag. She was as buzzed as someone who had risen in the afternoon after a sleep of sixteen hours.

Anneliese pulled herself over the rail of the landing. Fearing an imminent somersault, she tacitly treaded until she had come down the stairs.

The light was switched on in the kitchen. Susanna reached her hand into an opened cupboard. A blue sachet was pulled out; it resembled a teabag. Susanna examined it, attempting to read the text on the back. Then she neared it to her eyes and frowned. It was clear she was in dire need of glasses.

All of a sudden Anneliese could hear the tread of a delayed hippopotamus. Helga emerged in her white sleeveless nightgown, huffing and complaining without verbal execution. Anneliese was terrified that she might have the power of a teacher and rebuke her. In fact she swerved around her absent-mindedly – failing to notice she had taken refuge at the corner of the staircase.

Susanna heeded no attention to these footsteps. Helga finally stood at her back and snatched the blue sachet from the palm of her hand. Unruffled by this violent gesture, Susanna asked with an untethered volume:

'Are they the bluebell seeds?'

Helga issued a great 'Hmmph'.

'Can I have them?'

Thus began Helga's prattling in German:

'I know why you want to use them.'

'They have medicinal properties.' Susanna argued lazily in English.

'*Tish tosh!*' exclaimed Helga in German. 'You want to send them there to *her!*'

'She only needs the bluebell seeds.'

'And the postage – so expensive!'

'She only needs the bluebell seeds.' Susanna stressed more dryly.

'We made an arrangement.' Helga continued in German. 'My part of the garden is *mine*. Your peonies are *yours*. You want to send your mother bluebell seeds? You be a big girl and go out and get them and go to the post office *yourself.*'

Offering zero response, Susanna didn't wish Helga good night when she left. She merely stared into the contents of the cupboard and twisted her lips, seemingly in search of an appropriate substitute.

Helga had been gone for four minutes when the relaxed Anneliese heard Susanna declare:

'I'm not giving you barbiturates.'

Anneliese didn't budge. She scarcely even knew to whom this was addressed.

'Go up and read Tigerstedt.'

The girl cleared her throat. She stood up to confront her mistake and took stealthy steps to the kitchen.

'I came down to fetch a glass of water.'

Susanna opened another cupboard, extracted a glass and turned on the tap. Traipsing to the other side, she extended the glass as the tap ran. Anneliese circumambulated her without Susanna flicking either eyelid.

The flow of the tap stopped and Anneliese drank.

'If you're awake, why can't we have another session?'

'You have news since we last saw each other?'

'No.'

Susanna shut the cupboard forcefully, banging it accidentally. Sliding along the floor she returned to the dining room.

Anneliese slept for two hours that night. It would have been more if she hadn't been awakened by the sound of murmured discord slowly being amplified.

Clutching the schoolbag that stored all her plunder, she carefully came down the stairs. Quickly she observed how Susanna – newly attired in a light blue dress – made testy efforts to evade her maid and reimmerse herself in study but failed every time; parading back and forth in vain to stress her argument. At the conclusion of the debate all Anneliese heard was:

'It's about what your measuring tape has put *off*, Helga, not what any waist has put *on*.'

Helga served Anneliese pancakes with golden syrup. The wireless was reporting that transport was business as usual.

Susanna entered the kitchen momentarily, a pen and piece of paper in her hand.

'Helga – what's Czech for "plush velvet"?'

In response she received a boar's grunt and the German response:

'What the Hell do you want from me now?'

'"*Plüschsamt*" in Czech?'

Helga gave her the answer. Susanna swiftly returned to the dining room. Five minutes later she stood and waited at the threshold for the girl to finish breakfast. Anneliese interpreted her prominent impatience as an order to depart.

Outside the door of the house she enquired:

'Aren't you going out to get the bluebell seeds?'

Susanna's haughtiness was now glossed over by a brazen charm.

'Why – are you offering?'

Anneliese had no idea if she should take this seriously.

'I—'

'See you next week, Anneliese.'

When she closed the door her scar was visible again.

25.

Fastening the halyard

Isabel rushed down in a shimmery pale pink gown, a black shawl draped over her shoulders.

'You'll be cold.' Anneliese pointed out on that Saturday evening in February, wondering if Isabel had purchased the new dress with income from the sale of Josef's car.

'Oh . . .' She was short of breath, attempting to fix up her hair in the mirror. 'This young man who's,' – she had to catch her breath – 'who's taking me – he has a car.'

Anneliese put down the book she had been attempting to read.

'A young man with a car?'

'Mmm-hmm.'

'Oh.'

Isabel continued plying the comb through her hair. A few minutes later the doorbell rang.

'Oh, *Liesa*,' she hastened to add before heading to the door, 'could you put on your pretty red cardigan? You look a little . . . comfortable.'

Anneliese gazed at her clothes. She had deemed her checked red and black dress becoming.

'*No.*'

'Well, be nice to him. He's an *adult*.'

Isabel opened the door. In walked a blond-haired man of well over six feet who looked a little over twenty-five. Appearing adrift, his blue eyes targeted the ground and he muttered 'good evening' to Isabel. Both hands were in his pockets.

Anneliese volunteered her own greeting. He scratched his neck before a curt response:

'Good evening.'

Isabel excused herself, promising she would return in a matter of minutes. Anneliese and the still-nameless gentleman stood waiting in the corridor.

'Would you care to . . . come into the living room?'

He nodded without saying a word. As he entered the living room he scarcely acknowledged Anneliese, too busy trying to straighten his collar. The man's eyes were sunken in a frown.

Anneliese lingered without any dialogue to offer. Finally she opted to stretch out her hand.

'I'm Anneliese.'

Clearing his throat, he extended his own in a shake scarcely tenable.

'Edmund Sawyer.'

'Do . . . sit down.'

'No, no. I'll wait.'

Bothered was he and slightly aggravated; maybe even bored. Perhaps he was just arrogant.

Circumspecting the room with pursed lips, his tongue roving inside his mouth, he appeared to be looking with an air of expectancy.

'What do you do?'

'I . . . I go to Croham Hurst with Isabel.'

He slowly moved his head before unleashing a full nod.

'Yes, yes . . . It's not really great on the *alumni* front, is it?'

'I . . . I don't follow.'

'Well – you don't have – you know . . .' He sniffed and wiped his nostrils with the back of his finger. 'Many girls going to Newnham.'

'Newnham . . .'

'College, Cambridge. It's where my sister went.'

'Oh.'

He moved around a little in his spot and stared intently at his wristwatch.

Anneliese resumed her questioning.

'Do you . . . work?'

'Yes.'

She nodded again. Nonplussedness propelled her to detract her gaze.

'What field is it you—'

'I'm still studying to be a barrister.'

'At university?'

'No, no.' He laughed. 'For the bar.'

Anneliese clasped her hands together.

'Your name is Edmund Sawyer . . . Is your family related to the – to the family that runs the firm?'

He chuckled discomfitedly, looking up in the air.

'Yes . . . we're *notorious*.'

Anneliese's heart began to pound. When Isabel came down the stairs she informed Edmund in a gaspy voice:

'Would you just – excuse – for a moment. Thank you.'

Hurrying out of the room she grabbed Isabel by the wrist and dragged her against her will into the kitchen.

'Liesa!' she gasped in frustration.

'That young man is a *Sawyer*.'

'Well – yes, I know. That's his family.'

'No – he's a *Sawyer*. He comes from the *Sawyer* family of *lawyers*; the ones who're in the papers almost *every* day; the ones Daphne mentioned all those years ago. Everyone suspects them of being involved in East End gangs and . . .' She lowered her voice even more. 'All kinds of judicial . . . shenanigans.'

'I know, Liesa.'

'They ...' Inching closer to Isabel, Anneliese muttered hesitantly: 'They – palm – they lend London courts . . . *palm* oil.'

Isabel offered a naïve blink.

'Not . . . *vegetable* oil—'

Anneliese squeezed her hand round her wrist like an animal's halter.

'*Ow!*' Isabel yelled.

'For exorbitant fees they will represent murderers they know . . .' Anneliese cleared her throat. '*Did* . . . it. They even have rivals – the Remington firm, who are apparently *worse*; they reserve Oxford and Cambridge places for children of judges if they're willing to lead jurors . . . you *know.*'

Isabel was unmoved.

'*No.*'

'How could you . . . aren't you *frightened?* Do you know where he's going to *take* you?'

'He graduated only last year. He's only twenty-three; the youngest brother. He's taking me to see *Follow the Fleet.*'

'But you've already seen it.'

'And he's taking me to see it again. Now, *please*—' Relying on her domineering height she shifted Anneliese's shoulders with both hands. 'Would you *excuse* me?'

'Isabel!' hissed Anneliese. Having raced into the corridor, she was already attempting to take the arm of this remote, haughty male specimen. Rather than seizing hers he let it hang.

'I'll be back by eleven, Liesa.' Isabel called.

Anneliese spent the next three hours lying on the sofa in the living room; peeling herself from it to peer out of the window every five to ten minutes. She picked at the skin on her fingernails and buried her face in her arms. The clock struck eleven. Then it struck half past. Only at twelve minutes to midnight the bell rang.

She approached the door and looked through the keyhole. It was Isabel.

'Sorry. I left my key behind.' Anneliese looked at her as though she had an extra finger on her hand. Isabel took notice. 'Why are you . . . I actually enjoyed myself, and thank you.'

She dashed through the corridor and went to the kitchen to make herself cocoa.

Anneliese followed her and tried to lean against the kitchen wall.

'I don't think you should be implicated in that family.'

'*Family?*' Isabel bellowed. 'I've so far only met *him*.'

'I did assume you had the intention to *marry* at some point.'

'Not *yet*. It's merely a *rehearsal*.' She placed the pot on the stove. 'Do you want some?'Anneliese shook her head. 'Tough, 'cause I don't believe you.'

'Isabel . . . these aren't *rumours*. They're in the papers every day. I hear people discussing them at the bus stop. Four years ago a Remington got shot.'

'What has he got to do with the Remingtons?'

'They're all of the same *cloth*.'

'Oh, really?'

'Really.'

'Well, he told me his grandfather only opened their firm forty years ago. The Remingtons go back around a century, right?'

Anneliese inanely comforted herself by rubbing one arm with the other.

'You like him *so* much?'

Isabel was stirring little blocks of chocolate into steaming milk.

'Hmm?'

'Are you . . . really so keen on him?'

The entrails of Isabel began to coil round each other, plaiting like hemp in a halyard.

'He's unpredictable.'

Only one precedent persuaded her to harbour such a thought. He had spent half the film with his left hand high on her leg.

'So . . . should I expect to see more of him?'

'Yes.'

'For the near future?'

Isabel finished with the chocolate and placed it back into the cupboard.

'For a future broader than the "near".'

The cupboard door slapped as she closed it.

26.

Trekking hills without an overcoat

A landmark in her sister's social existence it was: one of those days when Anneliese would not be home.

Catching sight of her already dressed in a black and white three-quarter sleeve dress with a black jacket around it, Isabel slowly descended the stairs in a sleep-deprived stupor.

Her voice was uncustomarily croaky.

'Liesa, the tap . . .'

'The plumber should be coming after Easter.'

Anneliese picked up her bag.

'No, Liesa . . . you woke me up.'

'Oh, sorry!' She was too giddy to be sorry.

Isabel headed to the kitchen where, for cordiality's sake, Anneliese sprinted to issue a proper good morning.

'You look . . . decorous.' Isabel observed. 'Are you meeting Daphne?'

'No.'

'Vanessa?'

'No.'

'Who . . . would you be meeting?'

'Oh – I have an appointment with my epigraphist.'

'Your . . . is that like a . . .' Isabel scratched her scalp. 'Is that like an endocrinologist?'

Anneliese's eyes simmered with amusement.

'No. An epigraphist transcribes engraved text.'

'En . . .'

'I discovered some,' – she gulped and had to inhale – 'some documents whose penmanship was quite frankly, illegible . . . There's an epigraphist in the Classics Department at King's College . . . it's not his job but, erm . . .'

There was silence.

'He must be a very nice man to work on something totally irrelevant to him for free.'

'Yes, yes.' Anneliese omitted to mention the three pounds she had transferred to him.

'Did he know Papa?'

'Yes.' she lied.

'That's probably why. What are these papers?'

Her eyes grew taller.

'They're . . . they vary. The matters discussed are chemical, pharmacological, pathological, neurological . . .' She tucked in a strand of hair behind her ear. 'Do you remember when the Nobel Prizes were awarded in December?'

Taking a sip, Isabel hid her nose in her mug.

'No.'

Anneliese's speech was rushed and lined with a layer of polish: an emblem of glee.

'Otto Loewi, this German pharmacologist – he won for Medicine, having discovered there were synapses across the brain that were *chemical*.' She sighed melodically. 'Previously it had been believed all synapses could only be bioelectrical.' Isabel could barely muster the sufficient falsehood for a smile. 'So . . .' her voice became even breathier, 'I'm conducting some research and I'm going to my epigraphist.' The listener nodded. 'Have a good day.'

'Good – Oh Liesa, would you get some Easter eggs? I saw some with this decoration that I've never see—'

The door slammed shut.

Isabel passed the day dallying around shops, purchasing four bars of Fry's Five Centre to embellish their 'Chocolate Easter Cake': a new addition to their runty inventory of traditions.

Arriving at Professor Naumann's office at King's College, Anneliese found a man weathered by labour. His round black spectacles were sliding down his nose. It had been her initiative to meet with him on Good Friday despite his reluctance. For Easter 1937 he had bought tickets to fly back to Hamburg to be with his family. During his telephone call he had insisted on returning her papers at the beginning of April, a time which – to the ears of Anneliese who had anticipated this delivery for well over two months – did not appear appealing.

He was a ruffled and bulging man with dyed sandy hair unbecomingly curling in different directions.

'These papers . . .' he announced. 'The terminology contained . . . I think I had more success when transcribing the stone engravings of hendecasyllabic verse in Aeolic Greek.'

She nodded in uneasiness.

'I'll be able to suss, Professor Naumann—'

He presented approximately three hundred sheets to her.

'Take them away from me.'

'Those are the transcriptions?'

Resting his hands on his desk, he used it to set himself upright.

'In many drafts.'

'And the originals?'

'In the box.' He pointed to one on the desk.

Anneliese examined it.

'You did make sure that . . .'

'Yes, yes. Now, please – I must catch the fourteen-fifty-seven to the airport.'

He put on his coat.

'Thank you so much.'

'I am not a chemist, Miss van der Holt.'

'I know.'

'It's very possible I miswrote many, *many* terms.'

She rushed her acquiescent nod.

Isabel was making shepherd's pie for dinner. She had tried to sprinkle salt from its container on the baking tray; a pound of it had dashed through like an avalanche. Standing agog at the counter, she wondered how much she could sieve.

Anneliese half-ran and half-skipped home and through her journey could have sworn that the cool breeze outside was filtering her heart. With unbridled velocity she burst through the house:

'Liesa—'

'Not now, not now!!'

'Liesa, I made us shepherd's pie!' It was the first time Isabel had made them dinner in the past five months. 'I also made a chocolate cake!'

Already Anneliese was racing up the stairs.

She threw the bag down on her bed and took out the two piles of papers. Having jerked her bedside table's drawer, she hastily removed a bar of extra bitter Fry's: comfort to provide her either celebration or conciliation. Lying flat on the bed on her stomach Anneliese took out the chocolate to munch on the bar as she opened the folder of bulky transcriptions, stilling her quivering hand in the process. She could have told herself the papers would be full of fiction; either made-up wordings of Professor Naumann or deliberate fabrications by Susanna to deflect her readers' noses from the veritable theories they would never find.

Then again that was unlikely.

Isabel munched on a burnt, brick-like piece of shepherd's pie.

She spent three hours muffling Saint-Saëns' works for piano with the soft pedal. At two o'clock the light from Liesa's bedroom was aglow. She could not escort herself to bed before her sister was asleep: if anyone found out about it she would face social exclusion.

At quarter to four Anneliese emerged from her room astagger, pigments of beams asprawl over her eyes.

Isabel was in her nightdress.

'You aren't *tired?*'

'No.'

In fact her eyes were more alert than usual. She stood leaning on the banister looking exceedingly pleased with herself, smug with a haughty air that Isabel had met before.

'Did you know that a chemical called "levodopa" – which comes from broad beans – can be converted into dopamine to slow down degradation in a victim of Parkinson's disease?'

Isabel was worried.

Delighted with herself – so much that she mimed Susanna's righteous smirk and patted Isabel atop the head – Anneliese informed with pretend kindness:

'You did not. Only – *two* people in the world know that.'

Isabel was on the verge of entering her own room when Anneliese barricaded the doorknob.

'There are many incurable diseases, Isabel.'

'Mmm-hmm.'

'The absence of spingomyelin in cell membranes, for instance. It's fatal. Causes Niemann-Pick disease.'

'That's . . . a shame.'

'They break down lipids.'

'Lip . . . Anneliese, I'm off to *bed* now.'

'Don't you remember anything Miss Hampshire taught us?'

'I remember . . . "Reproduction is . . . *etc., etc.*" That's what I remember.'

'Lipids are molecules that contain fats.'

'That's nice.'

'Without them excessive fat accumulates in the liver and spleen and bone marrow and *brain*.'

'All right.'

'Well . . . it's not *really*. Children die from it, Isabel. Sometimes at two months; some more luckily at six.'

'Would you move away from the door?'

Anneliese shifted herself. Isabel grabbed the knob.

'Wouldn't it be wonderful if someone found a cure and stopped the children dying?'

Isabel closed her door. No response could be heard.

'Someone *has* done, Isabel. Does that not *interest* you?'

Isabel shut her door.

The ideas that she had just absorbed and the experiments whose details she had read would be enacted and twice proven, published globally, distributed to schools and universities and practised universally. Susanna's name would be on history. The names of girls her sister knew, a century from then, would live on only on their tombstones if they managed to survive the English climate.

Anneliese had almost nothing she could contribute. She was too challenged when it came to chemistry; her days of easy tests and quick analyses were long behind her, buried somewhere in the months preceding Josef's death.

A stamp in the world's annals she could scarcely seal: that Isabel would do if she could overcome her stagefright. The Younger Twin had always known she lacked the power to eradicate fatal diseases, steer the course of art or change the current jurisdiction. Her legacy would only be a tender stroke. Serving Susanna – who had trekked so many hills and would have done so even with no overcoat, and in a storm and through a heap of boulders – sufficed at this stage in her life to constitute her grounds for living.

The next morning Anneliese was sat on the sofa adjacent to the piano, her hand clutching the spine of a medical journal, her knees bent at her chest.

Isabel came in to take her keys.

Anneliese's voice was soft but brushed with condescension as she spoke.

'Are you going out with Edmund Sawyer tonight?'

Isabel refused to look at her.

'No.' Isabel took her keys from the little dish on the table and tucked them into her pocket. 'We last saw each other three weeks ago.'

She sensed that Anneliese was nodding but was loath to look at her.

'Oh. Was he—'

'I found him hideously *boring*, Anneliese.'

Isabel had long ago concluded that the truth regarding anything did not deserve an explanation. Details about this boy in particular she guarded even from Olivia.

27.

Caterpillar legs

Edmund Sawyer was the reason Isabel had taken to attending parties where the couples could be visible. She tended to deny herself Olivia's extravagant, loud bashes in a house that had innumerable rooms.

It was her sixth party of the school season. She was five weeks away from turning eighteen, three months apart from filling in four application forms with six months left till her conservatoire auditions. Two of her cello strings had snapped at her untethered violence in the past six weeks.

Having concluded that the infiltrating spirit of her sweltering surroundings was sufficient, Isabel abstained from alcohol that evening. At quarter to ten she sat on a high stool, her elbows on the counter of Vanessa Mardling's blue and pearl-white kitchen. The doorbell rang. No one else was there and neither did they enter: both the wine and beer were in the dining room. The doorbell rang again. She wasn't going to welcome such a late arrival in another person's house.

She fumbled a lot with her drink, knocking the straw on the edge of the glass. After a third ring of the doorbell she heard a latch lifted and footsteps resound in the corridor. Rashly scurrying feet were absorbed by her ears; rhythms obstructing those of a tinny piano recording of 'Just One of Those Things'. After a few moments the stomping desisted. As she sucked her straw the gentle footsteps rustled near her. A soft voice, somewhere between a tenor and a baritone, alerted her from somnolence.

'Excuse me.'

On this occasion she was forced to turn her head around. He was a young gentleman of some height with fair hair and tall eyes of a crystal blue clad in a suit with a black tie and jacket.

'Have you seen a medium-sized chap with brown hair and spectacles?'

She shook her head with overworked politeness.

'I didn't think so.'

He sighed in despair.

Gazing at him lengthily, the girl endeavoured to prepare a graceful, cool approach. It seemed he was too old to be a party guest; too young for her to be afraid of his advances. Dangling both hands at his sides, clenching his fists ever so slightly, he displayed a self-possession. His timbre was quite airy. The fellow was well-built, in better shape and obviously maturer than the young men she had known. Entirely harmless.

At a loss, she rubbed her forefinger over her thumb. As she strived to swivel on the stool Isabel all of a sudden felt her feet were plagued with pins and needles: she would totter if she volunteered to shake his hand.

'Is it someone important?' she asked with false concern.

'My brother.' the man clarified. 'He wasn't supposed to . . .' He stuck one hand in his pocket and his eyes darted left and right. 'I'm sorry, I'm being terribly rude.' Extending his right hand, he took the left out of his pocket. 'My name's Nathaniel Pillinger.'

Her voice emerged in a suppressed and nervous murmur.

'Isabel van der Holt.'

'A pleasure to meet you, Miss van der Holt.'

'Would you mind – is there someone sitting next to you?'

'No, no.'

'I . . .' He sat down. 'I'm meant to be a . . . a "chaperone" for my brother. Our . . .' He looked flustered. 'Our parents are on holiday and asked me to look after him – he's only fifteen . . . And I imagined . . .' He heaved a great sigh. 'There's a young lady – well, I imagined he would turn up *here*. But that's a boring story. Er . . . Is "van der Holt" a Dutch name?'

She drank a little more before she summoned proper courage.

'Yes. But that's my father's side. My mother's German.' It was a timid reply most unlike her. An image flashed before her eyes of how she had encountered Papa's colleague's son some years before; she must have been just eight – and how she had stood paralysed. Now she found herself glued to this stool, reluctant to peel herself off it, her feet pressed to its bar – dependent on the unsturdy thing. Continuing to stir her straw around, she heard:

'Aren't you cold? I don't think the – I don't think the heating's on.'

'I'm—' She blushed at thinking he had probably observed her dress was backless. 'Not really, no.'

'Have my jacket.' he insisted, removing it and wrapping it around her shoulders. There was a remarkable pause. 'If you don't mind my saying . . . You don't look as though you're enjoying yourself.'

She smiled, embarrassed. Had to suck her bottom lip to stop the smile from being overly revealing.

"Well . . . when you've been to *one* such an occasion, you've been to them all.' was the sole cliché that came from her mouth. 'Do you know Clive, erm . . . Vanessa's brother?'

'Who?' asked Mr Pillinger. 'The boy? No, I just came here to look out for Grant, my brother. He, er . . . He's liable to get himself into a rut.' He laughed lightly. 'What about you?'

'Well . . .' She pondered for a moment. 'I go to school with Vanessa.' It was his turn to nod. 'Are you at university?'

'I was.' he informed her. 'I've finished now.'

'Where were you?'

'Oxford.' he replied nonchalantly. This time she nodded once more and smiled. 'I read Economics. A lot of . . . stuffy people there. Do you have plans yet?'

'You mean . . . university?'

'Whatever holds your interest.'

She demurred and hesitated.

'I . . . I want to go to university.' she stated blandly. Shame prevented a disclosure of the truth. 'But I don't know which subject I want to read yet.'

'Which do you enjoy?'

'Erm . . ..' Unaware that it was not exactly ladylike, she scratched her head. 'History.'

'Oh, really? Which period?'

'The Tudors.' was her automatic answer.

'Fascinating.' her interlocutor replied. 'I read some Strachey recently – you know, *Elizabeth and Essex*. The style . . . perhaps a little monotonous for my taste.'

She nodded again. Soon he would think she was mute. A caterpillar's multiple, sinuous legs must have been climbing her flesh: she was frozen.

Warding it off, she scratched her knee a little, wondering which subject to undertake next.

'Do you like music?' she asked him, her voice tight.

'Well . . . yes.' he replied. 'In particular the Brandenburg concertos.'

Isabel was not aware that Mr Pillinger had never heard the Brandenburg concertos. She herself despised them.

Before she could prepare an adequate response a short and awkward boy appeared at the door's threshold.

'Grant!' Mr Pillinger cried. 'I told you not—' Rebounding from his seat he swiftly stormed to him and hissed through half-closed lips: 'Did I not say you *weren't* to go outside?'

Grant's voice was loud and scarcely understated as he looked at Isabel.

'Doesn't look as though you turned the whole house upside down on my *behalf*.'

Mr Pillinger turned around.

'Miss van der Holt, this is my brother, Grant.'

Grant offered her his hand but very hastily withdrew it once she took it. The 'how do you do's' were exchanged before Grant bellowed impatiently:

'There isn't much to do here, anyway. You brought the car?'

Mr Pillinger's gaze was too fixed on Isabel. Grant tried again:

'Tally?'

'I brought the car, yes.'

Isabel was perplexed. Very quickly Mr Pillinger explained:

'Nathaniel became "Tal" which subsequently became "Tally". It's a – an idiotic name.' He turned to Grant in agitation. 'Yes,' he replied to his brother. 'We can go.'

Isabel immediately began to take his coat off.

'Oh, no.' he insisted. 'I really don't need it. You can . . . you can keep it.'

Now she was tremendously confused. She couldn't recall manuals or romantic novels dwelling on the manner of suggested action if a young man wanted to donate his coat.

'It was a pleasure to meet you, Miss van der Holt.' He smiled, again extending his hand.

'Likewise.' She spoke rather softly.

'Are you being picked up?'

'Well . . . no. Why?' she asked, offering pretend naïvety.

'I could drive you home, if that would be convenient.'

Neither of them heard Grant tap his shoe on the ground and part his lips noisily.

'That would be charming.' she said in exultation, standing up. A little taken aback by her height, Mr Pillinger did his best not to betray his surprise.

She followed Mr Pillinger and Grant to the automobile. It was the first time a young gentleman had opened the car door for her.

'Grant – get in the back.'

'But—'

The boy had no choice.

On the way home Isabel and Mr Pillinger exchanged some trivial and meaningless words, much to Grant's manifest irritation.

'Do you work?'

'Do I? Ah, yes.' Mr Pillinger attempted to deliver the line with importance. 'Yes, in the City, for the moment. I'm an assistant to the manager of a hotel chain.'

'You work . . . in a hotel?'

'Erm, no, allow me to explain—'

'He labours for the filthy rich.' Grant yelled from behind. 'Have you heard of Sherborne Hotels?'

'Well, yes. Of course I have.' Isabel responded as softly as she could.

'He's the assistant to the Director of Operations in the London office. He's making *tons*, just so you know.'

Mr Pillinger's voice grew severe.

'*Grant*. There's no need for that commentary.' He turned to Isabel apologetically and whispered: 'I think he drank a little.'

'That's all right.'

'Which school do you go to?'

'Croham Hurst – in South Croydon. It's little and nobody's heard of it.'

'I've heard of it.'

'Oh?'

'Our school used to have balls with yours.'

'You went to Aylesbury?'

'Yes, I did. Quite a pretentious place, I must admit. Grant still goes there.'

'I hate the dump.' Grant snorted.

'So are you . . . do you want to work in management?'

Mr Pillinger sighed very slowly.

'None of that's decided yet.'

'He wants to do what Papa tells him!' was Grant's next avowal.

'Sorry.' Mr Pillinger once again whispered to Isabel.

'No, no. My sister's very different from me, too.'

'A younger sister?'

'Yes. Younger by six days.' She smiled. 'We're twins.'

'Born *six* days apart?'

'Yes.'

'They told me in biology that was impossible.'

'No, no – it's possible!'

When they arrived outside her home she tried in vain to give his coat back; he wholeheartedly refused. Beholding her as she arrived at the front door, he cast a wave.

Anneliese was less than pleased to see her sister exit a man's car.

'What are you *doing*?'

'A very kind gentleman gave me a ride home.' she explained.

'Is that his coat?'

'It *is*.'

'And what else did he want?'

'He was perfectly delightful. His name is Tally Pillinger.'

'His name is *what*?'

'His name is Nathaniel Pillinger. They call him "Tally".' She giggled slightly. 'Don't you think that's *sweet*?'

Anneliese was stymied. Her sister scurried up the stairs and spent a few hours alone in her room wide awake. The tenuous voice of Noël Coward poured down: 'We Were Dancing' and 'Just Let Me Look At You'. Isabel sang along to them in a murmured, sometimes deliberately off-key tone; harmonising at a lower or higher pitch as she desired.

The next morning she came down to breakfast humming tunes from *La traviata*. It was a Saturday and ten o'clock when she awoke.

'There's a bouquet for you.' Anneliese reluctantly informed her.

'Oh?' enquired Isabel with pretend shock. Anneliese responded by imitating her – only prosaically.

'Oh.'

Isabel noticed an arrangement of two dozen roses. Above them was a note that read:

> *Thank you for delightful conversation. Feel free to make use of my coat, and please forgive my brother – he knows not the straits of decency.*
>
> Sincerely, Tally Pillinger.

How quaint she found the inverted 'know not'; how endearing was his figurative 'straits of decency'. It was most poetic. A smile drove up her cheeks.

'This "Nathaniel" chap?' asked Anneliese.

'Mmm-hmm.' She cleared her throat and sat back down to breakfast.

28.

The carrot and stick

At forty-two minutes past two she would begin voraciously eyeing the clock – as though expecting a cuckoo to pop out. At ten to three she'd start to tap her right foot on her left. Twelve minutes later she was rubbing them together and creating friction; moisture on the back of her school skirt was not enough to spur on her excitement. A siren rang inside her with the long-anticipated buzzing of the bell.

The girls didn't like Tally. They openly declared him highly 'unfanciable'; too mature, lacking in spontaneity. Oddly enough it was Anneliese who ostentatiously made her approval known. She loved seeing her sister return in his coats. She loved seeing Tally adjust Isabel's straps when she had clumsily put on her dress.

Six weeks into their courtship Isabel had grown relaxed enough to sneeze in front of him. He carried a number of handkerchiefs just in case.

After three meetings he had started showing up at Croham Hurst at quarter to four, which was where he once met Anneliese.

A man's voice called one day:

'Excuse me.'

It took her a number of moments and a three hundred and sixty degree turn to discover the source.

'Yes?'

'Sorry for bothering you – I've seen you many times. I'm Tally Pillinger.'

'Oh, yes – I know, I recognise you!' He shook her hand thoroughly.

'Isabel said you were studying to be a doctor.'

'Erm – yes, possibly.'

'I've always been quite fascinated by medicine. Considered going into it myself but . . .' His head rotated. 'Never mind. Have you decided on a field yet?'

'Yes. Psychiatry.'

'Ah. How very . . .'

'*Modern?*'

'No – I was going to say . . . quaint.'

'Well – it's all right. I understand that many people think it . . . quite inferior.'

'No, no. Not at all. I've read some Emil Kraepelin.'

'You – you *have?*'

At times Anneliese marvelled how her sister could find such a cultured man engaging. Even by his brows' expression one could tell he was an educated fellow.

One afternoon Isabel came out of Croham Hurst and didn't see Tally. She panicked till her searching eyes had landed on another spot.

'You *moved!*' she accused him.

'There were many mothers there, gabbing away. I didn't want to appear to be eavesdropping.'

They stood and faced each other. She found it gloriously refreshing to be so at ease with him that neither had to say 'hello'.

He took her arm and they proceeded.

'Do you have homework?'

Adamantly Isabel shook her head.

'No.'

'I don't believe you. You had a lesson with Miss Clarendon today.'

'How did *you* know?'

Griping in his jacket pocket, he retrieved a folded paper square.

'I copied your timetable down to keep track.'

'Oh.' She squeezed his hand. 'But they're still showing—'

'No, I think we should go home and I'll explain the answers to you.'

Isabel giggled.

With every step their pace slowed.

'Very well.'

He rented her a car to mark her eighteenth birthday; for six months he would regale her with free driving lessons.

Isabel discovered Tally was more humorous than she assumed. Slyly he would make amusing observations, speculating whether the fat lady in the car in front could fill two seats. When at one point he observed a poodle running on the pavement, he began to race it with her car until the small dog lagged behind. Often he would speak to dogs outside – albeit to himself – and do the same with passers-by he never actually addressed. All of these performances intended only to squeeze laughs from Isabel: he worried her vivaciousness was thrice his own.

On one occasion before Christmas she insisted that he watch her as she forced her car across the snow. Spotting an icy road ahead of them, he warned:

'Don't go there.'

'Why not?'

'It's slippery – and you're not used to it.'

'That's why you're here.'

'No, Isabel – *really*.'

'Tally.' She sighed in frustration. 'First the faggots and now this?' she was referring to their fourth time at the Ritz when Tally had insisted she reject the meat dish to prevent a bout of late-night nausea.

'No, this is much different. You don't want to go down this road, Isabel – it's too icy. Park the car here.'

'What – Tally, we're in the middle of Maze Hill.'

'So? I'll take us home.'

'*I* want to take us home.'

'The conditions are not *fair*.'

'But – well, *fine*.'

An hour later Anneliese returned home from Susanna's and peered at Isabel, red and flustered, perching on the kitchen counter next to standing Tally.

'Four more lessons, and he says I'll pass.' she told her breathlessly.

Anneliese looked at them both in confusion.

'Did you . . . *race* the car?'

'No!' Isabel almost burst into giggles. 'We parked the car down on Old Dover Road, and then we raced to see who'd get here first. And he kept stopping me to tickle me 'cause . . .' She spluttered laughter. 'He thinks I'm his pet rabbit; he's my carrot and *stick*.'

Both of them chortled in one rhythm:

'And she won.'/'And he let me win.'

'My love's more generous than hers.' Tally mockingly proclaimed.

Isabel snorted inelegantly, slipping down from the counter to give him a kiss on the lips with her arms round his neck, nuzzling his cheek as she did so.

'Are you *neglected*?' she murmured tenderly.

Grasping her hand, he insisted:

'Very much so. When you're at the wheel the whole world is neglected.'

Isabel's smile was the arc of a sunrise.

The dalliance seemed adequate enough for Anneliese.

29.

Psychic cautery

In place of flourishing red flower heads a huddled clan of wilted tufts drooped at 9 Eversley Avenue.

The doorbell wasn't working. It took a few knocks on the glass pane of the door for Helga's head to finally bob up. The old lady was cleaning the kitchen floor with a mop and a bucket.

With the opening of the door Anneliese immediately launched into:

'Helga – the peonies, they're—'

'*Ja, ja.*' Helga quickly retorted in German. 'But when she comes back, she won't notice.'

Anneliese stepped in and took her scarf off.

'You mean she's *out?*'

'*Ja, ja.*'

'Why – did someone *die?*'

'Almost.'

Anneliese began to fiddle with her thumb.

'Oh. Only . . .' She stuttered. 'I-I rather meant that as a joke in poor taste . . .'

'She has this patient – a man, about thirty. He comes all the way here – he's bleeding to death. And instead of going to casualty he comes to his psychiatrist!'

The girl frowned.

'So she escorted him in the ambulance?'

'Been gone for almost two hours now. Told me to tell you not to wait for more than fifteen minutes; she has other hours in her schedule.'

'What was wrong with him?'

Helga shrugged.

'Got blood everywhere. Looked like a knife wound to me. She sure tied it up well, though. Had to use the kitchen towel, but you know the saying: "Desperate diseases *do* have desperate remedies."'

She didn't know the saying, not having spent a portion of her life in Germany or Austria-Hungary.

'Shall I wait in the . . .' She pointed to her left. 'Practice?'

'Yes, yes. Go ahead, don't mind me.'

The door was closed so it was up to Anneliese to press down on the handle. She stepped into a wet patch of cleaned rug. On the table a small splotch of blood was prominent.

Swiftly she headed to Susanna's chest of patients' books. Grabbing the first volume, Anneliese found a Spanish tome, *Les Atlántides*. Its spine was taken like a kitten lifted by its scruff. An envelope fell out. It was addressed, *S.Z. Černuška*, with 'Eversley' spelt 'Everly'. Then she heard a key turn in the front door.

Hastily she took the envelope and shoved it in her bag.

Before her eyes could meet Susanna's in the corridor they landed on her shoes: high heels of black and white patches of leather. The left shoe's white was splayed with blotches of red stains.

'Susanna, there's blood on—'

'I know.' Taking off her scarf, she seemed more agitated than was customary. 'A patient of mine came to me with a partially severed thigh.' The story ,made her seem almost impertinent with indignation. 'He'd been stabbed.'

Looking down at her heels, she appeared to lament their disfigurement.

A sigh accompanied Susanna as she reached into her rack to clasp a plain black pair. To herself she languidly remarked:

'This is *so* dull.'

Anneliese watched as she dropped the black pair on the floor and began loosing the ones on her feet.

'Was it a domestic conflict?'

'A mugging on his way here. It happened only ... four or five streets away.' Her gaze was stilled as she slipped on the shoes. Eyes squeezed in puzzlement – or from some bitter taste. 'He didn't know where else to go. Anyway ...' She headed to the chest of drawers that stood outside the living room, grabbed her perfume and immediately sprayed it on her neck and wrist. 'I called the ambulance and accompanied him and those dolts.'

'Those ... *dolts?*'

Susanna was already in her practice when Anneliese entered.

'The paramedics had no *idea* what they were doing. When I intervened they threatened to have me *arrested*. Funny when one considers that the ambulance was racing at approximately sixty miles an hour. So ...' she looked up and blinked six or seven times, 'I tourniquet-ed him, tied off the superfemoral artery, cleaned out the clots ...' She looked curiously challenging with her large eyes. 'And he's alive.'

'You saved his life?'

'The dolts did *not*.'

'I didn't even know you were a surgeon.'

'I'm not. I dabbled.'

'In surgery?'

'As a student at St Mary's.' Contemptuously she parted her lips. 'I would never have *chosen* that field. Surgeons are craftsmen; pianists harassed by the compulsion to do something *useful* with their hands.' Unhinging her hands from each other, she laid them on the arms of her chair. 'Have you decided on your specialty?'

'Yes, but . . . Why would you advise against surgery?'

'It's . . . mundanely uninteresting.' More blinks were unleashed. 'I cheated a little; that was how I got to do surgery.'

'What did "cheating" entail?'

'It wasn't part of my residency. I knew someone . . .' She cleared her throat and fiddled with her sleeve. The 'someone' probably aroused unwanted memories. ' . . .he let me in on a few surgeries. I practised – somewhat. I was conducting research for my doctorate at the same time. I wouldn't suggest that you to do the same thing. Apart from anything else . . .' Her hand stretched out, she tapped the arm of her chair three times in rhythm. 'It was illegal.'

'What was your "official" specialty?'

'I did three. I had two bachelor's degrees by then, had done seven internships . . . I immersed myself into neurology and twice into pathology. And only after that did I do one year at the Maudsley Hospital.'

'But then . . .' Anneliese had to sigh before completing her sentence. 'How couldn't you – how could you remember *all* . . .'

Susanna failed to understand this approach. She was studying her patient with superiority and specks of genuine confusion.

'Anatomy to any doctor is the cello to the player. I never believed that doctors *should* have specialties. That all resulted from an emphasis on students' limitations. It built this... overarching "general regulation". In truth a gastroenterologist should know as much about the larynx as an ENT.' She swayed the foot of her crossed leg a little. 'Given the narrow potential of most people . . . no one agrees with me.'

'Yet here you are.'

'That's right.'

'You're not a vascular surgeon and you're not an obstetrician and you certainly don't hold a *number* of posts.'

'Different subject.'

'How . . .'

'That was a choice.' Briefly a silent tension held its sway. 'So what *is* it?'

'Oh, well . . .'

'They're going to ask you at the interview, you know. At Lady Margaret Hall.'

'I know.'

'Which one is it?'

Anneliese interlocked her fingers, attempting shyly to smile.

'You're going to misinterpret this.'

Susanna crossed her legs the other way. Her comment was one weakly offered, almost inert:

'I see.'

'I scoured my options very *vastly*, Susanna.'

It almost seemed the latter's countenance was tired from its expressions.

'Anneliese . . . if tomorrow you were to meet some . . .' She used her hand to do explaining on her part again. ' . . .some *fascinating* individual, who by some pure coincidence happened to be an *ornithologist*, would you apply for Natural Sciences?'

'That wouldn't happen.'

'How do *you* know?'

'I've been ready to apply for Medicine since I was ten. You need to tell me why my choice is wrong.'

'Well there are . . . several reasons.' She looked at her with eyes half-hidden by their lids. 'Very few people *interest* you. You almost take *pleasure* from stereotyping people.'

'*You're* the most supercilious person in the world – and you call me judgmental.'

'You haven't seen me with many patients.'

'I've seen enough to know you condescend continuously – obstinately.' There was no response. 'I saw you with that girl . . .

You – you always – most of the time ... I'm not going to believe that when it comes to other patients you're a different person.'

'Don't believe it, then.'

Anneliese had no answer. Seeing the stymied girl, Susanna spent the time smoothing her thumb and forefinger first down then up a pencil. Eventually she grew bored of the exercise and threw it to one side.

'What's going to happen when one of your colleagues refers to you some schizophrenic who aspires to *cannibalism?* When another one wants you to understand the rituals of an ancient tribe in Guatemala? When a Romanian gypsy stuck in an asylum badgers you with the string bracelets that she's selling?'

Anneliese could not suppress the urge to take the upper hand.

'Neurologist, pathologist and polymath . . .. *You* chose it.'

'No – I *didn't*.'

Susanna was embarrassed for the first time she had ceded to her patient's provocation. It was a rut from which she had to climb.

'I didn't think so.'

'You would have to spend time in a mental hospital. And they don't *choose* to go there.'

Anneliese was unabashed.

'I'm mainly focussed on the area of psychoanalytical psychiatry. Freud treats patients who are none of those things.'

'How much has he accomplished to afford this luxury?'

Anneliese looked at the ceiling. The clock below it told her it was 7.20.

'It's in my nature to want to help, Susanna. And I have that ... that mathematical streak.'

'"Mathematical streak"?'

'The one that tells me, if there's an answer to a riddle, that I have to *grab* it. Patients could only bluff with me for so long.'

'Could they? You're too gentle.'

'That's a matter of style. We don't all have to be abrasive like *you* are. You practise psychic cautery.'

'I practise it with you because you're making this decision blindly. You only scrapped your prejudice against psychiatry because you met someone you felt could understand you. If you had been referred to someone else, your dream would still be being a neurologist like Papa.'

'See – now *you're* mistaken.' She ringed her fingers together. 'I didn't come here out of loneliness.'

'You said your reasoning was blotchy, knowing full well it wasn't "blotched".'

'According to that kind of grievance – you knew well I didn't need any real "treatment".'

'And?'

'And you *keep* me here!'

Susanna scarcely knew how to defeat a young descendant of her schooling. Her pupils focussed on the ceiling, came back down again, ruminated over something wrapped away and hidden far from Anneliese.

'Some man stopped me from getting killed.' Anneliese quietly announced.

'Hmm?'

'A few weeks after Papa's death I walked onto a road . . . . no, I was walking *on* the road. I used to . . . to *do* that, once in a while. A car passed by and almost hit me. That was the incident that . . . compelled me to come here.'

Susanna folded her hands on her crossed leg.

'You're telling me this *now?*'

'Yes.'

'Over two years since your first session?'

'Yes.'

'That's useful.' Her stare remained steady and fixed as she mulled over this. 'You didn't want to kill yourself.'

'Obviously – *no*.'

'You said you did it when you were little . . . even when you were happy?'

'Yes.'

'For what reason?'

'I . . . Isabel assumed I was crazy . . . I – I don't know.'

'There was some form of exhilaration?'

'I . . . suppose.' Anneliese adjusted the hem of her skirt. 'I haven't done it in . . . I don't know *how* long. Why would you take it seriously?'

'You know, if . . .' There was an algorithm being processed in Susanna's head. Anneliese imagined long rows of numbers being divided and multiplied to yield the output of a seventeen-digit-long decimal.

Done with its searching, abruptly the look on her face became sly and conceited.

'It's . . . it's very interesting.'

'What have you—'

'It's too early for that, Anneliese.'

She watched her patient as if Anneliese were just an animal on which she preyed. At once she was now menacingly incandescent and sadistically seductive.

'What does "too early" mean?'

'It would be unprofessional of me to put forward a theory without enough proof.'

'Don't be a coquette with me, Susanna. I'm not the "married man from whom you learnt English pronunciation".'

'Helga shared that with you?'

'She did.'

'Mmm.'

There was no admission on Susanna's part and yet her eyes suggested a familiarity with this. Anneliese wondered if that man – upon allowing his poor family to be a martyr to his cause of passion

– had been branded by the imprint of those instruments: an imprint that would char his harmony for years.

But quickly that self-serving glare dissolved into familiar drooping dismal eyes and a soft sigh.

Clearly this dalliance had suppurated rather messily.

'So, are you going to tell me this idea?'

'No. Without further precedent of your behaviour, it's only a . . .' She shook her head dismissively. 'A *draft.*' She took a deep breath. 'Consider it, and consider other aspects of your character you find anomalous when you compare yourself with other girls your age. And go.'

'Why?'

'Because I'm not planning to say anything else.'

'You're not going to stop me from becoming a psychiatrist?'

'I think experience will halt you.' Her hands joined together. 'Tell me if you ever do anything . . . "radical" again.'

30.

Orange tulips

Nobody among the Oxford academics held a great deal of respect for would-be psychoanalytical psychiatrists.

When Anneliese returned home after her botched interview at Lady Margaret Hall the house was empty.

Then paroxysms of giggles spewed:

'No, Tally – *Taallly!* She is *not* too fat! She *isn't!* No – she *isn't!*' Anneliese opened the door to her bedroom.

She found her lying on her bed with her feet on the headboard, her head at the foot of her blanket. Tally was sitting at a chair beside her dressing table.

A small kitten lay on Isabel's chest.

'Look, Liesa!!' Isabel exulted, cuddling the furry animal so tightly Anneliese feared it would burst. 'Isn't she *beautiful!*'

Indeed the grey and white tabby creature possessed clear blue eyes and a pointy pink nose. She was adorable.

Anneliese dimly muttered:

'Yes . . .'

'How was your interview?'

She searched for words.

'I'll probably be staying here.'

'That's not a bad thing . . . necessarily . . .'

'I suppose not.'

'We named her "Christina". We're going to share her till she grows into a *big* cat: one week here, one week at Tally's.' Isabel took the kitten, holding her up to Anneliese so she could see. Flipping onto her stomach, she placed Christina in front of her.

'Would you look after her while Tally takes me for a driving lesson?'

Anneliese grunted a little before her submission.

'Why . . . Well, yes – fine.'

Before she had a chance to resume speaking Isabel sprang up and thrust the kitten in her hands. Christina stared at Anneliese with forlorn eyes. Anneliese studied her before informing the little one:

'I suppose it's not your fault.'

Tally approached Anneliese when Isabel had exited the room.

'I'm sorry for not asking your permission—'

'No, no – there's no trouble with having a cat in the house.'

'I really should have done – it's just, Isabel told me she wanted a cat the day before you went up to Oxford; erm . . . I don't think she had a phone number to reach you.'

'That's all right.'

That evening in her cold and half-unheated room she dipped her hand into her bag and pulled out her new document.

It was a translation of the letter she had taken from Susanna's chest of drawers, newly collected from a freelancer whom she had paid the previous week. Her mother had sent it to the psychiatrist from Vysoké Mýto.

Anneliese had copied down the text for her translator. She had then taken an identical unused envelope and mimicked Susanna's mother's handwriting to write the address, tucked in the original letter and sealed the epistle with its crumpled-up stamp.

During another session a brief moment of Susanna's absence had allowed her to insert this substitute back in the Spanish novel in her chest of drawers.

Now the English version was awaiting her. She had been saving it for after her toil's end.

> *My little beetle,*
>
> *I've been sitting here wondering how many barons Magdalena is introducing you to. Any candidates?*
>
> *I know you said I should keep silent, but I didn't. Here it goes: your father refuses to send money; you know him – too heady with his causes. There is however, a young beau of mine who could transfer some funds. He has a friend who travels frequently to England – a sailor, no less. Provided that we put aside our little grudge and trust this measly fellow, we could organise a little trip for him. What do you think of that, my ladybird?*
>
> *Remember how many offers you had from the fellows at Hoechst? I wasn't going to let those paupers lay their hands on you. Of course, if you had stayed here then you could have met him over coffee during Love Feast. But this concept of Westernisation thumped you on the head like a club; you took up residence on some forgotten puny little island.*
>
> *I still remember all those banquets; little Šárka twirling her long hair and gloating of her projects to a band of counts and marquises who couldn't understand you. I told you then my beetle that men only know the territory of their courtship; no one's going to pander to the likes of Lise Meitner.*
>
> *Over here the scent of spring floats in the air. I've thought about it for a long time and I really think that orange tulips would be perfect lying down on Lili's grave.*

*Knowing the country where you live, it's most unlikely
that you'll find them anywhere. They're blooming right
outside the salon window; I can see them now.*

*Your father's bellowing again. You know how he gets
with his temper!*
God be with you,
Your Mother

Somewhere along these uncoagulated paragraphs were pumps that
sent a chill into their reader. Anneliese acknowledged that she was
incapable of understanding many references. She remembered
seeing the name 'Lily' on a blanket she had spotted in Susanna's
room a year before; she gathered that the reference to a 'Lili' was
the same one.

Nonetheless there was a stench of unfamiliarity in this epistle
and it paradoxically came from a blood relative: a butcher's apathy
towards his slaughtered creatures' equally mammalian flesh.
Anneliese could understand the writer of this letter was a human
being and could write to some extent.

She failed to understand how such a text bore any correlation
with Susanna.

Their first session after Christmas swiftly followed Lady
Margaret Hall's rejection. She cried a little bit – mostly because she
could envisage that her father would have been upset. Here was
one of his eighteen-year-old girls being warmly courted, her
marriage at this point *predestined*. On the other hand there was the
Younger Twin – without even a university.

Hoarse from a winter cold, Susanna was constantly gulping
down huge sips of water.

Her glass set, she resumed her speech with a voice some tones
lower.

'Are you going to marginalise the tiny chance you didn't want to
go there?'

'I *did* want to go there!'

'And yet before your interview . . .' She cleared her throat. 'You said they'd think you "mad" if you mentioned "psychiatry".'

'Well, I was right!' Anneliese's volume hoped to challenge her psychiatrist's subdued condition.

The latter sniffed before responding:

'You could have hidden it from them; you could have said "neurology" like Josef wanted.'

For a few moments Susanna squeezed her eyes tightly.

'Papa told me to be honest.'

'So you used one lesson from his upbringing to cancel out another.'

'What?!'

'You didn't want to go to Oxford, even though "Papa" desired it. You remembered something else he taught you. Via this substitute your conscience remains safe. Do you know what that means, Anneliese?'

She looked at Susanna despondently.

'It's suggestive of the idea that you're becoming independent. That's . . . a step. If this goes on, you won't need me anymore.'

Susanna radiated one of her faint, slight and temporary smiles.

Anneliese was displeased.

As Susanna closed her eyes again – applying such a mechanism to prevent herself from sneezing – Anneliese lunged forward with a long-anticipated query.

'Isn't there . . . don't you have a girl . . . called "Lily"?'

She blinked a few times.

'*Had.*'

'Oh.'

To preclude further enquiries Susanna added systematically:

'A car crash. Many years ago.'

Suddenly the tinkling warmth and scent of red peonies lost its balance. Anneliese was displaced.

'I'm so sorry.' she mumbled.

Susanna looked at her nonchalantly. Her temperament was pastel-coloured and phlegmatic. After a long pause she took a hefty breath and held it. It was probably another way to offset sneezing.

'You gave her an English name.'

'Yes.'

'Was she born here?'

'Where else would I have had her?'

'*You* weren't born here.'

'I *was* – in Salisbury. Into citizenship. We moved to Austria-Hungary when I was three.'

Anneliese kept wondering just how elaborate this filigree of fabrications was.

'Have you been taking walks on motorways of late?'

Anneliese's brows curved downwards. She could see the motive hidden by the decoy.

'No.'

31.

The tinkered teapot

The night was sweet yet stuffy. April had seen the influx of great sunbeams through their window pane together with an exodus of wind. It was seventeen minutes past two in the morning. The abstaining sun could scarcely curb the heat.

Isabel was sat on the piano stool. On the sofa Tally stroked Christina. There were two hours left before he had to go to work.

'Just . . . five minutes have gone past. Try it again.'

Her eyes were drooping. She lacked the energy even to face him.

'Tally . . . I have depleted my resources. There is no way I could perform much better.' She stood up. 'I'll bring you a blanket . . . not that you need it. But you should get some sleep.'

'No, no – I'll stay.'

'Of course you'll stay. But I'm not going to practise. Get some *sleep*. Mr Foster'll kill you.'

'I'm not going to be late.'

'Only drowsy. I'm going to *bed*, Tally.'

'You barely practised!'

If there was one trait in her beau she found repellent, it was this. Isabel had specified at least six times that she was no public performer.

This information appeared to have swelled in his brain and then burst like a pimple. He would chide her. He would ask her, with the best of intentions, which notes he could buy for her, whether she sought a new metronome, if maybe he ought to ask a friend of his – a violinist – for a second opinion.

She had expressed to him that it was not a medical condition. Simply put there was no way that she could do it.

'You know how poor I am; you know the situation . . .' she insisted. 'Thank you, but – really, it's hopeless. They won't take me.'

'Of course they'll take you.'

Rarely had she heard a comment so inane. The Royal College of Music, for which she was auditioning that day, could never take a student whose fingers tripped up on Liszt's Third Consolation. Isabel of all people knew they deserved better. His optimism was a cause of agitation for her.

'It's not a problem, Tally. Most girls don't bother going to university. Now – just, stop *worrying*. I'm going to sleep.'

She had already exited the room when once again he called her.

'Can you at least . . . explain the problem?'

Isabel was brash and brusque.

'*Why?*' Already she was primed for self-defence.

'It's just . . . I'd like to know. You said when you were six that some woman hailed you a "genius". I couldn't bear the thought of that being wasted.'

'Nothing's being "wasted" Tally; it just isn't *present*.'

'You said . . . *sometimes*, it is.'

'When I'm alone.'

'So what's the problem?'

She scratched her arm.

'It's a – it's . . . Tally, you know, those famous pianists – they're like circus performers. I'm a pianist; not a *presenter*. I need to be afforded . . . *intimacy* with my instrument. That won't happen if there's a spectator or listener, or a goddamn *metronome* in the room!' She grew short of breath. 'Sorry.'

'It's all right.' Tally reassured her.

'I mean to say that I don't want any rapport with the audience. It's not for them I play. My playing is a selfish act; I do it only for myself.'

'I'm sure that isn't true.'

'Get some *rest*, Tally.'

'But Isabel—'

'Get some *rest*.'

She disliked how much he wanted to believe that everything in her was good and noble when she knew it wasn't. The trickles down her flanks or through her chest or abdomen each time he touched her, for example, were deplorable – for they would slither in her also when she brushed past *other* men. Not long ago her physiology had plagued her with proclivities unquenchable. Waiting for Tally to propose in order to legitimise her longing quelled their urgency.

Rather than being hyped with nerves at the audition like her fellow candidates, Isabel was swiftly locked into a state of tedium that morning in the waiting room. Boasts were being flung without discrimination:

'Did you . . . They took me too. Yes, yes – and Guildhall too.'

'Did you apply to Oxford?'

'No. That's no *conservatoire!*'

'They did take me, you know.'

'Well – they'll take anyone! I got accepted into Juilliard.'

The girl sitting next to her demurred.

'Oh. My mother says no young lady should ever go to New York – so dangerous! Apparently there's *nowhere* you avoid the mugging.'

'They gave me a full scholarship.'

'Well, I got one from the American School at Fontainebleau.'

'Is that . . .'

'With Nadia Boulanger. So *lucky!* They say she *detests* foreigners.'

The prattling was perpetual.

Isabel had by that point received rejections from both Guildhall and the Royal Academy.

Her playing sounded like the unrelenting noise of someone tinkering with a defective teapot. After a few moments the adjudicator raised his hand.

'Thank you.'

She stood up and gathered her music. Then she remembered sombrely that protocol dictated that the judge give all the candidates the customary aural tests regardless of their playing. Upon his hastening to ask, 'Would you excuse me?' she foresaw his imminent return.

Isabel found it amusing. Certainly she bore no grudge against him or the RCM.

She plonked herself back down on the red velvet stool. Opening her score, she saw her notes were scribbled with expression markings: dynamics stressed on the left of the page, other indicators suffusing the right. Empty and inane, they were much like this hall in which she found herself: cold, no good for the fingers, echoing with poor acoustics. Even her abominable playing had allowed her to perceive that.

The adjudicator stayed away for long. She took her right hand and played the C-sharp chromatic scale, first *allegretto*, then *pianissimo, andante*.

Scarcely could she believe that the acoustics were this poor. Of course, she was well used to the abysmal sound cascading in the Royal Albert Hall: it had extinguished her attendance at the annual Proms. But she had always been convinced conservatoires were prone to *flaunt* their students; not present them at a disadvantage.

Two minutes later she was still alone. So she sat down to play and give her own examination – to the hall's acoustics.

The surroundings may as well have been slim glass. Rising sound diffused in a thin, hazy film of texture. It rang with the gossamer fibre of cricket-like chirping. *forte* and *mezzo forte* were the same.

Only towards the end of the first movement of the *Pathétique* sonata Isabel observed the judge was back – and jumped up in her seat.

'Much better.'

This time he sounded quite sincere.

Anneliese was glistening with radiance when she got home that evening.

'What happened?' Isabel enquired.

'No, you tell me – how did it go?'

Isabel folded her arms and leant against the corridor's wall.

'Well, eventually they took me.'

Anneliese had to force herself not to gasp.

'*Really?*'

'Yes.'

'I thought you said—'

'Well, the man – the professor went out of the room and . . . I had nothing to do. Turns out he heard me so . . . after the aural test he said I was accepted.'

Anneliese expelled a girlish laugh.

'That's wonderful.'

Isabel peeled herself away from the wall. She was fatigued.

'I suppose . . . I'm still not really keen on it. I mean, I know it won't change anything.'

'But . . . imagine the *connections!*'

Hastily Isabel averted her glance.

'Why are *you* happy, Liesa?'

'I'm going to St Mary's.'

'Where?'

'St Mary's Hospital Medical School. And that's where . . . that's where my tutor went.'

'Congratulations.'

'Thank you.'

That night it took too long for Isabel to fall asleep. Imagining Tally's unwanted cheer, she winced at the notion of feigning new joy.

32.

Chinese whispers

In winter her cheeks flushed and she would loose a long white swirl of air into the cloudy mist. Summer glee would coax from her the same reaction.

Isabel was traipsing across Knightsbridge in a pair of three-inch red high heels, dragging Daphne with her left arm and inadvertently provoking her to stumble over cobbles on the way.

The latter was a flustered one. She had received no university acceptances, her parents had no fortune and no suitor was in place. 'Not yet' was her response to people's poking noses.

'How long have you and Tally been together?'

'Oh, er . . . It's ten months now.'

She let out a nervous, breathy exultation.

'Wow.'

They stopped outside Selfridges. Daphne thought of the one shilling in her purse and gulped.

'Do you want to go in?'

Her companion was too dazzling and enthusiastic so she ceded.

'Yes, yes, of course.'

Isabel headed first to the door. She was wearing a pink dress

with short summery sleeves and apparently Tally had bought it
for her.

Two hours later she was on the third floor. Daphne was sitting
on a stool drinking an orange juice the clerk had brought her.
Isabel had dropped Tally's name seven times.

It was the fourth dress she was trying on: red, sleeveless, with a
train that laced the floor.

'Do you prefer this one or the black?'

Daphne could scarcely concentrate. Her eyes were fixed on
dozens of consumers racing through the halls.

'Erm . . . this one would suit you very well with, you know, lots of
rouge.'

Isabel darted her eyes down to look at the hem.

'It's a little uncomfortable to walk in, don't you think?'

A young male clerk approached her.

'Miss van der Holt?'

'Yes?'

'Mr Pillinger is on the telephone for you.'

'Ah, thank you.'

She came down from the platform. As she was handed the
receiver at the counter she began to scratch her neck.

'I wouldn't want to . . . No, Tally . . . I've chosen it. I've chosen
the one I'm going to wear. Mmm-hmm. Mmm-*hmm*. Yes.' She
began snickering with her mouth closed. 'No, I don't think that's
necessary . . . You really mustn't . . . .. All right. All right.'

Newly aglow, Isabel returned to Daphne. The expression of her
joy was modest and restrained; a little ill at ease. She articulated in
a whisper as though beggars sat nearby in shredded rags:

'He said I could have both.'

Daphne's efforts at pretence had not yet been exhausted.

'That's wonderful!'

The gowns were each packed up in an enormous box tied-up in
ribbons.

'We really could have them delivered, Miss van der Holt. I'm sure that Mr Pillinger would be most happy to oblige.' the gentleman clerk emphasised.

'No, no – that's quite all right.'

'A young lady of your pedigree oughtn't to carry items on the city streets all by *herself*.'

'Well – Daphne's with me.'

'One of our staff would be quite happy to escort you.'

'Oh, really – it's perfectly fine. Daphne, could you just . . .' She handed her one of the boxes. Daphne collected it in her arms.

'We really do look forward to seeing you again, Miss van der Holt.'

'Why, *thank* you.'

It was their fourth outing that year to Selfridges and it was only July. Three days later they would part and leave Croham Hurst. Anneliese was spending most days cooped up in a library.

Isabel returned at twilight that day. The pinkish sky was slowly being striped by a thick orange beacon.

Anneliese was on the staircase once again, her Czech dictionary splayed out on her knees.

'Have you been up to anything?'

Isabel marched up two steps.

'Do you remember that tonight . . . tonight's the night that Tally's taking me to the Criterion.'

Anneliese's head jerked up.

'The theatre?'

'No, the restaurant.'

'Oh.'

'Apparently it features in a Sherlock Holmes story.'

Anneliese tucked a small piece of paper into the dictionary. Disengaged was she from all reality.

'I'm listening.'

Isabel inflected her voice upwards, as though it were a question:

'That's nice to *know*.' She opened her pink boxes. 'I got two new dresses.'

'Tally?'

'Yes.' Isabel sucked on the inside of her cheek. 'I'm going to wear the black one.'

'It looks more becoming.'

Having replaced the boxes in the living room, she came back to her sister on the staircase. Her hands were clammy from the friction with the cardboard and the bath of sunlight dousing them. She rubbed her palms against each other wanting them to dry. In a simmering voice she effused:

'I think . . . it's . . . to- tonight.'

Anneliese eyes slid left and right.

'What's . . .'

'He . . .' Isabel's voice was even quieter. 'We've never been there before . . . he got me two dresses . . . he promised pink champagne because I asked him . . . And we're having this meringue that takes three hours to prepare . . .' Her palms met each other once again in their attempt to scrape each other's sweat off. 'I think it's tonight.'

'I don't – Isabel, I don't—'

This time she raised her hands and shook the pair as though they had been washed.

'I think he has a ring.'

Anneliese's heart leapt for a moment. Her voice was musical as she responded:

'*Oh . . .*'

'It would be a relief to you, huh?' Anneliese was unresponsive. 'Never mind. I understand where you're coming from.'

Since the advent of Tally Isabel understood almost everything. Accepting Anneliese's strange turns, she refrained from asking why she spent her time with a Czech dictionary and politely made enquiries about church. One subject she had barely mentioned was the Royal College. Miss Cunningham had almost thrown a fête for her: she was the first Crohamian to be admitted to a famed conservatoire.

Isabel had sat there quite subdued and taken little bits of cake in order to appreciate the flavour, stuff her mouth and be unable to respond.

Reservations were for nine and she was dressed at half past seven. It took her four attempts to properly apply all her cosmetics.

'*Liesa.*' It was the fourth disruption to her work on the Czech language. 'Could you check my eyes again?'

She responded by cupping her chin.

'It's fine.'

'Really? Is the pencil close enough to my lashes?'

'Yes.'

'Are you sure?' she sounded breathtaken. 'I don't want it to look as though I chose to paint a thick black circle round my eyes. It's meant to be a *border.*'

'That it *is.*'

The ring of Isabel's lips unleashed another swirl of air.

'Good.' Her eyes gazed at the clock once more. 'He's only coming in an hour. Why don't you entertain me?'

Anneliese looked as though someone had just asked her to dance.

'Erm—'

'Never mind, never mind – I've got some records that I haven't listened to yet.'

But for the next sixty minutes Anneliese heard neither Noël Coward nor Sibelius emerge from upstairs. It was silent. It had rarely been more silent.

It was twenty-eight minutes past eight when the doorbell rang. Isabel could see his Rolls outside and skipped down gently on the steps for fear of tumbling. It was Anneliese who answered the door.

'Evening, Anneliese. How is your research?'

'My . . . research?'

'I meant . . . your studying.'

Anneliese looked quizzical.

'Well – it's almost the summer holidays. I've been reading about the musculoskeletal system. It's not really . . . not really interesting compared to pathology.'

'And you've been reading a lot about *that*, have you?'

'Yes.'

Tally shook his head hurriedly.

'Good – good.' Isabel gazed at him persistently with her dilated eyes. He took one hand out of his pocket and proffered it in her direction. Anneliese had to step back.

'Shall we?'

Isabel nodded without saying a word.

'I'll have her back before eleven.'

'Well, it's not a . . . I mean . . . you can stay out later if you wish . . .'

'I wouldn't want her coming home after you'd gone to bed.'

'That wouldn't be a problem.'

Tally smiled timidly.

'Have a good evening, Anneliese.'

There was little conversation in the car. Isabel studied the street lights as they zoomed through the roads. No traffic interfered at that time of night.

'How did your meeting with Mr James go?'

'Very well, very well. There shouldn't be a problem with Delaney.'

Tally was even more distant than she. Moments later she could tell that he had lapsed: a formality had unforgivably escaped his mind.

'You look radiant.'

She pressed her fingers into her crossed knee.

'Thank you.'

'I'm sure the other gown was just as beautiful.'

The breeze was soft as she stepped out of the car. Purrs of skidding vehicles pocked the silence. With high heels three inches tall she paralleled his height.

When they entered the Criterion some fine saxophonist was drowsily performing a drab, melancholy ditty; effecting breathy tremolos on final notes of phrases. Strangely the restaurant was hardly busy. The saxophonist looked tired and played his riffs with sloth. Cigarette smoke oozed from women's holders everywhere. So intolerable was the heat that all the bodies in the hall had been enshrouded in a stifling sauna.

Isabel would happily have multiplied the ambience *twofold*.

'He's skipping some of the notes, isn't he?' Tally criticised.

A waiter escorted them to their table.

'Thank you. Erm . . . no, it's the style, Tally.'

'But . . . you see . . .. because of your career, I've been trying to listen very carefully, and am I not correct in saying that he's swaying from some of the notes?'

'It's deliberate.'

'But it's wrong.'

'It's . . . it's from New Orleans, this...' She shrugged. 'It's sad and atmospheric.' She buried her face in her menu. Without glancing at him she acknowledged, 'Thank you for taking me here.'

'You're welcome.' He was rather taut.

She cleared her throat.

'I'll have the nine-ounce – six-ounce Sirloin.' She closed her menu and looked at him. 'Miss Cunningham's making me play for assembly.'

'Well, Isabel . . . with only two days remaining, it was to be expected.'

She let out a sigh.

'Not really. I asked her not to.'

'Nonetheless . . . they should be allowed to hear you play once more.'

She was almost disputatiously discordant.

'Perhaps.'

They ordered. Isabel gulped down her glass of water and the waiter straightaway refilled it.

Uneasy banter poked the air for the next hour. Couples around them were exchanging raucous laughter and copious anecdotes, dabbing their cigarettes in ashtrays, letting their vocal pitches escalate and pop like fireworks.

Following her steak's consumption Isabel decided to recross her legs.

'I still think this musician is rather *subpar.*' Tally pointed out.

Isabel gazed once more at the saxophonist.

'It's a different genre, Tally. He's actually a professional.'

Tally nodded in a forced agreement. He reached into his jacket pocket.

Her feet were glazed in cold.

It was a handkerchief that he extracted.

A click of his fingers summoned the waiter; he bade him bring the pink champagne.

Isabel beheld the runty man with oval eyes.

'At what time would you like the meringue, madam?'

The question was redirected to her escort.

'Another ten minutes or so, thank you.'

Isabel stroked her right arm with her left.

'With this heat . . . do you think the candles are for decoration?'

'Why else?'

An ant was on her hand; she had to flick it off.

'Something the matter?'

'No, no – not at all.'

'I wanted to talk to you about—'

Her champagne flute was abruptly toppled: she'd extended her right arm to take a sip. A little pink stream dyed the tablecloth and dripped along her skirt.

The small man with oval eyes approached them once again.

'Not to worry, madam; not to worry.'

Mopping up the spillage, he insisted that the tablecloth be changed.

Tally waved his hand:

'That really isn't necessary.'

Isabel began to yearn for Anneliese's pocket-sized knowledge of cardiology. Her internal instrument was ticking far too violently to qualify as healthy.

'Isabel—'

'Mmm-hmm?'

'There's a – well . . . you see . . . I wanted to ask what date you started university.'

Could he have already been planning the honeymoon? So early?

Her heart slowed down.

'It can be delayed.'

'What can?'

'The . . . the start of term. The first days are nothing but introductions in any case.'

'But . . .' He stroked his brow. 'No, I was just, I was just wondering when you were obliged to be there.'

'That isn't important.'

'What do you – what do you mean?'

'The first days are just formal gatherings and parties.'

'When's the start of term?'

'The 19th September.'

To himself he murmured:

'So I'll see you before, then . . .'

'See me before . . . What's happening in *September*?'

'Hmm? Yes, well, Isabel, there is a – I have some news.'

Her instrument began to pound voluminously yet again.

'Is it about Sherborne?'

'Not... erm . . . not exactly.'

The little man with oval eyes walked up to them *again*.

'Would you like your meringues now, sir?'

'Er – yes, that would be lovely, thank you.'

Isabel continued to sit still, wondering whether her optical expression could be read as the first sign of madness.

'I have a place at Harvard Business School.'

She leant back in her chair. Frames of New York and glittering billboards of Schweppes and Wrigley's chewing gum bounced in her mind like Punch and Judy pranced at Covent Garden.

'So . . . Tally – do you mean to say we're – you mean to say . . . we're going to America?'

He loudly cleared his throat. He also relied on the back of his finger to massage the tip of his nose for some reason.

'Well, Isabel . . . You and the Royal College . . . it would be a robbery – from them, from *you*.'

A catapult was pelting bricks at her.

'Tally – that, that isn't even *pertinent*.'

'How is it not *pertinent*?'

'Because I'm totally incapable – I – de- I can't – Tally, that's *really* not an issue. I would very happily go with you to Harvard. I don't need – I don't – *they* don't even need me there.'

He began to stroke her left arm with his hand.

'You can't . . .' His voice was very soft. 'You can't abuse your art, Isabel.'

'My – my *what*? I'm not *Rubinstein*. I can't – I can't play a scale in front of my own teacher.'

He released what sounded like a simulated sigh.

'That's just young stagefright, Isabel.'

Her voice was small.

'Young . . . stagefright?'

'You're eighteen years old. You've been going through an awkward patch. It's a hard age to experience: so much uncertainty, so many worries. And it's very tough when one feels there are many expectations on one's shoulders.'

She was quick to correct him:

'No, Tally – I never felt burdened by my teachers' or my father's expectations. Not when it came to the *piano*.'

He shrugged.

'It doesn't even make a difference. You feel burdened because of some other responsibility you take on, and that makes you nervous. It comes out in the *piano*.'

'It *doesn't*.'

'At any rate, Harvard is not a place for you. I'm not going to steal your chance of being great.'

'I'm not *great!!*' She let out a choked laugh: the kind expelled when one fails quite explicitly to make excuses. 'I took that in my stride, Tally.' She took another sip of water. 'I understood and I accepted that I wouldn't be a pianist, and I can live with that. I can live with it more comfortably if it so happens that you want to share this with me.'

'But I'm not talking about *will*, Isabel—'

'You just said you don't want me to go *with* you!'

'For *your* sake!'

It was a case of ill-received Chinese whispers. The small man brought their lemon meringues.

Taking a spoonful, she began to chew until she safely felt she could resume her speech.

'In any case . . . it's not really a problem. I'll go to the Royal College, then at Christmas I'll go to Boston, then at Easter you'll come here. It's only . . . what? Two years . . .'

She tapped her spoon against the ramekin. His voice was so shy, it was almost blotted out by the saxophonist.

'Isabel . . . I'm not – I'm not talking about a . . . "hiatus".'

She played with her spoon.

'What's a . . . "hiatus"?'

He inhaled very loudly.

'My father wants me to attend the school to, er . . . Well – it's a very expensive course and it's – it's not a holiday.'

'Of course not.'

'He wants to – I'm the Assistant Director of Sherborne Hotels.'

'I know.'

'And my father's the Director.'

Isabel sniggered nervously.

'I *know* that.'

'He wants me to go to America because he wants to *expand*.'

She took another spoonful but the pudding felt intolerably stale.

'*What?*'

'He wants to expand Sherborne Hotels into other continents; firstly across the Atlantic. He thinks it's worthwhile, my going to Harvard . . . with the intention of – with the intention of familiarising myself with the market.'

Isabel shrugged.

'So . . . so I'll come to live there once I've finished my degree.'

He closed his eyes for a few moments.

'Isabel . . .' A large and taut exhalation poured out from his nostrils. 'That would really be a silly act on your part.'

Purposely she dropped her spoon into the ramekin, stirring a clatter.

'Because . . . because I'm supposed to be a great pianist?'

'Well . . . I don't think you'll find the onset of a great career in Cambridge, Massachusetts.'

'Even if that *were* my plan . . .' She almost had to laugh to cure the tension. 'It *isn't* – but even if it *were* – it can't be far away from New York, surely.'

'But – when I finish Harvard Business School, I . . . I'm afraid I don't know – I can't *possibly* say where I'll go.'

Absorbing all the words, she nodded very slowly.

'I can't follow you ...' Her voice withered. 'Because I have a "great career" to perfect?'

'I'm sorry, Isabel, it . . . it would be imprudent.'

'You won't stay here?'

'I . . .' His nostrils seemed to purr again. 'I can't.'

'Because your father . . . Right.'

She stood up.

'Where are you going?'

Isabel tucked her chair in.

'To the ladies.'

The door marked 'ladies' was on the right of the restaurant. Not far from it was the kitchen. Through the kitchen door she saw a dozen or so chefs bustling expressly back and forth, their frying pans tossing salads and meats through the air; another kneading dough with his bare, hairy hands. One of this entourage, a dark Mediterranean man, came out and approached her.

'Miss . . . can I help *you?*'

There was a fire exit door at the back of the kitchen.

The floor was slippery. Skidding as she raced amidst a string of cries and reprimands from chefs, she ended up outside on some wet pavement. She was without her coat; it had been raining.

There were three shillings in her purse; she caught a taxi. In constant combat with the urge to let her eyes get moist she sat behind the driver with her hands across her knees, wondering to whom to sell her dresses. It would pay for food and amenities. It could pay for Anneliese's birthday present five months later.

When she arrived home it was only half past ten. The only beaming light came from the corridor.

She understood that she would never get her coat back. That she could accept.

Isabel went upstairs on tiptoe. Anneliese was clearly fast asleep. So apathetic was she to her sister's fate, she hadn't even *fought* the urge to sleep. This realisation clamoured inside Isabel, stirring a loud and discommoding, suffocating kind of jazz in her: *crescendo* atonality.

She took it as a cue to wield her fury: for the moment she was desperately in need of it. Isabel banged on Liesa's door ferociously.

Inside the dark room Anneliese was roused. She could guess the outcome; could elicit from the frenzy that her sister was engaged. And yet her cheeks were stained from tears, she was engrossed in private sorrow and she wasn't in the mood for revelry.

Burying her left cheek in her pillow, she lay still with eyes closed.

In the disarray of her sister's room Isabel tripped over the Czech dictionary. She sought to grab it with her hands and rip the hardback covers from the pile of knitted sheets inside.

It flung open when it hit her foot and bruised it. A piece of paper lay inside in Anneliese's handwriting entitled: 'Paradubice Radical Arrested For Conspiracy To Murder Hlinka'. She could just about make out her sister's letters in the dark. It was an article, albeit poorly written – she supposed translated – about some revolutionary, a radical named Vladislav Černuška who had synthesised chlorine gas at the Hoechst factory during the Great War and plotted to assassinate Andrej Hlinka – whoever that was.

Quickly she stopped reading. Zealously she wished that she could throw off agitation, tell herself 'to each his own' again. She wished that she could understand why Anneliese had different interests; interests in some unrelated, unaffiliated Czechs.

She couldn't. She couldn't even make the proper effort to depart from Anneliese's room in peace. Isabel knocked over a trinket she kept on her chest of drawers quite deliberately. And when she shut the door the noise was closer to a slam than to a closure.

Three days had passed since Isabel had failed to be engaged. It was the last set of hours they would spend at Croham Hurst School: a bounty of hugs, parting gifts, presents for teachers and 'Jerusalem'. They sang it every year at the end of assembly.

It was Isabel who volunteered to enter Miss Butterworth's office at the end of the day. She and Anneliese had both chipped in to buy her an English first edition of Chekhov's four plays: one of her favourite dramas was *The Seagull*. Anneliese had bought the present by herself but she was presently held captive by Miss Hampshire who was feeding her Victoria sponge.

After the expected hug and perfunctory wishes, Miss Butterworth turned solemn and noted to Isabel:

'I haven't . . . I haven't seen your young man lately.'

Isabel shrugged.

Then she understood how stupid her reaction had appeared.

'He's – we don't see each other anymore.'

Miss Butterworth seemed rather taken aback.

'You don't?'

'No.'

'Ah.' She looked down. 'Well . . . I'm sure that . . . I'm sure that it won't be the last of your experience.'

Isabel knew not how to respond.

'You know, Isabel . . . I understand that playing isn't quite for you – at the moment. But those who can't *do* . . .'

Isabel was clueless. She imagined that her gaze might be the look of pigeons being trampled on by cars.

Miss Butterworth adjusted her planned course of speech.

'You're always welcome to come back and visit.'

33.

Diversion on the shopping list

Like a burnt, coarse chunk of steak that oozed blood at the piercing of a knife, Anneliese arrived at St Mary's Hospital Medical School frazzled and underdone after one hour of sleep.

Too many hours had been spent the previous night reading her tomes on biochemistry, pathology, the musculoskeletal system and physiology. As well as books by Freud and Jung and Adler.

The ratio of men to women in the classroom was approximately nine to one. All around her six-foot fellows discussed rugby, Arsenal unjustly getting penalties and Houses at their boarding schools. A marble bust of Alexander Fleming towered over the ensemble of some eighty first-years.

Keeping his height firmly erect – straight as a pencil – a sixty-something skinny man beset the room with the premeditated pace of military steps. His hair was shortly cropped and silver-grey, his eyelids heavy and twice-creased. There was a quilt of flakes across his facial skin; ill-treated eczema or psoriasis. After fixing his large eyeballs on the students with a still and manic expectation finally he whistled with his thumb and forefinger.

'Ladies and gentlemen.' His voice was thin and shrill. It sounded like a mercury thermometer being dropped along the floor. 'Could any of you tell me where you are now standing?'

A bespectacled boy with curly ginger hair extended a long hand.

'Not you, sir.' the professor quite briskly responded. 'You.' He addressed a petite red-haired girl with cheeks broadly bespeckled with freckles. 'Miss. Could you tell me what happened in the *precise* location where you are now standing?'

She wished she could obey him like a sycophantic soldier. Nonplussed, her blue eyes dallied like a group of dawdling girls stuck in the corner of a dance hall.

'Erm . . . Professor . . .'

Another boy – this time not bespectacled – shot up his hand as quick as cannon fire. The silver-haired professor nodded.

'Yes, Peterson?'

'The discovery of penicillin, sir.'

'Pre-*cise*-ly!' sang the professor – and he swung his left arm with such vigour, it was strange his elbow didn't dislocate itself.

Posing questions, he would slightly bow:

'Could any of you – *not* Peterson, if you please – tell me about "penicillin"?'

There was silence.

'Do none of you engage in *reading?*'

The silence recurred. Peterson at last raised his hand. Anneliese perceived how much his voice was high-pitched; like a countertenor's, similar to that of the *castrati* Isabel had once described to her.

'*Penicillium notatum*. It's a substance of fungi potentially capable of destroying bacteria.'

The silver-haired professor stuck his hands along his hips and began walking in small steps around the classroom.

'That is *correct*. As for the rest of you, if you are lacking a subscription to the *Journal of Experimental Pathology*, I suggest that you relinquish your positions here and leave immediately.'

A medium-sized boy with curly brown hair without delay took the advice.

The pedagogue approached the podium behind the desk and stood on it. He brushed his hands against each other as though wiping off some dust.

'Good riddance to *that* particular young gentleman.'

There were two other girls among the first-years. The first was the red-headed one who had risked fainting with her answer: shy and genteel Emily-Jane Stufflebeam. The other was a taller one whose profile Anneliese had scarcely seen; they hadn't yet met face-to-face. But somehow every time in the ensuing weeks she came across an essay labelled 'Excellent!' one name would feature at the top: *Melissa Gail Adams-Kennedy*.

Four weeks into their lessons Anneliese was yet to greet her. She could recognise that she was yet another redhead – one with a small nose, perhaps with skin as flaky as the silver-haired professor's. She knew of her by reputation only. In any case she didn't plan to socialise.

The experiments Anneliese found inconsequential. Everywhere people scattered the name 'Alexander Fleming' with the frequency with which they used the lexemes 'beaker', 'blade' and 'scalpel'.

Her partner – some Welsh blond athlete by the name of Aeron – couldn't handle it. He left the school on the seventeenth working day. She was assigned a new one. He made a point of going up to her before the start of their first lesson for the purpose of an introduction.

It was a boy with neatly cut black hair and a side fringe, spectacles and gleaming polished shoes. He didn't easily surpass her height of five foot three.

'Hello.' The student stretched his hand out. 'My name is Benjamin Levin.'

Anneliese nodded. Under the influence of his somnific voice she didn't offer him her own.

'Oh – sorry – Anneliese van der Holt.'

He smiled.

'You're Dutch?'

'Yes.'

'I'm Jewish.'

'So is my cousin.'

It was a faulty kind of meaningless exchange with which she was already too familiar – much to her dismay. But she pursued it for the sake of being polite, already sensing the impending tedium that being paired with Benjamin foreshadowed.

'Which school do you come from?'

'Westminster.'

There would begin a conversation during which she would inevitably have to cite her father who had died, then Benjamin would imitate faint sorrow, then a realm of silence would usurp them both.

It would be sequential – like a shopping list.

Just as her chronic nodding and smiling was waning she heard him declare:

' . . .but what I *really* want is to become a psychiatrist.'

'Oh.' Her mind stopped scouring for a figurative exit. 'So do I.'

He laughed a little warmly.

'Did "they" reject you too?'

'Oxford?'

'Well – Cambridge.' Benjamin clarified. 'It's the same thing.'

'Yes, "they" did.'

'We oughtn't to have bothered.'

'No, I suppose not.'

It was no grounds for kinship – but it sketched the makings of a tolerance towards him on her part.

Here at St Mary's Hospital Medical School came the epiphany

that Anneliese's hands were not faulty. The reason for this was a simple one: so poor were her performances on tests and essays, every time she had the chance to execute another exercise she rose to the occasion. Her dissections of a pancreas or lung or brain were fairly even. Most boys in their class were hopeless at it. It was the only moment Dr Viking would commend her work.

Isabel's contrasting morning ritual now consisted of the mutilation of unread and garrulous, explanatory letters sent first-class from Cambridge, Massachusetts.

34.

Ripe

Walking beneath the golden-brown and jaundiced leaves of trees she passed on Exhibition Road that morning in November, Isabel envisaged her bland future. The role of breadwinner would go to Anneliese. She would become a well-respected doctor, inter-marry someone in her field and probably maintain a home ornately furnished by a double income.

Her own part would be that of the 'inferior' sister. Amid roaring engines of taxis escorting commuters to work she eavesdropped on the augured conversation taking place in their bedroom:

'Anneliese, you told me she'd be gone by next week.'

'Yes, but, [Richard]/[Tom]/[Jack], you have to understand, she has nothing to do with herself, nowhere to go . . . You can't leave her with Mother. Mother rarely gets up in the morning.'

'And when do you think her situation might just change?' would ask, inevitably, Richard, Jack, or Tom.

Isabel already knew her fingers couldn't count the weeks that she would have to spend inhabiting their attic or their basement and playing the scavenger; gnawing on their food and utilities.

The College gave her time to comfortably defer these pictures' presence.

Yet they were already plastered on her psychic insides.

From the moment of her morning entrance there invariably would be some cellist or violinist practising the hardest piece ever composed, brandishing triple trills and staves of turns and portamentos mournfully amiss from her experience for five and a half years. Students' exchanges scarcely constituted conversations. 'Combat' should have been the name for them.

On that occasion as she headed down a corridor she heard emerging from behind her:

'It's at Wigmore Hall.'

It was a girl. A boy was trailing her.

'I didn't even know—'

'How could you not *know?*'

'I didn't see the noticeboard—'

The girl was even more blatant and louder.

'There *was* no notice on the board.'

The boy was silent for a while.

'So how did you—'

'This *wonderful* young man came in – truly remarkable – and told us Wigmore Hall was holding auditions for a showcase sometime next *week.*'

The girl chewed, salivating as she crunched her chocolate and made chomping noises. Isabel could hear saliva serving as the glue that stuck her lips together.

'I don't understand – how could you *not* have been there?'

'You mean . . . in the common room?'

'What *common room?* I mean the Elgar Gallery. It's where the whole clan meets, practically every day . . .' She chomped and chomped until it sounded like the item was en route along her windpipe. 'Anyway, it's over now.'

'What is?'

'The auditions. They'll never take you now. Well – have a nice day – cheerio!'

That banter permeated everywhere she went. The professors were a little gentler sometimes; either that, or irritable. Her piano teacher whipped her every lesson verbally, incriminated her and slammed his fist on the black top: yelling that if once again she failed to practise she would promptly be expelled.

Needless to say she never failed to practise.

Sometimes the conversations aroused more excitement when a few girls bragged about their 'covert' knowledge and 'spilled out' their secrets. Usually these would be overheard amidst the common room where some half-bearded boy with spots asprawl his nose and cheeks would sluggishly sit on the sofa, legs apart and eyes half-closed in semi-slumber. The girls would be hovering not far from him, dangling over the piano, munching on chocolate or – if they were vocalists – swigging great gulps of water.

That morning Isabel chanced on the following:

'But – Simon, Rebecca, what I'm saying is, I don't understand—'

The other two or three or four would rarely heed to listen to the first.

'The "Peabody" is a conservatoire somewhere in America.'

'It's like the Eastman.'

'It's *not* like the Eastman.'

'How would *you* know?'

'How would *I* know?'

'But, but – Simon, Simon, listen – did you ever get the scoop on that girl . . . what's her name?' A small and plump violinist by the name of Harriet heaved a great lazy sigh. 'Damn – what's her name?'

The boy among them raised his voice.

'You mean the . . . the Flemish?'

'Yes . . . yes, that's right, the *tall* one. She's Dutch, isn't she?'

The boy nodded vigorously.

'Yes, her name is . . . "van de" something. She's Flemish.'

'And then, then . . .' it was Plump Harriet speaking again. 'I heard her uncle sits on the Board.'

Another girl with jet black hair was quick to interrupt:

'I heard that she canoodled the *someone* on the Board.'

'"Canoodled"?' the boy asked.

'Yes.'

His eyebrows dug into the bridge along his nose.

'Who *uses* that word?'

Plump Harriet sucked on her lollypop.

'*God* . . .' She sat back in her chair and crossed her legs. 'I heard that she and Peter Connaught were . . .' Her fingers flickered to and fro. 'And that's why—'

The one with jet black hair consented.

'She must have . . .' Her voice became a melody and it was clear which schooling she was undertaking. '*Engaged* in a certain . . .' Then it was clear she was a soprano: '*Something* with a certain . . . *well-to-do* someone.'

Isabel had accompanied cello student Peter one night on piano. The only time that she had spread her legs was to perform the third movement of Dvořák's Cello Concerto.

It had failed miserably.

Sarah Tyde was one of the few nicer ones. Her manner was lukewarm and affable – traditional in the most English sense. She had attended Wycombe Abbey. Isabel had never heard her play. On this day, a week after her nineteenth birthday, she would familiarise herself with Sarah's art.

It was her professor who was monitoring this recital in the lunch hour. Each of them would have to play onstage at the Royal Albert Hall.

The order was unfortunately alphabetical: Isabel's 'van der Holt' immediately succeeded 'Tyde'. When it came to the latter's turn her bespectacled, bald teacher offered a radiant smile. It must have helped that Sarah Tyde's curvaceous contour was a heaving bosom bottomed by a modest waist.

'Would you care to play it for us, Sarah?'

He doted on the girl as if she were his favourite niece. Isabel found it quite sickening.

A breezy confidence enrobing her, Sarah had platinum blonde, long and free-flowing hair. Its strands curled up so wispily, her long skirt hung so delicately from her waist and most excruciatingly her broken chords bounced with a tender flexibility. It was the manner in which all her crescendos were gently *legato* – and all her staccatos were choppy and brisk. Even her calm expression as she played was a magnetic one, although it looked so out of order with the tragedy that she was striving to awaken in the piece.

All her other classmates looked on wondrously. Talented students were wont to incite others' rage. This was not one of those instances.

No disfigured, jagged strokes of feeling could contaminate the silken, airy Sarah: she had not been born with an inherent tapestry of scabrous scuffs of sentiment. The fear and gloom that touched on Isabel's interpretation would elude her always.

Yet the blonde girl's playing was the gradual hacking of a thin, serrated knife into her stomach: Madam Butterfly's own *harakiri*.

Isabel's performance that day was an indefatigable failure. She played, flushed her spectators who were languid in a dismal silence, got yelled at by Professor Perkins after the recital and avoided going home because she knew she couldn't practise. Anneliese was there.

Her sister would remark the sight of sombre Isabel whose eyes were puffier and redder than their usual selves from the bewailing she had wrought inside the toilet cubicle.

Lowered by several kinds of albatrosses, Isabel was sure a paperweight resided in her skull. She was in need of a new hobby so she reached into her purse. Economising was a gift not yet in her possession. Neither did she plan to work towards that goal.

At first she was conservative. It was only six o'clock. She took the bus to Charing Cross under the false pretence that she was heading home. Then she turned to Villiers Street.

Her dress was not formal enough for some restaurants. So her ravenous eyes spotted a wine bar.

It was a drop of sherry in a crystal glass that she imbibed, served by a dashing barman likely younger than her classmates. Unlike couples sitting at round tables, throwing themselves into mundane badinage, she perched on a high bar stool carefully removed from everyone's attention.

Twenty-one minutes passed. Looking at her pocket watch, she wondered how to make another glass of sherry last.

Port featured on the wine list but one shilling tinkled in her purse. That would suffice for one glass. She would have to make it durable.

Rummaging in search of other coins deep in her pocket, she abruptly heard a baritone voice stealthily command:

'Don't waste your resources.'

Isabel turned around. It was a gruff but handsome forty-something-year-old man clad in a suit. Flakes of beard extruded from his upper lip and chin as though he shaved in moderation; dark brown curls made up his chevelure.

He took his wallet from his inside jacket pocket.

'What's your poison?'

Isabel could have rebuffed his offer, made excuses, spoken of a sister who was ill or promised babysitting.

'The Tawny port. Thank you.'

His green eyes lingered on her as they might on some impoverished individual.

'I take it you don't drink the real stuff.'

'What's . . .' She gulped. '*Real?*'

'Men's liquor.'

She ended up appearing rather sorry.

'Calm down, no one's forcing you.'

'Good.' She sniggered nervously. Her port arrived.

He persisted in looking at her with a somewhat disgusted, somewhat intrigued gaze.

'Downing that won't fix you.'

'How would one plan to . . .' She wouldn't have uttered the sentence had a blazing conceit not ignited her mind. '*Fix* me?'

His voice dimmed.

'I'm sure there are many ways.'

Setting her glass to stretch her hand, she was still wondering if this was called for.

'Isabel van der Holt. I study at the Royal College of Music.'

From the corner of his eyes his pupils seemed quite focussed on the hand.

Physically he dismissed it. Even pretended that he hadn't seen it.

'Steven Hutchinson. I'm a barrister.'

'Is that . . . that's the defence?' Subdued laughter followed.

'Yes . . . that's the defence.'

It took her ten seconds to finish her port. His voice was throaty, a little constrained when he spoke. His eyes and frame would barely move. From his steadied focus she surmised that he was good at darts.

'Have you ever been to Crockfords?'

Her face was blank.

'You mean the, er . . .'

He leaned over the bar and looked at her more closely.

'It's a club.'

'Is it a . . . a gentlemen's club?'

'Not anymore. I can take you.'

She tried to play the role of the innocent – maybe a tad too theatrically.

'Well, may . . .'

'It's open now.'

'All right.'

Any escort of his was apparently admitted freely. They caught a taxi and sat far apart inside the car. Isabel peered out of the window the whole way. She was too frightened to say anything, fearing excessively she might seem like an idiot. She wanted him to see her as being nubile – not an idiot.

When they emerged half an hour later she realised that it was a club with a covert casino. The look of horror on her face was not one she could easily conceal.

'I'm not – I'm not properly dressed—'

'It doesn't matter. Take my arm.'

'Your—'

'Take my arm.'

She obliged. Upon entering she smiled to the porter; he accepted her coat. Not a word was said about her not-so-formal clothing or the fact that she was alien to them. She whispered to Mr Hutchinson:

'I've never – I've never played before.'

'*I* have.'

'I don't have – I can't really . . . *bet* . . .'

'I'll show you.'

'No, I mean – I don't – I'm a—' (her plan not to appear an idiot was faltering). 'I'm a student.'

'Bet on my money, then.'

'I'm sorry?'

'Bet on my money.'

Its underground resort was swarthy and luxurious. Mahogany chairs were coated in red velvet, spinning green and black and red roulettes dazzled her eyes. No one questioned her presence. All the attendants were reserved, aware exclusively of victories and losses. Everybody seemed adrift.

He instructed her to place five red chips on the number thirty-four. The automaton heeded his orders.

Ordering a sherry for her, he watched her pursue his commands. Throughout the evening they engaged in nothing but the art of losing. No conversations stirred; no questions, no impulsive actions.

Two hours later he approached her and suggested that they leave. The porter handed her her coat. Mr Hutchinson refrained from linking arms with her.

He caught her a taxi. Before she stepped inside he warily commanded:

'I'll see you tomorrow.'

'Where?'

'Here.'

'When?'

'The same time as today. Wear an appropriate gown.'

The cab driver was waiting. He bellowed quite discourteously:

'Hurry *up!*'

Isabel ignored him.

'But . . . shall we meet first?'

'Don't ask questions.'

He opened the door to the taxi and waited for her to climb in, all the while shooting stern eyes at her.

It really wasn't in her plans to go to Crockfords the next day. He was, after all, a stranger – one who hadn't made any enquiries; may not have given her his name had she not asked for it. He had presented her no warmth, offered no curiosity about her being; even neglected to ask for her telephone number or home address.

On the surface of her mind a moral conscience cautioned her, insisting what this gentleman had done was wrong. At least, it was not *right*. He was anticipatory. He was expecting something from a woman that remained ineffable. He sublimated his intentions into the magnetic prowess of his eyes.

So she showed up the next evening – this time in a scarlet dress, pretending she was in a hurry.

'I have to leave by half past nine.' she insisted.

'Why?'

'I'm meeting someone.'

'No, you're not.'

She scoffed sarcastically.

'How would you *know*?'

He looked at her once more with some form of revulsion.

'Your lipstick's smudged. Go to the ladies.'

Coldly she was subservient.

'Fine.'

It seemed again that Isabel's attempts at being a lady were in peril. She adjusted her cosmetics and returned. Mr Hutchinson stood waiting for her with his hands linked like a guard before a palace.

'Put it on twenty-two.'

She sat at the roulette. His hand was resting on her chair.

Looking up at him, she questioned:

'Is that how old you think I am?'

'Just do it.'

Isabel placed the chip on twenty-two. He won. He didn't seem the slightest pleased about it.

'Why did you ask me to come?' she demanded to know.

'I didn't *ask*.'

'Well then – why did you *tell* me?'

'Put the chip on thirty-one.'

'Why can't you just . . . answer the question?'

'Put the chip on thirty-one, and then I'll tell you.'

So she obeyed, if only for the sake of feeding curiosity. He won again.

He put his hands on her shoulders and lowered himself. The bottom of his chin haphazardly caressed her neck.

'All the most enjoyable activities take place between a man and woman.'

'And that's it?'

'Correct.'

Her shoulders were untouched again; he had removed his hands. Without looking up at him she asked by mirroring his drowsiness:

'Why did you take me and not another?'

'Put it on eighteen.'

This time he lost.

'You'll find out.'

'When?'

'Soon enough.'

Every night that week she came to Crockfords. She was running out of dresses. Every new experience would yield another morsel of progression; one more touch or whisper, one more truncated revelation. She came on Saturday and Sunday, saving her best dress for the following Tuesday.

That was their eighth meeting, by which time few questions had been asked and even fewer answers given. But she could recognise there was an apple to be tasted.

Neither Tally nor the young men she had known had offered a sneak peek. They had been inanely ignorant; almost effeminate. They had exercised the art the way that women assumed knitting as a hobby: the first loop by the needle being flattery, another courtship and the third a comely ring to finish off the tapestry.

Steven skipped these cultivated processes. The tug of war was one between the sexes: one of them en route to conquest and the other on the run in her resistance. Nothing could have been more primitive. Nothing could have made more sense to Isabel.

Habitually she told her sister she was meeting with some violinists. Anneliese did not believe her but she lied and said she did.

Wolves were not a timid bunch. In their third week of meetings Steven steadily began to be a little more aggressive in his tactics.

For every gesture, every intonation of his she could imitate he would reward her with another inhalation of the prize. That evening he allowed his lips to linger on her neck and started muttering obscenities beside her ear after their victories at Crockfords. He told her that the gift bequeathed upon a man and woman was a trove of pleasure: a perpetual source for drinking the delectable. Her heart leapt from the shock; from the indecency and immorality of the scenarios suggested.

And then she settled into these imaginings as she might mould her mattress with her frame. She learned to toy around with them inside her head throughout professors' sleep-inducing lectures. She watched the other girls around her picking at their nails, rummaging for handkerchiefs inside their bags or looking at some freckled boys beside whom Isabel would not have *sat*. Those girls would never be familiar with the meaning of the male-female entanglement. They focussed on the lectures about pentatonic scales and Dorian music; she imbibed another kind bestowed in nightly intimacy.

None of these attractions were enacted: therein lay the other fruit of her enjoyment. Most of the time envisaged images would conjure a reaction. Now an impassive partner took a share in this and aided her. It helped students' recitals pass as quickly for her as cascading water through a plughole.

By January they were still conducting the same meetings every evening. He invited her to dinner for the first time at a restaurant in Mayfair. In three courses all he said was 'pass the salt' and 'waiter'. Her delight proliferated.

35.

Musical quivers

Men had their own trend of idealisation: Anneliese understood that. They could ponder on a woman's beauty, eyes with upturned corners, lips and stains they left along her glass. Conjuring the figure of a goddess, they externalised their love in sensual gestures.

With all this knowledge at her helm she nonetheless allowed Benjamin Levin to hover around her. He was the kind of man one never needed to assuage; his was the role to mollify all others and withstand a pack of dimwits championing nonsense. Always able to restrain his nostrils' steam, the fellow was a tender sort of Mummy's boy: tranquil and compliant and discreetly dissident.

One December afternoon the two spent an entire lunchtime searching for a paper in the library that Dr Montague had told them was imperative. Seventeen drawers contained articles stored chronologically. The date of publication of this mandatory article had slipped their minds.

Anneliese searched through 1878–1900 while Benjamin scoured the following twenty-two years.

She decided that their small talk should be centred on a subject at least marginally interesting.

'I suppose that we're the only ones who want to be psychiatrists.'

'No, no . . .' Benjamin stammered a little. 'There are three of us, actually.'

'Really?'

'Yes. You, I, and Melissa Adams-Kennedy.'

'I still haven't met her.'

'I'm sure you will quite soon.'

'She's the one who gets excellent marks?'

'Oh, yes.' Benjamin hastened to add in a cautious whisper: 'She makes quite an exhibition of herself. Don't worry if you're not entranced.'

'I won't.'

'So – tell me, er . . . I don't believe we've had this conversation: who's *your* psychiatrist?'

Anneliese dropped a large stack of articles. He began picking them up, peering at their dates in a bid to assort them.

'Are you all right?'

'I'm fine. Yes, erm – what were you saying?'

'You have one of your own, don't you?'

'A psychiatrist? Well – erm – considering I'm going to be one – yes, I have one, yes.'

'Who is he?'

'Dr Westwood.'

'Who's that?'

'A woman.'

Benjamin betrayed no signs of awkwardness or lack of understanding.

'Would I have read any of her articles?'

'Probably not, no.'

He groaned in frustration.

'It's so difficult.'

'I'm sorry . . . What is?'

'Psychotherapy. I read a lot of Freud, some Jung, some papers of Melanie Klein. Do you know who she is?'

'Yes.'

Benjamin released a sigh that indicated stress.

'It's so hard – taking a patient's whole life and attempting to unstitch the components and then to secure them together. When I decided I would specialise in it, I got myself my own psychiatrist. I've been seeing him for just about six weeks now. How long have you seen Dr Westwood?'

She threw the number off the top of her head.

'Three.'

'Three weeks? You're more of a newcomer than I am! I must admit – it makes me feel more comfortable.'

Gravely she studied him.

'Three years.'

He looked impressed. Anneliese had no capacity to fathom why and how that information could impress someone.

'You must have a great mentor.' A long pause forced him to catch hold of her attention once again. '*Anneliese?*'

'Yes?'

'Is she?'

'Is she what?'

'A great mentor?'

Anneliese unfurled her bent legs and stretched them out over the carpet.

'Well . . . she—'

Not once in these three years had she addressed the subject of Susanna with another. Barely had she broached it even *with* Susanna.

'She's demanding.' Anneliese finally answered.

'You look upset.'

'I do? Oh . . .' She scratched her cheek.

'Is she hard on you?'

'Well . . . She's my Eumenides.'

It was apparent Benjamin's familiarity with Greek mythology was not so strong.

'So she's harsh, then?'

Anneliese wallowed in her despondency.

'Yes. But – but sometimes I think she needs her own psychiatrist.'

Benjamin took care to point out:

'Most of them have their own.'

'Oh – this one doesn't.'

'Maybe she does.'

'She *doesn't*.'

'Perhaps you'd like to tell me about her? Get it off your chest? Only, of course – only if you want to.'

Anneliese snatched a glance at the clock. She wondered whether speaking of Susanna would be less embarrassing than the discussion of the marks they had received for physiology exams that morning. There was no way a layman such as Benjamin would comprehend all of Susanna's sorcery.

Neither did she.

'Yes.' she conceded. 'All right. But we'll have to go somewhere private.'

Dumping the articles in a disoriented bunch, they sealed the drawers and left the library.

'Private' was a spot outside the hospital where patients went to weep after a terminal prognosis.

They sat down in a shaded corner that remained undrenched by rain. She leant her back against a wall and felt its cold across her skin.

Anneliese pursued the storyline in full – relating how Susanna had enticed her with some mention of "gamma-Amino-butyric acid" which they knew didn't exist yet; how she had snatched and read her private files; how she had rummaged through Czech newspapers and found out that her father was a radical political extremist. She ended up confessing that her therapy did not alleviate her life – that on the contrary it racked her brain;

condemning it to hibernate until she could resolve all of Susanna's problems.

Benjamin collected her admission with the temperance and goodwill of an aspiring saviour. He scrutinised this lonely girl and started to prepare a rescue mission.

Her conscience emptied, Anneliese looked at the sky and pondered.

'You wonder where it all fits.' She sniffed and rubbed her hands together from the cold. Benjamin offered his coat. 'No, thank you.' She folded her arms. After a few more lines of thought she replaced her deduction: 'It *fits*. She has a great capacity.'

'Erm . . . do you mean she's big boned?'

'A great vertical capacity.'

Benjamin was slow to understand. He diverted the course and landed on the more appropriate subject.

'You're certain that no one has looked at her papers?'

'I'm completely certain.' Anneliese examined her fingernails and decided she needed to trim them. 'Why else would she store them in the pillow cases in her attic?'

'Well . . .' Benjamin looked at his watch. 'Oh, dear. We're late.' They started heading back into the university. 'I have an uncle on my father's side who's a doctor at the National Hospital for Nervous Diseases.'

Anneliese kept her head down as they walked.

'Mmm . . .'

'What I meant to say was – I'm sure he'd be delighted to read any papers about innovative medical experiments.'

Her head was all of a sudden aloft.

'He must be very busy, though, with all his patients . . .'

'Not to worry, not to worry. We're very close. He'll fit it in his schedule if I ask him.'

'Oh . . .' The glacier symbolising her hostility towards the young began to melt. 'That's very kind of you.'

'Of course. It is no trouble *whatsoever*.'

That evening she spent nine hours copying – in the most legible handwriting possible – all the text, figures, diagrams and chemical formulae prolific throughout her psychiatrist's papers. Only one remained incomprehensible to her.

Sprinting to university the next day, she bumped into Benjamin – who was immediately handed a ponderous folder.

'That's everything.' He looked at her, bewildered. 'Oh – I mean – those are Susanna's papers, as transcribed first by some epigraphist at King's, then by me.'

'So—' He continued to be puzzled. 'These aren't the originals?'

'No, no – you couldn't read them. Her handwriting is . . .' She scratched behind her ear, exhaling. 'Anyway, they're accurate replicas. I used paperclips to attach little notes on the front of each with my own summaries about their contents, just in case your uncle was perplexed. I hope I'm not imposing too much.'

Benjamin raised his eyebrows.

'No, no!'

'I'm really so, *so* grateful!'

He liked her better when she was content; she almost always appeared dismal.

'Erm, Anneliese . . .'

'Yes?'

The pupils in her irises were now agleam.

'I have tickets for *Dr Faustus* – Marlowe's *Dr Faustus*. It's on 21st December. Would you care to join me?'

She looked dazed. Self-preservation immediately forged a response:

'Yes – of course! I'd love to.'

She had to do it for Susanna's sake. That evening she began to ask herself how many women, centuries before, had used their cunning wiles to reach a greater good. He was a gentle boy, a courteous boy with good intentions. And yet had she refused him he might just have 'lost' the papers; told her that his uncle was too *busy.*

None of her acquaintances were genuinely interested in papers or experiments or findings. If she didn't seize this prospect the committee for the Nobel Prize in Physiology or Medicine might never pick Susanna as its first female recipient.

Too quickly did her mind race for her concepts to make any sense.

Benjamin telephoned a week before the play to tell her that his mother 'unforgivably' had given its awaited tickets to his cousin Abraham. In lieu of this he had bought tickets to a rendering of Franz Liszt's *Transcendental Études*. She imposed it on herself to accept.

As she accoutred herself in a sleeveless, backless black gown that 21st December, Anneliese entered Isabel's room with the question:

'Liszt's *Transcendental Études*?'

'Yes...' Isabel gave out a smile whose sadness she desired to disguise. 'I used to play them once.'

'Are they pretty?'

'Very. Why on earth would you have heard of them? And why are you so beautiful? Are you—' Her speech spluttered into a guffaw.

'I'm . . . I'm going to hear them with Benjamin.'

'My, my . . . Liesa, you are in a *courtship!*'

Isabel sprang to her feet and jumped up and down, shaking the ceiling in the living room downstairs.

Then she flipped back on her bed.

Anneliese was unimpressed by these unnecessary calisthenics.

'It's not – Isabel! You have to taint everything with illusion! We're friends and we're going to listen to Liszt's *Transcendental Études!*' She heard her sister give a close-mouthed chuckle and responded with averting eyes. 'You're just like Susanna.'

Isabel sat up.

'You told your *tutor* that Benjamin asked you—'

'I tell her *many* things.'

'Hmm. Well, Anneliese, I must say, though it sounds mean, that that just shows how many friends you have. Enjoy yourself.'

Benjamin picked her up at a quarter to seven. Through the window Isabel pursued them with her eyes. He was driving her to Cadogan Hall by himself.

As they stepped out of the car he offered her his left arm and she reacquainted herself with her doubts. Benjamin wore a tuxedo. The spectators would assume they were husband and wife. The usher called them 'sir' and 'madam', making Anneliese feel even more remorseful.

She didn't really hear the *Transcendental Études* – instead fixing her eyes on strings atremble in the grand piano. Now she knew why arrows were called 'quivers'. The same strings must have also yielded to a tremor in her abdomen, extending from her lower right quadrant to the upper left quadrant and all of the sections she studied throughout her anatomy textbooks. This young man had taken her to hear a concert, dressed in a tuxedo, probably expecting her to gradually convert to Judaism.

By half past eleven Benjamin had driven them back. He had been warm without provoking a frisson. Stepping out of the car, she let herself yield to a long-winded sigh of relief.

'Cold?' Benjamin asked.

'No, no. In any case – I'm home now.'

'We should do this again.'

'Yes, of course.'

She stood before him and tried hard to recollect all that her father had once taught her on concluding statements.

'Thank you very much for taking me – it was a pleasure. I had never appreciated Liszt before.'

'He's a great composer.'

'He is.'

She scanned her memory for any other formal greeting. All of a sudden she saw Benjamin lunge forward and lean down: a clear attempt at an invasion of her private space. To save herself she oafishly began to stumble backwards.

'No, Benjamin, no – no ...' She wanted to sound less condemning than she did. Still in shock, she failed to muster her desired tone. 'No – I don't – I don't do that.'

'I'm so sorry. It was really very rash on my part—'

'No, no – Benjamin *I'm* sorry; I don't – I don't want any of that; I don't want *any* of it – not – not at *all*; I don't know if I'll *ever* want it.'

The defence was a little too brusque, too excessive, too revelatory.

Shaken by this exclamation, Benjamin could only nod in simulated sympathy. Anneliese continued:

'I'm so sorry – I care for you; I really do care for you, but I – I . . . there is no hope in trying to get me – trying to entangle me in a romance; I'm just not normal.'

Matter-of-factly he quipped:

'I'm quite sure you're *normal*, Anneliese, it's simply a question of preference.'

'I don't know, Benjamin. I don't think I want to marry. I don't want children. I don't know anything. I—' She stared into space for a few moments. 'I'm sounding very foolish and you must excuse me.'

She dashed off. With her back turned, he responded:

'You don't sound foolish at all. You're being frank.'

Anneliese gave way now to a different kind of sigh.

'Find yourself a good wife, Benjamin. I'm really not – not what you anticipated.'

She was quite more than what he had anticipated. Now there was a mystery to pick; a problem to unwind. This served to amplify his curiosity. As he watched Anneliese trying to ham-handedly pin her key in the door – shoving it left and right with no luck till her sister opened it – Benjamin realised he had never felt more needed.

She hated herself. She told herself that Benjamin must think she was some kind of *actress*. Susanna's chances of receiving any Nobel Prize were thwarted.

Her castigations huddled to become an endless flagellation.

Isabel knocked on her door before she went to bed at one am. She came in to find her sister puffy-eyed with moistened cheeks. So she sat down.

'It was rather too forward of him on the *first date*. Especially with someone like *you*.' Anneliese chose not to respond verbally. 'But you shouldn't take offence, Liesa—'

'I didn't find it anyhow offensive.'

'So, then—'

'I don't like the boy. Not in the way *you* would.'

'So you . . . went to a concert with him for no reason?'

'Yes.'

Isabel nodded complacently.

'Very well.'

She closed the door behind her as she left. Anneliese continued to pursue her punishment.

36.

Half-plucked

Preparing for their dinner to be held at Claridge's, Isabel excused herself to Anneliese for going to Plump Harriet's birthday party.

The Younger Twin had long ago renounced her quest for truth. In spite of everything she was completely certain Isabel was not a virgin. Susanna differed in opinion. She insisted that since Isabel was able to approach her sister without reddened cheeks and a distinctly altered set of intonations she was 'pure on paper'.

This was the veritable case. Isabel had been to Steven Hutchinson's Kensington mansion three times in four months. She had even met his parents, Ernest and Patricia: a barrister and a society hostess. During the dinner for the most part she had strived to stave off Steven's roaming hand along her upper thigh, attempting to suppress the urge to giggle as she did so. But 'on paper' – as Susanna would have put it – she was eligible for a white gown at her wedding.

That night she was the one who didn't want the games to stop. At eleven they sat on the ivory leather of his living room sofa savouring port. He took the initiative and began kissing her on the neck. Isabel sealed her mouth, fixing her lips together with a figurative clasp. When it was clear that she was still in no mood to relent he loathfully retreated.

After a long and clumsy sigh some words dashed from his mouth – all of them nonchalant:

'Are you referring to marriage?'

She set her glass of port.

'When?'

'Now.'

'I didn't say . . .' Then Isabel smirked. 'Yes.'

'Very well.'

'*Yes?*'

'Yes.'

Stepping out of the taxi car three hours later she skipped in jocoseness. Then Isabel asked herself what this particular scenario was. She was engaged – it seemed – to a much older man who barely questioned her, could still forget she had a twin and didn't know she played the cello.

Yet those anxieties were nothing but the deluge of a faulty tap. Isabel refused to be an ingénue straight out of a French novel who would be debauched then dumped in squalor. She had already lost a plenitude of battles and the swift path to a crystal reputation was the only door unclosed.

Anneliese was fast asleep. Isabel opened the door to her room and sat on the edge of her bed. Her hand began to rustle Anneliese's arm.

'Liesa!' she whispered. The dormant one did not react. Isabel jogged her arm violently. '*Liesa!*'

She tried flicking a finger at her earlobe. Anneliese was still dead to the world.

Finally she spoke aloud in a full voice.

'*Anneliese*, I'm engaged.'

The latter thought she could hear monstrous, feral noises coming from next door. Her eyes were glued together. As she struggled languidly to open them her sight was smeared by a dense, sticky element that looked like rain-doused windows.

Her voice was croaky; only half-alert.

'Wha . . . *what?*'

'I'm engaged, Liesa. I'm getting married. His name is Steven Hutchinson, he's older than I am, and he's a barrister.'

Anneliese sprung up and put the light on. She felt as though her soul were being used for chemical experiments; her sister was submerging it into a tank of pungent acid.

'You're . . .'

'Going to be a wife.'

Her hands extended on the bed to keep her upright.

'When did you . . .' She cleared her throat. 'When did you meet him?'

'Last year, in November. I didn't tell you because . . . I was anxious.'

'What – what about Tally?'

Isabel scoffed snidely.

'Write to him at *Harvard* if you want his tidings.'

'But . . .' Anneliese scratched at the back of her neck. 'Can I at least meet him?'

'Of *course*.'

Both relinquished themselves to silence for over a minute. It was Isabel who fractured it. Her voice assumed melodic cheer.

'Well . . . Aren't you going to . . .'

Anneliese rushed her argument. It didn't sound convincing.

'I'm very happy for you, Isabel.' She patted her arm. Isabel flung hers around her sister.

'Thank you.' She kissed her head.

37.

In the dark corner
of a drawer

18th April 1939 was the date of her wedding: it was to be held at some small London Lutheran church. On the fourteenth Anneliese was due to arrive at the National Hospital for Nervous Diseases where Benjamin's uncle, Dr Levin, had at last read and made sense of Susanna's collection of papers.

Steven disgusted Anneliese. They had met just once at his apartment. He had barely said a word to her. Throughout most of the evening he had put considerable effort into making Isabel spew boisterous laughs. He also couldn't peel his hand away from the north quarter of her leg.

Every time she asked herself what happened privately a shot of tart adrenalin sped up her spine and oozed a bitter taste into her windpipe.

The hospital was not far from the one on Great Ormond Street; her appointment was at 10.45.

She had to report to a receptionist.

'I'm here to see Dr Levin.'

The curly-haired, bespectacled young woman appeared quizzical. .

'Do you have an appointment?'

'Yes, yes. At quarter to eleven – Anneliese van der Holt.'

'All right love, take a seat.'

She nestled in her seat amidst a waiting room of highly incapacitated people: half of them somewhat immobile and the others laced with bandages around their heads. It serrated the tight edges of her moral conscience.

After being summoned by a nurse she was led to his office. Watched suspiciously by the infirm as she paraded through the corridor, Anneliese was discommoded.

Dr Levin on the other hand was more than welcoming.

'So, you are Benjamin's new sweetheart!' He was a mostly bald and rather plump short man with dark tufts of coarse hair, nearing on sixty. A hirsute hand was thrust into her sight. 'Delighted to meet you.'

As she took his hand her voice was hindered by the bees aswarm across her stomach.

'Thank you – thank you so much for reading Dr Westwood's papers.'

'Oh – that's *quite* all right, that's *quite* all right – won't you sit down?'

Anneliese obliged.

He took out the sheets she had given to Benjamin. They were crumpled; half the paper clips had been removed and probably were lost. She mourned their decadence.

'I found the papers of your aunt really quite – really quite startling, actually.'

The buzz in Anneliese's stomach grew stentorian.

'My . . . aunt?'

'Hmm? Yes, *yes*.'

He slapped the pile he was holding with the back of his hand. It took some time for Anneliese to gauge the nature of her friend's concoction.

'Ah – yes, yes, I know – they're – my aunt's papers are very surprising.'

Then Dr Levin heaved a great lingering sigh.

'But – not quite efficiently *supported*, I'm afraid.'

'What—' Anneliese swiped off her glasses. All of a sudden they seemed dirty. She began rubbing them with the hem of her skirt. Dr Levin handed her a cloth to use in lieu of it.

'Thank you. How *so?*'

He spread out the papers horizontally, aligning one against the other on his desk. Several times he cleared his throat.

'Miss van der Holt . . .' in a proud and stern voice – his hands dramatically aloft to aid his imminent avowal – he declaimed: 'This is all speculation.'

Her gut canal became a gutter drain imploding with stray leaves.

'But – Dr Westwood was Professor of Neurology and Associate Professor of Pathology at St Mary's.'

'Well – that's evident.'

'I'm sorry?'

'Miss van der Holt . . .' He cleared his throat. It sounded like he had a nasty cough. 'To a layman these experiments seem credible and . . . *astounding*. Hypothetically, they represent exciting samples of hypothesis.' He held his palms out in a hopeless gesture. 'But – that is all they are: *hypothesis*.'

Anneliese was timid but hard-pressed. She became more urgent and much louder than she understood she *could* be.

'Didn't you read the one about the boy with Niemann-Pick disease?'

'In my day – they called it "Niemann" disease. In fact, I still recall a time in which it didn't have a name.'

'Did you not read the addendum? Because of her it *worked* and the boy lived!' Unwittingly she started panting. 'The average life expectancy for a Niemann-Pick victim is usually *three* years!'

He nodded vigorously.

'Yes, and that is most impressive. It sounds . . . *wonderful*, for a novel, or a – a theatrical *drama*. But we're in the twentieth century, Miss van der Holt. Doctors can't administer experiments pell-mell. Do you realise what this doctor did? No board would have approved it. Furthermore, I can assume she would have got a sentence.'

'A . . . sentence?'

'No doubt two to four years in a local penitentiary.'

'But . . .' Anneliese grew even shorter of breath. 'She had the parents' consent; it was an emergency. She wrote down all her reasons – didn't you *read* her reasons?'

'Yes, yes, yes. But in real life – this kind of experiment just *cannot* be allowed.'

'If she hadn't performed the procedure the little boy would have *died*.'

'Yes.'

'So you . . . Dr Levin, do you believe her report?'

'Oh – yes, yes. And her method is revolutionary. Nevertheless, one must acknowledge that her actions were infringements of the law. Such an experiment would have to be approved by several boards and then await approval by approximately six committees of the British Medical Association.'

Anneliese had hoped to stretch her own hands out but they were far too sweaty by this point.

'If she *had* taken it to *any* board – by the time they would have granted her permission, the child would have been *dead!*'

He raised his eyebrows so high, they approached his hairline.

'I'm sorry Miss van der Holt, but it is a dangerous example of illegal medical experiment. Now, *if* – and I use the protasis deliberately – *if* she were to seek permission from all the committees, *and* the British Medical Association – and if she were to repeat her procedure, and if it worked – in *that* case this would be worthy of great commendation.'

'The Nobel Prize.'

Dr Levin raised his shoulders in doubt.

'Yes – *possibly*. But you are young, Miss van der Holt, and you must understand, that labour of this scale – even the fourth paper, which, between you and me and the lamppost, as they say – was really by far the most astonishing, revelatory work on Parkinson's that I have ever read—'

'What – what work on Parkinson's?'

'The fourth paper – the estimation on the vaccine.'

It was the one she hadn't understood.

'I – there's a paper on levodopa . . .'

'Yes, that was first *chronologically*. That was by far the most viable of the lot; I fail to understand why your aunt didn't *publish* that paper. It would serve clinicians a great deal of supplementary hours if they functioned under the belief that dopamine existed in the brains of several species. Regarding chemical synapses – I'm afraid Otto Loewi got ahead of her on that one.'

Anneliese had to blink a few times.

'Erm – you're wrong. Check the date.'

He took another look at the second paper.

'Ah, yes. '28.'

'Exactly. She discovered gamma-Amino-butyric acid.'

Dr Levin stroked his chin.

'What I was saying, Miss van der Holt – I was saying that, between you and me and the lamppost, her proposal for a vaccine for Parkinson's seems . . . hypothetically, to be quite credible.'

'She—' Anneliese had to swallow and take a great breath. 'That paper . . . the one I don't think that I understood . . . that was a proposal . . . for a vaccine . . . for Parkinson's?'

'Oh, yes. She tested it on mice.'

'Well, I remembered that part.'

He frowned.

'Strange – testing it on mice. Most doctors test on rats. In any case, the results thwarted my expectations. Mice that were predisposed genetically to have cells die in the *substantia nigra* experienced no such deterioration after her inoculation.'

'And she was – she was talking about a vaccine . . .'

'Yes.'

Anneliese remained open-mouthed.

'And so – and so – after all this, you still insist, er, Dr Levin, that this is nothing but kitchen sink talk?'

'Yes. For the sake of gossip – the results of these experiments sound very likely, very useful, really quite *plausible* in theory. They demonstrate a knowledge of both neuroscience and pathology I have yet to see paralleled. For the sake of kitchen sink talk, I'm not sure that in my lifetime I've encountered a single neurologist or even pharmacologist who would have used any like methods to draw similar *conclusions*. This conversation nonetheless has no bearing at *all*; it may as well be the likes of a – er . . . a fanciful exchange: the kind in which you no doubt frequently engage with your girlfriends.'

He handed back the papers. It took her a long time to realise that he was extending them.

'Professor Fleming published the results of *his* experiments in the *Journal for Experimental Pathology*.'

Dr Levin blinked several times and let thin air pass from his mouth in a sigh.

'Miss van der Holt, Professor Fleming treated fungi in a petri dish, not *dying children*.'

'In other words . . .' She let her fingers fiddle with each other. 'I could have these papers published in a journal or a newspaper and no one would be *interested*?'

'Well – when it comes to that child, I'm sure the police would be. I wouldn't advise that kind of action, Miss van der Holt.' He huffed a great deal and released a nasal waft. 'In any case, no professional would be interested in tests conducted without any affiliation to a well-known institute.'

'But he's – he's – that boy would have been dead, and he's *alive*. And – and so many doctors, so many research scientists, toil away night after night after night with *nothing* to produce at the end of a day's work – and he's alive because of *her*. You don't deem that a *miracle?*'

The doctor lifted his palms again.

'Who knows? Maybe. In any case, all her experiments – they *should* be overseen by the university. Where is she now?'

Suddenly a wave of weariness clenched Anneliese. She had to lie.

'Girton, Cambridge.'

'Well, then – where's the quandary? If she performs these and other experiments there, I'm sure in ten years' time I'll probably be reading of them in *The Lancet*.'

It felt like another door slammed loudly in her face.

'Well ...' Anneliese aimed faintly to obscure her obvious humiliation. 'I'll talk to Dr – I'll talk to my aunt.'

'I would advise you to do that.' he concluded. 'If these theories are to be realised, they shall take years of risky, dear trials.'

Anneliese stood up to leave, sullen and despondent. The murkiness was spilling out of her like waste in overflowing bins. She waited to depart in order to release this rubbish and diffuse it in her tears.

'Thank you.' She remembered to extend her hand. He shook it vigorously once again.

Stopping at the door, he took care to point out:

'And – Miss van der Holt, I'm really very, *very* happy that Benjamin has found himself a young lady as elegant as your *likeness*.'

The slowly wilting hours of the day were spent considering how the components of Susanna's mind and soul would wither.

They would endure her physical existence tucked askew in some dark corner of a drawer: a bent and defunct screw tossed carelessly amidst defective gadgets for the lack of energy for its disposal.

38.

The ménage and the metaphysical

When Isabel phoned Anneliese from Steven's home to tell her her fiancé planned to take her to his country home in Kent her sister was expectedly disdainful:

'Bu- I . . . Isn't, isn't it bad luck for you to see each other before the wedding?'

Isabel let out a breathy laugh.

'If a disaster's imminent, I don't think Fate is going to call on old folk superstition to unleash it.'

The laugh that followed was both long and choked: broken up by intervals of breaths.

'How many rooms are there?'

Isabel let her tongue beat the inside of her cheek.

'All of a sudden you're interested in *manors?*'

'Well . . . I've never heard of manors located in Kent.'

'Of course you have.'

'I don't read *Country Life* magazine.'

'I'll see you at home on Tuesday.'

'No, Isabel—'

'On Tuesday.'

She slammed down the phone.

With the exploitable funds of Steven's salary she had bought black and white dresses and suits, pencil skirts and jackets drawn in at the waist. She had informed the students of the RCM of her impending wedding only that day – leaving Plump Harriet open-mouthed as she sucked on her lollypop. The others had accumulated wrinkles like a bark asprawl with moss.

They travelled in his Cadillac. It was a better car than Tally's Rolls: more stylish and equipped with a new engine that abstained from spurting with the splutter of a chest cough. The vehicle's growling was subdued as they encountered the green pastures of quaint Kent; the branches of its olive rivers mirroring surrounding trees. He drove with one hand on the steering wheel, the other in between her lower thighs in its habitual haunt. Regardless of their whereabouts she never saw it as a hindrance: only as a sign of his possession.

It would serve as a premature honeymoon. With few churches free throughout the Easter period she had no choice but to marry during term time. The weekend prior to their wedding was their only chance to get away.

Steven never carried bags for her, and never held the door, and never put his arm around her waist and never kissed her on the lips. His parents had berated him for being disrespectful to her in their presence. Isabel decided that she treasured such a frosty manner. In her mind no elaborate words or excessive embraces were called for. Their tenor of relationship had been established in the first week of their meeting. It simply hadn't been enacted yet – just referenced parenthetically in casual whispers as she sat at Crockfords, or unprecedentedly whilst eating at a restaurant, or midway through a concert when the music's rhythm beat into the girl an urge to come unhinged.

He barged his way into the manor and demanded that the porter bring him brandy. Wearily and carelessly Steven explained the rooms' arrangement:

'The servants' quarters are here downstairs – on the left – nobody ever goes in there. Upstairs is our room, three guest rooms, two bathrooms—'

'I'm staying in the guest room, Steven.'

'The drawing room is straight ahead.'

He headed to it.

'Steven . . .' she called after him. 'I'm not – I'm not sleeping in "our" bedroom yet.'

Taking a copy of the *Financial Times* that lay aslant the coffee table, he sat down and placed a folded leg along his other. The porter came in with his brandy.

'Madam, anything to drink?'

'No, thank you.'

'Very good, madam.'

The porter left.

'Steven . . .' He didn't look at her. As he peered down at the newspaper, she noticed that his lips were thin and taut and almost white. He flicked a page. 'Steven—'

'Suit yourself.'

No piano stood in the estate. His parents had insisted that they had a Steinway there but Steven had abruptly cut their discourse and explained that it was 'broken'. When they had enquired how, he had retorted snidely that it had been 'out of tune since '32' and that he 'wasn't going to talk about it anymore'.

Steven spent the entire evening with the *Financial Times*. No indecent repartee coursed coolly to her ear at dinnertime; neither was a gaze most prurient cast shamelessly in her direction. Her next few hours were spent treading with her high heels on the marble staircase and the corridor upstairs and listening to their reverberating echo.

He didn't bid her good night and the next day he neglected to wish her good morning. Even the old porter who had served the family for fifty years would raise his eyebrows to her in a tacitly apologetic gesture.

All the windows in the dining room were besieged by great clusters of sunlight. Clad in a three-piece suit, Steven took hold of work files and then settled on a deck chair in the six-acre garden.

Isabel stumbled on an unappealing volume on the bookshelf: *Justine, or The Misfortunes of Virtue.*

She brought a deck chair next to his and settled down on it. Without opening her book she murmured in the form of a reminder:

'There are only two days left.' Once again he didn't answer. 'Steven—'

'Till what?'

She started fumbling with her skirt's hem. Her voice was dark; marked with a bitterness she didn't much care to conceal.

'I followed all your other orders.'

He scoffed.

'You *women*. Think you have a conscience.'

Isabel heaved a great sigh of nonplussedness.

Steven marked something on one of his sheets with red pen. He didn't look at Isabel when next he spoke.

'They shouldn't put up a resistance.' He narrowed his eyes pensively. 'It only makes them look more idiotic . . .' He chucked his pen onto the ground. 'In the end.'

Isabel tried to be appropriately menacing in her expression: a threatening tone that was nevertheless unconvincing.

'This isn't any kind of a rebuttal . . .' She bent her legs and tucked them under her. 'Two days hardly determines anything.'

'What charlatanism.'

'I don't – what would be . . .'

'You don't think that marriage should require preparation?'

'The wedding's scheduled for the day after tomorrow.'

'That isn't an answer.' Isabel's hand travelled to her shoe and nervously she started tugging at its heel. 'What makes you think I'll marry you if you overlook certain conditions?'

She twitched.

'What conditions?'

'Respect, for one thing.' He scratched his chin with thumb and forefinger. 'Women aren't born ready for us, you know; we have to break them in. Like horses. We—' He unsealed an icy chortle. 'We didn't even plan a *honeymoon*.'

His musing was pronounced in an austere and sanctimonious way: to Isabel it appeared glib. Lacking experience, she didn't have the clout to fight it.

'Most women blossom late. I thought you were an early riser; more mature than they are.' He stood up and grabbed his papers, ready to leave. 'It was my impression that you understood the order of proceedings.'

Lengthily she eyed him with a slovenly contempt.

'I don't respond to half-hearted efforts.'

That evening Isabel tried to sit at the other head of the table. Steven's hand motioned insistently: he was apparently telling a dog to jump down from the sofa.

'What?'

'Sit somewhere else.'

'Why?'

'Heads are for spouses.'

She sat one seat away and made a lot of clatter with her knife and fork throughout her dinner. Catching sight of servants' gazes of condolence, Isabel was starting to compare herself to a neglected beggar in the underground who made his living calling out for change.

That night she made use of both bolts on her door. Taking the book *Justine*, she planned to test its powers of sedation. Steven started punching at the door at midnight. She didn't budge. Her cognition hardly flickered as she let her eyes trail over *Justine*'s text. Numbness seized her intellect.

It took him just under ten minutes to break through the door. Grabbing her, he pressed his weight along her upper body and his hand on her left arm, digging his nails into her skin in order to disarm her.

Her primed resources used her fists and kicks to fight him off. The compulsive gestures of her arms and legs resembled pantomime; he laughed at them. Pressuring fingers weighed down on her thighs and a parade of scintillations marched up little hairs across her skin; lapping up effusive heat like petrol feeding on a flame. When his hand began to glide along her leg she felt her limbs assume a nimble texture, furling and convulsing to a choreography unnatural to her. His designs provoked their every movement. Naturally she let him take responsibility for their expression.

It would have been unjust to sabotage the exercises of a man so skilful in his craft.

She chose the pretext for her actions backwards – only after their completion. The idea that governed her mentality was based on principle. If she was to be honourable in this new role as wife it was her duty to establish her obedience in advance. Who was Isabel to argue with a man so thoroughly experienced in the field? He was reminding her that they were now in a relationship demanding her concession.

Anneliese received a call on the eve of their wedding. Isabel appeared uncommonly high-spirited and strangely supercilious.

'I won't be home, Liesa – we're staying here until tomorrow.'

'You're going to get married in *Kent?*'

'No. We've decided to come back tomorrow, at around midday. I'll see you at church; around three.'

'*In* the church?'

A brash beep pounded in the telephone before she could enquire further.

Anneliese journeyed to her sister's wedding with a pestilent aroma itching at her nose. Isabel was thanking school friends with the pomp and glamour of the hostess of a ball when she arrived. Designed and sewn exclusively for the occasion, her silky, v-neck pencil dress had no puffs and a train that travelled several yards across the floor.

She approached Isabel with rebellious apathy.

'Did you sleep well?'

An uncanny glimmer flickered in her sister's eyes.

'Mmm-hmm.'

Anneliese looked around the church before thinking of the next thing to say.

'Where's Steven?'

'He's coming.'

She wished she could have asked her sister why she was so happy.

The question would appear completely illegitimate.

'Did everything . . .' Anneliese's voice was excessively soft; almost inaudible. 'Did everything go . . . as planned at the . . . at the manor?'

'Mmm-hmm.'

'Good. Good.' Anneliese tickled her left cheek. Isabel was quiet for a little before whispering:

'I have a lot to look forward to.'

'Well, yes . . . You're getting married . . . It's a – it's a felicitous occasion.'

'Yes.' She drummed her fingers on a pew. 'I don't mean only that.'

'Hmm?'

'Well – I already know.'

'Know what?'

Isabel smirked.

'You know – it's funny, back at school I *hated* mock exams. I thought they were completely *pointless*. Now I more than understand the purpose. Sometimes it helps to have a dry run. Or not so dry.'

'What—'

'It's an American phrase, it means "practice".'

Thus the executioner dealt his last blow.

Anneliese abstained from applause at the end of her wedding. She spent the whole reception standing in a corner, resting her entire weight on the endurance of a single high-heeled foot. There were eventually so many pins and needles in her leg that she could barely walk.

It was insufferable for her to understand that Isabel was a poor loser. If she had ceded at the start of courtship, or a few months prior to the wedding, even to a man to whom she *hadn't* been engaged – it could have been excused by impulsivity or passion. But to resist the notion of procrastinating something for three days – a moment designated for a special time – was nothing but a lack of will on her part.

That night was another session with Susanna. In the morning she had visited a pharmacologist in order to identify the liquid taken from the doctor's bedroom two years previously. He hadn't recognised it and had told her that it probably had sedative effects; qualities of medical hypnotics. In order to remember it she had inscribed the formula in pen on her hand's heel.

Anneliese met with a fresh surprise: Susanna opened her own door.

'Helga's gone grocery shopping; there's a late-night market today.'

The patient nodded. Susanna followed her with furrowed eyebrows as she came into the house. Reasons for her surveillance surfaced in the practice – where Susanna took hold of her wrist and flipped it over to examine the nine digits. $C_{12}H_{18}N_2O_2S$ was their label. She studied it in silence until:

'That's a nice formula you have written there.'

Susanna released the hand.

Anneliese could say nothing, save to declare a quick:

'Thank you.'

The psychiatrist sat down hastily, taking care to tuck the back of her long skirt over her crossed legs.

'Did you come up with it yourself?'

'I must have read it somewhere.'

She shot a look of wide-eyed puzzlement.

'You can't remember where?'

Anneliese breathed out a:

'No . . .'

'Medicine must be progressing far more quickly than I had expected.' She took hold of her pencil from the table. 'So . . . she's married?'

Anneliese's sigh was prophetic.

'Yes.' She cleared her throat deliberately. 'Most girls look forward to a pretty dress and nice bouquet. My sister is depraved.'

'Is that some . . .' She glared at her dryly for a few moments. 'Circuitous way of informing me she didn't wait until marriage?'

'Yes. This morning I discovered that my sister's vocation in life is not music, marriage, even procreation, it's just . . .' She winced and almost shuddered. 'Intercourse.'

'You're hardly reading this in context.'

'Context?'

'You assume your sister is a beautiful young girl who has everything, and in spite of this "everything", hankered for *that*. She lost her art, lost her father. And she probably has quite a melancholy disposition to begin with.'

Anneliese's voice was too high-pitched as she responded:

'You *think* so?'

'From what you tell me . . . yes. Adding to her problems is the idea that you don't understand her. As we've learnt over four years – you don't *want* to.'

Anneliese scratched her left hand with her right.

'At the moment I'm too scared. It's ... she's some kind of barbarian; I don't think "understanding" would be any kind of balm.'

'You mean the concupiscence?'

'Yes.'

There was a pause in which only a rustle was heard as Anneliese straightened her skirt.

'This isn't just about Isabel.' Susanna pointed out.

'Probably not.'

'This is a general lack of understanding.'

Anneliese sniffed.

'Yes.'

'Josef would never have approved it.'

'Yes ... but that's not the point.' Susanna waited. Anneliese unsealed her mouth again. 'I don't understand it the same way I don't understand why a button in a lift would enjoy being pushed. If a mosquito bites me and it itches, I attain some tiny satisfaction if I scratch it – but I don't *remember* it; much less reserve some hours for it in my life.'

'A button in a lift is an inanimate object.'

'That's what makes it frightening.'

Susanna squinted for a few moments; tossed around some thoughts in her head.

'"Frightening" in what sense?'

'The idea that *thinking* human beings could relinquish a great deal of positive emotion, abandon some altruistic or cerebral task, all for the sake of these spontaneous bouts of hypersensitivity. I see this ... as something that makes us beasts. And I don't ...' She heaved a great sigh. 'I don't see how I can think that it has an individual meaning per person, per act.'

Susanna's voice grew dimmer.

'When did this congruence between inhumanity and copulation come to rear its head?'

Anneliese turned her eyes left and right.

'When it became relevant. I must have been fifteen when Isabel was reading... Something whose initials are "K.S."'

'And nothing's changed since then?'

'No.' Susanna looked at her blankly. Anneliese hastened to enquire, 'Is that bad?'

'It's not in *your* eyes.'

'Sorry?'

'If you inculcate yourself with such a principle, you can't expect to yield to these "spontaneous bouts of hypersensitivity" when they appear. So . . . is it *bad?*' She shot her a deliberately frazzled look. 'Is it bad for *whom* – it clearly isn't "bad" for *you* if that's your choice.' Susanna tapped her feet aground and ruminated. 'Of course ... wandering along a busy road was not, *so* ...' Mysteriously she shrugged. 'Who *knows?*'

Anneliese was slow to follow.

'So ... you think these sensations exist, but that I don't acknowledge them because I'm so immersed in my thoughts?'

There was no change in Susanna's reaction.

'I wouldn't know, Anneliese. I don't inhabit your physiology ... only you would be able to recognise that. Either in the comfort of your home or . . . afoot elsewhere.' She awaited a reaction but none came. 'If and when anything changes, you'll tell me?'

'You can't say "if and when", Susanna. It's either a temporal clause or a conditional one.'

'I know. It was a deliberate ploy.'

39.

Reeling in the beast

It was an honour to experience the pleasure women of her standing could procure exclusively through their illicit lovers via matrimonial privilege. This alone leant Isabel distinction.

Defeated by the prosecution, he would take her with no pause as soon as he came home. Victories stayed his grapple by ten minutes or three whiskeys.

A backwards schooling was the one that Steven used for discipline. Most forms of education and apprenticeship sought to uproot men from the borders of their physical existence. Steven's guided Isabel into rewinding progress fostered by millennia of homosapiens. He taught her to regress to her primeval origins and welcome self-abandon.

She never had to worry that this kind of instrumental practice would dry up and depart from her routine. She never worried that like Tally Steven would abruptly flee and leave her pitifully desperate and alone. This affair of theirs was therapeutic treatment unlike any other – and a suppler, more experimental method of distraction than the torpor of her wine consumption.

So adventurous was Steven that the tantalising juice of their liaison was a never-ending flow of nectar. Never would she have to live through the reverberating toil of a long-wearied housewife: that revolting fate had been averted on account of servants.

In a word she was no longer like the rest – no longer relegated to the clan of amateur musicians at the RCM obtusely bickering about their teachers' favourites. In the throes of mutual understanding she believed her life now had a purpose: something individual and unparalleled. For once she didn't need to fret that Anneliese was singular and she was not, or that she couldn't outstrip Sarah Tyde's fine craftsmanship, or that plump Harriet would be a world-known cellist. This was her mark of one-upmanship.

When her husband proposed paths as yet untaken, for the first time in her scholarly experience she answered like a deferential student. To verify that she was not transgressing social norms she would be sure to ask, 'Is that all right? Do people *do* that?' Invariably his answer would be 'yes'.

Such spontaneity spoilt Isabel for choice. On a daily basis she extracted both the aftershock of ecstasy and an insatiable discovery. In her rare moments of solitude she slouched back on the sofa with a glass of red wine, giddy at the role for which it seemed both destiny and her peculiar disposition had *designed* her. Unlike her instruments these gifts were simply not for public eyes.

He manoeuvred her like the accomplished driver of a loco- motive whose attentive knowledge of his personal machine had been well honed for years. The engine could be operated from a gamut of directions and a range of different buttons; it even had a mechanism for immediate response in unexpected lanes. With a fuel capacity inviting many unpremeditated uses of its function in an empty train, or in the guest room at the twins' home whilst her sister worked downstairs, or on the stairs it sparked a flame. Sat in an opera box he even dropped the kindling question:

'Which do you prefer – me or the music?'

Isabel was not discriminate. Hoisted in alleyways, hauled down in parks and fastened into place across an open field, she was unsettled by a thirsty agitation only he could sate; the liberty to jerk, jolt and convulse without the supervision of protective reflexes. Of the tremors, sways or shivers that she made she was completely unaware: they lay beyond her power. Shedding her self-mastery was her superlative indulgence.

As she bathed in her cold sweat on some hard surface she would feel her flesh sealed on a group of tiles and wonder how a slab of raw meat would have sizzled in her stead. She counted just how many of her adolescent years had been bestowed on lowly sportsmanship. Had she discovered that her being could procure such chemical reactions she would surely have aroused them in her tender years at the expense of many wasted hours spent on frigid instruments.

Little by little she became a paper copy of her husband. With every one of his libertine gestures, his wanton decisions, reckless choices or movements – he weathered her modesty, reserve and deportment. She became ravenous, animalistic: as shallow and unscrupulous as he.

Whenever Anneliese invited them for dinner she desired to eclipse the horrifying vision. In her mind there was no longer any Isabel. A self-absorbed, arrogant weasel would be dining at her table inexplicably; next to him his doting mistress – or another member of his adulating posse.

Moments were reserved for pleasure taken in deriding people. Isabel enjoyed resting her head against his shoulder as he did so. One night in June he made a point of interrogating Anneliese.

'So, sister-in-law . . . you don't have any chaps yet?'

Isabel squealed.

'Steven!'

'Well, I mean . . . you're what? Almost twenty? You want to end up an old maid?'

'That really isn't nice, Steven.' But Isabel's quick castigations were bereft of credence.

'You know, it's better to start early. Isabel's a musician – she can tell you that.'

'Steven . . .'

'I mean – women your age start getting on quite soon now, don't they?'

'Steven – stop it!' Isabel slapped him gently on the arm: a mother cheerily rebuking an endearing child.

He cursed a great deal also; muttering four-letter words if he spilled wine across his plate. Isabel found all this most amusing. She snickered and was forced to cover up her mouth, attempting to protect her reputation as she sat with Anneliese.

The summer holidays turned into Isabel's exasperating period. With no RCM and Steven working until after dark there was a constant restlessness that crept up through her entrails. Always she flitted hither-thither, dumping newspapers along a chair, then on the table, spinning in circles just to force herself to finally feel dizzy and be tired enough to sit and scrutinise the clock.

Usually the clock would show that it was only half past twelve.

The academic year ended and Isabel received Anneliese with a twitchy alacrity. Speaking velociously, the former swallowed rapidly after each of her sentences. When finally they sat and Steven's maid Marcella served them tea the young wife strived to manifest a simulated poise, resting her chin on the back of her forefinger. She studied Anneliese with a savage intensity – in fear that an unsteady gaze might clumsily betray the bounds and surges irrepressible inside her.

'How were your exams?' Isabel felt it was her obligation to ask.

'Well . . . they were difficult.' Anneliese confessed half-heartedly, reluctant to go into detail.

Isabel nodded. Taking a long strand of hair, she began twirling it.

'Hasn't Steven introduced you to his other friends? Some wives of husbands?'

'Yes.' Isabel spoke softly. 'I don't want to talk to them – what *would* we talk about? They have no fashion sense, I'm hardly interested in gossip and I don't know any of the people they're familiar with. And *they* don't know who Czerny is.' Neither did Anneliese. 'And you? Is there anyone who's caught your eye?'

'No, not at all.' Anneliese spoke in a rush. 'But I have plenty to do.' she pointed out almost snootily. 'What do you and Steven talk about?'

Isabel sniggered in a fashion not-so-ladylike. Anneliese imagined she was going to blow her nose.

'There's not a lot of – there isn't that much conversation.'

'Does he tell you about . . . cases? Or is that confidential?' Isabel appeared forlorn. She shrugged. 'So it's all . . . private?'

'I don't know.'

'But he does *like* his work?'

'I . . . I think so. He's very angry when he *does* lose a case.'

Anneliese made it her duty to nod.

'Where did he read law?'

She had never asked.

'I can't remember.'

'Does he like music?'

A thin-lipped smirk curled up the corners of her mouth.

'He enjoys taking advantage of its presence.'

'So . . . can he – can he speak any language other than English?'

Isabel frowned.

'Why would he?'

'We do.'

'So?'

'Is there really anything you know about him unconcerned with physicality?'

'Of course.'

'Such as . . .'

'He likes his steak rare-medium.'

Anneliese blinked. She was mimicking Susanna without any intention of doing so. Suddenly she understood what her profession would entail.

Isabel crossed her legs the other way.

'We know each other very well.'

'Well, yes . . .' Anneliese sighed. 'Your organs know each other very well.'

'That's *perverse*, Liesa.'

'Lesser, more radical physicians, could have called you schizophrenic.' claimed the charlatan.

'They could have called me *what?*'

'He enjoys fornication; you enjoy fornication. Very select reasons. Was a construction worker not enough for you? An ex-convict, perhaps?'

'You'll never understand the way it works.'

Anneliese rose. Without a single word she headed to the door.

In the forthcoming weeks Isabel began to languish from boredom. With every book she tried to read she felt as though her head were being pounded by a mallet.

With Steven absent during work hours those uninvited, old companions of her fears embarked on a retreat back to her being. She twiddled with her thumbs and fingers. Her home's design began to look like the interior of a prison cell. She wondered how much time would pass before her husband found her unattractive, whether he would one day ask her what her favourite pieces were or whether she had friends. She dreaded wondering how she would fill her time after her graduation. She didn't even know if she was going to graduate.

Now in the gloom of empty daylight she discovered this was not a home for her. There was no shadow of rapport that had been hers and Anneliese's years ago. There was no Papi, no piano that was unresponsive – let alone responsive. At best, even with Steven present, it was little but a well-lit cave.

But once her daily melancholy had subsided, once the sadness had sufficiently fatigued her to entrench her in the need for sleep she pined to be conveyed into her haven of elation. Steven was more than wary of her uninhibited dependence. Exploiting it, he amplified her crazed expectancy; intensified the languor of her heady wait.

Once in the middle of July he kept her in a trance for over ninety minutes. At the culmination of their tryst, as her lax body meditated the impending rapture of reward, a scratchy blade abruptly grazed her ankle with a different kind of apex. It was an incision: the shape of two crossed swords was etched into her skin. His hungry gaze implied it was her compensation for his service. Like a hungry fisherman enticing his new catch with dangling bait to wrench it from the reel and beat it moments later, he was sticking out his tongue in pleasure. For the first time in their union he discomfited her lust.

At night she saw the blood had dried. Faded spots of orange smudges now surrounded the engraving he had carved on her. She washed her wound and pulled a long sock over it.

From then on she began to carry out endeavours to deflect this circumstance. She went out for long periods and took long strolls at night, started attending concerts by herself and left the house pretending she was going to the RCM to practise.

In the context of their sessions these rebuttals were of no avail. Always he would wait until euphoria had plunged her into senselessness before inserting the cold, foreign edge of an external object in her flesh and prompting exhalations of another timbre. Failing to comply with these results, she would be starved of physical attention for a fortnight till she finally impelled him to be merciful: she craved the episodes of their first weeks as newlyweds. Their splendour was her only proof of life.

Yet her conciliatory prize would now involve the casualty of one limb or another.

Then there came the lengthened bouts of time in which she rubbed her wounds with antiseptic. Steven's encyclopaedia would be retrieved to check how she should staunch the bleeding.

Rain was plummeting one Sunday afternoon in August when her sister heard from her for the first time in seven weeks.

'Lie- Liesa—'

'Are you all right?'

'Yes, I'm fine.'

'You sound unnerved.'

'No, I'm – I'm perfectly fine. I've just been … listening to a frightening story on the wireless. Liesa, Steven cut himself slicing a cucumber. Is it right to put salt on a wound?'

'No …' Anneliese was silenced by this weak suggestion. 'Who told you to – put *salt* on a wound?'

'I just – I want to clean it up for him very, very, very well.'

She sounded fidgety. Anneliese had the distinct impression that her teeth were chattering.

'Is something wrong? Did you hurt yourself?'

'No. No I just – they were narrating some horrific tale on the radio. A man was disembowelled and they took out his organs.'

'They don't usually read that kind of fiction. Especially at three in the afternoon.'

Isabel simulated outrage:

'Well – they *did* today!'

Time spent outside now tripled in its length. She would parade about the rainy streets with no umbrella, loiter around Covent Garden in the midst of thunderstorms and take a walk for milk or bread when that task was assigned to servants.

Every time she came back home at night she knew what was in store for her. She never fought with him. This was in part because she still hoped he might take her painlessly. The loyal wife indulged him with his favourite carnal pastimes and debased herself as much as possible in an inane attempt to make their unions bloodless.

Steven would not relent. One night he garnished their performance with an unexpected final twist: at their ritual's apogee he wedged a knife's point straight into her lower flank, cracking the ivory with an unbridled flow of scarlet. Another sliding of the knife's blade up her leg created the thin slash of a red line. Resembling two folds stitched together, it was scarcely visible until she saw it bleeding.

The action urged her breath to swoop and then fly down.

Powerless was she to take the knife. She had no weapon of her own.

In a choked voice she asked him with the most docility that she could muster, struggling to restrain her stammer:

'Ste- Steven, Steven, just – just put it on the table.' She tried to reason with him in a language he could understand; to line her words with the serene perspective of a person who regarded this as foreplay. 'I'm prepared for anything.' she put in a whisper. 'You don't have to train me. I'm fixed. I'm fixed for you.' Her breaths were still shorter than normal. 'I've learned a lot.'

Leaving the knife stuck at the apex of her thigh, he went to take a shower. It was up to Isabel to take it out as carefully as possible and then cleanse her eleven-inch vertical wound and the hole in her side. She told herself from now on she would have to wear thick stockings in the summer.

A week later she found herself once again in the bathroom dabbing wet cotton wool on her legs. Isabel began at once to feel confused, dizzy and sick; disgusted at herself for this aberrance. There was a throbbing pain above her cut. The more she moved the injured foot the more she felt a breeze dash past the gash, affecting the exposed torn flesh.

She wore long skirts and other women looked at her outside as though she were beside herself. With a head that beat the rhythm of a noisy drill she languidly arrived at Anneliese's in a hazy stupefaction. Isabel was pressed to go inside before the latter had a chance to spot her bloodied ankle and the pinkish flesh surrounding it.

'Liesa . . . could I stay with you tonight? We've had a . . .' She wondered how to formulate her words without scaring her sister. 'We've had a spat.'

'There's no need to ask.' Anneliese bid her come in without taking her eyes off her. Isabel dashed upstairs.

'I'm just going to the bathroom.' she told Anneliese. And there in their old cabinet she found some bandages at her disposal.

Anneliese hovered outside the bathroom.

'Is everything all right?' she called.

'Yes.'

'Are you feeling sick?'

Isabel was struggling to prevent the bleeding.

'No, no. Let me be.'

Ten minutes later tighter bandages had halted the profusion.

When she came down she walked as giddily as possible to waive all possible suspicion. Joining Anneliese in the kitchen, she began peeling potatoes for dinner.

'Let me help. Erm – I'm not, I'm not intruding. I won't stay long. I just needed to get away to teach him a lesson.'

'This is your house. I don't see why you keep asking permission.'

Isabel sniffed several times and blamed the onions on the counter.

Four days later they both heard the wireless announce that Britain had declared a war on Germany. Isabel conversed about it to evade more discommoding subjects.

40.

Long division

Two weeks into the war it seemed that reading about casualties and gangrene was her daily dose of entertainment. It was the start of her first hospital rotation.

Anneliese made a point of following Emily-Jane Stufflebeam: the latter liked to gossip in hushed tones. Racing through St Mary's Hospital in their white coats, she wouldn't cease to prattle.

'They might send us to the Front – as nurses.'

'There's been no confirmation of that yet.'

'But it could *happen!*' Emily-Jane hissed.

'Do you think it's going to last so long?'

'Don't you remember what happened *last* time?'

Anneliese was so exhausted she could barely keep her eyelids trustily unsealed. It was time for her to practise intravenous work and she already knew that her house officer despised her.

On the patient's arm were faded traces of blue lines. Anneliese looked at her needle.

Still she failed to understand how these two features – blue and silver – were not mutually exclusive.

A few months previously she had exposed herself to human innards. Witnessing an autopsy, she had looked down to see an open chest with ribs cracked wide apart. Inside had been a well of blood with the pale centre of an asymmetrical pink ball; the mould of a soft paperweight. Throughout her scrutiny she had been at a loss to understand how surgeons could discern its outline in this tank of blood. In place of what her father called a 'soul' was nothing but a medium-sized blob.

Suddenly Emily-Jane flung open the door, taking little account of the patient before Anneliese. Perky and wide-eyed, she flung an offer at her classmate:

'Do you want to meet my supervisor?'

'You mean ... the doctor who's surveying you during your surgical rotation?'

'Mmm-hmm!'

Dashing aimlessly about the hospital was better for the girl's morale than failing to save lives. Excusing herself momentarily, she told her patient that a doctor would be with him shortly.

They took the stairs and mounted four long turquoise flights. By the time they got there Anneliese was short of breath and struggling to retain saliva in her mouth. Emily-Jane was placid. She raced ahead of her; Anneliese had to skip to catch up.

An operating theatre bade them enter. In it a bearded man with silver tufts of hair irreverently left uncoiffed was exercising a procedure on a woman's spine. Most of her back and rear were covered by a border of blue cloth that left a slender rectangle exposed. In that gap was her unmasked interior amidst a diamond-shaped incision. Anneliese could see the red sponge of her flesh inside and trace the ridges of her lower vertebrae.

He wasn't wearing a mask. A young lady in a nurse's outfit was repeatedly extracting and then reinserting a small cigarette between his lips. At intervals he coughed a little.

Taking notice of the girls, an overwhelming burden of fatigue oppressed him.

Emily-Jane called out:

'Dr Westwood!' Anneliese's heart was like a spring. 'This is my friend, Anneliese! She wants to be a psychiatrist.'

The blonde nurse removed the cigarette from Dr Westwood's mouth.

'Psychiatrist . . .' He scoffed, spluttering drops of saliva around him; possibly on the insides of his patient. 'Hopeless profession.'

'Is that a laminectomy you're doing, Dr Westwood?' Emily-Jane enthused.

Another inhalation of his cigarette was taken.

'Yes.'

Anneliese couldn't resist the temptation to whisper to Emily-Jane:

'Wouldn't that contaminate . . . he's not even wearing a mask.'

Her companion whispered far more loudly:

'Last time they told him off, he threatened to *retire*.'

A few moments passed; Emily-Jane's sprightliness slowly began to plateau. She grabbed Anneliese's hand.

'Let me go and introduce you to Dr Farnsley; he's a friend of my father's.'

'Erm . . .' Anneliese felt that familiar organ throbbing: the same one whose nakedness she had so recently espied. 'Just – just one moment. I . . . I have a question for Dr Westwood.'

She told herself it was a common surname. It didn't mean anything. It didn't suggest anything.

'Ah . . .' She stepped a little closer to him but the nurse obstructed her proximity. 'Sir . . . By any chance, are you – would you happen to be related to another "Dr Westwood"?'

Emily-Jane tut-tutted in the background. Questions of a personal nature were highly impertinent.

He mumbled with a strait of animosity.

'That depends what you mean by . . . "related".'

'Is there – would there—' She told herself to stop. Nothing

fruitful would transpire; no discovery would loftily take flight. She would neither stop her sessions *nor* make progress in them.

And yet she was so bad at listening to herself.

'Would there . . . happen to be another "Dr Westwood" who's . . . alive and related to you?'

'Candice . . .' he called.

Anneliese's shock was being put on hold. The nurse adhered, permitting him two languid inhalations.

'Are you referring to that *looney?*'

Anneliese gulped.

'About Dr Westwood . . . the psychiatrist. Susanna Westwood.'

He grunted almost inaudibly. Puffing smoke on his sterilised tools, he chewed on his cigarette whilst remarking:

'So that's her present name; she never *was* one for consistency. What happened to the girl?'

'What girl?'

'That girl of hers . . . what was her name – Lily? That Bohemian burick was sure she'd convinced me *I'd* sired her.'

Anneliese could only utter quietly:

'"Sired" what?'

'My daughter.'

She was frozen.

'Lily wasn't?'

He snorted in an ugly fashion.

'Between the Hun, Parsons and Turnover I wouldn't be surprised if there were six potential fathers.'

Anneliese was not ready to give up her fight.

'Lily – Lily died . . . in a car crash. But I . . . I . . .' She realised how foolish she sounded; she just didn't care. 'There's little chance she would have lied to you, er, *sir.*'

'Her gestation had begun before our marriage.' he informed her in a manner that was clinical.

'There could have been a misunderstanding—'

'*Anneliese.*' Emily-Jane rebuked, raising her voice.

'This Susanna Westwood lives on Eversley Avenue in Harrow.' she insisted.

'My house.' he continued. 'The whore took me for all I had.'

Emily-Jane couldn't detect the tension in the air. She didn't wait a second before sibilating:

'*Anneliese!*'

They left the operating theatre.

A pendulum not only hung her down but alternated between left and right.

The new mystery was an equation not unwindable. In this long line of addition and subtraction there was no explanatory calculation to accommodate such fraudulence.

To discover the unfathomable roots of this vile act it would be necessary to retrace Susanna's origins through long division. Why *would* she have convinced this ugly doctor she was carrying his baby? How could it *possibly* have been in Lily's interests to possess *that* kind of father? Could it be that he had clout with the *review* board that refused her grants for hazardous experiments?

She stroked her head. It was no use. She would have to eliminate Susanna altogether. That was the only surmisable quick fix.

Except it didn't work. For when she arrived home that night and Isabel was trying on another gown and humming as though war did not exist, immediately she yearned to be reanchored to her problem.

'The lace won't do up.' Isabel fiddled with the back of her dress.

She huffed and puffed some more as though to prove her point but Anneliese could not be sympathetic to the cause.

'It's a mystery ...' the Younger Twin responded. 'Like the Bermuda Triangle.'

She told herself it was just timing. In ten years' time she

would encounter many fascinating people and resist the need to see a therapist who plucked her intellect. Then she would get herself a standard therapist; a normal therapist. A therapist whose life was not a screwball of bizarre occurrences and withheld truths.

As usual she was ten minutes early that evening. Helga's voice was of a tone so elevated that she sounded like a stream of water gurgling down a pipe. An attempt was even made to speak in English:

'Good *evening!*'

Anneliese could barely nod in assent. She deliberately replied in German.

'*Guten Abend, Helga.*'

'Let me take your coat.'

It was bizarre to witness the old woman so enraptured. Anneliese addressed her in an apprehensive voice:

'What did she do?'

'Hmm? Oh – nothing at all! It's the day of St Wenceslas.'

'St Wenceslas . . .'

'Yes, yes – our patron saint.'

Only then did Anneliese behold a string of pearls and stones entwined around the staircase.

'You see these?' Helga pointed to them. 'They're symbols; this is what Charles IV put on his head this very day in 1347, during his coronation—'

'*Anneliese.*' The command came from the practice. 'Take them down.'

She failed to understand why her psychiatrist assumed she could exploit her to fulfil these menial instructions. Pushing the door of the practice, Anneliese fiercely retorted:

'Mistress – take them down *yourself.*'

Leaving the door somewhat ajar she heard Susanna proclaim humorously:

'That's a young one I have. Not *that* young anymore. *Your* age.'

'That's quite all right.'

Incensed by this demeaning reference, Anneliese approached her eyes to the inviting sliver of the open door. A young blond soldier sat before Susanna in his uniform of olive green. En route to Whitehall to enlist at the Recruiting Office, he was fiddling with the cap crouched in the middle of his lap.

Displeased with herself, Susanna shook her head.

'Sorry, we were saying ... I'm not sure that you should be compelled to stand the pressure.'

'Well ...' The man flipped his cap up. 'It's not as though I'm epileptic.'

'No ...' There was some irregular uncertainty about her. Her gaze couldn't be fixed. 'Frankly, I – I wrote the letter when the war began.'

'You wrote a doctor's note?'

'I wrote a doctor's note for all my patients.' She cleared her throat. 'Male patients.'

'Well, that's ... That's kind of you Susanna, but there really was no question of my turning them down—'

'Your father shouldn't play a role in your decision.'

'It's not my father who—'

'It depends ...' She looked at him and opened her eyes wider. They were engrossed in that magnetic stare. 'On whose judgment you trust.'

'Hmm.'

Leaning back uncomfortably, he seemed intent on taking thumb and forefinger to stroke his chin. Something hindered him: the presence of a poised and older woman.

'There's only one real fear I have.'

The magnetic stare pursued its course.

'I would think that it's the same for everyone in your position.'

'Maybe.'

Anneliese would have expected every other young man she had seen to scratch his head, sniff, interlock his fingers, stretch or exercise another symbol of uneasiness.

This one was in check.

'I'm going to war unmarried . . . without a young lady . . . no one's awaiting my return . . . and I always believed that young men shouldn't die without an opportunity to, er . . . to flex their muscles . . . so to speak.'

Her eyes narrowed to become austere. At the same time her voice grew smoother, more eventual; less firm.

'There wouldn't be a lack of that . . . at the Front.'

'But there aren't any women there.'

Zealous in resolve, his eyes sustained a steely look in her direction: she appeared to have outgrown it. For a second Anneliese witnessed her twitch, reminding her affected self that there was designated protocol she had to follow in these situations . . .

Yet her words were torn off at their ends and she was struggling.

'Eric, that wouldn't – it . . .'

Susanna's eyes were loosened from their customary pose. They now revealed another nature perpendicular to her premeditated guard. Here was the faint watermark of some young girl who had once lived in wonderment. Anneliese watched as her thumb and forefinger began to line the edges of a pencil she was tapping on her armchair. Susanna's cheeks grew pink. No longer were her eyes enrobed in mist and tinted with the gleam of melancholy. A shiny drop of coquetry was lingering instead.

Eric pursued his argument.

'A man can't live in a cocoon for his entire life.'

'No, but—'

'There'll be other lads there, awaiting the arrival of some hired floozy . . . Cabaret singers, the entertainers – they can barely strike a note. They barely know what perfume they douse themselves with; at any rate it doesn't *smell* like any fragrance. Whereas some women ...' He was almost stuttering by this point. 'You – you think they gleam because they're made of silver. And so you conjure this impression, over years, that if you lean on them you'll hear some hollow clang; some proof of hardness. Then you find out, when you least expect it, that behind that gleam is something soft, mollescent; tangible and malleable. And you can press on it.' He kept his fervid glance on her. 'If she were to let you.'

Susanna's normal self was now resumed.

Resting her chin atop her hand, she began stroking her cheek with her forefinger.

'*One* will.'

'But—'

'*Hypothetically* ...' She allowed her instrument to linger to create a wispy air about it. 'Resistance would be difficult.'

He forced a smile.

'Well.' He sprang up. The man was long: some inches above Isabel in height. He looked a little lachrymose.

The extension of his hand was cold and distanced.

'Thank you.'

It seemed that she was reticently willing to accept this stance. Concordant with his cavalier approach, the corners of her eyes were slanted upwards in her perspicacious cunning as she rose. She took his hand and closed the gap between them covertly to plant a tender kiss atop his cheek. After allowing it to linger for some seconds she retreated.

A species of flirtatious femininity had been uncorked.

Crumpled was the inner lining of her female patient's stomach. Droplets of sweat ran down her palms as she depended on the hinges of the door for physical support.

Flustered, the young man seemed pleased. He took Susanna's hand to squeeze it once again and left without observing Anneliese.

Clinging to a trance, Susanna welcomed her half-heartedly with a melodic sigh.

In a voice half on the verge of withering her patient asked:

'Are you going to speak?'

'Mmm-hmm.'

'You look as though you're on the verge of bursting into song.'

Some of her seriousness resurfaced. Susanna's gaze betrayed dismay. It seemed the spell had finally been broken.

'I don't know any music.'

'I suppose it's beneath you?'

She settled down into her armchair.

'It's an intellectual dearth.'

Anneliese tapped her fingers on the sides of her own chair.

'So?' Susanna seemed inquisitive.

The girl leant her chin on her hand.

'You don't seem that aggressive with *him*.'

'With whom?'

'With your last patient.'

She smirked.

'He's traversed a mileage of self-knowledge you have yet to mount.'

'Kindness gets awarded on the basis of merit?'

Susanna lowered her head, keeping only her eyes lifted. Her voice was the colour of tar.

'That wasn't kindness.'

'It must be very flattering to think you were the final woman that he lusted after.'

'He might survive.'

'For memory's sake . . . would you *want* him to?'

Quizzically narrow, Susanna's eyes were impatient.

'What *has* your head been spinning?'

'I don't have a *wheel* there.'

Smugly Susanna pointed out:

'You're against me this week.'

'It's no wonder.'

But she wasn't going to put in extra effort to be pleasing to her patient.

'Did you have a minute of silence at St Mary's?'

'Well . . . I don't know how many young men are affiliated . . . in any case, it's rather early.' Anneliese beheld Susanna's unmoved face. 'Oh, you mean – I thought you were talking about . . .' Only then did she recall that Freud had died. 'No.' She shifted her position on her chair. 'Did you?'

'I had an auto-da-fé.'

'What . . . *really?*'

'Of his books.'

'You burned *Beyond the Pleasure Principle?*'

Susanna held her patient in suspense, staring at her with suspicious eyes until her lips surrendered to a curve. Anneliese had to resist the urge to tut-tut like Emily-Jane.

'Oh – that's not *funny.*'

'It's plausible.'

'Yes, but . . .'

'I mean – why do you think I would *need* it?'

'Susanna . . .'

'Did you think I was Freudian?'

'Not exactly, no.'

'I'm not Freudian. Actually it was a quiet Saturday. None of my old colleagues called. Not even the Kleinians.'

'I would think . . . they've rather got a lot else on their plate.'

'And so it's all the more surprising that the wireless reported it.'

Anneliese sought to discuss some universal topic. Luckily the war provided that with ease.

'I don't know how well we can manage everything that's going on . . .'

'Is Isabel still staying with you?'

'Yes.'

'Hasn't it been four weeks now?'

'That's right.'

'So what happened with Steven?'

'I don't know.'

'You didn't ask her?'

'No. But I wasn't referring to that. I just mean that . . . I'm not sure I can believe our world has wrapped itself up in another global conflict – yet again.'

Susanna became solemn.

'So it . . . astounds you?'

'Yes.'

'Hmm.'

Anneliese waited for an unprecedented response.

'Well?'

'You're so young.'

'That's a dull reaction coming from you.'

'I meant that . . .' Susanna raised her head in contemplation. 'Dozens of countries living in a conglomeration since the Neolithic Era . . . that's almost twelve thousand years. Annexation has been taking place since Octavian seized Egypt in the Roman Empire. A war broke out not long ago over . . .' Horror in her expression met the names cited. 'The *Serbs*, because they shot an Austrian archduke. As though we really need *either* of those nations . . . but that's not the point. People expect siblings who grew up in the same house to bicker and then gasp and drop their jaws when a large pack of different countries start to wrangle. The only reason Europe hasn't blown itself to pieces is the length of time it took for arms of mass destruction to develop. And yet you and the world still think there'll be a time when peace will reign over this tiny continent that squeezes thirty nations in its borders.'

'I don't *think* that.'

'Why're you shocked?'

'I'm unprepared.'

'What are you frightened about?'

'Weapons of mass destruction.'

'That's logical.' Susanna allowed. 'In our time war is facile, travel and communication run as quickly as a bumble bee and medicine is so advanced, the population's tripled in a hundred years. There's no room for evolution. In the nineteenth century there still remained a great deal to accomplish. We're in the wrong half of history.' she drew her conclusion. 'So you ought to be scared.'

Anneliese found it difficult to ignore omens.

'You say that as though it is irrelevant whether we live or die because the globe will be destroyed in any case.'

Susanna switched her intonation. It sounded mockingly dramatic.

'Are *you* going to change it?'

'Well, no. I don't have the . . . I don't have *anything*. But *you* . . .'

'Failed the audition.'

'How is that . . .'

Anneliese sat in wait. Yet every footprint that Susanna left behind tacked on her trail more twisted prongs.

'Could we return to the original affair we were discussing?' she requested.

'According to your reasoning, there's no point talking about anything.'

'Yes, but I work for *you* and your reasoning's different. Do you want to tell me what they're making you do at St Mary's?'

Anneliese gazed at her dismally.

'Do you have influence there?'

It was the second time that day Susanna seemed off-balance.

'I'm not answering that one.'

'Well... fine. Dr Viking brought in this dead badger—'

'Just one moment, Anneliese—'

'Yes?'

'Before I forget – ask her what happened with Steven.'

The patient interlocked her hands.

'Erm – all right.'

Three hours later Anneliese came home to hear the syncopated beats of Gershwin being pumped along the ceiling. She gathered Isabel had made no further progress with returning to her marital abode.

Anneliese called her name. Isabel came sprinting down, effusing pride.

'I made mashed potato with cheddar. It actually turned out *splendourfully* well.'

'Well, that's . . .' Anneliese itched behind her ear. 'Splendourful. You never told me why you left.'

Isabel looked as though she had remembered something.

'I happened to have gone there this morning.'

'Oh?'

'I think he's gone.'

'"*Gone*"?'

'I think he went to Whitehall to enlist.'

Anneliese hung her coat on the rack.

'I'm sorry to hear that.'

Isabel barely seemed sorrowful. Gleefully she asked:

'Is it all right if I stay here, Liesa?'

'Of course.'

So Anneliese's ears became accustomed to the sound of saxophones, Sibelius and Noël Coward once again; feet banging down the stairs spontaneously at night and tinny notes of the piano cracking sombre daybreak. She had missed Isabel. But that kind of admission would have dampened Anneliese's honour.

41.

The war tally

Isabel's relationship with rationing was faring poorly. A year had passed since the beginning of the war. Benjamin Levin still pined for Anneliese, Steven was still (allegedly) at the Front. The twins were still living in Blackheath.

In an endeavour to communicate they met in Hyde Park on a brisk day that September 1940, helplessly enshrouded in the backdrop of a leafy golden brown. Slow to surface, twilight was arriving at 6.50. They sat on a black bench before a pond where Isabel withdrew a small brown bag of bread chunks. Anneliese regarded them in horror.

'How old is the bread?'

'Very, very, *very* stale.'

Anneliese snatched some pieces from Isabel's hands.

'It's still soft.'

'We didn't have any old bread.'

'Everyone is coping with one loaf a week at best – and you are going to share ours with the ducks.'

Isabel turned sullen all of a sudden. Without facing Anneliese she notified her:

'Yes.'

'There are different ways of being magnanimous, you know.'

She threw some pieces of the crust at an endearing, doe-eyed duckling.

'I know.'

'You're not doing anything for the war effort.'

'I know.'

'With Steven absent, there's no reason why you can't volunteer at a hospital.'

'Too many hours in the day. In any case, my holidays from the RCM aren't *that* long.'

'You could be a searchlight operator.'

'I would likely . . . break the light. What are *you* doing?'

'We have soldiers at St Mary's Hospital.'

'But you're studying there; you're not *tending*.'

'We all tend. They use the students too; we need it for our clinical training.'

'Oh.'

Uncomfortably a pause ensued whilst Isabel continued pelting bread across the pond. So paltry was her aim, the pieces never reached the ducks. Anneliese grabbed a few cubes and chomped on them.

'When Steven – if Steven comes back from the Front, do you think that you'll have children . . . sometime?'

'Yes. Sometime.'

Once more it was the turn of silence to regurgitate its echo.

Two minutes later Isabel observed in giddiness:

'There's a woodpecker on that tree.'

This deliberate avoidance sparked impromptu rage on Anneliese's part.

'You must be happy – I mean, having already got married. I guess that's most of your destiny accomplished, huh?'

Isabel listened to the tap of the woodpecker's beak on the bark.

'Well, not really.'

'Why not?'

'He . . . I didn't really marry – I didn't really marry . . . I'm not . . .' She swallowed and then cleared her throat. 'I think . . . maybe . . . I'm disturbed . . . somehow.'

Anneliese hoped swallowing would sink the newly surfaced bulbs of moss that choked her soul.

'Why would you *say* that?'

'Because . . . I just didn't experience anything most girls experience before marriage.'

'Meaning?'

'I think . . .' She scratched her neck. A profound sigh lapsed from Anneliese's mouth could have enveloped the two sisters in a mist. 'Maybe Tally I was in love with. But Steven . . . he's – he's responsible. He takes control very well. Those are good qualities to find in a husband.' the wife reasoned unsatisfactorily.

'Why are you "disturbed", Isabel?'

'Because I – I just feel very peculiar.'

'What does—'

The howling of an air raid nixed their speech. Isabel repeatedly shook her head in a kind of convulsion; the sound was too unmusical and she was hypersensitive to noise.

Savagely incorrigible was the feral beast. Anneliese was the one to seize Isabel's hand; the last time they had raced out of their house to find the nearest underground the older sister had approached them *closer* to the bombs. Anneliese had considered having an Anderson shelter built. She had even contemplated using her inheritance to rent them an apartment somewhere out of London.

'It's early!' Isabel squealed. Anneliese didn't have the time to pay attention. '*Liesa!*'

'I heard you.'

They escalated down the steps of Hyde Park Corner underground. Inside was huddled a dense bustle of three hundred people: adolescent boys sliding across the ground as though it were a frozen lake and school were shut because of snow; uproarious policemen yelling 'calm down, ma'am' and 'quiet – quiet!'; breathy whistles and a band of housewives garrulous and taking up much space akimbo.

In a corner near the platform's end they sat together. Obscured by the coarse canopy of babble the two girls could barely hear each other speak.

'Isabel, I'm going to have a shelter built.' Anneliese flung her words over the underground storm.

'Good.'

'What were you saying about . . . being "*disturbed*"?'

Deafened by the sound of children's cries, a violinist perched along a train rail practising his scales, a mother shouting at her toddler and a horde of drunken men discussing Arsenal, she barely concentrated on her sister.

'*What?*' Her gaze was unbeknownst to her averted. 'Oh – I'll tell you later.'

Three weeks thence six hundred perished in the bombing of the Balham underground shelter. Anneliese insisted that the girls use their inheritance to rent a furnished flat outside of central London.

Her sister's face was blank as she alerted her to the idea one overcast, dark grey November evening.

'*Isabel?*'

The latter's voice was dim.

'Yes.'

'We'll have to get up early and it'll take us longer to get home, but . . . Better to err on caution's side. I don't trust these shelters anymore; I don't trust *any* shelters.'

'Yes.'

'So I'll pay half and you'll pay half.'

'Mmm-hmm.'

Anneliese dawdled outside her door.

'I'll ask Mother to come, but . . .' Anneliese let out a quick breath. 'We can't exactly . . . manoeuvre her.'

Isabel nodded.

It was a two-room apartment only twenty metres wide on Cromwell Road in Elstree. After drawing straws it was decided Isabel would sleep in the main living room and Anneliese would have the bedroom opposite.

When Dr Viking was abruptly taken ill one afternoon and lessons finished early Benjamin drove Anneliese to Prince Consort Road on his way home. She stood outside the Royal College of Music until five o'clock.

Crisp was the nipping frost encircling both her gloves and wrapped-up neck; she buried the hands of her folded arms in the hearths of her flanks. A young gentleman emerged from the college. Anneliese could vaguely recognise him from her sister's mandatory string quartet.

'Excuse me.' she alerted him. 'By any chance, have you seen Isabel van der Holt – she studies the piano and cello?'

'Inside.' He pointed. 'First room on your right.'

She thanked him and ascended the steps. With a coat of stuffy warmth around her face her ears met with the velvet timbre of a lowly voice lending 'We'll Meet Again' a suave vibrato.

In a smoky practice room sat Isabel in a long-sleeved and chestnut dress, her crossed legs dangling from the grand piano as she gently swayed in song. A young male pianist chewed on the end of his cigar as he accompanied their free performance to a crowd of some three dozen drinking, chomping, smoking students. Anneliese's hand became a muzzle to prevent a cough from spluttering, her gaze betraying nothing but neutrality.

Twenty-five yards from the college, Isabel cautiously whispered:

'That's as much as I *can* do.'

'Hmm?'

'*Sing* to them; not much else. If I could play and entertain them – if someone hauled down a piano to the air raid shelter, then . . . I couldn't play – but I could sing again . . .' she broke off. 'I need a piano to keep me in tune. That's what I do. You asked what I could do; that's it.'

They boarded the presently uncluttered Northern line in the underground. Each day it took them a little over an hour to reach their new home.

Jostling to and fro, the train tugged them in different directions. Isabel turned to look at her sister.

'What were you doing today?'

Anneliese appeared perturbed.

'You wouldn't want to know . . .'

'No – *really*.' Isabel insisted. 'What were you doing today?'

She frowned and looked at Isabel in some distress.

'We were extracting saliva from locusts and examining the fluid.'

'Oh.'

'I told you that you didn't want to know . . .'

'If you dislike it,' Isabel began, 'then why do you continue with—'

'Because – as I've *told* you – I have to know anatomy and physiology to become a psychiatrist. Otherwise I'm just some theorist who speculates about the human mind. And there are far too many of those around.' She gestured with her hand by way of introduction: 'Isabel van der Holt – Nietzsche. Have you *met*?' Isabel shot a look of confusion at her. 'In my opinion he's the one responsible for all of *this*.'

'Of *what*?'

'*This*.' Anneliese pointed her finger down. 'Especially the purging of Jews. That's *his* fault.'

'God – *why*?' addled Isabel wanted to know.

'He was the one who said there was a "superman", and . . .' Anneliese very briefly awaited her sister's reaction. 'Never mind.'

'So you didn't save a life today?'

'No. I didn't do any clinical work today.'

'So . . . nothing for the war effort?'

'Not today, no.'

Isabel tapped her fingers on the bar to the left of her.

'So we're even.'

Anneliese failed to understand.

42.

Stray smoke

Confronting the concept of the Aryan race, Anneliese was ashamed of her feelings. No resolve could sustain her resistance. She had sunk into hatred.

It wasn't as though she and Hitler had an unpronounced affinity. Towards the Jews she only felt a cosy warmth; the gypsies she had circumspected never bothered her and she had no desire for the human race to be blue-eyed and blond.

One species alone repelled her undeservedly. While Isabel would crave the act that led to reproduction Anneliese began to fantasise about annihilation.

Its name was Melissa Adams-Kennedy; perfunctorily it signed itself "Melissa Gail Adams-Kennedy". Now that Benjamin was goading Anneliese to come with him to social gatherings around the university their introduction had been made.

Since their first meeting a loud cymbal had made Anneliese's soul its habitat. Battered were her insides every time she heard that shrill and flexile voice; they echoed with scared shock with every sight of that dyed hair. Melissa was a natural redhead who – on grounds that were completely inexplicable – would dye her strands a bolder shade.

Her waves appeared to have been drenched in Heinz tomato ketchup. Placed too correctly, each lock dented in proportion to the other so the tresses stuck together like a stack of straw. The face was round and of a heart shape with a tapered chin; her forehead was so large it was an awning for a pair of eyes that strained to offer modesty. So often did Melissa appear stunned that one surmised a pricking needle mercilessly poked her neck.

She was Dr Viking's favourite and Professor Treadwell's favourite and was growing to be popular among their classmates. Only Anneliese and Benjamin would keep themselves secluded from her pack. She liked to interrupt the lunches in the dining hall in order to announce that she was raising funds for the Red Cross. These sermons would abound in references to casualties:

'Out there on the Front are young men – cousins, brothers, fathers, nephews – they are *dying*. Soldiers need new uniforms; they need our cans and condiments.' Melissa relished applauding herself in the midst of her speech. 'So let's give, give, give – and *rally* for the cause!'

When she affected sadness in attempts to stir compassion it was with bizarre and calculated episodes of vocal tremors. Every intake of her voice propelled a fetid breeze to climb up Anneliese's throat until her appetite had vanished.

Benjamin received all her confessions with a look of under-standing. They alone were sure Melissa was a fraud.

Most lessons would proceed like that of 17th January, 1941:

'By golly!' Dr Viking exclaimed upon examination of Melissa's work: two cleft halves of a human brain. 'This is the finest dissection I have ever witnessed! Class – gather around to see the work of Miss Adams-Kennedy.'

They were forced to circle him as he referred to her invaluable artistic virtues.

'I'm sure someday I'll hear your name in conjunction with the word "Nobel", Miss Adams-Kennedy.'

The sound of smashing glass turned everybody's heads.

Anneliese had accidentally dropped and cracked a beaker.

'*Do* try to be more careful, Miss Vanholt.' instructed Dr Viking.

Studying the night before exams in the school library became impossible. Melissa would be rubbing her thin lips against some small boy's ear and giggling in a manner that was heinously high-pitched even for *her*: scraping like a sheet of foil. Snickers came at rhythmic intervals that were in no way regular so Anneliese would struggle to foresee their onset.

Doubtless Melissa Adams-Kennedy received full marks in the exams of February 1941. Anneliese discovered that apparently this was the way in which the world rotated: she would work for hours late at night to memorise these convoluted facts while her antagonist attended parties and downed liquors; Melissa would be crowned the victor. Susanna gave her life to diagnosing, testing, proving, charting, documenting – and the artificial, tawdry specimen that was Melissa Adams-Kennedy would take her share of plaudits.

There were no other free seats in the library except for those in front of her that afternoon in March. Benjamin had gone home early for the Sabbath. Henry Blankett entered with four books and sat beside Melissa. She listened to him more than avidly without once blinking.

'You remember my uncle, the psychiatrist?' he was telling her.

'Absolutely.'

'He has a patient now; a young woman. Of course he won't tell me much about her. Father died when she was six; she's never had any romantic interests. I'm afraid she's stumbled into transference.'

Melissa longed to proffer sympathy.

'That's *so* common, nowadays.'

'My uncle's hard-pressed to convince her of the truth: that, at this juncture in the psychotherapeutic evolution, this tenor of occurrence is almost a *sine qua non*.'

Again Melissa nodded, this time very slowly, as though her pace meant to denote the great profundity of her incisive understanding. She launched into her own opinion.

'Personally, *I* think patients should be warned of potential transference before the commencement of therapy.'

Henry was swift to agree.

'So do I!'

Anneliese would not have trespassed on the conversation had there been a chance to work in peace. As circumstances stood that was impossible.

On her way out she made a point of intervening:

'Excuse me, Henry, I couldn't help but overhearing: what else did your uncle tell you of this case?'

Blond Henry shrugged.

'Not a lot. It's all strictly confidential, of course.'

'So ... why are you certain that the young woman is experiencing transference?'

Melissa looked at Anneliese like a parishioner examining a heretic.

'*Anneliese* ...' she began in her slender voice, 'transference is by *far* the greatest and most common danger to the analytical exchange. Aren't you familiar with Jung's works about it?'

'Yes, and Freud's.' Anneliese brandished her shield: a pronounced blink.

Henry now engaged himself.

'So ... what would be your – your thesis on the subject?'

'I don't deny that transference happens many times. But sometimes a ...' Anneliese cleared her throat. 'One has to have an object from *whom* to transfer ... The patient doesn't necessarily liken your uncle to her father, Henry. And her absence in romantic interests could just be ... evidence of a delayed libido or ... asexuality. Unless your uncle personally knew her father, how can he pass judgment on potential transference?'

Melissa was taken aback.

'I think you should read Freud's study on Dora. It's available right here, you know – on the fourth shelf.'

'I've read it twice.' She recalled the attraction of Susanna's red peonies. 'You don't believe every patient has their own aesthetic criteria, personal ethics and preferences about how they would like their therapist to look and sound and move?'

Henry was conclusive. He seemed bored by now.

'I think this patient wished she had a father.'

'You have to think more . . .' Melissa feigned a struggle to articulate her point. '*Broadly*, Anneliese.' Her hands stretched out like those of someone making a cat's cradle. 'It's not just *longitude*, it's also . . . latitude. And *volume*.'

Anneliese was silent in her ire.

In the meantime Isabel's existence had been little more than an array of bland routines. That night however she was gone.

By 11 pm Anneliese was astir in her panic. The jarring siren from a mile away was stretching its vibrations to their flat and Isabel was probably in central London. Accoutred in her coat, she was about go out looking for her sister when she pulled the door and found her with her left hand pressed against its casing.

She was smug, sunny, sprightly and sly.

'Melissa Adams-Kennedy is a cheat of the first order.'

Isabel entered with a classy swagger.

'I've been waiting here and staggering – losing my marbles – all this time you've hunted down Melissa Adams-*Kennedy*?'

'Mmm-hmm. And her "rich daddy" is no daddy. He's a *client*.'

She was already in their kitchen pouring herself wine.

'What does she do . . . run a business?'

'M.A.K has no *time* for schoolwork; all her statistics and examples are *forged*. She goes by another name in her domestic hours: Betsy Mince.'

'Who's "*Betsy Mince*"?'

She swung around to face Anneliese. The corners of her lips were lifted.

'A hooker.' Isabel took her unfinished glass of wine and set it at her hip. 'How'd you like her *after-school* job?'

'How did you . . .'

'I saw the *process*, Liesa. She was standing outside some pub in black high heels, leaning one foot against the wall. A young man came up to her – I heard their conversation. She kept on citing "rates an hour". They stole into an alleyway. I didn't need to *follow* them.'

The noisy, tambourine-like rustle that had quivered throughout Anneliese's innards halted. Overcome was she with a professional concern.

'She must be living on that money, saving up to pay for training at the Institute.'

'What institute?'

'The one I'm going to. For budding psychoanalysts.' Anneliese tucked a lock of hair behind her ear in pensiveness. 'Poor girl.'

Isabel's high spirits were blown out.

'Why is she *poor*? She treats you horribly. I went out to give you *leverage*.' She sat down next to Anneliese. 'So the next time she bothers you . . .'

Isabel took a chocolate bar out of her pocket and started to stuff a chunk into her mouth. Anneliese was hardly entertained.

'Isabel – Isabel, stop *chewing*. I'm not going to blackmail her because she hasn't done anything *wrong*.'

'But you said she was being a—'

'It won't hold up before a *jury*. It would be *egregious* if I – and *stupid*.'

Isabel demurred.

'Oh. Well – apologies for my new *war* effort!'

She retired to her room.

The next evening Anneliese had to call Isabel from St Mary's to tell her that she would be staying late. She and Benjamin were preparing charts and a report due the following morning.

They left at eight o'clock at night, hoping to be home before the raid began. Benjamin offered to drive Anneliese back to Elstree; she still had to take the keys to the administrator's office. He told her he'd be waiting in the car and left the building.

When Anneliese came out she headed for the car park. Posited against a wet brick wall, stood in a pair of four-inch high heels was Melissa. It was the preamble to her night shift.

A short red skirt clad legs painted with gravy to give the impression of stockings. Hardly complimentary to the skirt's shade was a maroon-hued waistcoat hung over a white chiffon blouse with some scarcely perceptible drawn-on design. It was too blistery outside for this kind of attire.

One hand was on a khaki brown square satchel hanging from her shoulder. The other clutched a pack of Wrigley's chewing gum, a sample of which speedily degenerated in her masticating mouth.

Maybe it was Anneliese's favoured vision of her that took note of her rough, scaly skin bestrewn with eczema; maybe she sought to stamp inside her memory the clash of peeling flakes with a cosmetic crust of artifice.

And yet a small ounce of compassion trickled slitheringly to her heart. Like outdoor cigarette smoke rising to the open window of her flat, it came to her in little and unwanted gulps; a swirl ephemeral yet palpable.

'Melissa, erm . . .' Anneliese parted her lips mistakenly noisily and pressed them together again. 'Benjamin's giving me a lift to Elstree. Could we take you home, perhaps?'

Melissa's eyebrows sank as their corners simultaneously rose. For a moment they looked painted-on, as though belonging to some child's impression of the devil.

Anneliese attempted the delivery again with more panache.

'It's very late and I'm not even sure it's safe to be *here*. Bombs could rain down any minute.'

Melissa was dry. Her voice was high-pitched, taut and flat at the same time. Atonal.

'I know where the shelter is.'

'It's in the underground at Paddington.'

For a few seconds she stopped chewing.

'I *know*.'

'If you turn left and then—' A scoffing Melissa neglected the girl's unsolicited presence. 'I only wanted to say that . . .' By lowering her voice she strived to make it gentler. 'I don't know what transport you employ to get home—'

'Why *would* you know?'

Had Professor Treadwell caught these fibres in Melissa's voice he would have been aghast.

'If I could assist you . . .'

'You're not getting any help from *me*. It's not *my* job to do dissections for you and it's not my fault you can't do *pipsqueak*.'

Melissa carried on chewing. Her hand was still gripping her satchel.

'I have . . .' Anneliese's voice withered. 'I didn't mean academic help. I just meant that – my sister and I are staying in a flat in Elstree, and if you need accommodation—'

'*Three* hours away?'

And the chewing progressed. Out of sight of medical practitioners her voice grew burrs and shrivelled to become a hoarser instrument. Anneliese began to wonder if she was intentionally dropping 't's.

'No . . .' This time Anneliese's voice was even softer. 'It's not so far – in any *case*, should you ever find yourself—'

'*Homeless?* Do I look like a *tramp* to you?'

'No, no. But, ah . . . We have something to spare at our apartment.'

'Good. Set up a veterans' charity if you've got nowhere else to dump yer *chicken-feed*.'

In some bedevilled corner of her psyche Anneliese imagined spreading rumours and the way that she would smear a sacred reputation with a personal assortment of brown, slimy oil paints. It was an area of her mind she had to keep securely closed.

Yet recognition of it sent a spiral of excitement through her ribcage.

43.

10th May 1941

It was Anneliese's turn to travel to the shops and trade in ration coupons. Most weeks it was her turn since Isabel was barely trustworthy; six times now in the past nine months the words 'black market' had escaped her mouth.

11.11 am

Anneliese ascended from the underground and made her way towards Victoria station. She and Isabel had made a pact to check their mother was alive each fortnight. Almost two hours it took them to commute from East London to Blackheath.

Sunlight was pounding on her skin but scarcely heating it. It was a cold May day and the deceiving spray of yellow she beheld on the horizon served as no more than a decorative tint. Leather winter gloves enrobed her hands.

The train journey was lengthy and exhausting. Anneliese watched fleeting images: battered, perforated roofs on homes and splintered boards askew along street corners. Wooden balustrades were loitering amidst the cloven pavements and sprayed gravel:

shards of stones and dust that had embellished slates of avenues. At least a third of London was a wasteland for collapsed furniture and severed buildings.

The train's pace floundered growingly. It puffed, emitted steam into the foggy air and nestled finally at Westcombe Park.

Anneliese's foot stepped out into a coating plaster of mixed sand and rubble. Looking out at the horizon she observed a row of mostly upright houses punctured by a single blank hole in the middle. Turning the corner, she passed a mechanic's garage. A middle-aged man stained in grease put forth the consolation of a yell:

'Cheer up, love. It might never happen.'

She eyed him absolutely clueless. He slapped his hands together, rubbing them ferociously. Slippery from oil, the fingers skidded off each other.

'Few more months and this'll all be ovah; bloody 'uns don't know what's *comin'* to 'em.'

Forcing an uncomfortable smile, Anneliese replied loudly enough for his hearing:

'We can only hope. Have a nice day.'

It barely dawned on her that half her blood was of a 'bloody 'un's'.

Ascending their old road she saw a large hole in the concrete that resembled an unfinished well. Glass in nearby houses had been shattered; flowers in front gardens wilted. Burnt rubber flaunted its infesting stench. It was still prominent after two weeks; Isabel had told her about it a fortnight before.

The force of the bomb half a mile away had ripped off their front gate but it had long been in a state of disrepair. Glass and bricks and mortar in the building were intact.

Isabel's visits to their home were brief and curt. Anneliese made greater efforts trying to persuade Mother Elise that it was dangerous for her; that bombers weren't discriminate about the victims of their targets. The explosive that had landed in the middle of their road had merely incapacitated drivers: it could easily have hit their home and blown her mother into pieces. Elise often emitted witch-like howls or threw a book as her response.

Both Anneliese and Isabel had for the most part ceased to care. It would have scarcely been the city's greatest loss.

Anneliese left after twenty-five minutes with both medical journals and leather-bound volumes of Josef's compressed in her satchel. She feared Elise would burn them on a whim someday.

12.49 pm

The queue for rationing was taking hours. Anneliese had to return home by four o'clock for another departure. For the first time Susanna had cancelled their session: her only free hour that week was at six o'clock, Saturday.

Middle-aged women were gabbing in front of her. They were discussing at great length how the McFarlanes' house had stood untouched not far from Holland Park until a bomb had ripped off wooden paling from their neighbours' gate and tossed a bar inside their window – knocking over their ignited candles and incinerating the entire home. The family was still alive but residentially there was no proof of it. A pitch black orbit had replaced their former territory.

2.13 pm

Anneliese received her set of goods around two hours behind schedule. As she took the brown bag from the dusty hands of the plump gentleman she suddenly felt moist around her palm: the butter from inside already melting.

She approached the gentleman again.

'Excuse me, sir—'

'You're gonna 'ave to go to the back of the queue, me love.'

'It's just the butt—'

'There's a *queue.*'

She looked inside the bag and felt the wrapped-up butter. It was challengingly solid. If she could get to Elstree within ninety minutes it would stand a chance to safely reach the destination of the fridge.

4.21 pm

Over two hours later she lingered at Catford Bridge station having awaited the train for well over an hour. The butter had devolved into a viscous slush but she was still at loss to find a rubbish bin and part ways with its dribbling mess. Anneliese had searched for one all over the platform; this goose chase had propelled her to miss the first train. Now the second train seemed destined never to appear and she was holding a brown bag of meat, sugar, confectionery and a butter she was sure would turn them all into distasteful, oily substances.

Anneliese had to preserve their weekly share. Dipping her fingers into the bag, she extracted the runny slab. It started dampening her hands. She looked around her. The train was far away and only two remaining passengers still waited. Tacitly making her way to the end of the platform, she sought to deposit the butter in some well-shaded corner.

The train came. The signalman immediately blew his whistle. She had to board the carriage with a lump of runny butter.

6.14 pm

London transport was upended by technical problems. Strangely they were completely unrelated to the war; the same ones

Anneliese had heard about prior to 1939. She was now close to their station in Elstree and Borehamwood. The only problem was the train was stuck, she could see nothing but green hills outside and now her skirt was the accommodation of a deluge of fast-running butter.

7.19 pm

'Liesa!'

Anneliese entered their flat with her soaked, greasy hands. The butter had dripped out onto the platform from the moment she had stepped down from the carriage. Most of it however clung in desperation to her person.

'What happened?'

Anneliese shook her head.

'We don't have any butter this week.'

Isabel looked startled.

'Why not?'

'I don't think you want to know.'

She removed her coat. There was no chance she could alight at Harrow before 9 pm. Changing her clothes, Anneliese headed downstairs to use the communal telephone. A man was standing there and chatting with his son who was now living with a family in Shropshire. It was twenty-four minutes past seven. She could have stood behind the poor man who was missing his son, silently pressuring him to suspend his long-winded discussion and hand her the phone.

She evaded this option.

After all – what would Susanna be doing on a Saturday evening? What could have been the primary difference between six, a quarter to eight, nine or ten? It wasn't as though she was busy in her ripe seduction of another married man.

If she would encumber her . . . so be it.

Anneliese skipped her way back upstairs.

'Isabel, I'm going to Susanna's.'

'But it's—' She was aghast. 'Don't you remember when the siren sounded at six thirty-*six?* It isn't really safe to—'

'There's always the underground.'

Anneliese clasped her satchel.

'You need a lesson with your tutor late on a *Saturday* evening?'

'Apparently I do. Don't fret for me; I'll call you before leaving her house.'

9.11 pm

The idea was a crazy one. It was almost nine fifteen when Anneliese approached Wembley Park station; another abundance of technical problems had followed. The sky was still a pastel blue. For the past two months the city's raids had gradually grown scarcer; with the exception of a few it was a little quieter. The habitual tense state of its commuters had already slackened and she wasn't frightened.

9.43 pm

By the time Anneliese exited the station pallor in the sky had been suctioned in favour of navy. A full moon beamed that night. Stars were puncturing the landscape with their silver shards. Absconding to Susanna's, she could still get back in time. If on the other hand she loitered in the underground and came much later there would be a chance Susanna let her spend the night there. The house had been issued an Anderson shelter; few homes were safer. Harrow was outside the core of sites the Luftwaffe intended to destroy.

These were the explanations she related to herself.

10.15 pm

Anneliese rehearsed her speech. She would tell Susanna that the window in their home in Blackheath had been shattered by a bomb, that she had known Elise would never have it fixed, that she had waited for repairmen who'd arrived at an ungodly hour – it being Saturday. This event had so fatigued and stressed her that she needed more than anything to talk about it with her therapist. It made sense in her head.

Never would she have the actor's strength to actually *relay* it.

She rang the doorbell. Light blazed in the corridor.

Helga flounced towards the door and swung it open.

'She is *out*.' she announced.

'*Now?*'

Anneliese imagined that her hearing was deceiving her.

'Yes, yes. She goes out three times a week. At night.'

'So . . . she's out when the sirens go off?'

Helga nodded adamantly.

'Most nights. She comes back at midnight.'

'And she's . . .'

Helga shrugged from cluelessness.

'Still in one piece.'

In her anxiety Anneliese groped at the sleeve of her coat. Blending her voice into a whisper, she enquired: 'Does she have a . . . a . . .' She recalled the German word. 'Lover?'

A vast cackle burst from Helga's mouth.

'A *lover*? *Her* with a *lover*? Hee hee!' Helga stroked Anneliese on the head. 'It's been a long, long time since that, my *Liebling*.'

'Is this . . .' Helga traipsed into the practice to collect the open books, shut them and stick them back into Susanna's shelves. Anneliese followed. 'Is this recent?'

'For the past few months.'

'So . . . only since they started bombing very heavily?'

Helga lifted her forefinger to the side of her head, tapping it.

'Some people, eh? They think that God will spare them even through the *flames*.'

Anneliese was swallowed by dismality. Encrusted in the concept that inside Susanna was a bottle stopper staunching all her sentimental flow, it had escaped her mind to ponder on the overall effect her failed career, dead daughter and a string of terminated love affairs had had on her.

Her conscience had forgotten to denote that crucial temple on the map: the one whose supplicants would pray for the reward of death. It started to occur to Anneliese that her psychiatrist and the explosives were twin entities that shared the single quest of lifelessness.

Helga stepped onto a stool to reach a shelf and reinsert a large tome.

'Lucky that we got the Anderson.'

'Yes. Yes, I considered getting one of those before Isabel and I chose to move away.'

'Mistress never uses it, though.'

Anneliese's head was static.

'What do you mean, she "never uses it"?'

Keys chinking fractured their evolving conversation. She heard Susanna burst in through the door and sprinted to the corridor to greet her.

Susanna didn't bother to look down at Anneliese. She merely sensed the presence of some smaller creature scampering; the rustling of a squeaky mouse. Taking off her double-breasted navy coat, she hung it on the rail.

'*Jesus*, Anneliese . . .'

Anneliese disposed of her premeditated plan.

'The underground was late and then they cancelled it and then I took *another* one and by the time I got here this young girl – she must have been no more than twelve – asked me how she could get to Westminster. So I was really shocked because we're *miles* from Westminster—'

Susanna had already sped into the kitchen and was reaching for her foot to take one of her heels off. Helga showed up. She shoved the shoe into her maid's left hand.

Swifter than usual and more irritable, she was being swatted by some pest – for when she spoke her thinner voice betrayed unflappable vexation:

'Fix it, would you?'

Helga shook her head in dismay and took hold of the shoe.

Heading to her rack of high heels, Susanna extracted another pair Helga had made for her: stitched patches of white and black and brown leather.

Putting them on, she steadied her gaze and her ears led her elsewhere. The radio had bid her come into the kitchen: some foreign woman was discussing economic policy in a Slavonic language. Marching to the wireless, Susanna spun its left dial anti-clockwise.

Defensively Helga cried out in German:

'How else am I supposed to know what happens there if you switch off the damn thing every time they *talk* about it?'

She heeded Helga no attention. Looking up diagonally to the left, Susanna remained stuck in thought. Her tone was weary with exasperation; riddled with contempt.

'That vernacular . . .' She almost clicked her fingers – but abstained. 'The twang of an elastic band.'

Anneliese gathered the language had been Czech. Its words could aptly shred Susanna's nerves.

She began slamming her cupboard doors open and scouring them.

'Helga . . .' she yelled without espying her still standing in the kitchen. 'Where's the lime cordial?'

The maid slowly proceeded to one of the cabinets under the sink. Anneliese waited before commencing another address. Timidity harnessed her speech.

'I hope you weren't worried about me.' Susanna seemed not to have heard. 'Susanna—'

'Why would I have fretted for you, Anneliese?'

'Well, with the war on—'

'Hardly an excuse for everything.'

She poured herself a glass of water and inserted droplets of lime cordial. The liquid morphed into a spread of green.

'So . . . did you just assume I was late?'

'I assumed you would be typically bearing some tenacious grudge.'

'*Hmm?*' Anneliese scratched her head.

'I don't know – frustrated with my choosing not to share all my inventions with the world; maybe you'd found out about my ex-fiancé who donated money for the Parsons Wing, had some other "epiphany" – it didn't cross my mind.'

There was a pause. Susanna drank and closed her eyes to try to coax new calm out of her psyche.

'What "ex-fiancé"?' Anneliese asked.

Susanna leant her glass against her cheek. After a long lingering gaze of hopelessness in Anneliese's direction she posited the glass on the counter and flounced out of the kitchen. A soft recording of some Fred Astaire songs murmured in the dining room. It wasn't long before Susanna pulled the needle off.

Helga had gone upstairs. Anneliese watched as Susanna yelled in her direction with an instrument louder and tenser than usual:

'How do you maintain my house with all this rattling *din?*'

It was her impression that Susanna started watching her with flat neutrality or nonchalance. Yet Anneliese eventually looked up to see those eyes were acrimonious and still. Doubtlessly Susanna understood she was an object of surveillance.

'Go to a *circus*, Anneliese.'

She swept right past her back into the kitchen. Anneliese was tentative to follow her but did it for the sake of parting.

Susanna's eyes were slightly softer now but nonetheless evasive and belligerent.

'Leave my house.' she suddenly insisted.

Anneliese then turned around and headed to the door.

10.39 pm

She stood not far from Wembley station, having now been seized by a presentiment. It was pitch black outside and she was waiting for the siren. She didn't want to go inside the station now; she didn't want to have to tolerate the loathsome hygiene of its occupants.

Slow rustling bubbled not so far: uneven steps. Her heart jumped from the fear that it could be a mugger and she raised a foot to dash into the underground.

'Anneliese.'

It was Helga.

'The mistress says you can come back now.'

They strode up the hill to the house. It took Helga a few minutes to take out her keys from her bag.

Standing in the corridor, Susanna hugged another full glass of lime cordial.

'So she came after all.'

In its contrived theatricality her voice almost became endowed with music – the phenomenon she called an 'intellectual dearth'.

Helga took Anneliese's coat again. She wrapped her arms around herself, now shuddering.

'There's going to be a raid tonight.'

Susanna stalled, leaning against the wall in contemplation.

'There hasn't been one in three weeks.'

'That's why there'll be one tonight. Hitler's been hatching something.'

'And he's keeping it a secret from Miss van der Holt.' Cautiously she sipped from her glass. 'Helga – bring Cassandra some pyjamas.'

Anneliese leant against the banister of the stairs.

'Do you drink anything except for water and lime cordial?'

'No.'

'Helga told me you drank champagne at fourteen.'

'I did.'

'You stopped?'

'Yes.'

'Why was that?'

'There was enough filling my system for the need of much else.'

Helga came down with a small pile of her clothes. Anneliese responded with a proposition:

'We could have the session now; I'm not tired.'

Handing Helga her glass, Susanna pushed open the door to the practice.

11.02 pm

Anneliese was sitting in her chair, hands diligently crossed along her lap. No concentration would lay hold of her. She merely repeated her augury.

'It'll start any minute now.'

Susanna stared at her dryly. No nerves seemed to rack her now. Her voice was regulated, dim and languid.

'You all attribute too much value to this puny little island.'

Anneliese was certain she had heard the phrase before. Then she remembered seeing it in the epistle from Susanna's mother.

'Hitler has a whole continent to conquer – including one third of the world – and all of you are hares before a hunter frozen in their tracks – "Oh, he'll definitely pick on *us*." The British have no concept of tactical strategy.'

Anneliese was not defensive but she frowned.

'How would *you* know?'

Studying a bookshelf to her left, Susanna squinted – probably because a tome was out of place.

'Susanna?'

'I learned about these things.'

'At school?'

She was clueless.

'What school?'

Anneliese tapped one of her feet on the other.

'I don't know. Here? *There?* I – I never even told you . . . that time, when the war had just begun, and I came here and saw you with that soldier . . . Emily-Jane Stufflebeam had taken me to meet her supervisor at St Mary's.'

There was a pause. Blankly Susanna stared.

'Well . . . he turned out to be your ex-husband. That's where he works now.'

Susanna crossed one leg over the other.

'I know.'

'I would *think* you would . . . I was somewhat shaken, though . . . particularly when he called you a "Bohemian burick"—'

Susanna looked distracted: she was focussed elsewhere. Anneliese imagined she was wallowing in some distressing memory. That was her theory till Susanna raised a pensive, erect finger:

'You were right.'

'I'm sorry?'

'You can't hear it yet?'

'Hear what?'

Two seconds went by and the hooting of a wolf beset the tunnel of her ears. She heard its sound approach more closely till it blasted through the building at full force, rattling the window panes with its convulsions.

Anneliese's skin was suddenly abuzz with the loud sprinkles from the roaring shower's onslaught.

'Is it always so – is this what happens here when they *start*?' she yelled helplessly.

'Yes. Go to the kitchen.'

Anneliese could barely hear Susanna.

'*What?*'

'Helga will take you to the shelter.'

Helplessly she looked around.

'Aren't you going to—'

'*Go.*'

Anneliese obeyed. It was the first time in her life that she recalled the bluster of the aeroplane the day they had departed Zurich. Isabel had wept and pressed her hands close to her ears; Anneliese had feared she would be swept away by raging wind. Now in the warm, domestic comfort of Susanna's home she was reliving this commotion.

Helga was already in the kitchen. She opened the door to the garden and they scurried outside.

More forceful was the penetrating blast. At their flat in Elstree they would hear explosions at a distance; here Anneliese was dizzied by the notion that not far from her the earth was being hacked by blows of a tenacious axe. She heard the first crash. Casting her eyes over the fence she saw a red and orange splotch: a swellingly florescent cloud of flames. That smell of burning rubber made her want to sneeze again.

'Get in there quickly, child!'

She rushed into the shelter; Helga followed suit. Anneliese had never seen an Anderson. The ground was wet; two narrow wooden benches lined the cave. It felt colder *inside* than out. Helga's knitting kit and an unfinished woollen scarf lay on the seat beside a pile of gas masks hatting gas lamps.

'Sit down, *Liebling*; it isn't as bad as it looks.'

From the sanctuary of the underground she had been spared the sight of happenings recalled in newspapers. Always she would witness the events in two dimension, black and white. Her eyes would slowly process them as she traversed the streets and saw the debris scattered across roads and rubble nesting at suburban doors. The cause that triggered the effect had hitherto escaped them.

Popping sounds outside began to swell in their intensity; she thought she heard the ball being disgorged, tackling the air and altercating with the foe of gravity.

Helga stroked her head.

'You're safe here, *Liebling*. Be a good girl and put your *mask* on.'

Anneliese swung her head to look at her.

'Where's Susanna?'

Helga shed a lengthy sigh, grabbing a couple of masks.

'Helga – you, you . . . you said she didn't *come* here. What do you mean she didn't come here? She's going to—'

She heard another bomb plummet nearby. Helga turned a gas lamp on.

'She's going to – just, just stay inside . . . for the whole night?'

Helga looked despondent.

'It's what she does.'

11.59 pm

Helga had brought one of Susanna's shawls with her and wrapped it over Anneliese's shoulders.

'No, no.' Anneliese removed her mask to tell her, attempting to take the shawl off and wrap it round Helga. Helga failed to comprehend. Anneliese was too exhausted to argue.

After another period of shivering she sought to know again:

'You're sure she isn't going to *come*?'

The siren's high-pitched squeal barbarically stomped across her words. Helga was not surprised. Muttering Czech words, she raised her finger to her head again to mime her mistress's insanity.

Clashes outside were indefatigable. It was a torrential rain of clangour that grew more destructive with each passing second. Anneliese closed her eyes in a bid to convince herself if she couldn't see it, it didn't exist. The fusion of the siren and the bombs kept her alert.

'Is she—' she was about to ask Helga. Instead she opened the door of the shelter. The lights in the house were still on.

'*Close* it!' Helga screeched.

She heeded.

She heard another bomb exploding somewhere in the neighbourhood.

Her heart began to mercilessly throb. It occurred to her that if the bombs reached Harrow they could land in Elstree also. Isabel would be in the apartment. Anneliese had brought her there with the intention of eschewing searches for an underground to sleep in, certain that the fighter pilots wouldn't target this periphery. She may have been mistaken. A shard of shrapnel could slice through her window; glass could hit her eye and blind her. Isabel could possibly have been naïve enough to step outside at some point in the evening. She could be hurled across the street by the explosive's furore; toppled backwards by its might.

Some flashing images began to intersect with her brain's wires: Josef telling her about the frontal lobe and Isabel commanding that she tend more closely to her fashion; aromatic inhalations of red peonies. She knew that all her life her mornings would be marked by looking at her hands in search of glasses then at hands across a clock.

She also knew the souls outside her frame could migrate. They would flock to death, or far across the seas, or miles away from her, until not even a faint echo of their voice would still be palpable;

until five decades from the present time there would remain those hands and those clock's hands – and no one. The sequence would forever be one image trumping its precursor; a long line of substitutes. People's permanence was as secure as the abode of swallows after winter's dawn. Those birds would fly down south to Africa; those of her nest flocked *farther*.

As she sat on the uncomfortable bench feeling its end etch a dent in her thighs, the statistics in the air became numerable. Those noises chipped away at totals; they obliterated figures from the population, striking digits off the Census. With Isabel that number could have been two thousand, three hundred and forty-seven; without her it would be two thousand, three hundred and forty-six. All it took was one small prick of shrapnel at the right site to exhaust the blood supply.

Anneliese sat listening to those statistics: the transcendence from existence to abrupt annihilation. She foresaw the Germans clinking their champagne flutes as they heard the death toll.

Two thousand, three hundred and forty-seven *vs.* two thousand, three hundred and forty-six.

She wrapped the shawl around her head as though it were a helmet.

'What are you doing?' Helga screamed.

Anneliese flung open the door.

'Come back! Anneliese!'

Decrying Helga's entreaties, she had already run out of the shelter. Metal clashed with asphalt at a nearby distance. Pounding her fist on the door, she could hear no response. Anneliese took to twisting the handle. It was tightly locked. She had to push it open with her side and subsequently broke the hinge.

Still clad in her burnt umber dress, Susanna leant over the counter. On it was some simple decorative plate with a design of a tall, lustrous vase displaying its red peonies. Acrylic paint stood next to them. Between Susanna's forefinger and middle finger was a brush splashed red. As Anneliese regarded her she felt as though someone had knocked her senseless with a slingshot's rocks.

Her presence thrust Susanna into fury.

'Are you *insane?*'

'Am *I?*'

No trance held sway over Susanna. Her mind was uneclipsed by fog: clear, cold and in co-ordination. She was imperative.

'Get back there – I'll come.'

'*No.*' Anneliese insisted. Walls crumbled somewhere down the street. She switched the kitchen light off. '*Now*, Susanna!'

Anneliese scurried to her. Unthinkingly she freed the paintbrush from Susanna's fingers, yanking at her hand. Susanna didn't slide across the tiles so easily. She forced her hand from Anneliese's tug. The latter waited in insistence.

Susanna walked in resignation. Her pace was mellow and her manner wouldn't yield to all this mania her patient was exhibiting. It took them a full minute to enter the shelter as crashes dispersed everywhere.

Anneliese was out of breath, swallowing very hard and shutting her eyes to regain her composure. Loose breaths turned into coughs as she inhaled the rancid odour of compulsive burning. Helga looked over at Susanna and tut-tutted. Susanna didn't move. She remarked matter-of-factly:

'You should breathe more slowly; you could hyperventilate.'

Distracted from her shortness of breath, Anneliese glared in contempt:

'*I'm* fine.' She continued coughing and taking great breaths.

'Breathe slowly.'

Susanna handed her a gas mask.

At that point she was contrarily determined *not* to take her advice. She coughed a little more and gave Helga the shawl.

'No, no, no.' Helga insisted. 'It's for—'

'Take it. I'm all right.'

Attempting to contain herself, she closed her eyes. She exerted efforts to erase the thought that pulling Isabel into a shelter was impossible. So Anneliese took that anxiety and funnelled it into her rage.

'Do *you* have a psychiatrist?' she addressed Susanna with disdain.

After a short pause Susanna answered in another dry tone:

'No.'

'You should get one.' Anneliese folded her arms and tried to warm herself. 'You're very clumsy at trying to seem normal.'

Helga let her head drop. In a few seconds she had fallen asleep.

Some moments later the onset of cold masked her fear. Following the panic came the realisation. To the fore came the awareness that she might come back to find a decimated home; its windows wrenched asunder and its top half snapped-off like a missing button. They lived on the fifth floor.

She looked down.

'I feel sick.'

Susanna maintained her serenity.

'Everyone you care about is safe.'

'I don't know that.' She inhaled and exhaled multiple times, taking some breaths in and out of the gas mask. They were as uneven as coarse bouts of gargling. 'It sounds very close.'

'It won't fall near Elstree.'

'How do you know?'

'They're targeting *ports*, Anneliese.'

Stifling the urge to cry, she almost giggled.

'There's a huge hole in the road we used to live on. "They're targeting ports," she says. Are you *that* sure of your immortality? They could hit *anywhere*. I told her not to leave the flat.'

'Anneliese—'

'So if she dies, it's my fault.'

Tears began to stream down from her eyes and prickle her pink cheeks.

'Anneliese . . .'

She refused to look at her.

'Anneliese . . . there are people at Victoria who don't die. There are more injuries than fatalities. Your sister's in a safe area, you live near a golf course miles away from the centre, miles away from any harbours. She is safe.'

But Anneliese continued blubbering. She put her knees up on the bench and laid her folded arms on them and started sobbing in her self-constructed nook. Her gas mask collected the tears.

'Anneliese . . . she won't die. It's not planned that way.'

She raised her head.

'What isn't?'

Slightly helpless and by now submissive to compulsive blinking, Susanna could only respond:

'I thought you were a fatalist.'

Anneliese scoffed.

'I wouldn't believe *your* thoughts on fate if you supported them with facts and data. You go out three times a week . . . with London under siege. You want to *die*.'

That phrase spewed further sobbing. Susanna was eclipsed by moisture bubbling in her eyes.

The latter reached inside her sleeve to take a handkerchief. Anneliese tried to use it in spite of its miniature size.

Susanna crossed her legs and sighed throughout her patient's wailing.

Now Anneliese began shuddering.

'Helga.' Susanna addressed her.

Helga wouldn't budge. Susanna raised her voice.

'Helga.'

She was still wrapped-up in the shawl, fast asleep and with a drooping head.

Susanna looked down at her crossed leg, which was parallel to

Helga's. She kicked the old lady's foot with the tip of her high heel. It was in vain.

Finally she stood up and took the blanket off Helga, proceeding to wrap it around Anneliese, smoothing it out at the top and eventually fastening it.

The latter looked at her as though she had an upset stomach and was being offered *cough* drops.

Her face still wet with tears, Anneliese explained:

'I'm not cold, it's psychologi—'

'I know.'

A cloud of weariness dawned over her. Now that her eyes could open fully she could see her spectacles were smeared with fog and dust. She took them off and rubbed them with her fingers.

Susanna watched in horror.

'You're making them dirtier.'

She put them on and found Susanna was correct. Her glasses were so smudged they seemed to have been whitewashed. Closing her eyes again most tightly, she removed them, felt for the shawl with her left hand and started rubbing one lens with its silk.

In a burdensome tone she made sure to utter:

'I'm sorry.'

'You're not . . .' Susanna exhaled through her nose. It was difficult for her to yield to sympathy. 'Your lenses won't leave a stain on my shawl, Anneliese.' After a while she muttered to herself, 'I should have brought a book down here.'

No response ensued. Susanna eyed the contents of the shelter in pursuit of an activity. She recrossed her legs and ordered Anneliese:

'Tell me about Melissa Adams-Kennedy.'

'What?'

'Melissa Adams-Kennedy.'

'Why would you want to know about Melissa Adams-Kennedy?'

Susanna shrugged.

'I'm not really very busy at the moment.'

Anneliese let her head sink.

'I'm not in the mood to talk about anything.'

'You won't fall asleep.'

Anneliese looked at Helga as a fine example. Susanna got the point.

'She's seventy-two. She's seen it all.'

'So have *you*.' Anneliese released a hat-trick of sniffs before she continued. 'What's *your* excuse?'

Susanna shifted somewhat. The bench was obviously too small to bear her length.

'I never really . . .' She closed her mouth and tried to rephrase it but it came out as planned. '*Do*.'

Anneliese hugged her knees.

'Fate seems to place us in these situations where we must engage in conversation.'

Susanna raised her eyebrows.

'You think that,' (she both emphasised and understated the next word) "Fate" provoked the Luftwaffe to pelt the city with hundreds of tonnes of bombs so that we could . . . "converse"?'

Humiliation hit Anneliese. She scratched her arm through the gap in Susanna's shawl.

'Were you in Vysoké Mýto during the war?' She had to blink to correct herself. 'The *last* war?'

Susanna's eyelids seemed too heavy for her eyes.

'Hohenmauth.'

Anneliese recalled the little Czech that she had learnt and coupled it with her restrictive German. The two names meant the same.

'Were any of your siblings killed?'

'No.'

'None?'

'None.'

'Your brothers didn't fight at the front?'

'What makes you think I had brothers?'

'Helga said there are eleven of you.'

'That's right.'

'So there must have been . . .'

'None of my siblings were soldiers.'

'But you *do* have brothers?'

Brandishing one of those looks too cryptic and ambivalent for a name, she was silent.

'Yes.'

Anneliese switched course in case she might appear too pestilent.

'When you were at St Mary's, didn't you work with Alexander Fleming?'

'Little. Not often.'

'Weren't you both pathologists?'

'He was Professor of Bacteriology; I was one of the professors of neurology and an Associate Professor of Pathology . . .' She moved her fingers somewhat. 'Our paths didn't cross.'

'You didn't want to?'

'Vice versa.'

'He held something against you?'

'I corrected him once . . .' she recalled it gradually with subdued fondness. 'In the third floor lecture hall . . . in front of . . .' She rummaged in her mind. 'Two hundred and ninety-six students.'

'I wouldn't think – I wouldn't think a man of his standing would mind a little . . . competition.'

A thin smile moulded her lips.

'I was a graduate student at the time.'

Anneliese nodded swiftly. The bombs were scarcer now. No one in the shelter had a watch. Helga was snoring.

Her terror having subsided, she griped at the chance to refer to substantial developments.

'I stole some of your papers.'

Susanna's expression didn't change.

'I know. They went missing.'

'You're not cross with me?'

'Well ...' She had to twist her mouth to stop potential chuckling. 'Nobody was going to get something from them *alone*.' Her look was begrudgingly sympathetic. She did her best to straighten it into passivity.

'But you still have me as a patient.'

'Yes ...' This time she had to look down to suppress the possibility of lapsing into laughter. 'Any wonder *why?!*'

'That's not the point. You must have hoped someday that they might help some dying people?'

'A great deal of authority it has.'

'What?'

'Hope.'

'If you had published the results of your experiments, you would have brought about such *change*. Those lives being lost now – *they* would have been lost – but *others'* wouldn't have. Life expectancy would have been up because of *you*.'

Susanna looked at her as though she were a waif.

'Who sent you?'

'What do you mean?'

'The oracle at Delphi?'

Anneliese ran out of things to say and tried to slouch. It was too hard for her to position herself comfortably.

She pursued her lecture.

'Individuals aren't lavished with gifts so they can go unused and *wasted*.'

Susanna let her eyelids droop again.

'They say that Einstein is a great violinist. I'm sure we'll never hear him play.'

Anneliese hoped that her prodding would prevail but she

was drowned in lassitude. A great yawn surfaced from her mouth.

'Sleep on Helga's shoulder, she won't mind.'

After the heart-pumping adrenalin, corrosive anger, acrid bartering and sorrow came the physical acceptance. Anneliese's corporal resources were diminished.

A few hours passed. She started to unstick her eyes and felt a headache.

Susanna was still wide awake and thoroughly complacent. It was lighter in the shelter.

'What time is it?'

'Sunrise must have been around two hours ago. The last bomb I heard was dropped a while after that.'

'There hasn't been the all-clear yet?'

'No.'

'God.' She rubbed her eyes. 'Isabel must be terrified – if she's . . . if she's all right. You don't think it's safe to come out yet?'

'*I* would.'

The pain in Anneliese's head was indomitable.

'Susanna . . .' She coughed and sniffled. 'The experiment in your papers . . . was it true?'

'Which one?'

'The boy with Niemann-Pick?'

Susanna was less condescending than habitually; even voluntarily sincere.

'Mmm-hmm. Yes.'

'You conducted illegal medical testing?'

'Yes.'

'It doesn't sound like you.'

'In that case . . . it wasn't "like me".' Recrossing her legs, she looked at Anneliese from the corner of her eyes as she spoke. 'My last "work of art" didn't turn out so well. It took nine years.'

Anneliese failed to understand the pretext for this phrase.

'The boy who had Niemann-Pick . . . is he still alive?'

Susanna almost chided her with her eyes' scarring bolts.

Seconds later the glare drifted aside.

She surveyed the ceiling of the air raid shelter for a moment then embarked on a familiar tirade:

'Helga.'

The old lady didn't stir. Susanna grew her volume.

'Helga.'

This time her head shot up. Startled, she mumbled some complaint in Czech that Anneliese could scarcely understand.

'Did you reattach the heel?'

Helga's response was something Anneliese translated in her head to be:

'You're like a bat with all your squawking.'

Finally the all-clear surfaced. Anneliese grunted.

'What's the point of having a symbol of freedom as ugly as the siren itself?'

Susanna sprang out of the shelter first, eager to busy her hands. The day was blue and frosty; the air – with its erosive fumes and stench of rubber – suffocated Anneliese's nostrils.

A bright glow flickered from afar.

'The sun looks so beautiful . . .' she mused aloud.

Susanna looked at her in an austere and dismal fashion. Her height enabled her to see above the fence.

'That isn't the sun.'

'What is it?'

'Maybe the Houses of Parliament. Or St Paul's.'

'Hmm?'

'A landmark on fire.'

By the time Anneliese reached the house Susanna was already handing her her coat.

'I – thank you for . . . You frightened me but . . .'

Susanna tested her patience with the girl for a few moments as she stared at her, awaiting the end of her garrulous spillage. Anneliese was too perturbed. She inhaled and wanted to recite a monologue that she had pre-prepared a host of years ago. It didn't happen. She traded in the possibility of speech for a long sigh.

'We'll resume at the usual time on Wednesday, Anneliese.'

Susanna disappeared into the living room without a parting. Helga went upstairs, most probably to 'reattach the heel'.

Throughout her underground journey Anneliese aimed to divine the nature of Susanna's 'last work'. She had been unable to discover this from her snatched papers.

At Kilburn a young woman and her toddler boarded. The little girl was strapped into a harness, her mouth smeared in chocolate.

'Mama, can I have more?' the girl asked.

The mother answered sharply.

'No.'

'But – *pleeeease?*'

'I have told you once, Rose, and I won't tell you again. You are *not* having any more.'

'But Mama, Mama *pleeease!*'

'Goodness!' the young woman exclaimed to herself. 'It's nothing but hard manual labour with you youngsters!'

Anneliese conjoined the pieces. The 'work' at hand was Rose. In Susanna's case it had been Lily.

By the time she reached home it was almost 7.30. Isabel was loitering outside their building in her coat. Mascara stains were helter-skelter on her crimson cheeks.

'*Liesa!!!*' she gasped, approaching her in an exhausted stagger. 'You said you'd telephone me when you left Susanna's!'

Anneliese was dazed.

'What?'

'You said . . . I didn't even have Susanna's phone number!'

Anneliese flung her arms around her sister.

'I'm sorry.'

'But, Liesa, Liesa . . .' She kept on panting. 'I had no idea what to do. I went outside when the siren began—'

'How could you *do* that kind of—'

'I found Susanna's address in your book. I tried to get to the station – the men there told me no transport was working and I didn't want to walk to Harrow – Liesa, I didn't want to walk to *Harrow!* The bombs were everywhere! So I had to go back home! I had to go back home but I *hated* it! I *wanted* to get there – but they told me not to *move!'*

She continued sobbing and gulping. Taking her hand, Anneliese led her back to their building.

'Susanna said there wouldn't be any bombs in Elstree.'

'I only heard one close to us.' Isabel started coughing. 'I was—' She gulped, apparently swallowing one of her tears. 'I was te-*terrified!'*

No hot cocoas warmed them up. The radio limned the inferno that had swallowed St Paul's Cathedral, the melted asphalt at Waterloo Station, the cracked organ at the now defunct Queen's Hall where Malcolm Sargent had conducted Elgar's *Dream of Gerontius* hours before. The girls sat wondering about the status of Croham Hurst, their house on Glenluce Road, Cousin Elise in Bethnal Green. Even their mother.

Without purpose.